THE
EYE OF
MADNESS

THE
EYE OF
MADNESS

THE TESLA GATE BOOK 3

JOHN D. MIMMS

Distributed in 2016 by Open Road Distribution
180 Maiden Lane
New York, NY 10038
www.openroadmedia.com

THE
EYE OF
MADNESS

"Deep into that darkness peering, long I stood there, wondering, fearing, doubting, dreaming dreams no mortal ever dared to dream before."
~Edgar Allan Poe

"...while the sons of the kingdom will be thrown into the outer darkness. In that place there will be weeping and gnashing of teeth."
~Matthew 8:12

"There are dark shadows on the earth, but its lights are stronger in the contrast."
~Charles Dickens

CHAPTER I

ENGLAND

"No excellent soul is exempt from a mixture of madness."
~Aristotle

THEY FOUND LIEUTENANT WILLIAM LANGFORD in the general area of his post, though not in the condition expected. He was at the end of a rope, five feet off the ground, and twisting in the chilly Scottish wind. As the eye of the cosmic storm encompassed the Earth last night, a cold front moved through Northern England causing a great deal of rain. The torrential downpour soaked the lieutenant to the bone. Not that it mattered, because he was dead.

Someone pointed out that there was no mud on his shoes and no tracks below him. This suggested he was hanging and dead when the rain began. Why was it important? It was not, except for one small thing. The entire battalion had heard his screams last night after the rain started. It was soon after the Impals began to disappear all over the planet. They were not the screams of a depressed and suicidal person. They were of a man in tremendous physical and mental agony, or perhaps more accurately . . . terror.

"I haven't heard such screaming since I was a battlefield medic," the base physician reported. "The cries of men with agonizing injuries did not compare to what I heard last night. At least those brave soldiers clung to some small degree of hope, a faint belief of my ability to perform a miracle and heal them. What I heard last night was pure agony, completely devoid of hope."

The Headquarters of the 1st Signal Brigade in Gloucester was the primary staging base for the relocation of Impals to the Channel Islands. It also funneled several refugees to a few secluded locations in Northern Scotland and Ireland. Almost two thousand Impals had resided here until last night when, what many are calling, the 'eye' of the cosmic storm arrived over the Earth. All Impals everywhere vanished and were replaced with something . . . well; no one knows what or who it is. It's as if shadows gained consciousness, a sentient purpose with equal intelligence and malice.

Lieutenant Langford was by himself last night, with only one small light under a wooden guard booth. The light still glowed in the morning sun, but the door to the small building was standing wide open. Like a good soldier, he had gone outside to investigate the strange noises in the dark. He paid for performing his duty with his life.

The logistics of hanging oneself from a tree are not easy. The lieutenant was quite efficient with his impromptu suicide. The rope was three-quarter-inch braided natural Manila, standard military issue. It was easily strong enough to handle him; he weighed 170 pounds a month earlier at his annual physical.

One end was tied to a lower branch of the same tree and secured with a slapdash mix of knots and lashings. The other end looped over a higher branch, two feet in girth and exactly twenty-one feet from the ground. From there it fell about nine feet, culminating in a perfect hangman's knot. The noose was straight from the textbook with thirteen coils designed to collapse the loop under pressure. A true hangman's knot snaps the neck, making death quicker and less painful. It appeared the lieutenant knew what he was doing. Other than what was apparent, there was no sign of a struggle. The cause of death was obvious due to the unnatural twist in his neck. The rope worked with its intended efficiency and death was quick. He did not strangle or suffer, at least not when his life ended.

This was all a textbook hanging–suicide except for one small detail. There was no ladder, no chair, stool, stump or crate anywhere in the vicinity. No one could have carried them off without leaving footprints in the muddy ground beneath. So how did he get up there? It would have been difficult enough to strangle himself without some sort of step up. He would have to climb to get high enough to accomplish a fall with the required height and velocity to snap his neck. The mysterious lack of evidence was as disturbing as the poor soldier, swinging in the breeze like a ghastly piñata. His lifeless eyes stared at nothing. Their last terrible sight made them protrude from the sockets as if trying to abandon his skull and flee from the horror. Lieutenant Langford's final countenance had been molded by the darkness, which now held terrible secrets.

"What in the bloody Hell is going on?" Private Jack Abernathy asked his partner on guard duty. They watched from across the parade grounds as Langford's body was cut down and carried to the waiting ambulance.

"I dunno," Private Sean Poindexter admitted. He removed his scarlet beret and ran his fingers through his short red hair. "It was damn creepy, wasn't it?"

Both men were of similar height and build and wore the standard issue British Army green camo. The scarlet beret on their heads and their matching armband identified them as Royal Military Police. They had been on guard duty in one of barracks housing Impals the previous evening when all of them vanished without a trace. They were fortunate they were not outside.

"The noise . . . I'll never forget that noise . . ." Private Abernathy said. "It was this damn humming. It was like wind blowing across an open pipe. No . . . or maybe an inhuman choir uttering the same openthroated syllable in unison, *hhhhhhhhhhhh . . .*"

Private Poindexter shuddered. "I would say you gave it a pretty damn good description, mate . . . except for one thing. It wasn't like any choir I've ever heard. It was more like a pit of snakes, all hissing in unison."

Private Abernathy did not respond, his was attention focused on the nearby woods. He stared into a dark area beyond the tree line. Private Poindexter turned to follow his gaze. At first he saw nothing, and then it hit him. The dark area in the woods was moving. It was not random movement of smoke or fog wafting in the wind, there seemed to be intelligence to it . . . a purpose. Chills ran up the spines of both men as they stood transfixed by what they saw in the woods. They had no idea what it was, but they did share one common certainty. Whatever it was, it was malicious.

"That killed Langford," Poindexter croaked. "He didn't bloody kill himself. If he did, it made him do it," he said, pointing a shaky finger.

Private Abernathy nodded in agreement. There was nothing to say. Everybody thought the same thing, but no one wanted to say it aloud. It was crazy, right? Perhaps no more crazy than the souls of the dead materializing on Earth. Most people believed in the existence of the soul and held some concept of life after death. However, this . . . this darkness had no logical concept. It was an unknown, a horrible unknown, which made people as uncomfortable to speculate about it as it was to look at it. The darkness was intelligent, malignant, and calculating. It was a conglomeration of man's most primal fears . . . the dark and the unknown. A plan of action would have to be determined before nightfall.

"Do you think the Impals turned into that?" Private Poindexter asked, tearing his gaze away from the forest.

"No, not from what I saw," Private Abernathy said. "I can feel the bloody thing thinking as it watches us . . . if it makes any sense. It's got an intelligence different from the Impals, it . . . it . . . well, it wants something."

"That makes sense . . . I feel the same way. Although I don't know what the hell it is thinking or what it wants. I don't think I want to know," Private Poindexter said, knots twisting in his stomach. The potential scenarios played through his mind in a montage of snuff films. "Where do you think the Impals are?" he asked, attempting to shake his mind of the macabre imagery.

Abernathy shrugged. "Heaven, Valhalla, the great beyond . . . Neverland," he said, recalling an Impal he befriended in the barracks, J.M. Barrie, the creator of *Peter Pan*. Barrie had kept everyone entertained in the barracks with his stories. He told Private Abernathy he chose to remain behind after he died because he refused to grow up and moving on was the ultimate form of growing up. "Someplace better than here, I hope," he said, taking a quick glance back at the woods.

A short time later, the order came down from the base commander. All electrical systems from transformers and generators to wiring and light bulbs should be inspected. Any necessary maintenance would be completed by sunset. *Every* light must be available at dusk. The base was also tasked with stocking up on fuel, light bulbs, extra generators and as many Powermoon portable lights as could be requisitioned. These powerful lights were utilized a great deal by mining operations and road construction crews doing night work. A handful of these powerful lights could illuminate most of the base like a sports stadium.

"I got the call from the surviving government in London," the base commander said. "We need to prepare for an influx of refugees. Any persons who do not have adequate lighting in their residence should go to military bases or designated facilities in London, Liverpool, Gloucester and Edinburgh. It is not a mandatory relocation, but people would be bloody fools if they do not comply."

Lieutenant Langford was not the only victim: there had been tens of thousands. Not all were fatal, some survived their encounter with the shadows, but mentally and emotionally, death may have been preferable. No one who survived was able to articulate their experience, at least not with any coherence. Whatever they experienced threw them into such shock, social interaction was impossible.

"We're going to need a lot more food," Private Poindexter remarked as they walked back to the mess hall. "The Impals had an appetite, but not like flesh and blood people. I would guess we are going to have a lot more than two thousand," he said, pointing at the line of people filing in through the base's main gate.

"Shite," Abernathy said. "We better let the mess officer know he's got some shopping to do."

Poindexter halted with disgust on his face.

"What is it?" Abernathy asked.

"We're not going to have enough latrines," he said. "It was easy enough with just a bunch of buckets for the Impals, but . . ." he trailed off and Private Abernathy finished for him.

"The task is going to fall on us," he said with a grimace.

Abernathy turned to watch the people stream in. Memories of digging and maintaining latrines in basic training resurfaced in his mind.

He thought his head might explode when he saw the multitudes pouring through the gates. There were four restrooms, each with five heads servicing the four barracks buildings. There were never more than a couple of hundred soldiers there at any one time. Tonight they would have thousands of people. He hurried to his commanding officer to discuss the possibility of acquiring several portaloos.

Poindexter stopped to watch as his partner dashed towards the officer's quarters. The people filed up the road about forty yards from the forest. It was now close to noon and the sun was a great deal higher in the sky, causing the shadows in the forest to grow and elongate. The darkness in the woods had grown. It seemed to writhe like a wild animal trying to escape its tether. It was now bigger, yes, but it was more than that. The people excited it, to energize it similar to a shark smelling blood in the water. The daylight outside the woods was the only thing keeping this horror at bay.

The next six hours would be crucial in getting everyone settled and the lighting in place. Otherwise, when the sun went down, there would be nothing left to keep *it* away. The regions of the world now in daylight hours raced against the clock to do as much as possible to protect themselves from the dark. The unfortunate areas of the globe where it was now night could only hang on and endure until the sunrise.

CHAPTER 2

ISRAEL

"Like a muddied spring or a polluted fountain is a righteous
man who gives way before the wicked."
~Proverbs 25:26

EVEN THOUGH ONLY TWO HOURS separate London and Jerusalem, the eye did not arrive two hours before or two hours after it came to England. It arrived about eight hours later. The eye spread over the planet erratically, taking a total of almost fourteen hours to envelope the entire world. For many, it was a blessing, especially where it was night.

Malakhi Gavish lived in a small apartment in a lower middle class area in northern Jerusalem. Malakhi shared the small three room apartment with his mother and, as of late, his grandfather. His grandfather, who had owned a small restaurant in a nearby market, passed away before he was born.

Nehemya Gavish had chosen to remain behind and not crossover ten years ago after suffering a fatal heart attack. He stayed because he felt it his duty to watch over his grandson. Rebekah, Malakhi's mother, was six months pregnant with him when Nehemya died. Malakhi's father had disappeared soon after he found out about Rebekah's pregnancy. They never saw him again. In truth, Nehemya felt his daughter needed to be watched over almost as much Malakhi. She was just nineteen years old when her son was born.

Malakhi and Nehemya were having breakfast together, as they had done so many times in the last couple of months.

"Do you know what I enjoy most about breakfast?" Nehemya asked, giving his grandson a wink.

"Blintzes and bagels?" Malakhi asked. Bagels were a staple in the Gavish home, but Malakhi didn't care for them unless they were slathered with cream cheese and lox. However, they reserved these treats to special occasions because of their shoestring budget. Rebekah Gavin earned a meager living as a waitress in the restaurant formerly owned by her father. The new owners were not generous with their employees.

"No . . ." Nehemya laughed and patted his grandson's head with a cold hand characteristic of Impals. Malakhi had gotten so used to this interaction he didn't notice the chill anymore. He was just glad to have his granddad here. "The thing I like best about breakfast is getting to share it with my handsome grandson!"

Malakhi giggled as Nehemya reached down and gave him a cold poke in the belly. He flashed a sly grin and then handed him a bagel he had been concealing under the table. A generous portion of cream cheese and lox topped it.

"Where . . . ?" Malakhi began but Nehemya held up a single luminescent finger to his lips. He glanced over his shoulder towards the next room where his daughter was getting ready for work, and then turned back to Malakhi. "It's our little secret, okay?"

Malakhi beamed from ear to ear at his grandfather's surprise. Being the well-mannered boy he was, he could not accept it without some reciprocation. Seeing Nehemya's plain bagel, Malakhi took his knife and sliced the loaded bagel in two equal halves. He placed one half on his grandfather's plate as he took a slow and savory bite of the other half.

Malakhi thought of all the things he and his grandfather had done the last couple of months, this moment was one of the best. They had visited the ocean on more than one occasion. He remembered Nehemya joking that he didn't think he would need to use sunscreen due to his current skin condition. In some ways it was a disturbing thought, but it was just another example of Nehemya's good humor about any situation. He was always in a joking mood. Malakhi was not sure if this was his normal personality or it was because he was an Impal. His mother assured him his grandfather was the same as ever.

"He looks like I remembered him when I was six years old," Rebekah told him. "He used to be slim before he got older."

Impals never resembled their appearance at death. Their eternal appearance seemed to hail from a time when they were happiest and most comfortable.

They travelled together free from worry of detention or harassment. The Israeli government was tolerant of the Impals. They were probably the most tolerant government on the planet. Most other nations were rounding them up and relocating them. Of course, there was the extreme example of the United States under the leadership of General Ott Garrison. He was putting them through the Tesla Gates as fast as he could capture them. Publicly he was rounding them up for their own safety; privately he was sending what he believed to be demons back to Hell. It didn't matter to him if they were shredded out of existence or transported back. He was doing his service for God and country.

The Jewish community as a whole had seen these tactics before, used with similar mantras and motivations. They learned from the mistakes of history, even though the mistakes were not their own.

Many Israelis had adopted the symbol made popular by the American resistance. They now displayed it almost as prominently as the Star of David. The Myriad, a half solid and half transparent infinity symbol, was an icon representing man's eternal existence. It suggested that flesh and spirit are both an important part of infinity. It recognized that flesh and blood are not a requirement for being a human being. This symbol was called the Myriad because it represents many for infinity.

Malakhi owned one which he wore on a dingy red string around his neck. It resembled a sideways number '8'; made from half pewter and half clear plastic. He got it for his birthday present a couple of weeks earlier at the local bazaar. His mother remarked that when the sun hit the plastic it shimmered like an Impal. He wore it with pride.

His pendant made an ethical statement, but also reminded him of his grandfather.

It shimmered in the light of the morning sun coming through the small kitchen window, drawing his eyes down as he placed the cream cheese and lox covered bagel on Nehemya's plate. It was a distraction that would haunt him because, when he looked back up, his grandfather seemed strange.

Malakhi first thought Nehemya was upset that he gave half of his bagel back. This was before the unsettled expression grew into one of panic. His grandfather was fading. When Nehemya was little more than a vapor he heard his grandfather's faint voice say, "I love you, Malakhi." Then, he was gone. A half-eaten bagel on his plate and crumbs in his seat were the only evidence he ever existed.

Malakhi shrieked, causing his mother to charge from the other room, her hair still in rollers. They cried and called for Nehemya for several minutes before they realized their search was fruitless. Malakhi collapsed in his mother's arms and wept for the loss of his grandfather. Rebekah mourned the loss of her father, now for the second time.

The landlord of their small apartment complex was not tolerant of noise in the thin walled building. He also happened to live right next door. He was a heavy set, balding man whose harsh facial features were a perfect match for his unforgiving personality. He never spoke to Rebekah unless it was to collect the rent money. Malakhi knew to tread lightly in the hall, lest he receive a scathing lecture from the man.

The knocking at the door did not register with them. When their landlord began to scream in agony they forgot their grief. The knocking was replaced with a dull thumping as if someone were taking deliberate steps down the hallway. The thumping, however, was barely audible over the man's horrified screams. The odd thing, the thing that made the hair stand up on the back of their necks, was the noise. It permeated through the thin walls with horrifying clarity. *Hhhhhhhhhh.* It was as if a reptilian choir filled the hallway, all humming the same note. As horrible as the poor man's screams were, this noise was worse.

Malakhi started to walk to the door, but Rebekah stopped him. The small closet next to the front door was open a crack. In the sliver of darkness, she saw unnatural movement. It was as if the dark itself struggled to get out. The only thing keeping it back was the light streaming in through the window. She did not know how or why, but Rebekah knew the absurdity in the closet was somehow related to what was happening to their landlord. She threw herself across the room, slamming the closet door with one fluid motion. She grabbed Malakhi and rolled into the warm sunlight.

The room closest to the front door was little more than a sitting room. It would seem cramped if more than three people sat there. Malakhi and Rebekah's apartment was a mirror image of their land-lord's. His sitting room was on the other side of the wall.

As Rebekah lay under the window cradling her frightened child, the floor vibrated. The noise was still drowned by the man's screams, but she could feel someone taking hard and deliberate steps on the other side of the wall. He was no longer outside their door; he had gone back into his apartment. His screams ripped through the thin wall making it seem as if he were right beside them. The single noted hiss underscored his cries like a thousand slithering creatures, all locked in a chorus of wicked synchronicity.

Just when they thought they could no longer take the noise, they heard a crash. Rebekah's head shot up, her eyes drawn towards the source of the shattered glass . . . towards the window. The sitting room windows in the two apartments were only about three feet apart, so Rebekah had a clear view. Their apartment was about four stories above the busy street below. Mr. Zahavi, the landlord, flew through his window in a fatal dive toward the hard concrete. Seeing a man die was horrible enough, but the truly horrible thing was that there seemed to be no fear in the man, none whatsoever. There was no flailing of arms, and no screams. In fact, the man could have been on trampoline for all the fear he showed. It was a stark contrast to the screams of pure horror from seconds before.

"It was almost as if he were relieved to die," Rebekah thought to herself, but never shared with another soul.

She wanted to turn away, wanted to hide her face from the grue-some act. Yet, she found she could not tear her gaze from Mr. Zahavi as he fell lower, lower, lower . . .

He landed on the hood of a taxicab with an impact hard enough to collapse it and shatter the windshield. His body was thrown forward where it smashed into the back of a bus before crumpling on the pavement in a bloody and battered mess. He was dead, there was no doubt, but something was peculiar.

Rebekah saw two people die in the last two months. One was an elderly man who suffered a heart attack in her restaurant and the other was a young boy who was hit on his bicycle by a city bus. Both of them were still there, or at least their spirit was. They all remained, trapped by the cosmic storm. The man and the boy both remained, standing over their body in a state of shock and bewilderment. But they were here, and they were visible. Mr. Zahavi was not standing over his mangled body, he was gone like her father and all the Impals around the world.

Rebekah squeezed Malakhi tight and tore her eyes from the sickening scene below. As she held her weeping boy, her own grief began to wash back over her. She replayed the image in her mind of her father vanishing. His terrified face etched in her psyche for eternity. This played over and over in her head in a never-ending loop. The more she tried to block the image out, other unpleasant memories drifted into her head. The day of her father's funeral was now spliced into this tormenting mental movie.

As she wept, something else crept into her mind, another memory more recent and every bit as horrible. She opened her eyes and turned her head toward the closet door. It opened with an ominous groan. She held her breath as she focused on the door. Her breath escaped in a single blood-curdling scream at what she saw in the moving and undulating darkness.

CHAPTER 3

MAJOR GARRISON

"Listen to them, the children of the night. What music they make!"
~Bram Stoker

MAJOR CECIL GARRISON had endured more in the past twenty-four hours than most people do in a lifetime. Up until yesterday, he worked with a covert organization, made up of both military and civilian combatants. Their sole objective was the rescue of Impals from the clutches of Major Garrison's own father, General Ott Garrison. Yesterday, they evacuated several hundred Impals to an island in the English Channel. The success of this mission came with great costs.

The leader of the resistance, Colonel Danny Bradley, was killed. Cecil had returned to their base later to find their camp raided by the military. Everyone, including his wife and daughters were gone. He received the emotional jolt of his life when he found that his wife and others managed to escape. However, his youngest daughter was the one who betrayed them to the military. His oldest daughter died in the raid, but her Impal managed to escape with his wife and make it back to him. Cecil decided to cling to the hope that his father would not hurt his youngest daughter.

The eye of the storm passed over the United States several hours before it did Europe, but the results were the same all over the world.

The Impals vanished, including his eldest daughter. The darkness was no longer a figure of speech or a metaphor for evil and despair. It had become those things incarnate. Cecil was outside when he heard the screams of his wife from the upstairs bedroom of their secluded cabin. His wife, Barbara, was now alone in a dark room.

Cecil bounded up the stairs to the cabin porch and flung open the front door, knocking over a rocking chair sitting nearby. Upon hearing the screams, everyone emerged from the kitchen. They were about to ascend the stairs when Garrison flew past them, taking three steps at a time. He bolted through the bedroom door before any of them reached the first step.

As Cecil clambered into the darkness, he found himself no longer in a dark room, but in bright sunlight. He was lying face down, staring at white fiberglass. The dull and dingy white he recognized as the bottom of a canoe. It was the same canoe from when he was a boy at church camp. Something slimy and cold moved over his lower calf and a moment later he felt white-hot pain light up the back of his leg. In an instant, he forgot about his wife, forgot about Impals, and forgot about the past thirty years. He was twelve years old again and he was a terrified little boy trying to escape a nest of angry water moccasins.

Jerking his body up, he spun around on his seat. The snake still clamped its fangs into his lower calf. He screamed and yanked the snake lose, pulling a small divot of flesh from his leg with it. He tried to fling the snake overboard, but the motion seemed to take an eternity. The snake turned and glared at him. Cecil's blood dripped from a sinister reptilian smile. In an instant, he saw something that froze his heart. The eyes were not the slitted eyes of a reptile. There was intelligence in these eyes. These eyes projected an evil only humans are capable of committing. He knew what and who he was facing.

This serpent abducted six children, five boys and one girl. He killed her the most brutally because she had made him angry. Her short haircut and football jersey caused him to mistake her for a boy. This was what he loved, catching little boys and molesting them with a sickening perverted creativity. He then took his time dismembering them while they were still alive. After flying into a rage on discovering the seven year old girl's true gender, he sodomized her. Instead of beginning his dismemberment at the shoulders and hips, he started at the first knuckle of each finger. He took his time worked his way up in three-inch intervals. It took all night and the poor girl lived through most of it.

Cecil did not have the time to ask the question of how a snake, a slimy slithering reptile, could have accomplished this, yet he knew somehow. This was once a person who had lived as flesh and blood, yet they were not an Impal. As he flung the squirming abomination into the water, he saw more movement out of the corner of his eye. At the back of the boat five more snakes slithered over the side. They plopped into the bottom of the water-logged canoe with a vile splash. He searched wildly for a paddle, but there were none. He watched in horror as more snakes peered over the edge of the canoe, ready to drop in and come after him. Their eyes were the same as the first serpent, all with a sickening human intelligence. All contained a ghoulish story in their cold and calculating eyes. Rape, murder, molestation, and genocide were the common themes emanating from the nest of snakes. As they slithered over the side of his boat, Garrison saw no alternative. He let out a scream and threw himself over the side. He began to swim as hard as he could toward the shore.

He had only swum a few strokes when he felt several cold and scaly bodies wrapping around his legs. Numerous sharp pains ran from his ankles to his hips. He screamed and thrashed, trying to propel himself faster, but it was no use. A moment later, he felt them wrap around his torso and arms. This was followed by more brilliant pain as they began to bite again. The pain was more than he could stand. He cried out but it was a muffled, gurgling shriek as his head was now a foot under the murky water.

The serpents covered his entire body. He was bitten so many times from head to toe his whole body was one sharp piercing pain. The agony and the vivid evil memories he gleaned from the sentient reptiles were maddening. Death was preferable to this; death seemed as welcoming as a soft bed at the end of a long hard day. It was the only way, the only way to stop the pain and to purge his mind of the dozens of sick memories. Major Cecil Garrison let go. He ceased to struggle and prepared to draw a deep breath of lake water into his lungs, but then something happened.

He felt himself being pulled upward and then thrown back onto a hard surface. Instead of inhaling, the breath was knocked out of him and he lay on his back gasping for air. He was wet, but he was no longer underwater. The pain and the slithering feeling were still there, but it was fading. His eyes flew open as he sucked in air. Cecil blinked up into the bright sunlight. He realized he was underneath the upstairs bathroom window of the cabin. Burt and Derek stared down at him.

"You okay, Cecil?" Burt croaked, his face ashen white.

"Jesus . . . what the hell was that?" Derek asked, wide-eyed and waving a large flashlight around the room.

Cecil didn't respond to either of them. The dark green bathroom curtain was torn from the wall, rod and all. It lay a few feet away in a crumpled heap on the wet tile floor. Every light in the bathroom was on, including the overhead fan. Cecil made a move to sit up, but Derek and Burt each grabbed an arm and raised him off of the cold wet floor. He leaned back against the wall and pulled his knees in close for warmth. Even though it was not a cold day, he couldn't remember when he had ever been this chilled. Soon his eyes fell on the claw foot bathtub sitting in the corner. The water inside sloshed about as if there were an earthquake.

"What happened?" Cecil asked.

"What happened?" Burt snapped. "I'll tell you what happened! You came running into the bedroom and then the next thing we knew, you were screaming your head off and running into the bathroom."

Burt stopped as Dr. Winder entered the room. The doctor walked to Cecil's side and knelt down.

"Are you okay, major?" he asked.

"Thanks to you!" Burt said. "Thank God you stopped us before we wandered in here. We might have all wound up . . ." his voice trailed off sheepishly.

It was then that the hazy, confused fog lifted from Cecil's head. He remembered why he stormed into the bedroom in the first place.

"Barbara . . . where's Barbara!?" he shouted trying to scramble to his feet. He slipped on the slick tile, but Burt and Derek caught him.

"Easy, Cecil," Derek whispered. "She's right out here. We'll take you to her."

They escorted him from the swamped bathroom with Burt on one side and Derek on the other. Cecil jumped at a sloshing and gurgling noise behind them. Gazing back over his shoulder, he saw that Dr. Winder had just pulled the plug on the bathtub.

He was about to ask why the bathtub was full when he saw Barbara lying on the bed. Charlotte sat beside her and held her hand while Sam Andrews ran a cold beer bottle back and forth across her forehead. Despite his concern for his wife, a burst of anger ran through him at the sight of a beer bottle being used to cool his wife. Sam Andrews was an alcoholic and a pretty bad one. He let his withdrawals get the best of him for the couple of weeks they were in the secluded Impal refugee camp. He almost murdered the president. Andrews also displayed several other temperamental outbursts that could have put them in jeopardy. Now here he was, drinking and acting the part of a concerned citizen.

"He's mocking me," Cecil thought as he strode across the room and knocked Andrews out of the way.

Judging by Andrews's face, he considered beaning the major over the head with his bottle. If he did, he reconsidered. The bottle was over half full. It would be a terrible waste. Instead he sauntered into the bathroom to join Dr. Winder who was staring out the window as if gazing at death itself.

Every light possible was turned on and every blind and shutter was torn down. The room was so bright; it almost made it necessary to squint. Barbara's tan skin was pallid. Cecil peered into her hollow and haunted eyes. They were wide open, frozen in terror, unblinking and unresponsive. She did not even react when Cecil bent down and kissed her on the cheek. She was alive, as evidenced by her rising chest and a raspy snorting exhale, but she was in deep shock.

"Oh dear God, did she see the snakes too?" Cecil thought as he brought her limp hand to his mouth and kissed it.

But how could she? That was something Cecil had experienced when he was a boy. He never discussed the details with anybody, not even Barbara.

Cecil turned to Charlotte who was sitting at the foot of the bed.

"What happened to her?" he whispered.

Charlotte fought back tears and put a fist over her mouth to stifle a sob.

"She—she was in the floor. She looked as if someone was attacking her," she said as tears burst down her cheeks.

"Attacking . . . how?" Cecil pressed.

"She . . . she . . . she was being raped," Charlotte said, wiping tears away.

"Did you see anybody?" Cecil asked. His insides started to twist in knots at the thought of his beautiful wife enduring this despicable violation.

"No one visible . . . it was almost as if she was acting. But, the terror in her screams and on her face . . . she wasn't acting."

He kissed Barbara's cheek and squeezed her hand while stroking her forearm. Her eyes were still fixed on an invisible spot on the ceiling. Her terrified expression burned a little deeper hole into his heart with every glance. Her chest heaved up and down with rapid regularity, as if she completed a rigorous workout.

Cecil closed his eyes. His experience was much more than a vivid recollection of a childhood incident, it was far worse. This was a true nightmare. He had no idea his experience was not real until he was pulled out of the bathtub. How the bathtub was filled in the first place was a question he brushed to the back of his mind. Right now, the logistics did not seem as important as the encounter itself.

He did not know how or why, but he knew what each one of the snakes, these *things*, had done at one time. It was as if a demented movie played out in each of their eyes, a movie full of a lifetime of horrific atrocities. These brutalities gave each and every one of them a high level of satisfaction. There was no remorse in the entities minds. Every murder, rape and abuse was as benign and pleasant to them as taking a trip to Disneyland. They had injected their horrible deeds into his soul like poisonous venom with every vicious bite. He felt frigid as if he sat with a high fever in a deep freeze. Cecil did not realize how much he was shaking until Charlotte reached out and clasped his free hand between her palms. She gently rubbed as if treating someone with frostbite. Her hands vibrated in response to his trembling. She tightened her grasp, soon managing to reduce his shivering to a dull quake.

Even though he felt cold, his heart burned red hot with anger and hatred of these things. To call these things human was unfathomable, but then Cecil knew that they all were at one time. His anger skyrocketed when he thought about how these things violated Barbara. They had tormented her into this pathetic petrified state. But, if they used to be human, what were they now? They were not Impals. If they were, they would no longer be here. A troubling thought crossed his mind . . . could his father have been right? Could the eye of the storm have revealed the Impals's true nature? Perhaps they hadn't disappeared at all, but instead reverted back to their natural state. He found this thought disgusting and downright absurd. He had interacted with Impals, his own daughter was now one, and he knew there was no malice, no hidden agenda in her. They were good, frightened people who were trying to make the best of their circumstances. Sure, there were some 'bad' ones. The two prison guards who beat him and the two bounty hunters shot by Colonel Bradley came to mind. One thing became evident to Cecil in the past two weeks— 'bad' was a subjective term. The bad he just experienced was worse than anything he ever felt before. The evil of the unrepentant entities and their enjoyment in their deeds made the 'bad' Impals seem like saints. They may have once been human, like the Impals, but they were different . . . very different.

An overwhelming feeling of terror washed over Cecil. It was not for fear of what the darkness would do to him, but what it would do to his loved ones. He thought of his youngest daughter, Steff, who was now in the custody of his father. Was she safe? Was she in the light? Did she know what the dark could do to her? He felt tears of frustration and worry beading at the corners of his eyes. He bent down and gently pulled Barbara up into a sitting position and rested her head on his chest. He would not let her out of his sight again, not until this thing was over and the darkness was gone. He kissed the top of her head as he squeezed her close. Cecil shut his eyes and said a prayer for his wife; he also said a prayer for both of his daughters, wherever they may be. Then he said a prayer for the world.

CHAPTER 4

WINDER

*"When the unclean spirit has gone out of a person, it passes
through waterless places seeking rest, but finds none."*
~Matthew 12:43

BY THE TIME BURT AND SALLY put loving hands of support on his shoulders, Cecil had prayed for several minutes. He jumped with surprise at their touch, but he did not loosen his grip on his wife.

"Cecil, will you join us downstairs?" Burt asked gently. "We have some work to do before it gets dark."

It took an enormous amount of will power, but he lowered Barbara's head to her pillow. He closed his eyes, kissed her on the forehead and turned to face them.

"Sally and Charlotte will stay here with Barbara," Burt said. "It will be okay."

Andrews, Vandeputte and Dr. Winder walked out of the bathroom together. Each gave Cecil a respectful smile before going out the door and down the stairs. He could hear the slurping noise of the bathtub drain as the last vestiges of water drained away. What the hell happened in there? He hoped the answer awaited downstairs.

Cecil turned and gave his wife one last loving glance. Charlotte and Sally smiled reassuringly. He turned and walked downstairs.

He noticed the house was much brighter. Every light was on and every curtain, blind or shutter was torn down. There didn't seem to be a single dark spot or shadow anywhere, except outside in the woods. Cecil could see several dark spaces in the forest outside the living room window. These sunless areas seemed to pulsate with a living presence. It was evil. Chills ran up his spine as he gazed at one particular dark spot; he was sure the darkness watched him.

The men stood in a semi-circle around a rustic cedar coffee table. Everyone was too keyed up and on edge to sit. Cecil tried to ignore the shadows outside and grabbed a nearby rocking chair. He pulled it to the open end of the semi-circle, but did not sit down. He stood facing the group with his hands grasping the wicker back of the chair. Everyone seemed terrified of even the darkness cast by the shadow of the furniture. They stood with their legs as far as possible from the blackness underneath. That is, all but Sam Andrews. He was content to plop down on the sofa with his mud-crusted boots propped up on the coffee table, and a beer in his hand.

They all regarded Cecil as if he was damaged goods and the wrong word could tip him over the edge of sanity. After several moments of uncomfortable silence, Cecil finally broke the ice.

"Tell me, why was the bathtub full of water?" he asked.

They glanced at each other with blank expressions. Finally Cecil's best friend, Burt, spoke up. "You climbed in there, Cecil. You lay face down and turned on the water. You were screaming and thrashing bloody murder. We couldn't get to you at first because of the dark room, but when we could, we were afraid to touch you."

"Why couldn't you get to me and why were you afraid to touch me?" Cecil asked.

Burt frowned. He answered the question, remaining as clear and concise as possible. "Because you went charging right into the darkness," he said. "Andrews and I were about to run in behind you when Dr. Winder warned us off. He told us not to go into the dark."

Cecil glanced at Dr. Winder who was staring at the floor, listening. He remembered Dr. Winder had called him down to observe the change in the sky and to listen to radio reports. People from China to Europe were warning about the 'living darkness'.

"How did you get in the room without being affected?" Cecil asked.

"We grabbed a broom handle and stuck it into the room to turn on the lights," Andrews interjected with slurred speech. "I'll be damned if it didn't feel like something was pulling on it." Andrews took a final drag on his beer bottle and sat it on the end table next to him. He achieved a pretty good buzz this morning judging by the empty bottles lined up on the coffee table. Under normal circumstances, Cecil would have thought it was the alcohol talking. However, these were not normal circumstances. Normality in the world had been on vacation the past couple of months and incongruity took its place.

"After we got the light on," Burt interrupted before Andrews could say something stupid. "Barbara was writhing on the floor and we heard you screaming in the bathroom. Turning the light on only forced whatever it was into the corners and shadows. The damned, well . . . darkness was still there like it was waiting for the light to go out again."

"I ran over and tore the curtains and shutters down," Derek said. "It all seemed to disappear and retreat into the bathroom. That's when Andrews tossed me the broom and I managed to flick the bathroom light on, and then tear down the curtains."

"Then we saw your ass going all Dennis Wilson on us," Andrews drawled. He was making a crass reference to the Beach Boys drummer who drowned while out on his yacht. "It was freaky . . . you were trying to swim through the bottom of the tub."

"The important thing is," Burt said, giving Andrews a cutting glare, "you and Barbara are all right."

Andrews grinned back at Burt, but nobody noticed because Cecil exploded.

"Barbara is not okay!" he hissed through clinched teeth. "She is damn far from okay!"

Everyone stared at Cecil. This outburst was way out of character for him. Even Andrews seemed to sober a little.

"No . . . no, she's not," Burt said. "But Cecil, at least she is alive. Dr. Winder says this dark crap is killing people all over the world . . . it almost killed you, buddy."

Everyone, including Cecil, turned their attention to Dr. Winder who was still staring at the floor. He slowly raised his head and nodded.

"It's not so much the dark is killing people, it's more like the dark is causing them to kill themselves," Dr. Winder said.

"Huh?" Derek blurted.

"It makes sense," Burt said. "Cecil had no idea what he was doing, but he managed to fill up the bathtub and almost drown himself." He paused and whispered to his friend. "What did you see, Cecil?"

It was as if Burt's voice was coming from somewhere far away, a safe distance from the canoe and the snakes. For an instant, Cecil was back there . . . remembering the horror, the terror and the pain. He shivered as if something cold and slimy slithered down his spine. He did not reply, he didn't have to because everyone understood. The details were not important, yet this was one case when the devil was definitely in the details.

He saw the snakes in his mind's eye and remembered the brutal cruelties committed by each one. These snakes must be the manifestation of humans who had committed horrible acts. An understanding began to form in his head, coalescing into a single word.

"Impals," he muttered in a breathless whisper.

"Are you saying your father was right?" Burt said. "Are you saying this darkness is Impals?"

Cecil shook his head and sat down in the rocking chair. He rested his elbows on his knees and stared at the floor. He then raised his head and scanned the faces of everyone in the group, finally coming to rest on Dr. Winder.

"No . . . something different," he said, keeping his eyes on Dr. Winder as if seeking confirmation.

Dr. Winder glanced away. Everyone now turned to the doctor.

"How should I know what it is?" Dr. Winder snapped.

"You said the eye of the storm contained a different type of energy than the rest of the storm," Burt said. "Is it possible this new energy could have manifested something else?"

"Of course it's possible!" Dr. Winder said. "But I don't know why in the hell you think I have any idea what it is!"

He reached in his shirt pocket and fished out a cigarette. With trembling hands he inserted it between his lips and lit it. He took a deep drag and exhaled a large puff of smoke, causing everyone to move back a few paces.

"Doctor," Burt said in an even tone. "Do you think this darkness is Impals as we knew them?"

He took another drag off his cigarette and shook his head.

"No . . . no, not possible. The Impals disappeared, and then there was darkness. The energy was different, very different from the initial storm. A different manifestation . . . different energy . . . something new, something different . . . dark . . ." Dr. Winder's answer deteriorated into what sounded as incoherent rambling, although what he said made sense. Dr. Winder walked to the window and peered up at the sky. "Sky different . . . clouds different . . . different energy . . . not Impals," he rambled.

As Dr. Winder continued his blathering, the men gaped at each other. Even Andrews seemed concerned.

"So, if it's not Impals," Derek said, "then what is it?"

"Did you ever meet an evil Impal?" Cecil asked.

"Well . . . sure," Burt said. "We ran into several real jerks."

Cecil shook his head. "No, I'm not talking about jerks . . . I'm talking about evil," he said.

"Well, what about those two pricks who beat you in your prison cell, or the two jerks who shot me for bounty money?" Burt suggested.

"They definitely fell into the category of a-hole, jerk and prick . . . and some a little on the stupid side, but . . . evil? They were not even close to the blackness I saw. I'm not just talking about an absence of light. I mean their heart and soul were black . . . uncaring and unremitting hatred . . . profound wickedness."

"How the hell could you see that in all of them?" Burt asked.

Cecil shrugged. "I don't know, I can only tell you that I did. I know it as well as I know you, Burt."

Burt shook his head, keeping his eyes fixed on Cecil. "Jesus, what did you see, man?" he asked.

Cecil didn't reply, but Burt could tell by his expression that he should not press the question. He decided to approach from another angle. "So . . . they used to be human?" he asked.

Cecil nodded. "Well . . . they used to occupy a human body, but to call them human, well . . ." Cecil trailed off, he was at a loss of how to explain it to his friend.

"Demons?" Derek asked.

"I don't think so," Cecil said. "Demons serve Satan. These things seemed to serve nothing but themselves and their own twisted desires. They were, well . . . black souls."

The men sat in silence until Burt jumped up. "Hey, where's Dr. Winder?" he shouted.

They turned toward the window where he stood moments before. He was not there. It didn't take long to figure out where he went because the front door was standing wide open.

Almost tripping over each other, they sprinted to the door. Clambering onto the porch and down the steps, they spotted Dr. Winder a short distance away. He resembled a turkey caught outside in a rainstorm. He stared skyward with his mouth agape, mumbling nonsensical phrases.

"Einstein . . . thermodynamics . . . energy, different . . . very different . . . not Impals . . . different, different . . . the dark, energy," he muttered then began pointing skywards as he walked towards the woods. "Sky . . . color . . . different," he repeated over and over again.

The sky was different. When the Impals were here; it was lavender colored with yellowish clouds. Now it was a reddish tint with orange clouds. Nobody had any idea what it meant. The general consensus was it had something to do with the energy of the storm and now the mysterious energy of the eye.

The time to process what Dr. Winder was saying would come later because it suddenly occurred to everyone he was in grave danger. He was wandering toward the woods and the shadows.

"Dr. Winder!" Cecil screamed, his heart in his throat. "Don't go into the woods!"

Winder may as well have been a hundred miles away because he did not react to the screams of Cecil or anyone else. He stayed on course.

His head in the air, he stumbled towards the darkest and most volatile area in the woods. The dark shadow cast by the massive canopy of trees seemed to undulate with excitement as Dr. Winder wandered closer. He would be in the shade in a matter of seconds. Everyone ran after him, trying to catch the doctor before it was too late, but he was too far away. By the time they reached the tree line, the screaming already started.

Dr. Winder shrieked in agony as the darkness engulfed him in a thick bank of smoke. It was all they could do to not go in after him, but the men knew better than to get any closer. Even though they were several yards away, they could still feel the dark. It seemed to be an impalpable, yet tangible, wave of hatred and malice radiating with the intensity of a forest fire. A moment later, Dr. Winder made an impossible leap. He shot straight up from the blackness and grasped the trunk of a large pine tree about seven feet off the ground. He then proceeded to climb with incredible speed and agility. He ascended more than thirty feet in a few seconds.

Dr. Winder climbed higher and higher, a column of smoky darkness trailing behind like an umbilical to Hell. A moment later he was out of sight. The screaming stopped and the woods fell silent. For a few seconds, they only heard the chilling hissing and clicking from the darkness.

"Dr. Winder?" Burt screamed.

In almost an answer to Burt's call, a blood-curdling scream erupted from high above. An instant later a silent flash of something, or someone, dropped from the trees and hit the ground with a sickening thud. Dr. Winder lay in a crumpled and disfigured mass a few feet from the darkness. He was dead.

CHAPTER 5

THE GENERAL

"There is a Destiny which has the control of our actions, not to be resisted by the strongest efforts of Human Nature."
~George Washington

THE ROOM WAS AS DARK as a crypt. All of the lighting was shutoff . . . lamps, light fixtures, and even security lighting. The curtains were drawn tight over the three massive Bow windows. It was a bright and sunny day outside, but not a single speck of light made it into the old room. A room completely devoid of light in the middle of the day was unusual. Of course, it was not as odd as the circumstances. The eye of the cosmic storm now encompassed the Earth and this room, this dark room, was the Oval Office.

One person alone was supposed to sit behind the Resolute Desk, but he was now dead. The vice president had served as a puppet leader since the death of the president. Earlier, when the eye of the storm arrived, he was found in his bedroom upstairs lying in the bottom of a large walk-in closet. A foot-long wooden shoehorn protruded from his throat. The evidence suggested that the fatal wound was self-inflicted.

Two secret service agents wound up in the hospital trying to reach him. This was before someone brought in several large flashlights.

The darkness managed to take the most important man in the world, even though he was only a life sized marionette. The puppet master sat alone in the Oval Office, listening to the whisperings of the dark and gloating.

"I was right," General Ott Garrison thought to himself. "Now the Impals are showing their true face."

He knew what the darkness was doing to people around the world, not to mention the former president/vice president, however . . . it did not bother him. Sure, he could hear the terrifying whispering and hissing coming from the dark, yet he was in no way bothered. Quite simply, he could pass through the darkness unmolested and unscathed. He was empowered and he was boastful. Arrogance swelled through him as he held up an unseen middle finger to the dark.

"Screw you!" he muttered, clenching his jaws.

The cadence and frequency of the inhuman whisperings changed. It was enough to satisfy the general that his taunt was received. After passing through a dark hallway of the White House, he noted how the darkness seemed to part in front of him. Making the Oval Office a 'light free zone' was the final confirmation of what he believed.

"God chose me to rid the world of Impals," he thought to himself. "Now he has shielded me from their evil. He has chosen me for a higher purpose."

He slid out of the high backed leather chair and onto his knees between the desk and the window. He began praying, silently at first, and then raised his voice from a faint whisper to almost a yell.

"Dear Heavenly Father,
I pray this prayer in the power of the Holy Spirit. In the name of Jesus Christ your one and only Son who died and rose again for remission of sin. I bind, rebuke and render powerless: all division, discord, disunity, strife, wrath, murder, criticism, condemnation, pride, envy, jealousy, gossip, slander, evil speaking, lying, false manifestations, lying signs and wonders, fear of deceiving spirits, and all familiar and territorial spirits.
I AM GOD'S CHILD! I RESIST THE DEVIL AND DECLARE THAT NO WEAPON FORMED AGAINST ME

31

SHALL PROSPER. I AM THE RIGHTOUSNESS OF GOD IN
CHRIST JESUS . . . AMEN!"

He did not move and did not open his eyes for several moments
after completing his prayer. He listened to the darkness, a faint grin
forming at the corners of his mouth. The darkness . . . the Impals . . .
the true face of evil was afraid of him. The relentless noise of the dark
had subsided tenfold since he finished his prayer. The sound was now
little more than a faint whisper from a distant room.

General Garrison rose to his feet and opened his eyes. He looked
around him, seeing nothing in the pitch darkness, but, then again, he
was seeing everything, wasn't he? He saw his destiny, his purpose, his
important place in God's plan. He, and he alone, was chosen. Nothing
could touch him because this was God's will and he was more than
ready and able to carry out His will.

"This is the end times," he whispered as he walked towards the
door, "and God has chosen me to help usher in his new kingdom."

The general had no idea exactly how the recent world events played
in to the prophecy of the end of days. He wasn't worried because he
knew God would make it clear to him soon. The book of Revelations
is thick with symbolism and metaphors for things yet to come. It is not
easily understandable, even to the most astute Biblical scholars. Was this
the prelude to the rapture . . . or perhaps the seven year tribulation? The
Bible did say there would be false prophets and deceivers in the end
days. To General Garrison, that was exactly what the Impals were.

He threw open the doors to the Oval Office, letting in a flood of
light and screams from the well-lit administrative area. Secretaries,
military personnel and Secret Service agents all regarded him with
wild-eyed horror. When he stepped out and shut the door behind him,
the expressions turned from horror to confusion. They stared at the
general, and then each other with bewilderment.

"S-sir, are you okay?" one of the Secret Service agents stammered.

"I've never been better in my life . . . praise the Lord!" he boasted
with a wide grin.

"But, but sir . . . it was dark in there, are . . . are . . ." one of the secretaries asked through a flood of terrified tears.

"Am I alive? Am I in injured? Am I real?" General Garrison finished for her. He gave her a large toothy smile and said, "Yes, no and yes."

A man in a dress Marines uniform stepped forward. He squinted at the general with intense scrutiny as if he were about to disarm an explosive device.

"Sir . . . do you need assistance?" he asked.

The general held up his hands in a calming motion. His face beamed with peaceful serenity. It made chills run up their spines, considering they all knew something horrific was in the darkness on the other side of the door.

"Please . . . everyone take a seat," he said, shielding his eyes from the bright auxiliary lighting. He couldn't help thinking this bright lighting was akin to being in the presence of God.

Once everyone took a seat, he stood where the lights were not in his eyes. Garrison smiled at them, resembling a preacher about to deliver a meaningful sermon. "My friends, we have experienced an unprecedented tragedy in our country . . . two of them in as many weeks. We have lost two presidents, two great and noble men who will be missed."

He scanned the faces of his captive audience with confident empathy. He understood their tragedy and grief, he felt their pain and . . . why not? He was one of them, wasn't he? No, he corrected himself. He was different; he was chosen . . . he was better. God had shown him this. The general knew he could turn around and walk back into the darkness of the Oval Office and survive, but none of them could. God protected the general because he was righteous in his convictions, he was special.

"As tragic as things have been, I believe all things happen for a reason. There is a reason God has put me in this place at this point in time."

"To do what, sir?" the Marine asked.

General Garrison regarded him with casual indifference. "Why . . . to lead the country of course," he replied as if he was speaking to a dense child.

"Sir . . ." the Marine began again. "The vice president never appointed a successor when he took over the presidency. Shouldn't the Speaker of the House be taking the oath of office today?"

The general felt a sudden flash of anger. He hated the Speaker, hated him with a passion. He was one of the most vocal objectors to the government's plan, the general's plan, for rounding up Impals. The speaker was not a Godly man, in the general's opinion. He was Catholic or Presbyterian . . . one of those denominations not true to God's word. Garrison had seen fit to ally himself with the leaders of those denominations and other religions when it suited his needs. It did not suit his needs anymore. The true dark nature of the Impals revealed were all the validity he needed. God's special protection from this evil was just icing on the cake. Besides, the general believed the speaker was an idiot. The very thought of the imbecile taking over the presidency made his stomach burn.

"I am above such petty human prejudice," he thought to himself. "God has seen fit to place me there."

General Garrison forced a smile and grasped the man's shoulder like a prideful father greeting his son. "You raise good points, Captain . . . ?" he said, examining the man's rank insignia.

"Captain Paladino, sir," the Marine said, straightening his posture.

"Well, Captain Paladino, the problem is that we have no time, no way of knowing if the speaker is still alive. After all, we are still on lockdown here. I'm quite sure the Capitol is as well."

Captain Paladino glanced at the phone on the desk beside them.

"We could call, sir," he suggested.

"Captain, I believe it would be dangerous to transfer leadership at this time. It would be dangerous for our country and, quite frankly, the world."

"But, it's the law sir . . . it's in the Constitution," Captain Paladino insisted.

Garrison smiled at him. "Captain, please allow me to show you why it is dangerous," he said, stepping back a couple of feet. He then motioned towards the door to the Oval Office.

Everyone stared with horror at the general. What would he do to demonstrate the dangerous situation of the country? Captain Paladino knew, after all, he was a Marine. His training enabled him to analyze and recognize a situation. He knew what General Garrison intended when he motioned toward the door. He was trained to be fearless, like all Marines, but the word has always been a misnomer. Any Marine worth his salt knew there was no such thing as fearless, fear was natural and unavoidable. The key was to control it and make it useful. Captain Paladino did a good job masking his fear, but he was at a loss on how to control it and use it in this situation. He walked a few steps forward, standing less than a foot away from the general. Captain Paladino then turned and looked him in the eyes.

Garrison smirked, his face brimming with arrogance and confidence. The general walked to the Oval Office door, the whole time keeping his eyes on the unfortunate Marine. He turned the handle then pushed the door open, revealing the pitch-dark interior. The hissing and whispering radiated from the dark opening in a demonic chorus. The general gave the others in the room a wink before giving Captain Paladino a wry smile. Garrison then confidently stepped inside, disappearing into the darkness. A few moments, later the general called out from somewhere deep inside the room.

"Captain Paladino, will you join me in the Oval Office, please?" he called in a sing-song voice.

"Why sir?" Paladino asked, his mouth as dry as sandpaper.

"I need you to join me for a meeting, Captain . . . so we can discuss the dangers that a leadership transferal would pose to our country."

There was a long pause before Captain Paladino responded. "Sir . . . I don't think it would be a good idea," he said.

The tension in the room was palpable. Everyone's hearts almost stopped when General Garrison spoke again. "I GAVE YOU AN ORDER, CAPTAIN! I EXPECT YOU TO OBEY IT!" he boomed, not with the forceful tone of a drill instructor, but of a man about to go out of his head with rage.

"Sir?" Captain Paladino called. Calm still registered on his face even though his heart was about to hammer out of his chest.

"GET YOUR ASS IN HERE NOW, CAPTAIN!" Garrison screamed.

The captain glanced at the others. They were frozen in terror.

Captain Paladino was a good soldier and Marine. He would not allow himself to disobey the orders of a superior officer, even if they were from an Army officer. But even more important, he would not let his fear control him, his fear of what waited for him in the darkness. He tightened his jaw, stood up straight, and then stuck his chest out before starting a slow march towards the door.

One of the Secret Service Agents handed Captain Paladino a flashlight as the two men exchanged somber smiles. They both knew the flashlight would be inadequate to fend off the complete darkness of the sealed room. Captain Paladino clicked it on and shone the beam through the open door. The darkness seemed to swirl around the narrow ray of light like rushing water over a clear tube. The hissing and clicking changed cadence and pitch. It was as if something or some 'things' were agitated by the presence of the light.

He paused for a second and then started once again.

"I DON'T HAVE ALL DAY, CAPTAIN!" the general shrieked.

A second later, the darkness enveloped the Marine. A single scream came from the open door, but that was all. They heard a series of loud bangs as if someone were taking a sledge hammer to the walls. The Secret Service agents scrambled to move some of the supplemental lighting to the door of the Oval Office, but it was no use. The banging stopped almost as fast as it began.

Everyone in the room held their breath as their hearts throbbed between air-deprived lungs. Heavy footsteps began to pound towards the door. A moment later, the smug face of General Garrison emerged from the darkness. He gave everybody an insincere look of sympathy then reached inside the door and flicked on the light switch. The interior of the Oval Office materialized, appearing as benign as ever. The hissing and scratching stopped.

"I'm sorry to report that our meeting did not go well," the general said in a matter of fact tone. "But I am sure you all see why change is a bad idea. I have been chosen to lead and I will do it," he said brushing his hands together as if eager to begin a challenging task. He then walked past everyone to the corridor beyond. He paused and turned before rounding the corner.

"Oh . . . please take care of the captain," he said flippantly. "He was a good man, but he just could not understand. I'm going to go check on my granddaughter, Steff," he said, and then waved as if he was leaving on a trip.

Everyone felt hollow and numb, but the general's final words sent a chill through them all. Most people would have checked on their child or grandchild immediately in a situation such as this. Of course, General Garrison wasn't most people. He was acting as the hand of God, everything, and everyone else, be damned.

CHAPTER 6

PRIVATE ABERNATHY

"A human life is a story told by God."
~Hans Christian Andersen

PRIVATE JACK ABERNATHY managed to avoid latrine duty, but his partner was not so fortunate. Jack received permission to return to his flat and pick up a few personal belongings before nightfall. He was sure he would get an earful when he returned, considering the spiteful stare he received from Sean. By the time he returned in a few hours, the work would be done.

The road leading into town was choked with the dispossessed as hundreds, if not thousands, made their way to the base. The barracks would be full soon, leaving only the parade grounds and a handful of open areas for the remaining refugees to settle. People from all walks of life and socioeconomic classes trudged along on foot with a common purpose, to escape the dark.

Jack watched in disbelief as the civilians passed. Some dragged boxes with rope or their bare hands. Others pushed wheelbarrows or pulled carts overloaded with personal possessions. Several people toted stuffed backpacks, while others clutched their belongings in their arms. He at first thought it odd that these people were walking to the base, especially the ones with heavy loads. However, when he

38

got a short distance up the road he understood. A military blockade was set up forcing anyone in an auto or other motorized vehicle to pull over and leave them. Space was a premium in the base and automobiles would crowd out people. A large pasture served as a makeshift parking lot. The field across the road was littered by what seemed to be a number of blankets or perhaps rolled rugs. When Jack drew even with the field, he could see it was not abandoned possessions. This pasture had become a makeshift morgue. A toe, an arm, wisps of hair could be seen protruding from under some of the sheets. A few of the lighter colored linens were spotted with stains of blood. Jack stopped and stared at the grotesque menagerie.

"Bloody sad, isn't it?" one of the blockade guards said.

Jack jumped as if received a shock. "What?" he stammered.

"Sorry mate, didn't mean to scare you. It is enough to make the best of us squeamish," the guard said with a shudder as he waved a small convertible into the parking lot.

"What happened?" Jack asked. "There must be hundreds of them!"

"Last night happened," he said. "When we reached four hundred, I stopped counting."

"All of them from town?"

"I don't know, it has been a damn fight all day . . . people insisting on taking their loved one on to the base with them."

"Fight?" Jack asked.

The guard raised an eyebrow. "Wouldn't you fight if someone told you to leave your child or parent's body behind?"

Jack shrugged, then without another word he continued his journey. He had to hurry; it would be dark in a few hours.

The road was luckily free of shade. Cattle grazing land bordered both sides and the nearest patches of woods were no closer than twenty meters from the road. In contrast, the town was a sadistic minefield. Shadows cast from buildings and trees threatened to block his path at every turn. The shady patches on every street and sidewalk writhed and undulated in a hungry, shapeless mass. After a half hour of careful maneuvering, he managed to traverse the five blocks to his flat.

The blinds were pulled shut as usual because Jack enjoyed his privacy. He picked up a fallen branch from the yard and then carefully unlocked the door. He stuck the branch in through the opening and fumbled about until he found the light switch. He flicked it upward with one quick motion. Tossing the branch aside, he slipped inside.

Jack's flat was of greater than average size. He could have stayed in base housing for much less money, but there was little solitude. The private's apartment could have accommodated two grown men with plenty of room left over. Three bedroom flats were almost unheard of in this small town. It may not have been a necessity to live in a place with this much space, but for Jack, it was almost as important as the very air he breathed. He had just started to gather a few personal items into his duffel when he heard a noise.

A whimpering sound came from outside his kitchen window. It was faint at first, but as he stopped to listen, it grew louder. Jack walked to his kitchen window and peered out. Dark shadows crisscrossed the yard from several elm trees. They made the yard seem as if it contained dark and surging tentacles. As he screwed up his eyes, he saw something that resembled a pile of laundry, until it started to move. An elderly woman was lying face down in a sunlit area, inches from a dark patch.

Jack stared, mesmerized. This had to be a sign. Everyone left town, or so he thought. It was his destiny to come back, to find this old lady crawling about in his backyard. Excitement leapt inside him when he realized what he must do. He grabbed a couple of high beam flashlights from a desk drawer and eased out the backdoor. He aimed the beams straight ahead and crept towards the old woman. The powerful light parted the shadows a little easier than he thought they would and he soon reached the old woman.

She stared straight ahead, whimpering and crying, taking no notice of his presence. Not until he knelt down and spoke to her.

"Are you okay, dear?" he asked.

She shrieked so loud he thought his eardrum might rupture. The poor woman began to scoot along on her belly as if the devil himself was after her. Jack managed to grab her by the hem of her cotton gown as she tried to scurry into one of the shadows. She screamed and writhed, but she was not strong enough to pull away. The woman was fortunate that the fabric in her gown was strong enough to resist their tug of war.

"Calm down . . . its okay!" Jack assured her.

She did calm down, but Jack wasn't sure if it was because of his reassurance or because she was tired. She was injured, as evidenced by the blood on her gown and deep gash in her right forearm. However, it wasn't until she tried to look at him before Jack discovered why she did not acknowledge him before he spoke. The old lady was blind.

"What's your name?" Jack asked.

She tried to focus on where she believed his face was, but she ended up peering over his shoulder. "Agnes," she croaked.

"Well, Agnes, how did you wind up in my backyard?"

She shook her head, her eyes vacant and distant. "Crawled," she whispered.

Jack noticed a gash in her arm as she shifted her weight onto her side. This was not the worst injury the woman suffered, not by a long shot. The skin on her lower legs from her knees to her ankles was one bloody mess. Exposed bone protruded from below her left knee.

"Can you walk, Agnes?" he asked. The answer should have been obvious.

She started to emit a high-pitched whine.

Jack got to his feet and scooped Agnes's tiny frame up in one fluid motion and threw her over his shoulder. She screamed in agony as his arm brushed over her legs, and then she passed out. He headed back to the house toting a ninety-pound payload, his ten thousand-candle power flashlight clearing the way.

Jack laid Agnes on his small vinyl sofa and then continued to gather miscellaneous items to take back to base. He stopped and stared at the old woman for several moments, as if he had forgotten his purpose. In truth, he hadn't forgotten. His purpose came into full relief. He was meant to come home today. No, it was more of a gift and he intended to appreciate it to the fullest. Life on the base had been dragging him down as of late, especially since the Impals arrived. He hadn't enjoyed the privacy he so craved. It was a little over two months, a couple of days before the storm arrived, since he had the alone time he desired.

He didn't need to come back home, he kept everything back at the base, well . . . almost everything.

Jack walked into his bedroom and opened the door to a large walk-in closet. The closet had a motion-activated light and the five foot by six foot nook glowed with one hundred watt brilliance. The closet was empty except for one very strange thing. An iron cage occupied over half its volume. He smiled at the cage with satisfaction.

"Good, the bitch is finally gone," he murmured through clinched teeth.

Jack caressed the metal bars as if its cold surface was the skin of a lover. He was lost in the moment; spellbound, enthralled, rapturous, at peace . . . remembering . . . remembering . . . remembering . . . what was that?

Agnes had awakened in the other room and was making her pitiful whining noise again. Anger welled up in Jack.

"The stupid old crone!" he raved. "Whining, like they all do. Whining and getting blood on my carpet!"

He patted the bars to the cage and then turned and strode into the other room. He found Agnes lying face down and moving her arms as if she were swimming. She had managed to move a few feet from the sofa and trailed blood behind her in crimson tire tracks.

"Damn you!" Jack shouted and grabbed her by the back of the hair. He jerked her up on her toes to where her neck supported the entire weight of her body. Her unseeing eyes flashed with terror and she tried to scream, but she didn't have any air left in her tired old lungs. He threw her over his shoulder and charged into the bedroom, banging her head on the doorframe in the process. He jerked open the door to the cage and flung her inside. She collapsed in a sobbing heap on the cold metal floor. Jack slammed the door and jingled it a few times to make sure it latched properly. He then sat across the room on the edge of his bed and watched.

Agnes was not the first elderly woman to pay Jack Abernathy a visit, over the years there were dozens. Some came as voluntary trusting guests, but most had been abducted and brought here. Some might say it was all for Jack's twisted amusement. Of course, Jack would disagree. He served a purpose, clearing society of old, weak, and dead weight. Jack believed this made the world a better place, pruning the demographic garden. Besides, they were not long for the grave anyway. His service also came with fringe benefits, he enjoyed every second of it.

To Jack, the elderly were a useless drain on society. Their weakened state and infirmities were a burden and what did they contribute? Not a damn thing. Old ladies were the worst. The putrid smell of age, mingled with a heavy scent of lotion and cheap dime store perfume was enough to make his head explode. Yet, it wasn't the worst of it. They all held an opinion. They all exuded a self-righteous attitude, damning anyone who didn't fall in line with their antiquated view of the world. They were selfish, they were gossips, they were burdens who begged to be removed like the malignant tumors they were. Jack was a social surgeon, he prided himself in this, but first and foremost he was a teacher. What good did it do to punish someone if they did not know what they were being punished for?

The cage was his classroom; a classroom where a captive audience of one could receive an education. They all learned the lesson of their inadequacy to society. His students always misbehaved though. The screaming, the pleading, and the crying was more than he could stand. Very few pupils got to hear Jack's entire lecture. Most were expelled on the first day, eternal expulsion to the murky depths of the nearby moors.

Some of his pupils had made the news, but not many. Most were forgotten by their families and society a long time ago. He was careful in his choices. Forgotten old ladies were the best candidates.

He prided himself in his neatness. No blood, no mess . . . just a slow suffocation with a thin link of rope. His favorite way was to lure them to the side of the cage with a false promise of release, or perhaps to offer them a drink of water. Then he would pounce and wrap the rope around their neck. Once secure, he would apply more and more pressure, and then release it. This gave them a second or two to pull air into their restricted airway. Then he would start the pressure again. Sometimes he would let this process go on for hours before ending it with one hard yank.

No, the real reason Jack returned home today was to see if his houseguest of two months was gone. An elderly woman named

Gwenda Harcourt from Comstock was his latest pupil. He trailed her home one Sunday morning after worship service at the Comstock Presbyterian Church. Jack thought that church services were the best place to find aging parishioners. If they attended church alone, they likely lived alone, easy pickings.

Gwenda received her final lesson the morning the cosmic storm arrived. Before Jack had time to take her out of the cage and deposit her in the moors, he was shocked to see two Gwenda Harcourts in the cage. One was old, pallid and dead. One was young and beautiful with a shimmering luminescence like a lake on a sunny day. Jack fled from the house in terror, only to return later when he realized what was happening. He held the Impal, Gwenda, at bay with an iron bar as he dragged her body out of the cage. After disposing of the corpse, he returned to marvel at the being now inhabiting his iron classroom.

But Gwenda was no longer a member of his murderous demographic. She was a young version of her former self, probably as she appeared in her mid-30s. She seemed sad and frightened, yet she was not vengeful, even though she realized what Jack had done to her. She didn't qualify to be one of his condemned students. What good would it do to lecture her on the evils of the old when she was not elderly? Of course, she wasn't human either, but he couldn't let her go. She would leave and she would tell . . . he couldn't have that.

His flat had no neighbors within fifty yards and the walls of his home were thick cinder blocks. It would be difficult to hear the screams of an Impal closed up in the closet. Jack had become so confident in his seclusion; he began to have great fun every time he came home by prodding Gwenda with an iron bar. Her tinny, high-pitched scream gave him chills at first. After a while, he found it exhilarating. He was glad his unwanted house guest was now gone, but he also kind of missed her.

"It is okay," he thought to himself. He had a new pupil now, something he desperately needed, a Godsend. It was over two months since anyone occupied his cage other than an Impal. He was craving another pupil. With everything locked down on the base, who knew how long it would be before another opportunity?

He didn't believe in God. Jack was not a religious man and church was nothing more than a hunting ground for him. Even so, he gave a silent prayer of thanks for this opportunity to make the world a little better place. His prayer was more an act of self-gratification than it was a profession of thankfulness to a deity.

When he finished his hollow prayer, he regarded Gwenda with a soul-freezing smile. She knew what was coming and there was nothing she could do about it. She pushed herself as far away from the door to the iron cage as she could, her arthritic legs drawn as close as possible to her body. Jack casually got up and strolled to his dresser where he opened a drawer and produced a thin link of nylon rope. He rolled it up and shoved it in his pocket. He then strolled back to the cage and knelt down. Jack put his nose and mouth through one of the narrow openings in the bars and puckered his lips as if he wanted to give her a big goodbye kiss.

He wanted to taunt her, but he knew he must move fast because there were only a few hours left until sunset. What happened next, Jack did not anticipate or even imagine in his wildest dreams. He saw a quick flash and then felt excruciating pain as something impacted his lips and chin. He flew backwards and hit his head on the seat of a wooden footstool. Consciousness left his body in a dissipating fog.

Jack did not know that Gwenda had very long legs for her small frame. Though injured, the leverage provided by the back of the cage made them formidable weapons. He also did not know her right fibula was shattered in the attack. She writhed on the bottom of the cage in pain. He would have enjoyed that.

Jack didn't know anything right now. He would not know anything for several hours, if and when he regained consciousness. The sunlight streaming in his large picture window would be gone by the time he awakened. The bedroom and the closet would be dark.

CHAPTER 7

ON BOARD

"Whoever is out of patience is out of possession of their soul."
~Francis Bacon

DR. WINDER LAY IN THE WOODS for over an hour before the men could retrieve his body. They gathered every flashlight and built a small fire to cast enough light to cross the short distance to his mangled corpse. Cecil and Burt were not up to the task. They tried to assist, but they knew the man. Not to mention, he was not recognizable as his former self. No one knew for sure how high he climbed before his fatal dive, but every bone in his body was shattered. Cecil and Burt sat on the front steps of the cabin wiping tendrils of vomit from their chins.

Sam Andrews made the crude comment that he was like dragging a bag full of jelly. Cecil had to restrain himself from picking up one of Sam's discarded beer bottles and pelting him in the head. He wasn't sure whether they were glad Charlotte's father kept the cabin well stocked with beer or not. Andrews had been a violent and short-tempered ass at the Impal camp. All that time without a drink was enough to push any alcoholic to the edge. He was still an ass, but the alcohol seemed to have quelled his temper for now. The beer wouldn't last forever.

Cecil glanced over at the metal canisters of gasoline stored beside the house for the generator. There were twelve in all and they already went through two in a little over ten hours. He did a quick calculation in his head and figured the generator would be able to run another ninety-six hours. Only four days until the gas was gone. Of course, this was assuming the electric consumption remained at the same level, which he knew it would not. The nights would put a strain on their electrical needs. They could cut back during the daylight and spend time outside. Nevertheless, the increased need at night would knock about a day off their time. They had three days to find a safe way out of the woods or succumb to the darkness.

They would discuss a plan soon, but right now they had more pressing matters. As luck would have it, there was a tool rack mounted on the house next to the gas canisters. An assortment of rusty garden tools hung on its weathered pegs. Cecil and Burt each grabbed an old shovel and dug a grave in a well-lit area to the side of the drive. When they finished, Sam and Derek deposited Dr. Winder's body in the hole. Cecil did not want to see the doctor, not in this state. He handed his shovel to Derek and strode towards the house.

"I'm going to check on Barbara," he called, keeping his eyes on the house.

Burt handed his shovel to Sam. "I'll go get the ladies so we can have a service for the doctor," he said and turned to follow his friend inside.

"Why bother," Sam mumbled. "He was an jerk anyway."

Without thought, Burt rounded on him with his uninjured arm and clocked him on the jaw. He had wanted to hit Andrews for a long time, but he immediately regretted it. The motion strained his injured arm sending a stabbing pain through his shoulder. However, the pain was secondary to his nausea as Andrews tumbled backward into the hole. He landed on top of Dr. Winder with a sickening smack.

Burt turned and headed back toward the house. He glanced at Derek who wore a strange expression of horror and amusement on his face. A stream of slurred curses flew from Andrews as he struggled to pull himself out of the hole. Burt couldn't help smiling.

Soon he was upstairs where Sally met him at the door in a tight embrace. Cecil had given the women the sad news and Charlotte sat on the edge of the bed crying. Barbara still lay unmoving with her eyes closed. She breathed in and out in an awkward, yet rhythmic, cadence. Cecil sat beside her and stroked her hair while whispering in her ear.

Cecil carried Barbara downstairs and placed her on the sofa. It was much brighter and he wanted to keep an eye on her. He left the front door open while they conducted a brief service for Dr. Winder. There was a clear view from the grave to the sofa. Cecil never took his eyes off of her, even when he said a few kind words about the former scientist. He found it hard to concentrate on his words as he watched his wife and listened to the inhuman hissing and clicking. They were a chorus of hellish insects and reptiles trying to form cruel words.

Cecil was so engrossed, he did not notice Andrews's irreverent behavior, but everyone else did. He stood by the grave taking long swigs of beer, while acting impatient and bored. He emphasized his boredom with an occasional belch. When the service was over he took his empty bottle and shoved it neck first into the soft dirt of Dr. Winder's grave.

"Have a drink," he murmured.

Burt wanted to deck him again and moved in his direction, but Derek moved to intercept him. "Come on, let's go talk to the major," he said, giving Burt a reassuring pat on his uninjured shoulder. "Maybe the lush will get drunk and stumble into the woods."

Even though they both hated Andrews, Derek immediately wanted to take it back. The thought of anyone stumbling into the woods sent a clammy coldness through them.

They went into the kitchen and poured themselves a cup of coffee while they waited on Cecil to sit with Barbara. A few minutes later, Sally and Charlotte came in and sat with her so Cecil got up and trudged to the kitchen. He was a hollow shell of his former self. His gaunt and pale countenance resembled a man who just crawled to Hell and back. They couldn't imagine Hell being much worse than today.

"Where's Andrews?" Burt asked, glancing at the windows.

"On the front porch drinking another cold one," Derek said, motioning toward the door. "You better hope he doesn't sober up," he added with a grin. "He is liable to come looking for payback."

"He probably won't even remember it," Burt growled.

When Burt told Cecil the story, the dark cloud dominating the major's features seemed to break, if only for a moment or two. He grinned and tapped his fingers on the tabletop. "Damn, I wish I had been there to see it," he said.

"Well it's obvious we can't count on him," Burt said. "Especially as long as there is alcohol in the house . . . and even if he runs out, well, you remember what he was like at the camp."

The three men agreed that any plans made would not include Sam Andrews in the discussions. They would take turns babysitting him to make sure he didn't do anything stupid to harm himself or someone else.

They also agreed that there were about three days of gasoline left, give or take a few hours. It was the take part that worried them. They must prepare a Plan B in case they were unable to get more gas. The problem was, there was no Plan B, at least not a feasible one. No gas meant no electricity, which meant no light, which meant no protection from the dark. They could make it through the days with caution, but the nights would be indefensible. Also, God forbid a thunderstorm came through in the middle of the day. The unanimous decision was that they must figure some way to get out and get gas. There was no alternative. In just three days, unless this phenomenon passed, they would all be taken by the dark.

The three men walked out onto the front porch and scanned the woods and the road leading to the house. The whole area was pocked with dark patches.

"How many flashlights do we have?" Burt asked.

"Not enough," Derek replied. "Maybe three or so and I'm not sure the batteries are good on all of those. I found a fourth one upstairs, but it did not even have any batteries in it."

"Well, damn," Burt muttered. "The ones we have don't put out enough light to find a shiny penny in a shadow."

They pondered their dilemma. Would the overhead light in the vehicle be enough to protect them if it was subsidized by a few discount store flashlights? Cecil was hopeful, but he didn't truly believe they had a chance to make it out. There were too many dark patches in the woods. No, the only safe option was to wait a month and let fall do its thing. Of course, they didn't have a month and fall was far behind this year. In spite of several cool spells the last couple of weeks, not a single leaf had changed color yet.

"We're going to have to try," Derek said, breaking the tense silence.

"I'll do it," Cecil said.

"The hell you will!" Burt shouted. "You have a wife and daugh— daughter who needs you!" He stopped himself from saying daughters because Abigail Garrison, Abbs, had been killed yesterday. She disappeared with the other Impals around the world that morning. Cecil's youngest daughter was in the clutches of General Garrison. Whether he went on this mission or not would not help her. He couldn't get to her even if he knew where she was.

"You have a wife, Burt!" Cecil snapped. "Besides, I'm the ranking person here and it's my decision!"

"With all due respect, *major*. I'm not sure our ranks mean a whole hell of a lot right now!' Burt retorted. "I'm the logical choice."

Cecil glanced over his shoulder and saw Charlotte and Sally watching them. He jerked his head towards Burt, indicating they needed to tone the volume down.

"I don't care what the ranks are here; I'm a civilian in any case," Derek said, dropping his voice to a whisper. "I'm not married, I have no kids, and I have a mother I haven't seen since before I graduated high school. You want to talk about logical choices? Well I am the clear cut choice to do this!"

The argument of who was the most qualified to die continued for several minutes before it was broken up by Sally and Charlotte. The women insisted that nobody was going, not until certain it would be safe. This was their official, public stance, but deep down they knew the men were right. Safe or not, somebody was going to have to attempt it.

Everyone had become so involved in the argument; nobody took notice of Andrews who lounged a few feet away. They didn't notice when he rolled off the glider swing after he drained the remainder of a six-pack. He lay face down on the edge of the porch, one arm dangling mere inches from the dark underside of the porch. If he were awake, if he were sober, he might hear the faint clicking and hissing noise coming from the darkness beneath.

The women went back inside and started to prepare lunch. Nobody was hungry, however they had to eat. Ranking person or not, Major Garrison ordered it so. He felt like a jerk telling everyone to eat now, but he knew it was important they all keep their strength up. Most of all, he worried about Barbara. She couldn't eat.

Cecil sat down and gently rubbed her throat. He wasn't sure if she was in shock or a coma. She didn't appear to have any outward signs of injury, which was good. If her comatose state was psychological, it would be easier to deal with. The one thing he did know was that she could not eat or drink in her current nonresponsive state. To Cecil, this was as bad as anything else they faced. He knew Barbara could go for weeks without food, but she would only last a few days without drinking.

He thought about sitting her up and trying to get her to sip on a glass of water, but the last thing he needed to do was pour water down her lungs. Remembering his Army medical training, he went back into the kitchen and put several ice cubes into a metal mixing bowl. He then found a meat-tenderizing hammer and crushed them into a fine icy powder. He then took the bowl back into the living room and sat down beside her. Taking a pinch of ice between his thumb and forefinger with one hand, he parted Barbara's lips with the other. He then placed the pinch of ice between her cheek and gums. Cecil grabbed another pinch and repeated the process. After a few attempts, he sat back and watched with hopeful anticipation.

At first, she did not move and Cecil's heart began to sink. He tried to fight back the tears when the reaction he hoped for didn't occur, yet just before he lost hope, it happened. Barbara's throat moved ever so slightly; she swallowed the melted ice. Cecil's tears turned to tears of joy as he bent down and kissed her on the forehead. He then sat back down beside her and began the slow process of feeding her ice.

Cecil was so engrossed with Barbara, he did not notice Andrews come in from the porch and now stood a few feet away. He remained quite steady for a man who put away a half case of beer. The strange thing was that his countenance was lucid; one might even say he was stone sober. Andrews stood as rigid as a statue, watching until Burt entered the room.

"What the hell are you staring at?" Burt snapped.

Andrews's body remained still while his head swiveled ninety degrees until his eyes fell on Burt. The unnatural movement gave both men a moment of pause.

Terror flooded over them when they saw his eyes. Those were not the eyes of the temperamental jerk and alcoholic they knew. There was somebody else staring out through Sam Andrews's eyes. Someone calm, someone sober, someone calculating . . . someone who called the dark their home.

"What . . . what the hell?" Cecil stammered, moving to protect Barbara.

"Who the hell are you?" Burt demanded as he snatched a fireplace poker from the hearth.

Four words came out of the mouth of Andrews's. These four words were in his voice, but annunciated in such a way there was no doubt that Sam Andrews was not the one doing the speaking.

"My name is Musial."

CHAPTER 8

REBEKAH AND MALAKHI

"In Israel, in order to be a realist you must believe in miracles."
~David Ben-Gurion

REBEKAH HELD HER SON in her lap for what seemed like hours. The world outside was a faraway and distant concept. The only thing they were conscious of was their hammering hearts, and the hideous hissing of the dark. Emergency vehicle sirens wailed outside. The living darkness was responsible for it all.

They were shaken out of their terrified state when another scream rang out from somewhere below. Even though it was muted by distance and walls, it drowned out the high pitched wail of the sirens. Someone else was in the dark.

Rebekah poked her head up and peered down into the street. She took a deep, shuddering breath when she beheld the chaos. People ran, jumped, climbed, crawled and drove over one another in a mad dash to escape the dark. It was a bright sunny day, but it didn't matter because the dark was everywhere. It was in every shade and shadow. The darkness waited for the next person to stumble into the shadows like an insect in a web.

Rebekah clutched Malakhi as another blood curdling cry erupted from the street. A woman crawled about in the darkness beneath a large city bus. She shuffled on all fours from one tire to the next, screaming and throwing her head from side to side. She finally settled on the right rear tire. With a sudden serene calm, she laid her head in front of it as if taking a nap, letting the massive bus drive over her head. Rebekah gasped and ducked under the window. She still heard the sickening crunch and pop of the poor woman's skull in spite of the other noise.

"Momma, what is it?" Malakhi wailed. "Where did grandpa go?"

"I don't know baby, I'm sure he is fine," she lied. She wasn't sure about anything.

Sensing movement, she turned back towards the closet. Had the door opened more? She could have sworn it was only open a couple of inches, but now the dark slit was at least a foot wide. The volume of the dark chorus grew. It seemed to both echo and permeate from the walls around them. They must get out, but she did not know how.

The hallway was the only direct route to the stairs and elevator, yet it was completely dark and windowless. The only other way was air vents, which were too small for both of them, not to mention they were dark inside. The building had no fire escapes; however there was an exterior metal staircase at the end of the hall past the elevator. The problem was they needed to traverse about sixty feet of dark hallway to get there.

There was only one small flashlight in the apartment and it was not bright enough to search for loose change under the sofa cushions. The one thing they had an abundance of was candles. Being a waitress was not a lucrative profession. It was not uncommon for them to have power shut off for a day or two before Rebekah could scrape up the money for their bill. Candles and a small battery powered radio helped then to get through those times. They owned a large Menorah they kept for Hanukah which held nine candles. She also had two regular seven candle menorahs. There were enough candles to fill all of those with several to spare.

It just might provide them the light they needed to make it down the hallway. A spark of hope started to grow until she remembered the candles *and* the menorahs were in the closet. Their tiny flashlight would not make a dent in the closet's dark interior.

Rebekah searched for a solution to their dilemma. Desperation was about to consume her when something met her eye, something bright and shiny. As she moved her head backwards she was blinded by a brilliant flash of light. The sun was reflecting off of the bathroom mirror. Inspiration took over.

"If I can reflect light into the closet," she thought. "It might be enough to drive back the darkness long enough to grab the candles."

Another thought hit her, one more exciting than the last.

"Could the mirror be used to reflect light down the hallway?"

After a quick mental calculation she did not believe so. No, the closet would have to do.

Rebekah tried to rise to her feet, but Malakhi clung to her.

"Don't go, momma!" he pleaded, burying his head in her chest.

"I'm not leaving you baby," she said, stroking his dark locks. She kissed him on top of the head and whispered. "We are both going to leave, sweetheart."

Reluctantly, he released his grip and slid to the floor, curling into the fetal position. Another scream stabbed the air, making them both flinch. Rebekah knew they must act fast. It was still late morning, but the afternoon sun would cast long shadows through their small apartment. If they didn't hurry, they would be trapped.

She looked at the closet. The door had not opened any wider, yet the darkness seemed to radiate an unnatural excitement. It was like throwing breadcrumbs into a pond of hungry fish. It watched her, it anticipated, it longed for her to come inside. However, Rebekah had no intention of being fish food today. She strode to the bathroom, where she had left on both the overhead and vanity light.

She fumbled with the large mirror frame for a few moments. Once she pulled it free of the wall, she turned to leave the bathroom. As she cleared the bathroom door, something happened that scared her to the very core of her being. The power went out. Her back had not cleared the door frame yet when the bathroom was plunged into darkness. For an instant, she got a sample of what the darkness held. Every square inch of her body felt as if it were violated by a wickedness transcending anything she knew. In an instant, she experienced an eternity of hopelessness and hate. If she had lingered a second longer in the bathroom, she would be as dead as their landlord. Maybe not a dive from the window, but perhaps a broken mirror and a glass shard to the neck or wrists. Her heart throbbed in her ears. She leaned against the door, panting and clutching her chest. She opened her eyes and shrieked when she saw movement in the mirror as it reflected the bathroom door.

The darkness swirled. The insane chorus intensified and changed cadence, almost as if it summoned her. Rebekah pulled herself together and positioned the mirror on the wall opposite the closet. She turned it at different angles until a blinding bright beam of sunlight reflected on the closet door. The darkness disappeared from the crack and the hissing quickened as if agitated. Satisfied the mirror would stay in place; she cautiously approached the closet and flung open the door. The inside of the closet was cast into full relief. The darkness disappeared with an unsettling noise like ripping sackcloth.

Inside were their coats, shoes, and a few assorted boxes. At first, she did not see it. Then she glanced to a side shelf. There sat a box marked 'candles' and on the shelf above were the menorahs. Taking great care, she reached in and grabbed the items that would potentially save their lives. "How fitting they were Hebrew religious items," Rebekah thought. She said a silent prayer as she placed the menorah and candles in the middle of the living room. Malakhi watched her with round eyes. She managed a smile and beckoned him to join her.

"Did you find grandpa?" he asked.

"No, baby," she said, and then pointed to the items on the floor. "But I found something that will help us leave here and search for him."

A small trace of hope started to spread across his face. "Did you get matches?" he asked after checking the items.

Rebekah's stomach lurched.

"Did they have matches?" . . . "Were they out?" . . . "Had she picked more up on her last trip to the market?"

"No," she said and began to search the room.

"It's okay, Momma. I know where they are!" he said springing to his feet. He was about to run and retrieve them when he stopped in his tracks. The darkness swirled in the bathroom at the prospect of another victim. He stared with horror as the malevolent chorus urged him to enter.

"Don't look at it, baby," Rebekah said. "Just stay out of the dark and shadows and you'll be fine."

Malakhi was terrified, but he trusted his mother. He tiptoed into the well-lit kitchen as if the slightest noise might send the darkness charging after him. He retrieved a box of matches concealed behind a stack of dish towels. He returned to his mother's side and handed her the matches.

She told him her plan, trying to be as casual as discussing a trip to the beach. Both of them were terrified, but the knowledge they would be doing this together gave both of them an uneasy peace. Malaki helped her arrange the candles in the menorahs. When she was satisfied the candles were stable, she lit one of the extra candles. Rebekah proceeded to drip hot wax onto the bottom of each candle for a little added reinforcement. Once complete, she used the candle to light the remaining ones. She then told Malakhi to stay put as she picked up one of the flaming menorahs and crept to the hallway door.

Holding the menorah in front of her as a shield, she threw open the door. As expected, the dark was the same as their bathroom and closet. The hissing and clicking noise rose to a maddening volume. The dark in the bathroom and the hallway sounded as if they were communicating with each other, plotting a plan of attack. Reminiscent of Moses parting the Red Sea, she poked her menorah through the door and the darkness parted in front of her.

She poked her head into the hall then withdrew it when a disturbing thought crossed her mind. She remembered her recent experience in the bathroom. Her back was in the darkness for a split second. She knew if it had been longer, she would have died. What would happen if she ventured into the hall with the candles in front of her, allowing the darkness to close in from the rear? She knew the answer and was grateful for the second menorah. Stepping back inside, she told Malakhi her revised plan.

"I've got to walk backwards, momma?" he frowned.

He was not an athletic child, so coordination was not one of his strongpoints. Stumbling and falling was a real possibility.

"It's okay, baby . . . I'll be right there with you."

He didn't seem very assured, and she needed inspiration. Her eyes fell on one of her father's old trench coats in the closet. She saved them after he passed away because she intended to give them to Malakhi when he was big enough. She also kept it for herself. She missed Nehemya as much as Malakhi did and the coats still smelled like him. Just opening the closet on occasion was enough to give her a small degree of comfort. She almost forgot about the coats since Nehemya returned with the other Impals. Now, there they were like a long lost friend.

She walked over; shielding her eyes from the reflection cast by the mirror, and took a coat off the hanger. She held it up inches from her nose and inhaled, taking in the nostalgic and comforting scent of her father. She then reached down and removed the long belt from the waist of the coat.

"Look here Malakhi," she said, holding the belt out reverently. "This was your grandfather's . . . with this you will always be safe."

Malaki regarded the belt with a frown. He reached up and stroked the leather dangling from his mother's hands.

"How?" he whispered.

She handed the belt to him and then turned him around. She fit the belt snug under his arms and then turned around. When they were standing back to back, she took the loose ends of the belt and tied them tight around her waist. They were tied so secure; there was no way for Malakhi to fall down if he tripped. He was a small child and even if he lost his footing, Rebekah could still support his weight. The next trick was for each of them to squat low enough to pick up their menorah. They accomplished this with relative ease.

"Okay, baby . . . remember to hold your candles out in front of you at all times . . . no matter what happens. I'll go slow, so don't worry about tripping."

The concern now was not so much for tripping as it was for dropping the menorah in the event of a stumble.

Malakhi did not answer, but she felt him nod his head against her lower back.

Steady, they made their way into the hallway, parting the darkness in both directions. Once they were squared in the middle of the hall, they resembled the beacon of a great lighthouse, frozen in mid turn.

The darkness parted, yet the gruesome chorus grew in intensity like a nest of agitated snakes. The dark was angry for this violation; angry and ravenous for the prey now in its midst. They trudged along at a snail's pace; the fifty feet or so to the door leading to the outside stairs seemed fifty miles away. Their hearts hammered and their breathing was labored, but still they inched forward.

They were a little over halfway to salvation, when a breeze wafted up the hallway. It came from Mr. Zahavi, the landlord's, open apartment door. Under normal conditions, this might have been a welcome refreshment considering what a warm day it was. However, normal conditions no longer held meaning in the world.

The breeze caused Malaki's candles to flicker. The sudden disruption made shadows bounce off the walls, causing him to panic and stumble. His grandfather's belt held him tight to his mother's back, but the menorah flew from his grip in a wide arc. The child watched helpless, as if in slow motion, while the menorah flew out of his hand and onto the carpeted floor of the hallway.

CHAPTER 9

STEFF

"A torn jacket is soon mended; but hard words bruise the heart of a child."
~Henry Wadsworth Longfellow

THE GEORGETOWN BROWNSTONE home of General Ott Garrison was an elegant residence. It rested in the center of one of Washington's most elite and historic neighborhoods. He lived there by himself since his wife died. He did not host guests often, outside of select dignitaries and an occasional mistress. Of course, he made sure that these iniquitous women never stayed all night. If they did, his staff escorted them from the premises with great discretion. A Godly man could not let such knowledge become public. He believed God made certain allowances for those who are righteous. The general was not blasphemous enough to believe himself perfect, but he *was* chosen by God for his righteousness.

One of his upstairs guest rooms looked out onto the quaint cobblestone street below. The street was normally busy with tourists and the typical metro area traffic. This morning, however, it was quiet as death itself. The current atmosphere was a stark contrast from a couple of hours earlier; before the Impals were replaced by the darkness.

The street in front of the general's home was shaded from the morning sun. The high rooflines and a plethora of ancient elm and oak trees gave the streets the appearance of dusk. It was October and the shade lasted longer in the fall than any other time of the year.

In the high arched window of the upstairs bedroom, a single figure sat. She stared at an invisible point outside the window. This person saw both the gruesome aftermath left by the dark and, at the same time, saw nothing at all. She was lonely. For twenty-four hours she had stayed in this room with a pair of Army sentries stationed outside the door. She had not heard anything from the Army men since the screaming started. They were dead now . . . she was sure of it. So were the dozens of corpses littering the street. She tried to count the variety of ways these people met their demise, but she stopped somewhere around thirty. It made her both numb and sick. She wasn't sure which feeling was worse.

A man hung from a tree across the street, dangling back and forth in the breeze. The girl saw him die first. He brought a link of chain out of his car trunk before climbing on top of the car. He wrapped the chain around the limb, and then around his neck. He jumped off as if doing a cannonball into a pool. Unfortunately, he did not die right away. Instead, he suffered a slow and painful strangulation. During the whole ordeal, he screamed as if he were on fire. His cries muted into a faint gurgling noise after he jumped, finally stopping several minutes later. She thought she could still hear his gruesome shrieks over the rustle of the wind and the demented hissing from her hallway and closet.

Steffanie Garrison knew what was going on because there was a small clock radio beside her bed. The room contained a TV, but television broadcasts had not worked for almost three months.

She listened to the reports warning of the dangers posed by the darkness shortly after she heard the screams of her guards. She knew better than to go bolting from the room because the hallway outside the door was dark.

She spent the next hour staring in horror at the tragedy unfolding below. At first, she was paralyzed by terror, unable to move. She sat in the window seat with her head against the trim, feeling terrified, confused, empty and alone. She wondered where her grandpa was. The man, who after last night's radio appearance, locked her away in his house like a bothersome pet.

Steff was startled out of her trance when she heard the front door slam. This was followed by heavy footsteps on the hardwood floor of the foyer and then up the staircase. Her view of the driveway was obstructed by the roofline. Otherwise, she would have seen her grandfather followed by a parade of Humvees pull up and park.

She slid off of the window seat and to her knees. She didn't have the strength or courage to stand. An instant later, she heard the footsteps clomping up the hallway toward her door. Her heart began hammering.

"How could anyone be coming up the hallway? It was still dark out there," she thought to herself, but then her breathing hitched when she heard a voice outside. She wasn't sure if it was from terror or relief.

"Damn, you unfortunate bastards," General Garrison remarked, discovering the remains of the two guards. He then gave an amused chuckle as if he caught a child doing something cute.

Steffanie Garrison was young and naïve about a lot of things. She was immature for a twelve year old and a little spoiled. She turned her family and friends in at the Impal camp because she didn't like the living conditions. She risked everything to call her grandfather, but now he had her locked up. At least at the Impal camp, she enjoyed freedom. Confinement was not the worst of it. Her grandfather's cavalier attitude was not lost on her. He was laughing about the death of two men under his command. He did not seem to care that his granddaughter might be in the same state.

Her insides turned to jelly when she heard the latch click on the bedroom door. A moment later her grandfather stood there with a smug grin.

"Why Steff, are you okay?" he cooed without conviction.

She gazed up at him and tried to speak, but all she could manage to do was nod her head. Her favorite China doll sat propped in a nearby wicker rocker. Its frozen and inanimate features conveyed more pity than her grandfather could ever conceive. Steff was convinced he loved her, at least at one time, but something had changed. He became so consumed with his own ambitions and self-righteousness, there

was no room left in him for anything else. Or perhaps his own arrogance made everything else, including his granddaughter, seem un-
important. The worst thought that ran through her mind was simple,
yet powerful— "Was his love real in the first place?" She thought it
was, but, in the past twenty-four hours she learned a powerful lesson.
Things are not always as they seem.

He walked over to her and offered his hand to help her out of the
floor. She raised a trembling arm only to be grasped by his large hand
and jerked up a little too rough. She gave a small yelp of pain before
retreating to the wicker rocker next to her doll.

"Come on, get your stuff together, you're moving," the general
huffed.

"Where?" she chirped.

The sly and arrogant grin smoothed the wrinkles on his face. "The
White House, of course. And you are going to be the first daughter,
or . . . granddaughter in this case," he chuckled humorlessly.

She stared at him for several long moments, not believing her ears.
"Why?" she asked.

Steff saw a flash of anger in his eyes that vanished almost as fast
as it appeared. He took a deep breath and sat down on the bed, never
taking his eyes from her.

"Well, for starters everyone is dead," he said with a smile that
seemed inappropriate. "But most important, God has chosen me."

"How?" she asked with wide eyes.

He stood up and walked to her closet door where the dark chorus
hummed. He opened the door and the noise filled the room, sending chills down Steff's back. The general then gave a sly grin over
his shoulder and stepped inside, closing the door behind him. She
shrieked with horror and covered her mouth, but after several long
moments of silence, something began to occur to her. How had he
gotten to her room in the dark hallway? He didn't seem to have any
kind of light with him. As she pondered this, she almost jumped out
of the chair when a heavy knocking resounded on her closet door. She
stared at the door, transfixed with terror. A few moments later, there
was another knocking at the door. This time it was followed by the
sing-song voice of her grandfather.

"Oh Steff . . . let me out . . ."

She forced herself to stand, and then wobbled to the closet door. She grabbed the latch and took a deep breath, before turning it and stepping back. As the door swung open, it revealed her grandfather grinning with satisfaction. Steff recalled a vampire movie she watched at a friend's house. It caused her nightmares for weeks about the coffin lid swinging open, revealing the monster inside. A fright induced sickness overcame her. Steff stumbled backwards and collapsed on the foot of her bed.

The general stepped out of the closet, no worse for wear, and closed the door behind him.

"Do you see?" he boasted. "Do you see how I am chosen?"

All Steff could see was the room swimming about her. She clutched her stomach and shut her eyes tight. She did not have time to catch her breath before her grandfather jerked her off the bed.

"Come on, let's go!" he snapped.

"How did you do that?" Steff asked.

"God," he said as if it should be obvious. He then forced her to her knees; before dropping to his knees beside her. "I need you to pray with me before we leave."

She looked at him as if she were expecting a punch line to a joke. Steff said her prayers every night and was not opposed to praying with her grandfather, but not now. She saw his eyes were shut tight with deep concentration on his face. When she realized he was serious about his invitation, she shut her eyes and clasped her hands under her chin. Her eyes were not completely shut though. She watched the general through parted eyes as he began his prayer.

"Dear Heavenly Father,

I and my granddaughter, Steffanie pray this prayer in the power of the Holy Spirit. In the name of Jesus Christ Your one and only Son who died and rose again for remission of sin, we bind, rebuke and render powerless: all division, discord, disunity, strife, wrath, murder, criticism, condemnation, pride, envy, jealously, gossip, slander, evil speaking, complaining, lying, false teaching, false gifts, false manifestations, fear of spirits, deceiving spirits, religious spirits, hindering spirits, retaliatory spirits, occult spirits, witchcraft spirits, spirits of antichrist and all familiar and territorial spirits.

WE ARE GOD'S CHILDREN! WE RESIST THE DEVIL AND DECLARE THAT NO WEAPON FORMED AGAINST US SHALL PROSPER. WE ARE THE RIGHTOUSNESS OF GOD IN CHRIST JESUS . . . AMEN!"

He recited the prayer almost word for word as the one he prayed earlier in the Oval Office, but with one small revision. He used plural instead of the singular. Garrison increased the volume gradually, reciting the last paragraph in a defiant yell. This caused Steff to gasp and cringe, but she held her composure. She answered her grandfather with a final, "*Amen.*" This caused the general to grin with satisfaction. This relieved her some, but only a little.

General Garrison rose to his feet. With the gentlest of motions, he stroked Steff's hair and lovingly scooped her into his arms. She shivered like a frightened rabbit as he whispered in her ear. "It's okay, you're safe now. Grandpa will protect you."

He then began to carry his granddaughter towards the hallway door. Even the general was not certain if this were an act of faith or an experiment. Garrison was so arrogant in his faith; he believed God would give him the ability to carry Steff through the darkness. If she did not survive then it was the Lord's will.

Steff cringed and pulled herself tight against him. She heard the hallway door creak open, giving way to the terrible choir of the dark. In her mind's eye, Steff saw the hallway populated with a multitude of insects and snakes. She held her breath for whatever horrific fate awaited. In the end, nothing happened. She remained snug in her grandfather's grasp as he trudged through the darkness and descended the stairs.

She began to whimper as she felt the sensation of icy cold fingers running up and down her legs and arms, through her hair and between her legs. She shrieked as every muscle on her body clenched, but he held her tight.

"Away you deceiving Impal!" he barked with venomous hatred. "Go back to Hell where you belong!"

A few moments later, the whispering and icy fingers were gone. She felt the warm sunlight on her face as they emerged out the front door. A dozen soldiers encircled them and escorted them to a waiting Humvee.

As the convoy began to pull away, Steff opened her eyes just in time to see the dangling feet of the hanged man across the street. One of his shoes was untied. The next two miles of the trip took the better part of an hour. They drove back and forth in an attempt to avoid the multitude of bodies littering the neighborhoods. On a few occasions, there was no way around them. The vehicle jumped with a sickening splat and crunch as they rolled over victims of the darkness.

They eventually pulled up in front of the White House. Steff gaped in awe at the famous residence. She had never been this close before. She got out and followed her grandfather inside, a torrent of thoughts and emotions swirled inside her. She thought she made a mistake by calling him, but after seeing how he defied the darkness, she wasn't so sure. Either way, it still scared the hell out of her. Still skeptical, yet willing to keep an open mind, she followed him inside the monstrous doors. They slammed shut with an echo reminiscent of a tomb.

CHAPTER 10

MUSIAL, THE MENORAH, AND THE MURDERER

"Some say the world will end in fire, some say in ice."
~Robert Frost

SAM ANDREWS, or at least the body of Sam Andrews, lay in a crumpled heap on the floor. Burt wielded the fireplace poker and clubbed him across the back of the head. Everyone in the group wanted to club him at one time or another in the past few weeks.

As warranted as their reasons seemed before, Burt did not act on those impulses. He acted out of pure fear. The thing speaking through Andrews's mouth and watching through his eyes was not him, and it was not the alcohol talking. They didn't know how, but they were certain that this new persona known as Musial was a product of the dark.

"What happened?" Charlotte shrieked as she ran into the room and cupped her hands over her mouth.

"He finally pushed the envelope too far?" Derek asked with an amused grin.

Sally was speechless. She could only stand in the doorway and gape from her poker-wielding husband to the slumbering jackass on the floor.

Burt and Cecil stared at each other as if they were trying to psychically communicate the best answer. Finally, Cecil said, "It wasn't Andrews."

Everybody except Burt seemed incredulous.

"What do you mean it wasn't him?" Sally croaked.

Burt gave them an explanation. Their faces fell gaunt with horror. The thing possessed Andrews somehow; it didn't drive him mad with an unyielding desire to end his own life. It seemed calm and collected. It now walked among them, even in the light. The realization that it could be any one of them at any moment brought a deathly silence to the room. They regarded each other with great scrutiny.

Cecil and Burt hoisted Andrews into a large oak chair in the corner. They held his feet and shoulders while Derek bound him with a combination of rope and iron chains. They all sat down and stared at the slumbering . . . what? Andrews, Musial . . . it? They found it hard to focus on anything else, even though night would be coming soon. There was something unusual, something sinister about the sleeping form in the chair. He could be pretending to sleep, or 'playing possum' as the saying goes. He might throw open his eyes at any moment and yell *boo*.

Malakhi shrieked with horror before the menorah hit the ground. He felt the terrible oppression of the dark moving in and encircling him. Surrender consumed him. Malakhi saw the bullies who had so tormented him in school. They were relentless in their persecution, but today they were unbearable. He was ready to grasp the menorah and bash his own head in because he wanted the torment to stop at any cost. It was the one escape the bullies offered. He might have accomplished this if he were not bound to his mother. All he could think of was how bad his head hurt, how hopeless life is, and what a terrible burden he was to his poor mother. In all this darkness and despair, he held one small glimmer of hope. His knowledge that ending his own life would make things better, would make things right, and would end his suffering. This was what the voices told him. The voices that were mere hissing and clicking moments earlier now spoke with crystal clarity.

As he struggled against his bonds, he pulled his mother backwards, almost causing her to lose her menorah. Her back was now bathed in the darkness and she could feel the icy fingers again.

"Malakhi, stop!" she shrieked, but it was no good because he did not hear her.

The only thing he heard was the cunning words of the chorus, over and over, "Take the Menorah . . . be quick . . . put it to an end . . . sleep, peaceful sleep."

Rebekah pulled forward as hard as she could in an attempt to pull her tormented son toward the outside door. As she took a few steps, something popped in her back and she screamed with agony. The stabbing pain radiated every time Malakhi struggled. When the pain became unendurable, she saw a bright light behind her, as if someone opened a window. However, it wasn't sunlight; the light was much too erratic. It flickered and jumped, casting her shadow toward the far door. Then it began to spread and grow. She felt the heat and knew exactly what it was. Malakhi's menorah had caught the hallway on fire. What would have been a horrific situation suddenly sent a wave of relief over Rebekah. As the fire blazed higher, the darkness shrank and retreated.

Empowered by a newfound hope, she bit her lip and pushed the pain aside. She began to trudge forward, dragging the dead weight of her limp son. The question as to whether he was unconscious or dead didn't have time to register with her. Rebekah's only thought was to get them outside before the fire consumed them or it went out and the darkness returned. Still holding her menorah in front of her, she stumbled forward like a person in a one-legged relay race.

Smoke began to fill the hallway, threatening to obscure the light and bring the darkness back. Rebekah didn't have the time or luxury to worry about it, so she picked up the pace. As breathing became almost impossible, they reached the metal door. She pushed hard. It wouldn't open. She shrieked with determination and pain as she threw herself against the rusty metal. Finally, with a loud scraping, the door swung open and warm sunlight poured in. Rebekah coughed and sputtered before inhaling a lungful of fresh air. She tumbled onto the landing of the stairs, and then unfastened the belt binding her to her Malakhi. She turned and laid him across her lap.

"Thank God . . . he is still breathing," she thought as she pulled him close. This small assurance would have to suffice for now because the fire was spreading. The smoke swirled in the wind resembling small tornadoes, burning their eyes and throats. She scooped Malakhi up and half slid and half crawled down the stairs. A few moments later, they were lying in the green grass of the park. Rebekah lay on her back, trying to suppress the pain as she held her son close. She squinted up at the inferno that was their home for the last few years. She wasn't sure whether to feel relieved they escaped the dark, or to cry because everything they owned was going up in flames. The only thing she could do right now is hug her son and cry. When she ran out of tears, feeling hurt, lost, injured, and alone; she got to her feet. For the first time since they arrived outside, she noticed the chaos around them. People ran in panic, sirens wailed, crashes and explosions thundered in the distance. The smoke plumes towering in all directions suggested that not just their building was burning. Malakhi sat up and rubbed his terror-filled eyes.

"Momma?" he asked with pitiful hopelessness. Rebekah's heart melted.

"It's okay, sweetie," she said as she reached down and helped him to his feet.

He stood and clutched the hem of her skirt for support. She massaged her sore back for a long time while she spoke comforting words to her son. She seemed to have only pulled a muscle and not ruptured or dislocated anything. She could deal with the inconvenience of a strained muscle, even though it hurt.

Rebekah scanned their surroundings, trying to make some sense of the world. There seemed to be no logic. Pandemonium and fear ruled. The one positive was that the surrounding fires had obliterated all the shaded areas nearby. The dark was gone in those areas, but where the smoke blacked out the sun it still raged. Rebekah gave a silent thanks that the wind was blowing away from them.

She grabbed Malakhi's hand and began walking in the direction of the market where she worked. The way was familiar and she knew there should be lots of people. The further they travelled the more she saw how right and how wrong she was. There were people, lots of them scattered here and there, but most of them were dead. Rebekah tried to keep Malakhi's eyes covered. It was no use, he saw. Her heart wilted each time Malakhi squeaked with terror. All she could do was hold on to him tight and keep moving.

After an eternity of walking through the corpse littered streets, they rounded a corner and stopped. About two blocks ahead, by a large soccer field, there was a line of flatbed military trucks. The vehicles were all crammed with as many civilians as they could carry. A solitary soldier in fatigues paced back and forth beside the trucks carrying a large megaphone.

"We need as many people on board as possible," he called. "Everyone will be taken to safety where you will receive good care."

"Where?" a man holding a little girl asked.

"Camp Anatot," the soldier replied, and then went back to barking commands.

Rebekah knew this was the best opportunity for her and her son to survive. It would soon be dark and they wouldn't survive the night here, especially since a good deal of the power was out. Grabbing Malakhi's hand, she began to run towards the trucks. Her back tinged with each deep breath, but they finally made it as the last of a large family climbed on back of one of the trucks.

"Two more?" Rebekah asked, pulling Malakhi in front of her so the soldier could see both of them.

He studied them doubtfully and was about to turn them away when an old woman spoke up. "There's plenty of room here," she said, scooting over about a foot. Her long white hair was disheveled; she looked as if she just rolled out of bed and then ran through a wind tunnel. Her wrinkled face was streaked with dirt and soot as well as her long blue cotton gown. She resembled someone who travelled to Hell and back. Despite her disturbing appearance, she was kind and empathetic.

"Okay," the soldier said and motioned with his thumb over his shoulder for them to climb on.

He didn't help them, in fact nobody did. Everyone else refused to make eye contact. The refugees all displayed a haunted, drawn countenance. The old woman, who introduced herself as Ruth, was a light in a dark room. She beamed with the hopeful face of a child, as if the trucks were headed for Disneyland.

Ruth talked with great excitement to Rebekah and Malakhi. She didn't divulge a lot of personal information other than she lived in an old neighborhood of Jerusalem. Rebekah thought it odd because she remembered seeing where Ruth's neighborhood was now a grand office complex. She didn't question it. Rebekah had never been to Ruth's section of the city and she didn't want to hurt her feelings. Judging by her appearance, she could well be a homeless person residing there, sleeping under a bridge or on a park bench. Rebekah was polite and nodded at Ruth's stories.

"Did you hear that this eye . . . this storm, center thing, didn't hit the world at the same time?" Ruth said. "It kind of spread over the planet like thick glue." She held her hands out in front of her, palms facing down, and wriggled her fingers to demonstrate something oozing over a sphere.

After a while, Ruth tired of talking, which was okay because Rebekah zoned her out a long time ago. By the time they reached Camp Anatot, a drive normally taking a little over thirty minutes, more than five hours had passed. The convoy took dozens of detours while avoiding the streets choked with debris, bodies, and shade. When they pulled through the gates of Camp Anatot, the sun was hanging low in the west. It would be dark in less than an hour

The road coming into the base and all open areas were illuminated by dozens of Powermoon portable lights. These lights were fed by a series of generators buzzing and humming every hundred feet or so.

They sat on the truck until after dark in the middle of a large, well-lit field. They slipped away from the needy grasp of Ruth and made their way to a group of white linen tents a short distance away. Each tent was lit up by the portable lights and a battery powered lantern inside. The cloth on the tents was so light and thin, the lanterns were probably not necessary. With the powerful lights around them, Rebekah and Malakhi did not even realize that night had fallen. Not until they travelled a short distance from the chattering diesel engines of the trucks and generators did they hear the dark beyond the perimeter. It was night in Jerusalem and soon it would be in England. Nightfall would arrive in the United States a short time later.

A piercing pain ran through Private Abernathy's skull as he sat up in the floor.

"Where am I?" he thought as he rubbed the back of his head.

Suddenly, it hit him. He was at home, knocked out by the stupid skank in the cage. As he slowly opened his eyes the final realization sunk in . . . it was dark. This chilling fact was reinforced by the hissing and clicking chorus surrounding him. He sat up and saw the dark moving and pulsing like a living thing. It was not just one place; it was everywhere . . . beside him, above him, under him, beneath every piece of furniture, and in every corner. It covered the entire volume of the room. It was an omnipotent entity focused on malice. He should be terrified, in truth, he should be dead . . . but he wasn't. Then the strangest thing happened, a calm peace settled over him. His breathing slowed and he regarded the room as serenely as if he were observing a school of fish underwater.

"Is this what happens when I die?" he thought.

Of course, he wasn't dead. He could tell by the stabbing pain in the back of his head. He sat up and gingerly touched it with his fingertips. His hair was matted and sticky from dried blood. The wooden surface of the footstool he fell on was smeared with a red glob of blood.

"Damn her!" he muttered and then glared at the closet.

He could see the outline of the cage as his eyes began to adjust. There was something lying in the bottom. He retrieved one of the flashlights off his dresser. Flicking it on, he shone it at the closet. In spite of the grotesque atrocities he had enjoyed his entire life, an involuntary gasp of horror spewed from his lips. He saw the form, rather what the form was. The old woman had shoved her head through the narrow bars. Her head was compacted into a deformed lump of jelly as the sides of her skull were crushed in. She was dead; there was no doubt about it. Jack experienced a sudden twinge of regret. Not because the old lady was dead. He regretted he was not the one who enjoyed the pleasure of killing her.

CHAPTER 11

SECRETS IN THE DARK

"People find meaning and redemption in the most unusual human connections."
~Khaled Hosseini

THE MID-AFTERNOON SUN shone through the rear windows of the cabin. A large field separated them from the woods allowing plenty of light inside. A light shone through to the living room and onto the unconscious Andrews, giving him an angelic appearance. Of course, Andrews was no angel. The thing inside him was even further from righteousness.

Sally and Charlotte sat on the opposite side of the room. They had been keeping an eye on Barbara as much they were watching the thing bound to the chair. Cecil, Derek, and Burt discussed plans and scouted the perimeter of the cabin. There was one subject which they were all in total agreement. They either needed to get to a safer location or they would need several more gallons of gas for the generator. Neither one seemed to be an easy or realistic task.

They could follow the driveway for about a half mile as it wound down the hillside and through the woods. There were several clear areas where the sun shone through. The problem is there were also an equal number of dark areas alive with murderous living shadows.

There were not enough flashlights on hand to light up all the dark areas in a vehicle. Derek suggested they go in a group with each of them holding a flashlight in a different direction as they moved. However, when they examined their inventory, they decided it would not be feasible.

"We only have three workable flashlights," Cecil said. "Only one of those is bright enough to do us much good in the really dark areas."

They assessed the gas inventory again and did another calculation. The news was not good. They only had enough for less than three days. It was hard for any of them to keep their minds on the dilemma with the potential danger bound in the house. Charlotte and Sally both owned guns and knew how to use them. Andrews was also trussed up so tight, the only part of his body he would be able to move is his head. Nevertheless, this provided little comfort given their circumstances.

A little over an hour before nightfall, Andrews stirred and stared at them. They weren't sure who awakened in the chair until he spoke.

"I almost forgot what an uncomfortable nuisance a body is," Musial said. He shook his head from side to side as a wry grin spread over his face.

"Musial?" Cecil asked, stepping forward and crossing his arms.

The smile did not falter as he replied. "Ah . . . yes, I did introduce myself, didn't I?"

"Who the hell are you?" Cecil demanded.

Musial regarded him with an exasperated frown, which soon morphed to a bemused grin. "You mean who *was* I. Right, major?"

"How did you know I am a major?"

He shook his head and shrugged as if to say it didn't matter. He then addressed Charlotte. "Would you mind untying me sweetheart?" he asked in a sappy, yet polite tone. "I find this an undignified way to carry on a conversation."

Charlotte glanced at Cecil and Burt, before shaking her head. "No, I'm sorry," she squeaked.

His mouth leveled to an indifferent thin line. "Never hurts to ask," he said.

"Why did you ask her?" Burt demanded, stepping forward and standing shoulder to shoulder with Cecil.

"I thought I would pay her the respect you do not offer," he said, staring into their eyes. "This *is* her house, is it not?"

Everyone turned to Charlotte. She ducked her head and nodded. She said '*yes*' but it was so quiet, no one heard her, except for maybe Musial.

Musial smirked. "You have this poor girl so submissive, so down trodden, she seems afraid of her own shadow," he said, then paused and smiled. "Of course, right now it is not an unhealthy fear," he said nodding at the window towards a dark area of the woods.

"Is that where you come from?" Cecil asked.

He nodded and smiled. His expression was awkward, as if embarrassed by the admission.

"What the hell *are* you?" Burt demanded.

"Am I a shade, specter, spirit, soul, essence, phantom, vision, apparition, wraith, ghost? Is that what you are asking?"

"Are you an Impal?" Cecil asked, his stomach turning in knots. He was afraid of the answer.

Musial's eyes narrowed for several long and torturous moments.

"Yes and no," he answered.

Cecil's heart stretched in two different directions. The *no* was encouraging, but the *yes* worried him.

"What the hell? What kind of answer is that?" Burt snapped.

"The most honest answer I can give so you might understand. I guess . . ." he began then trailed off as if in deep thought. "I guess what you refer to as "Impal" is what I strive to be."

"Are you a demon?" Sally asked.

Musial broke into laughter, albeit polite laughter.

"No . . . no, my dear . . . demons are much more subtle than my bloodthirsty lot," he chuckled. "And demons were never human."

"You were human?" Burt spat.

"As human as you," he said in a matter of fact tone.

"But are you an Impal?" Cecil insisted, taking a step closer.

Again he stared at Cecil for a while. The frustration was about to rise to a crescendo when Musial finally replied. "Yes, but not like the nice ones you knew for the past three months. We're different."

"How different?" Cecil prodded.

"Well . . . segregation has ended, for the most part, in your world. In mine, it is the status quo."

"Are you saying the devils in the darkness are human souls?" Cecil asked.

"I am indeed."

"Why are you segregated?" Burt asked. He felt he already knew the answer, but wanted to hear it aloud.

"I believe you already know that, but I am a polite guest and I will humor you with an answer." He took a deep breath before replying. When he spoke, he wore a shameful frown. "Because we are bad . . . because we are all bad."

"Bad, how?" Cecil asked.

Musial glanced at the women and then turned to Burt and Cecil with a half-smile. "I could regale you with all the nasty details, but there are ladies present. Besides . . ." he said, focusing on Cecil. "You already have a pretty good idea, don't you?"

The cold chills of the serpents touch, the sharp sting of their bites, and their horrific deeds gave Cecil a chill. He knew better than anyone what the darkness held. The only image that came to mind, the only way he could describe it to anyone else, was the scene from the movie *Silence of the Lambs*. In the scene, Agent Clarice Starling walks the basement hallway of the asylum to interview Dr. Hannibal Lecter. As she walked, she passed several cells, each containing the darkest and disturbed minds known to man. Each committed horrific deeds deserving of confinement to such a place. They had all forfeited their humanity to the point where segregation from others was necessary. They took great pride in their acts and felt no remorse at all. The only thing they felt was the strong and primal desire to do it again and again and again.

Everyone turned to Cecil. He pinched the bridge of his nose as if he were trying to quell a strong migraine, and then collapsed into a wicker rocker. Cecil kept his eyes shut and breathed deep until Musial spoke again.

"I wasn't there when it happened. I want you to know this," Musial said with deep sincerity.

"You expect us to believe it?" Burt said. "After you killed Dr. Winder and attacked Cecil and his wife?"

He moved toward him as if he was going to strike the bound entity, but Cecil grabbed his arm. "Wait," he said then got up. "Are you saying all the evil people who existed are in the darkness?"

"Most of them," Musial said.

"What . . . you mean Hitler is running around in the dark?" Burt asked, incredulous.

"No, not running around . . . waiting. Right out there," Musial said nodding his head at the window again toward the large shaded area in the woods.

Burt let out a barking laugh. "Ha, you mean to tell me Adolf Hitler is right out there?"

Musial nodded.

"All the way from Germany?" Burt laughed.

"The dark knows no borders, Mr. Golden. I think I have been everywhere in the world at one time or another."

"Doing what?" Cecil asked.

A troubled expression washed over his face and he looked away.

"Doing what?" Cecil repeated.

Musial stared straight ahead, refusing eye contact as he spoke. "Seeking to satisfy our nature."

"What exactly is your nature and how did you satisfy it?" Burt asked.

When Musial answered, he spoke with the voice of a shy individual forced to describe his nude form.

"We are black souls. Our nature is a twisted view of the world and its values. We see death as a cleansing mechanism. A perfect and natural mechanism. Death is an end to a means which we strive to fulfill. We have no greater satisfaction"

"Jesus, you believe you are doing good?" Burt said.

Musial nodded. "It starts out that way. Then there starts to be an enjoyment in the work, an intoxicating addiction to the act consumes and drives us."

"Why so vicious? Why now?" Charlotte asked, her voice cracking.

Musial smiled at her and answered her question in a polite and gentlemanly tone. "For decades, for centuries, for millennia the dark void imprisoned us. Sometimes we were aware of the world around us, but most of the time we just whispered to each other in the abyss. Our frustration grew in proportion to our insatiable desire to return to our nature. On a few rare occasions we could break through and cause damage through a weak minded and ignorant individual. We have contributed to your news over the centuries more than you know."

He started to smile, but thought better of it. Instead, he returned to his same respectful tone. "It was never physical, always suggestions whispered to a like-minded party. We were the voices in their head, the enablers convincing them that their cause and methods were fair and true."

"Where are those individuals now?" Cecil asked.

"Most joined us in the void; a few of the weak minded . . . well, we're not sure what happened to them. Maybe they got a pass for their stupidity." He turned back to Charlotte. "Now that this storm has freed us, we are able to have much more influence. Now it is not just the weak and like-minded who are susceptible, everyone is. Every time a person steps into the dark it is akin to throwing a raw steak into a cage with a starved dog."

"Why do you make them kill themselves?" Burt asked. "Why don't you do it yourself?"

Musial looked at him as if it was the most stupid question he ever heard. "Kind of hard when you don't have a body, don't you think?"

"Why are you only in the dark?" Cecil asked, trying to diffuse Burt's anger at Musial's sarcasm.

"We are dark souls; we have lived in the dark since we died. We cannot enter the light. That is all I know."

"You're in the light right now," Sally said, noting the ray of sun still shining on him.

"No, I'm in the good Mr. Andrews," he corrected. "He gives me a lot of freedom."

Burt seemed to ignore everything else Musial said. He was still focused on his former comment.

"So, you're trying to tell me Adolf Hitler is right out there?" Burt asked again.

"Yes, among many others," Musial said and then spoke as if he was divulging confidential information. "I must warn you, he has an exceptional desire for you and your wife to wander into the dark . . . just fair warning."

Burt knew what Musial was implying.

"We're not Jewish!" he protested. "I was raised Methodist!"

Musial shrugged. "Doesn't matter to him, it's all in the name."

"So you can take possession of someone and can . . . move around?" Cecil asked.

"If only it were that easy," Musial said. Then he sounded as if he were reading a grocery list. "First we have to be willing to leave the comfort of the dark, not many of us are. Then we have to find a host without inhibitions . . . in this case drunk. Last but not least, we have to get to them before the rest of the dark."

"So why did you take control over Andrews? Trying to kill all of us yourself and not share the fun with your buddies?" Burt snorted.

"I assure you sir, if I wanted you dead, you would be. I would not have gone through the trouble of introducing myself."

"Then what do you want?" Cecil asked, his patience wearing thin.

Musial turned regarded him with the most desperate and longing expression imaginable. In another time, place, or lifetime perhaps, Cecil might have felt sorry for him. "Salvation," Musial pleaded. "I want salvation."

CHAPTER 12

THE BRETHREN

"For judgment will be without mercy to anyone who has shown no mercy, mercy triumphs over judgment."
~The Holy Bible, King James Version, James 2:13

STEFFANIE GARRISON DIDN'T SEE her grandfather after they entered the White House. A pair of armed guards ushered her upstairs as General Garrison went to the Oval Office. She covered her eyes to shield them from the glare of the powerful supplemental lights.

It reminded her of an image of Heaven she saw in a movie once. A large, bright, and airy room with the chorus of angels serenading new arrivals. The booming, authoritative voice of God speaking from somewhere out of sight. No, the inside of the White House wasn't quite the same. The angelic chorus was the stomping and murmuring of soldiers. The voice of God was the loud voice of her grandfather barking commands. Steff, while maybe immature and naïve, was also intelligent. She was beginning to suspect these soldiers and her grandfather were as far away from angels and God as one could get. General Garrison thought his demonstration of immunity to the darkness would impress his granddaughter. Instead, it terrified her. She loved her grandfather and admired him. This internal conflict made her feel sick to her stomach. A lot of emotions swirled about inside.

The soldiers escorted her down a hallway. About halfway, they stopped in front of a green door and ushered her inside. The small bedroom with white painted walls seemed the most well lit of all. The soldiers closed the door without a word and left her alone. Steff sat on the bed and stared at the bright wooden floor for a while before she started to cry. She missed her mother, she missed her sister and, in spite of her misplaced anger; she missed her father. She wanted to go home.

General Garrison led a small group of advisors into the Oval Office, and asked them to sit. Once they settled on the sofa and chairs in front of the Resolute desk, he closed the door and reached for the light switch. To the men's surprise and horror, he flicked the switch. The large Bow windows were still covered so the room fell into complete darkness. As if a radio were switched on, the insidious hissing and clicking returned, followed by several agonized screams. After a long two seconds, he flicked the switch back on, vanquishing the dark. The room was quiet except for the labored breathing of the advisors. They stared at him with bulging and horrified eyes.

"What the hell are you doing?" one of them sputtered.

"You can't—," another one began. He let out a tormented cry when General Garrison flicked the switch again.

"Oh yes, I can," Garrison thought. "I'll show you how much I can."

This time, he paused a second longer before flicking the switch back on.

The men stared at him with desperation, yet they remained defiant.

"Screw you!" one chubby officer spat.

General Garrison shook his head as his mouth creased into a wan smile. He started to speak, but thought better of it. Garrison flicked the switch again, yielding the same terrible result. This time, he held it for an additional two seconds.

"How dare the punk use such profane language towards God's chosen leader," Garrison thought. "He may have to be taught a lesson."

Yes indeed. A lesson seemed in order for this fat and profane colonel, but not now. When he turned the light back on for the third and final time, he folded his arms and spoke as if he were addressing a room full of children.

"Now that you see what the dark can do, know this. It has no effect on me. And why, do you ask?" Garrison said as he walked over and sat down behind the desk.

They stared at him with horror. The resentment was still there, buried deep in each of them. They were all too afraid to show it. After a long dramatic pause, Garrison spoke again. "The reason is quite simple. God has chosen me to lead against these demonic Impals. Therefore, he has made a shield about me to protect me from their evil intentions. I, and I alone, must lead."

He closed his eyes and, without invitation to the others to join in, he began a loud prayer. By the time he finished, each of the men had chills running down their spines. It was arrogant, it was forceful, and the implications were horrifying. In short it made each of them question their own good judgment because it was also very persuasive. Perhaps he was right. The main points of his prayer seemed to fit the facts. He had demonstrated his immunity to the dark. The last thing any of them wanted was for the general to turn the lights off again.

"What do we need to do, general?" the chubby colonel asked.

"Stay in the light and follow my lead," he said in a distant voice.

The five men, a Marine colonel, Army general, Air Force general, and a Navy rear admiral had all served the two former presidents. However, they all reported to the president via General Garrison who was the Chairman of the Joint Chiefs. Now the president was gone from the chain of command, leaving only the general. All of them, without exception, questioned the constitutionality of what was happening. They all knew better than to voice their concerns. They all knew of the general's track record for brutality. Being God's chosen leader would not quell this propensity; if anything it would enhance it. They all gave a stiff nod of agreement.

"I'm going to be making a radio address right before nightfall. I want all of you to be present with me when I do."

Again they all nodded.

General Garrison stood up and checked his watch. "One hour gentlemen, meet me in the ready room in one hour."

He then got up and strode across the room to the door. As he opened it, he heard something behind him. It was very faint, but still audible in the silent still of the house.

"He's bat shit crazy!" one of the men hissed.

"Where the hell did he get the authority?" another whispered.

General Garrison shook his head with disappointment as he shut the door behind him. He might have to make a few small revisions for his radio announcement.

Jack had been down to the nearby moor to dispose of the body, so he didn't hear his phone ring. In fact, it rang several times in the past hour. His commanding officer, Colonel Fielder, started calling just before dark. His friend, Sean, tried to call as well. They continued at regular intervals. Jack walked back inside as his phone began to ring yet again. At first, it startled him, and then he experienced a moment of panic. He knew who was calling without listening to the messages. The question was— what the hell was he going to tell them?

He frowned and placed his hands on his hips as he stared at the silhouette of the phone in the dark. The whispers of the dark were miles away from his attention. Maybe he would tell them he fell asleep and woke up after dark? No, that was stupid; nobody in his right mind would fall asleep in this situation. But, was Jack in his right mind? He believed he was. He couldn't tell them he was immune to the dark. It would bring questions and scrutiny he did not want. He needed to make up an excuse and he must do it fast. He wasn't sure if they could search for him in the dark, but he had to assume it was possible. He strode across the room and snatched up the receiver.

"Hello?" he said.

"Jesus . . . Jack!" rasped the familiar voice of his friend, Sean Poindexter. "Are you okay? We've been calling all night! What happened?"

Jack touched the back of his head as he thought of an excuse. It dawned on him to tell the truth; at least some of it.

"Oh, thank God I left the lights on!" he said breathlessly as he relished the dark room.

"What happened?" Sean repeated.

Jack took a deep breath and then exhaled, playing for dramatic effect.

"I-I fell in my bedroom and hit my head. I was out cold."

"Do you need medical help?"

"No . . . besides you couldn't get to me anyway, could you?" he asked. He didn't care other than to test the possibility of receiving an unwanted visit before he could cover his tracks.

"No," Sean admitted. "But . . . bloody hell, mate . . . are you going to make it okay tonight?"

Again Jack took another dramatic deep breath. "Well . . . I've got lights. As long as the power holds out I think I will be fine."

There was a long silence on the other end of the line before Sean spoke in a quiet voice. "There is talk of cutting power to nonessential areas and reserving it for relocation bases," he said.

"Well am I in a nonessential area?" Jack asked, feigning worry.

"They think everyone has evacuated from there, Jack. It's going to shut off soon. I hope not until tomorrow."

"I guess," Jack began. He was starting to enjoy the game he now played with his friend. Perhaps it wasn't right to do that to a friend, but what Sean didn't know wouldn't hurt him. "I guess I can light a bunch of candles and get a few flashlights. I can sleep in the bathroom. It's small enough. They should provide enough light in case the power goes out."

"Yes, yes do that," Sean agreed. "With the commander's permission, I'll be out first thing in the morning to get you."

"Thanks, buddy," Jack said. "Thanks for watching out for me."

"You stay safe, mate," Sean said. "Don't do anything bloody stupid."

"Okay," he said with thick apprehension. "I'll be careful and will see you in the morning." He didn't think there was any danger of visitors tonight, but why break character? "And Sean . . ." he said.

"Yes?"

"Pray for me," he said, and then hung up the phone. He smiled with satisfaction as he placed the receiver back on the cradle. He had plenty of time to scour his flat for traces of the old woman and to dismantle and store the cage in the attic. This was where he kept it for the brief period of time when he had a girlfriend, but it was several months since he last entertained visitors. He grew rather complacent and a little over confident leaving it assembled in his closet. This proved to be a good wake up call.

Jack would not spend a night cowering in his bathroom; he would spend it in relative peace and harmony. After he performed his clean up duties, he would spend a restful night in his own bed. Of course, he was no fool; he would still leave a light on. He may be immune to the darkness, but things could change. As bizarre as it seemed to him, the whispering of the dark gave him comfort. There was not a living soul for miles, yet he did not feel alone. He may feel comforted by the dark, but he still wouldn't turn his back on it.

When satisfied that all evidence of Gwenda or any of his previous guests was wiped clean, he stored the cage in the attic. Jack walked outside and gazed up at the constellations in the moonless sky. He marveled at their majestic beauty, which he felt he was seeing for the first time in his life. The whispering and clicking of the dark came from everywhere, it even sounded as if it came from the stars. He smiled with satisfaction. The dark had terrified him when he saw it in the woods that morning, but now his fear was as far away as the stars above. Jack went back in the house and lay down on his bed. With little effort, he drifted into a deep and restful sleep.

General Garrison sat in the bright situation room waiting for his associates to arrive. Night had fallen moments earlier and he sat ready to make the most important radio broadcast of his life. He would tell the nation and the world that he and he alone, was ready to lead.

The door opened behind him and the Joint Chiefs entered the room. Each took a seat at the round wooden conference table where Garrison sat in front of a large microphone. They all gave a half-hearted, yet polite smile.

Their demeanor and countenance was amiable, but their intentions were nothing of the sort. The men convened a private meeting a short time after their torturous incident in the Oval Office. They all felt a measured degree of loyalty to General Garrison, after all; he was their chairman. But after a short debate, they recognized their greatest loyalty was not to the general. They all swore to preserve, protect, and defend the United States and its Constitution. He was so far outside the boundaries of the Constitution, even a novice of the law could see. He had assumed control, blocking out the Speaker of the House. There was no way he would relinquish control without a direct order from God or a bullet to the head. The men decided the latter was their best and only option. Garrison must die.

The Marine colonel was the only man who carried a sidearm when he wore his dress uniform. As a result, they nominated him as the assassin. He sat down to the left of Garrison and casually flicked open the holster flap. He was going to do it. The only thing he was uncertain of was when. Should he do it now, or should he wait and do it live on the air, or should he wait until after the broadcast? Perhaps doing it live would kill two birds with one stone. He could eliminate the threat and show the American public what a fraud the general is. Of course, there was always the chance it would make him a martyr. The chiefs did not discuss the timing of the act.

After several long moments of silent pondering, he decided now was the time. The sooner the better. He slipped his hand towards the butt of his pistol. As his fingertips slid over the smooth wooden handle, he started with surprise as the door jerked opened. A stoic Secret Service Agent stuck his head inside.

"One minute, sir," he said and then closed the door behind him.

"My God," the colonel thought, "he's already got the Secret Service treating him as the president."

The colonel's pulse quickened as he glanced at his peers. They all sat still with placid and unreadable faces, waiting for what was to come. The colonel could see in the men's eyes the confident urging for him to carry out the plan. He had their support. At least, he thought so. Maybe it was fear. God knows, it was eating him up inside. It was a difficult task to kill a man even if you happen to be a trained soldier. There was something different about the general, something special. The dark seemed to obey him. He tamped his fears down deep and tried to focus on the task at hand. The colonel had just slipped his hand back to the holster when the red light in front of the microphone came on. The general cleared his throat and then began to speak.

CHAPTER 13

TRUE NATURE

"The true nature of evil is that it is so very casual."
~James St. James

THE LAST RAYS OF SUNLIGHT disappeared across the western valley. The dark engulfed the outside of the cabin and the horrific noise invaded the walls and windows. Cecil, Derek and Burt spent the past two hours refueling the generators and setting up as many lights as possible. They decided to abandon the upstairs, especially during the night. They stockpiled every sheet, pillow, lamp, and toiletries downstairs. They stacked sheets, blankets, and pillows in a pile in the middle of the room. No one would sleep in a bedroom, the living room area would suffice for tonight and as many nights as necessary. It was easier to light and to defend than any other area of the house. In truth, even though no one said it aloud, nobody wanted to be alone. They cleared the furniture back against the walls before dark, but no one moved to claim a spot on the floor. Even though they were all exhausted, sleep was the last thing on anyone's mind.

Sam Andrews, a.k.a. Musial, sat in silence for the last couple of hours, staring out the window. He gave everyone the creeps with the strange mixture of expectancy and fear on his face. It was as if he was hopeful for something a great distance away, but at the same time, the hope terrified him. He had not said a word since he announced he wanted salvation, even though Cecil and Burt questioned him for an hour about what he meant. He seemed frustrated and maybe a little aggravated with himself. Perhaps he tipped his hand and revealed his true motive too soon. Musial refused eye contact and continued to stare out the window and into the woods until they gave up. Burt considered shutting the curtains to change the unnerving countenance on his face. However, he thought better of it. They needed all the sunlight they could get. Closing the curtains on the large picture window would have created a dangerous dark spot in the room.

Everyone sat around the living room with unease. They felt as if they were sitting in a small and untethered shark cage in the middle of the ocean; a school of enormous great white sharks circling just out of view in the murky waters. Derek brought the radio from the kitchen and set it up in the middle of the room. They hoped to get some news about what was going on in the world. It surprised them to hear a live broadcast from General Garrison.

Cecil sat on the sofa caressing Barbara's hand. His stomach twisted into knots when he heard his father's voice. It had been just twenty-four hours since he last heard the arrogant tone of General Garrison as he used Steff to further his cause. He could feel the pitiable stares of everyone, but he focused his attention on Barbara as the general began to speak.

"My fellow Americans and fellow citizens around the world. I bid you all a good evening, morning or day, wherever you may be in God's beautiful world. Times are dark right now and I can assure you I mean no pun by my statement. This is not the time for jokes. I believe this to be mankind's most serious hour since the great flood so many years ago. God chose Noah to lead his living creations onto the ark to escape the punishment for the world's iniquities. Today is different because we do not have a flood of water, but instead a flood of darkness. It is a dark evil that will drown each and every one in its wake more ruthlessly than any flood ever could." He took a deep breath and continued in an 'I told you so' voice. "I warned about these Impals for weeks on end, but there were many who refused to listen. I warned they were deceiving demons and now they are showing their true nature. I have prayed for God's protection and guidance. He has seen fit to speak to me today."

Everyone exchanged glances at this pronouncement. Even Cecil lifted his head and exchanged frowns with Burt. He could feel something devious, something big coming . . . he knew his father. He knew he rarely, if ever, bluffed. He also knew that what he said was always literal. General Garrison was as literal as ever tonight.

General Garrison's voice dropped to a somber and reverent tone. "The president was killed by Impals a few weeks ago. Our new president, who was the former vice-president, was killed by Impals this morning. The Speaker of the House is locked down at the capitol. This puts the line of succession in a sticky mess. But, this is not what is important . . ." he continued, his voice a little more upbeat. "The important thing is that God has shown me today what needs to be done. He gave me a great gift to accomplish the task. He-."

The general was cut off by an incoherent shout and a single gunshot. Next they heard the tormented screams of several men. There was another gunshot followed by three more and then silence. The only noise was the uncanny whispering and clicking. It now not only came from outside, but also from the radio speakers.

Everyone sitting around the radio sat bolt upright in surprise. Cecil's guts filled with a kaleidoscope of emotions. It surprised him, but he also harbored a small degree of hope. Did someone do the right thing and put this mad man down? He felt guilty for harboring this thought. After all, this was his father, but he was also the tyrant who believed in the genocide of the soul. He was also the bastard who held his youngest daughter and was responsible for the death of his oldest. When he focused on this perspective, a bullet hole in the old man's head seemed an appealing prospect. This hope was dashed a moment later. There was a shuffling noise on the radio and then two deep breaths. Then came the firm and defiant words of General Garrison. "I apologize for the interruption folks, but if you would indulge me, I would like to paint you a picture. A member of my own staff, under the control of the Impals, just tried to assassinate me while I was attempting to bring comfort to the world. God is good, God is great, and God has spoken again tonight for all to hear!"

He stopped for a long dramatic pause before continuing. Cecil focused his attention back on Barbara as she slumbered beside him. Her safety was the only thing he controlled and that control was fragile at best. Maybe it was a good thing his father wasn't assassinated then. What would have happened to Steff? She was very much on his mind as well, but he was powerless to help her until they got away from this cabin . . . if they got away. Perhaps the devil you know is better than the devil you don't know.

"Ladies and gentleman," the general continued. "Let me finish painting this picture for you. I am sitting in the situation room of the White House, around the oval conference table. I have a microphone in front of me. All the joint chiefs are here with me, but all of them are now dead. We were all sitting here and the lights went out during the incident. I am sure as you may have guessed by the noise coming through your radio; we are all in the dark."

He paused for several long moments to give his audience a chance to absorb and process this information.

"How?" Burt sputtered, but before anyone could reply, the general continued.

"Yes, that's right ladies and gentlemen . . . I am sitting in the dark . . . unharmed and unmolested by these Impals. This is the proof I spoke of, the proof that God has seen fit to protect and shield me from this evil so I may lead my people through it."

He paused and cleared his throat. "I am now going to turn the lights back on. You should be able to hear the difference," he said.

A second later, the whispering and clicking vanished from the speakers. It was replaced by the sound of shuffling papers and General Garrison's calm and steady breathing.

"Ladies and gentleman, I am thankful this is not television. The sight of my comrades is quite horrifying. Let's all observe a moment of silent prayer for their souls."

The general was anything but silent as he loudly whispered a prayer into the microphone. It was not reverent. Instead, it was arrogant and self-serving. Cecil backhanded a sofa cushion with his free hand. The hypocrisy coming over the airwaves was infuriating.

"Maybe it would have been a good thing if the assassin had succeeded," he thought to himself. He suddenly found it hard to breathe as a panic attack started to wash over him. His breathing was rapid and shallow as he stood up and began to pace. He felt the overwhelming urge to get out of there, to get away. Not because the darkness scared him, but because he couldn't do anything for Steff. They were sitting helpless in the middle of the woods. He wanted to get out and save Steff and, if necessary, he would take care of his father himself.

"Cecil, are you all right?" Charlotte asked.

He put his hands on his hips as he continued to pace and then nodded his head. Before anyone else could speak, the general finished his 'silent' prayer. He began to address the radio audience once again.

"My first order of business tonight is to urge everyone to remain indoors with as many lights on as possible. I am ordering energy reserves opened immediately to compensate for increased power needs. However, we can only sustain for a few days. Three days from now, all power will be redirected to military bases around the country. I am ordering extra lighting and accommodations be set up on these bases. I am not ordering everyone to relocate, this is America after all. Of course, I must warn you, if you do not, you may not have access to power for the foreseeable future. The darkness will consume you."

"This is America after all" Burt spat under his breath.

The general paused and it sounded as if he were shuffling papers, then he took a deep breath and continued. "As your government, we are dedicated to keeping you safe through this trying time. It is up to each of you as to what you choose to do. Today is Wednesday. As of this Saturday night, most civilian locations . . . towns, cities and so forth may not have power. Transportation will be available starting at 8 AM tomorrow local time. Check with your respective municipality."

He paused for a moment and took on a somber, grandfatherly tone. This may have been effective for those who did not know the true General Garrison, but it was sickening for those who did.

"Please people . . . please stay inside, please keep the lights on, please stay safe . . . your government is here to protect you. I'm here to protect you. God has chosen and blessed me so I have no doubt we will get through this. I will bring you another update in the morning. Good night, stay safe and God bless us all."

The broadcast transitioned to a recording of the national anthem on a repeating loop. It replayed three times before anyone spoke.

"That sounds like the Impal camps all over again," Sally said with a shiver.

"Are they going to start putting people into the Tesla Gates now?" Charlotte asked.

To everyone's surprise, Burt was a little more optimistic. "No, I don't think he will. He needs to keep the heart and soul of the people. That won't last long if he turns them into death camps."

Cecil stopped pacing and sneered. "Why should he electrocute them in the Tesla Gate?" He asked. "If they get out of line, he can just turn the lights off and claim it was an accident or malfunction. Besides, I don't think he would use the tremendous amount of electricity it takes to keep those damned things running. He is many things, but he is not stupid."

"Do you think it is necessary?" Charlotte asked.

"Maybe," Burt admitted. "Pooling resources seems the most practical way to go. I just wish—," Burt said, but Cecil cut him short.

"I just wish that brave assassin succeeded," Cecil finished. "Necessary or not, it's only another ploy for him to solidify his power."

"Of course," Burt said. "I wasn't taking his side, Cecil. God help me I wasn't. I was just speaking from a pure logistical point of view."

Cecil ignored Burt's comment as he continued with another thought. "Has anyone considered the big question here? Does anyone wonder how he can enter the dark without harm?"

"He was lying!" Derek said. "No one could see him . . . he could tell us anything and expect us to believe it!"

Everyone nodded in agreement, everyone but Cecil. Instead, he shook his head. "He wasn't lying," Cecil said.

"How can you tell?" Burt asked.

"The screams, the noise . . . they were too real to have been canned sound effects for our amusement."

"But how do you know he was telling the truth . . . how do you know he was really in the dark?" Derek prodded.

Cecil shrugged. "I know my father," he said, pronouncing the last word as if something were foul in his mouth. "I know how misguided and full of crap he is, but I have always been able to tell when he was lying. This is not one of those times."

"Okay," Burt said. "Assuming he is telling the truth, how the hell is it possible?"

"I don't know," Cecil said. "Of course I don't buy his explanation of God choosing him. The God I know is not that misguided. I haven't got a clue."

"Don't you?" a new voice to the conversation asked.

Everyone turned to see Musial staring sedately at them.

"Don't we what?" Burt asked.

Musial didn't even acknowledge Burt's presence; instead he focused his gaze on Cecil.

"What should I know?" Cecil asked.

"One of the oldest truisms of mankind, human nature, and nature itself," Musial said.

"What the hell are you talking about?" Burt demanded.

"Well, I think it was best put by William Turner in the mid-16th century. Of course I wasn't around yet back then, but I do remember reading his paptist satire—*The Rescuing of Romish Fox*. I believe the line went something like this: "Birds of one kind and color flock and fly always together.""

Everyone stared at him, uncomprehending. Everyone, but Charlotte.

"Birds of a feather flock together," she muttered.

"Precisely!" Musial grinned. "It's nice to know there is at least one intelligent person in this pitiful little band."

"Are you saying . . ." Cecil asked, and then trailed off with disgust on his face.

"I'm saying," Musial said, staring fixedly at Cecil, "your father is a kindred spirit to the dark. He is no different than me or any one of the thousands out there," he said, tipping his head toward the window.

Deep down, Cecil knew what Musial said was true, in fact he had suspected it before Musial ever opened his mouth. So why did he feel so sick, so hollow? Because it is a difficult thing to hate and loathe one's own father, but Cecil seemed to be accomplishing it with relative ease. He sat back down on the sofa and took Barbara's hand. He finally pushed his father and the dark to the back of his mind. He closed his eyes and soon his thoughts coalesced into one disturbing thought. Is my father the only one?

The thing Cecil, General Garrison, and even Musial did not know is that immunity to the dark was not unique. In fact, many kindred individuals passed unmolested through the darkness around the world tonight. They all shared the same unique distinction of being kindred counterparts of the dark. They were all 'chosen' in their own way, in their own minds, and they would make the most out of their opportunity.

CHAPTER 14

RUTH

"You cannot be responsible for salvation until first you've been responsible for sin."
~Edwin Louis Cole

JACK ENJOYED HIS UNIQUE STANDING in the world. He had no illusions of being chosen by God, or even the Devil. Whether it was brutal self-honesty or a special perception, he knew the dark, in many ways, was a reflection of himself. It made him comfortable, and it made him relax. As he lay on his bed with eyes shut and his lamp casting a trusting perimeter, he listened to the soothing whispers of the shadows. They served as a sinister lullaby as he drifted off to sleep.

Jack's eyes flew open and he sat up. His heart fluttered in his chest. Something awakened him, something loud, something forceful and something very near. The dark may be a comfort to him, but Jack was no fool. He still didn't trust it and with good reason . . . he knew how it thought. How long had he been asleep? He wasn't sure because the batteries in his wall clock died more than a year ago. He looked for his watch until he remembered placing it on the dresser. He was about to get up and retrieve it, when a loud rapping noise made him jump. He whirled about and stared at his bedroom window. Someone was out there knocking on the glass. They wanted in.

* * *

It took over an hour for Malaki and Rebekah to get settled into a tent. The living area was small, no more than ten feet by twelve feet. At least six people packed each of the hundreds filling the field. The soldiers tried to keep families together and divide living quarters by gender, but there was limited space. Malakhi and Rebecca ended up sharing a tent with three other women and an emaciated teenage boy. His appearance and odor suggested he had been living on the streets for weeks. He didn't say a word and took his assigned sleeping bag. The boy huddled against the rear wall of the tent with his back to everyone. A few moments later, they heard a loud fart followed by a couple of grunts, and then the heavy breathing of the sleeping teen.

The inside of the tents were almost as bright as the outside. Their thin fabric allowed plenty of the powerful portable lights to penetrate. However, if they got a heavy rainfall, the tent would not provide a lot of protection. Two kerosene lanterns hung inside. Each burned at full capacity, making a loud hissing noise as the flame flickered. It made Rebekah shiver when she noticed how similar it sounded to the darkness.

Malakhi lay down against the opposite wall from the flatulent boy and pulled himself into a ball. He was cold, but he was also terrified. Rebekah stroked his head as she talked with the other women. Two of them were dark haired and about her age. One was older with long salt and pepper hair and a plump mid-section and bosom. Her voice was raspy as if a dedicated smoker most of her life. They all recounted a near death experience for the day, but none seemed as harrowing as Rebekah and Malakhi's escape. The women were stretching out their sleeping bags, when they heard the rustling of footsteps outside the tent door. A moment later, the timid voice of a male soldier called out.

"Ladies, can we come in?"

They exchanged puzzled glances. The older woman, whose name was Andrea, rasped like a foghorn. "Come in!"

The flap of the door opened and a young and blushing soldier poked his head in. "I'm sorry but we have run out of room, we're going to have to bunk one more with you," he said.

Before anyone could respond, he stepped to the side and a mop of long white hair appeared in the doorway. The other three women blinked at the old, smiling woman. Rebekah recognized her at once. It was Ruth, the homeless lady who sat by her on the truck.

Ruth smile and plopped down on the floor next to Rebekah, wrapping her in a tight embrace. The smell of body odor and dirt was overwhelming. She was forced to suppress a gag.

"I just knew I would see you again!" Ruth said. "It's fate, that's what it is!"

The other women watched with polite interest. It was evident from their crinkled noses and watery eyes, the old lady's stench had wafted to their side of the tent. As soon as she greeted Rebekah, she made her way to the other ladies in the tent, introducing herself and hugging each one of them in turn. As offensive as it was, Rebekah couldn't help cracking a tiny smile at the women's revulsion.

Rebekah took the opportunity to roll out her sleeping bag next to Malakhi. She cuddled up as close to him as she could manage with her back to the tent. Her stomach twisted when Ruth rolled out her sleeping bag right next to her.

"So . . . what do you do for a living?" Ruth asked.

She was close enough that Rebekah could not only smell her rancid breath, but could feel its warmth blow across her ear. She cupped her hand over her nose and mouth then answered in a muffled voice. "I'm a waitress."

"You don't say?" Ruth said. "You know I used to do that too. It was years ago though."

The conversation was pretty much one sided with Ruth doing most of the talking. Most of the responses to her questions just required a simple yes or no. Everything Ruth asked was a question about her and Malakhi. After an hour of yammering, she didn't know anything about Ruth outside of her name and the fact she used to be a waitress years ago. Rebekah tried to endure the interrogation without passing out from halitosis overload. She kept hoping the next question would be her last. At last, the questions stopped and Rebekah heard faint and even breathing behind her. It seemed Ruth was asleep.

Rebekah relaxed a little, yet she found it impossible to go to sleep.

Even though she had shut her eyes many times during the day, she couldn't shake a feeling. She feared that if she gave in to sleep, if she closed her eyes, the darkness inside her own eyelids would somehow put a horrible end to her life. It was a rational fear, considering. She smiled when she felt Malakhi's steady breathing as he slept in her arms. He was unharmed and he was resting. A pang of guilt stabbed her when she considered the possibility that she used her own son as a Guinea pig. It was not her intent, but it still didn't make her feel better. She pulled him closer and kissed him on the cheek. Malakhi snorted and mumbled before settling back into his deep slumber. Rebekah closed her eyes and tried to envision a bright, sunny day. She was about to fall asleep, when she heard a voice inches from her ear. It was Ruth.

"Mighty fine boy you've got here," she said dreamily. It was as if Malakhi was the most precious thing she had ever seen in her life.

The foul breath of the woman was up Rebekah's nose before she could do anything and she couldn't help coughing.

"I'm sorry dear, are you sick?" Ruth asked, her voice dripping with sympathy.

Rebekah coughed a few more times then sat up. She shook her head as she scooted a few feet on her butt towards the front of the tent. She wanted to put as much distance as possible between herself and the toxic breath. "No, only tired," she said. "It's been a long day."

"Tell me about it!" Ruth cackled. "Sometimes I feel I have endured a thousand years of misery."

"Shhhhh!" the heavy woman on the other side of the tent scolded.

"I guess we'd better keep it down," Ruth whispered, scooting closer to Rebekah. As luck would have it, Ruth stopped when she was still a few feet away.

"Yes, we all better try to get some sleep," Rebekah said, but Ruth either didn't hear or just ignored her.

"I wonder how long this is going to last," she said thoughtfully.

"I don't know," Rebekah said. "I hope it ends any second."

Ruth regarded her a long time from her narrowed and wrinkled eyes. Rebekah couldn't tell if her expression was one of contemplation, anger, or longing. It seemed to be a strange combination of all three and it gave her the creeps. She encountered homeless people before, but none were this persistent about asking questions. From her experience, most would be grateful to have a bed and a roof over their head, not to mention the promise of three square meals a day. Ruth was a different animal. Rebekah was not sure whether to be troubled that she was so hard to read, or pleased that the old lady was a refreshing change of pace. Maybe she would feel different if Ruth were able to take a proper shower and brush her teeth. Rebekah made herself a promise that seeing to Ruth's cleanliness would be a priority for her in the morning. Even if it meant putting her hygiene second. Ruth hadn't bathed in a long, long time, and they were likely to be in close quarters for a while.

"Well," Ruth said, her pleasant demeanor melting, "we have to make the best of it until it does."

"Yes, that's true," Rebekah said. "I feel a lot safer here with all the soldiers and all the lights."

"It won't last forever," Ruth said. "Nothing ever does."

"What do you mean?" Rebekah asked.

Ruth shrugged and poked at her front teeth as if she were trying to dislodge a stubborn piece of food. "The Impals didn't stay long, did they?" she said.

Rebekah grimaced when she recalled the image of her father fading out of existence. She felt tears welling in her eyes. Not only for reliving the painful memory, but also because she felt guilty about almost forgetting it. Yes, she had been through a lot today, more than some people endure in a lifetime. Of course, that was no excuse to forget about her father. "No," Rebekah whispered.

Ruth switched gears quickly. "I hope they don't have kosher food for breakfast in the morning. I could go for some steak and eggs or maybe even ham and eggs," she said in a distant voice. "God, it has been a long time."

Rebekah shrugged. The thought had not even occurred to her. She was pretty certain that since they were on an Israeli military base, there would be kosher food. Considering the number of people the military had to feed, bagels and blintz would be the solitary menu item. Perhaps, if they were fortunate, maybe some canned fish or chicken. She had never eaten steak or ham in her life. It surprised her at first because she assumed that everyone there was Jewish. It seemed Ruth was not.

"I don't know," Rebekah said. "Probably rations."

Ruth wrinkled her nose as if they would be dining on freeze dried turds. Rebekah didn't think she had eaten a meal, let alone a good one, in ages. She thought it odd that Ruth would hold such high expectations.

"Are you Christian?" Rebekah asked.

Ruth stared at the floor as if terrified to make eye contact. She mumbled in a voice barely audible over the constant hissing outside. "Maybe, I suppose."

Before Rebekah could muster a response, Ruth switched gears again and said cheerily, "Well dear, I'm tired and I'm sure you must be exhausted. Why don't we get some sleep?"

A wave of relief washed over Rebekah. Moments ago, she was certain that she was in for a long winded talk, stretching into the wee hours of the morning. "That's great," she said. "I am exhausted and I'm sure Malakhi will be up at first light as usual."

Ruth scooted over and gave her plenty of room to stretch out and not feel crowded. She was still close enough that Rebekah could smell her, but it was unavoidable in this tiny living space.

"Good night," Rebekah said as she rolled close to her son and draped her arm over him.

"Good night," Ruth said.

Rebekah was so exhausted that, in spite of her apprehension, sleep came very fast. It may not have come so easy if she knew the conflict playing out in Ruth's mind. She lay on her side facing them, her eyes wide open. She watched the sleeping mother and son with the hungry zeal of a lion watching a sleeping gazelle. It was not hunger pangs pulling at her, it was the insatiable desire for rape, mutilation, and murder. The same desire that overwhelmed her a hundred times before. She wanted to take the pair out into the woods and play. They would have such a good time and it would rid the world of another single mother. God knows there were enough of them around nowadays.

She could have found a way to accomplish this; after all, she had learned to be crafty. However, there were two factors that stayed her hand. First, Ruth was not a she. Oh sure the body might be, but the consciousness was that of a man. A man who had been dead for thousands of years. Ruth was his mother's name. He had no idea what the real name was of the slumbering, geriatric, wino he inhabited. As far as he was concerned, it didn't matter. She was better off now anyway.

His dark nature pulled at him to act, to fulfill his perceived purpose, but he resisted. He resisted with one word replaying through his mind . . . salvation.

CHAPTER 15

DANGEROUS BEDFELLOWS

"Trust not too much to appearances."
~Virgil

GENERAL GARRISON SAT IN THE OVAL OFFICE staring at the far wall. He was alone, but he would not be for long. He sought the privacy of the famous room when he first heard about the arrivals. He wanted to pray and seek guidance, but it seemed God was not in a talking mood tonight. He knew God chose him and blessed him, but it no longer seemed that he was special and unique. It hurt his pride and ego, though he would never admit it. He arrived at the conclusion that he was certain must be the truth. God sent him helpers. He couldn't be expected to carry out this enormous task on his own. He couldn't lead with people who did not understand what it meant to be chosen.

Ever since the general's horrific radio address, there had been a steady stream of visitors showing up at the White House. These pilgrims' backgrounds were as diverse as their origins, yet they all held one thing in common. They all moved through the dark unharmed as General Garrison did. This small band assembled at the north gate by Lafayette Square was a tiny drop in a large bucket. Hundreds, if not thousands of immune people existed worldwide. Yet, the vast majority of these unique individuals bore no desire to broadcast their special

ability. They were afraid of persecution. Most important, they had secrets to protect, secrets as black as the deepest darkest hole imaginable. They were all arrogant in their own way.

"General, there are several people asking to see you at the north gate," an aide said as she peaked through the door. She was a short mousy woman who seemed as nervous as one in a room full of cats. Her hand trembled on the door handle, making a faint rattling noise.

"I know!" he boomed, causing her to step back a few paces and almost fall. "We're not in the habit of letting anyone into the White House uninvited, are we?"

"No sir," she squeaked. "I just thought you should know."

"Do you take me for an idiot, Miss Smith?" he asked. He had no idea what the poor woman's name was, nor did he care. If her name was not Smith, she made no attempt to correct him.

"No general, I don't," she said.

"And that's another thing," he said, stepping out from behind the desk. He eyed the poor woman with folded arms and a piercing scowl. "I think it is about time everyone starts referring to me as Mr. President . . . don't you?"

Her eyes filled with terror. "Yes, Mr. President," she whispered.

"What did you say?" he asked, cupping his palm to his ear, feigning deafness.

"Yes, Mr. President," she said a little louder.

He stood and stared at her for several uncomfortable moments. She managed to summon enough courage to clear her throat and say, "Mr. President, would you like for me to have security remove them?"

He was sure that this intrusive woman knew security could not venture past the lighted perimeter. This group of people assembled in a dark area between the White House fence and the lights of Lafayette Square. The general, now claiming the presidency, knew exactly what he would do. He would go out to them. He strode out the door, elbowing her out of the way.

"But . . . sir," was all she could manage as she landed on her rear. It was too late; he had already passed her and turned the corner.

Garrison came across a young Marine guard toting an M-16 assault rifle. He demanded the weapon and, after minimal protest, the soldier handed it over. Garrison inspected the gun as any good soldier would. He ejected and then reinserted the ammo clip. Once satisfied, he flicked the safety off and held the weapon at the ready. He moved towards the nearest door leading to the north lawn. The Marine followed, though he didn't dare protest. He saw the countenance in the new president's face, one he had seen once before. The murderous gaze of an insurgent, hell bent on killing him and his entire platoon. He would not let Garrison out of his sight, not only for everyone else's safety, but for Garrison's as well. The soldier rounded a corner just in time to see a door to the outside slam shut. He quickened his pace and began to sprint down the hallway. There were other guards out there, but he was the only one who knew Garrison was coming.

By the time he opened the door, Garrison had already forced the exterior guards to stand down and fall back. He was now at the iron fence bordering the north lawn of the White House, pointing his weapon through the bars. The Marine caught the eye of one of the outside guards and they stared at each other.

General Garrison, now the self-proclaimed President Garrison, was a soldier first. A politician would not have made such a bold and foolish move, but Garrison was no politician. He was a commander, he was a leader, and he was hardcore. Not to mention, he was chosen by God.

"State your business!" he demanded, leveling the rifle at the center of the group.

"We're all chosen, general . . . just like you!" a short fat man shouted and stepped forward.

The crowd flinched and hit the ground as a single shot rang out. The man, who dared to speak first, lay on his back with his arms and legs splayed wide. Blood pooled under the back of his head, or what was left of it. The people nearest to him picked brains and bits of scalp off their faces and clothing.

The Secret Service agents and military guards rushed forward at once, causing Garrison to turn. "I told you morons to stay back!" he roared.

It was difficult to go against their training and instincts, but the men complied. They didn't retreat that far back though.

"It's Mr. President!" he spat as he trained the rifle back and forth over the cowering crowd as if he were trying to decide on his next target. "Now does anyone else want to 'correctly' address me with your business?"

Garrison was about to squeeze off another random shot when a strong and forceful voice spoke up. It was a voice he recognized.

"Mr. President, we only want to serve God, you, and our country . . . as I always have," the man said.

Garrison squinted into the darkness then lowered the barrel of the rifle. "Avery?" he said.

"Yes, yes . . . it's me, Mr. President. I'm here to serve you again."

Avery Cooper had served under Garrison's command off and on for several years. He thought of him as a good and trusted soldier, not to mention a loyal ally. They were of the same mindset on most issues, including the way they handled things in Central America many years ago. The last time Garrison saw him was two years ago when Avery was a colonel stationed at the Pentagon.

"Where did you come from?" Garrison growled.

"The Pentagon sir, I walked all the way here . . . it's a bit of a hike," he said with a soft chuckle.

Garrison didn't find it amusing. "Come closer so I can see you!" he snapped. A couple of the others crouched on the ground began to get to their feet, but Garrison fired off a shot inches over their heads.

"Stay down!" he barked.

Each one froze like a statue and an eerie silence fell over the area. The only noises were the fading echo of the rifle blast and the sounds of the dark.

"It's me," Avery said, holding up his hands in surrender as he approached the fence.

As he entered the lights from the White House grounds, Garrison saw his face and lowered the weapon.

"Dammit, Avery! I almost shot you!" he barked.

"I'm glad you didn't," he said with a smile and offered his hand to Garrison through the bars.

Garrison studied his friend carefully before shaking his hand. He then motioned for him to go to the gate about thirty yards away. As

Avery began walking, Garrison shouted to the guards. "Let him in . . . but search him first!"

Avery jerked in surprise, but made no comment or argument. It would be unwise with someone carrying a deadly assault rifle in a very agitated mood. A few moments later, Avery was patted down and a small pistol removed from his pocket. Once cleared, he walked back to join his friend.

"What's with the gun?" Garrison asked.

"Do you really think I am stupid enough to go out with all these crazies about and not have protection?"

"Touché," Garrison said with a half smirk. He then turned his attention back to the crowd. "So . . . are any of them useful?" he asked, making another sweep of the crowd with his rifle.

"A couple," Avery said. "What are you going to do with the rest?" he asked with a sparkle in his eye.

"The Lord never wants us to take more than we need . . . waste not, want not," Garrison said with a heart-chilling smile.

Avery was excited and perhaps a little giddy.

"Go and pick them out," Garrison said with a wink and a nod toward the gate.

Avery turned and strode back to the gate.

"Sergeant, a word please!" Garrison yelled to a nearby Marine guard watching from beneath a tree. The soldier approached, eyeing Garrison and his weapon with suspicion. When he approached, Garrison motioned for him to lean close. He shared a special secret with the young guard. As Garrison whispered, the expression on the Marine's face melted into disgusted horror. "Sir?" was all he could manage to say when the president stopped talking.

He handed Garrison his rifle as he glanced toward the other guards. None of them would make eye contact; they were all scared and confused. They were all trained to protect the president, but then Garrison was technically not the president. The one thing never covered in their training was what to do if the president goes berserk with a gun. The sharp shooters were off the roof of the White House tonight because it was too dark up there. All security focused inside and on the well-lit lawn. The guards on the north side fell back in a row against the north wall of the residence, their guns out and ready.

The poor sergeant who handed his weapon to Garrison backed away and joined his comrades against the wall. As his back touched the side of the house, he had a disturbing thought. It seemed as if all of them were in one big firing line. The only thing missing was a blindfold and cigarette. Maybe they should act, maybe they should save Garrison from himself, but none of them seemed able to move. Did he have some mysterious control over them or were they too scared to intervene? Maybe it was a mix of both, the dark terrified them all and Garrison seemed to have control over it.

Garrison checked the new weapon and then slung it over his shoulder. He walked back to the fence and watched as Avery picked three people out of the crowd. One was a young man of slender build with unkempt hair, carrying a backpack over one shoulder. The next was a stocky, balding man wearing a business suit and chewing on a cigar. The final person picked was a woman with shoulder length hair, wearing blue jeans and a denim shirt. It was too dark to tell, but judging by the sound of her footfalls, she wore cowboy boots.

"What's so special about these bozos?" Garrison thought as he watched them parade through the gate behind Avery.

They stopped a few feet away from Garrison and then Avery turned and pointed at the young man.

"Sebastian Gardner. A computer geek, intelligence freelancer and a man who will do *anything* for his country," he said with a knowing grin.

He then pointed at the heavy set man with the suit.

"Robby Johns, *business* man," he said, giving no more introduction. The man chomped on his cigar and stared at Garrison through narrowed eyes. Unlike most people, he showed no fear of the new president.

Avery then walked over and put his arm around the woman.

"Joan Titsworth . . . what a name, huh?" he said looking from the woman's face to her well-endowed chest. She glared at him with a murderous stare. "She'll do anything for her country, but she'll also do anyone," he grinned.

Joan clouted him on the side of his head.

"Shut up you pompous, self-righteous ass!" she hissed with as much venom as anything in the darkness. "I'll split your damned skull!"

Avery rubbed the side of his head. He was about to respond when Garrison interrupted.

"Enough of this, Avery. We have business to take care of," he spat.

Avery's mood improved as a sly grin spread across his face. He held out his hand and Garrison gave him one of the rifles. "I haven't used one of these in years," he said.

"Since Panama?" Garrison remarked.

Avery nodded and began to walk toward the fence as Garrison followed.

"How do you know those people?" Garrison asked as they walked.

"I may be at the Pentagon, Mr. President, but that doesn't mean I'm not still involved with intelligence. Those three are some of the best domestic operatives we have. None of them will bat an eyelash at doing what must be done."

"Giving the government plausible deniability," Garrison said with a crooked smile.

Avery nodded.

When they reached the fence, Garrison leaned up against the bars and stared at the small group still milling about in the dark. "You sure you got all the useful ones?" he asked.

Avery shrugged. "I got you the ones I know. Do you want to conduct interviews with the rest of them?" he said impatiently.

Garrison glared at him. "You're damn lucky I let y'all in here, yourself included, colonel."

When Garrison first heard of the crowd gathering outside, he was terrified. He feared that he had been wrong in his assumption that God chose him. Of course, his terror was short lived. He realized God was testing him, giving him his first challenge of his new administration.

By the time he arrived at the fence, he was still hell bent on destruction. However, going out and just mowing everyone down was not practical because it was too easy. This was a challenge and shooting fish in a barrel was no challenge at all. He knew God sent these people here for a reason. When he saw his friend, Avery, he had no doubt. He thought of Proverbs 21:5: '*The plans of the diligent lead surely to abundance, but everyone who is hasty comes only to poverty.*'

He had done his diligence. He separated the wheat from the chafe. He identified those who God sent to assist his administration. The others must die. As long as there were others who could move through the dark, a great shadow of doubt was cast on his divine providence. He could not allow it.

"Are you ready?" Garrison asked, flicking the safety off and raising the rifle through the bars of the fence.

"You start left and I start right then work our way in?" Avery asked.

Garrison nodded then turned and shouted at the group. "Okay, people nothing more to see here, it's time to move along!"

As some began to turn and walk away, he gave the word.

"Now!" Garrison snapped, loud enough for only Avery to hear.

The deafening roar of automatic weapons fire echoed off the buildings. Lafayette Square was lit up like strobe lights. It was over almost as fast as it began, twenty-eight men and ten women lay dead in pools of blood, a mere stone's throw from the White House. The guards watching the mayhem tensed and a few raised their rifles across their chests, but no one dared to act.

Garrison and Avery beamed at each other with wide smiles of satisfaction.

"Thank you Lord for choosing me and guiding me tonight. Thy will be done," Garrison said.

As the two men were about to walk back to the White House with their three helpers, one of the guards summoned the courage to approach them.

"Sir . . . why?" he asked.

Garrison felt a surge of rage because his divine mission was being questioned. Even so, he was not a fool. As much as he wanted to shoot this man, he knew that discretion was the best policy. His quick thinking took over and he created a lie, a very convincing one. It would become his official stance on the incident. If over thirty of these people tried to crash the White House, no telling how many more there were around the country, not to mention the world. He was special and he must remain so. God's plan depended on it.

"Sergeant, I couldn't ask you and your men to carry out judgment, not in good conscious," he said.

The sergeant seemed confused.

"You see, those people were taken over by the damned Impals. Instead of killing them, they were controlling them. We . . . we had to put them down," he said with false remorse.

"But . . . what about them?" he asked, glancing at Avery and the other three.

"They were too strong for the Impals; their faith in God is pure. They mustered the strength to resist. Now, I'm going to take them in and let them recover from their traumatic ordeal."

The sergeant still seemed confused, but he nodded and stepped aside.

Garrison returned the weapon to the guard he borrowed it from. "It handles well," he said with a smile and a pat on the shoulder.

Garrison was about to walk on when something caught his eye above the sergeant's head. Someone was at one of the windows on the second floor. Steff stood there with her hands cupped over her mouth in horror.

CHAPTER 16

LITTLE DONNA

"It's fun to have a partner who understands your life and lets you be you."
~Kim Kardashian

JACK'S HEART PULSED in every inch of his body. For someone who was so content and restful moments earlier, the knocking at his window terrified him. Not because he thought it was one of the beings from the dark, but because he was afraid it may be the police or, even worse, his base. Did he thoroughly dispose of the evidence? He never welcomed an uninvited guest before, at least not one who left alive.

He glanced about the room, keeping one eye on the window. He jumped when a white hand rapped on the glass again followed by the top of a head peering over the windowsill. Whoever was outside was either crouching on their knees or quite short and standing on their tiptoes. He watched paralyzed until he heard the muffled voice of a woman.

"Hello . . . I see you . . . can I come in?"

When the eyes of the person peeked over the sill again, he absently pointed towards the back door in the next room.

"Okay," she said, and then disappeared.

Jack walked to the other room and flipped on the outside light. When he saw who was outside, he didn't know whether to laugh or to scream. A young girl, in her early teens, stood in the shadows peering up at him. Her grey eyes beckoned to him from underneath a mop of tangled black curls. Her ruby red lips twisted in a sardonic grimace. The first thing he noticed was that she used way too much make up. If not for her torn jeans, filthy trainers, and an unassuming green hoodie, she would have passed as a short prostitute. Jack hesitated before opening the door. This was not because he was afraid of the girl; it was because he had *some* honor. He might be a murderer, but he was not a pedophile. He did not believe her intentions to be honorable. He opened the door only a crack, but she bolted inside and plopped down at his kitchen table as if she belonged there.

"Hi sweetie, what's your name?" she said in a sultry voice way beyond her years. She propped her feet on the table and gave him a seductive wink.

Jack didn't answer at first; instead he studied her in the ambient light coming in from outside. He experienced a mixture of emotions. He wasn't sure whether he was happy to have someone to share the dark with or whether it was time to get his cage back out. He never caged anyone this young because it served no purpose. It wouldn't serve a greater good. However, in this case, he could make an exception. He didn't trust her and he wasn't sure why.

Jack sat down across from her at the table. His mood and posture were rigid. Finally, he answered through clinched jaws. "Jack." He reached up and pulled the string, turning on the light above the table. The room flooded with light, driving the whispers to the far corners of his flat. Once he got a proper look at his guest, she wasn't quite as she had appeared. She was definitely young, no doubt a teenager. Her physical maturity was blemished by a rough existence. A large scar corkscrewed her right cheek, ending an inch from her eye. Small purple blotches peppered her neck and the top of her hands. He couldn't tell if it was due to mottling from drug abuse or a bruise from an injury. Perhaps her makeup was not a symbol of promiscuity, but rather a cover for a life of shame and humiliation. However, her voice and tone suggested otherwise.

"My name is Donna, darlin'," she said with a wink, making the scar on her cheek jump.

He thought it strange that this girl did not have a British accent. She had an American one, although it sounded fake. Donna spoke in an accent of the American south to be exact. She took her legs down and dangled them over the edge of the chair. She leaned forward with her elbows propped on the tabletop and rested her head in her hands. She regarded him with dreamy eyes.

"Well, Donna," he began. "Where are you from?"

She rolled her eyes back and forth as if trying to recall some elusive fact. "Manchester," she said after several long moments. "I'm from Manchester, England."

"I figured it was the Manchester you were referring to," Jack said. "You don't sound like you're from Manchester."

She shrugged and frowned at him. "What the hell am I supposed to sound like?" she yelled and folded her arms over her heaving chest.

"Well, you sound as if you are from the States . . . Georgia or Alabama or somewhere," he said, making no effort at apology.

"Is this bloody better?" she said using an exaggerated British accent.

Jack stared at her. He was starting to consider getting his cage back out. This girl was not in his modus operandi, but he would still be doing the world a great service if he took care of her. He could be quick and merciful, unlike how he had treated most of his guests . . . besides he was tired and needed to get some sleep. He didn't need this aggravation. As tempting a thought as this was, one thing stayed his hand. She was like him. She could move about in the lethal darkness. This small woman-child humbled Jack in a way others had never been able to. He felt foolish that he was naïve enough to believe he was the only one with this special immunity. Of course there were others out there . . . there had to be. It was a mathematical certainty.

When she did not immediately get a response, she continued her tirade. "What say we go nick a bloody lorry and roam about town like a couple of bobbies while we search for any tossers hanging about after dark?" she said, thickening the accent and using British slang.

Jack felt anger rising. He didn't appreciate being patronized, especially not by a kid. He leaned forward and stared into Donna's eyes. "Listen Donna, you are in my house and if you want to remain in my house I expect you to show some respect. Judging by your appearance, you don't respect yourself."

He could see the anger kindling in Donna's eyes, but he didn't care. "Whatever rules you lived by before don't mean a bloody thing now. You are in my house. My house, my rules . . ." he said trailing off with a broad and patronizing smile of his own.

"You know nothing of me," Donna snapped, the southern American accent was gone momentarily, replaced by something that sounded British, but different from anything he ever heard before.

It was true. Jack knew nothing about her, but he didn't care. He meant what he said. The two of them stared at each other, neither one wanting to show weakness by breaking eye contact. Finally, Donna flinched. The flame in her eyes dimmed a little and she sat back in her chair. She yawned as she propped her feet on the table.

"So . . . why doesn't the dark affect us?" she asked in a neutral accent.

"I don't know," Jack said, nodding his head at her trainers. He wanted her to remove them from the table. She ignored him.

"Maybe this is just a shot in the dark here," Donna said, studying him from head to toe. "I would guess that you are in the military."

Jack still wore his uniform. He only planned on making a quick trip home and back. He had not anticipated staying. He frowned and said, "You could say that."

"What do you do in the military?" she prodded.

"I'm an MP," he said.

Donna laughed. "So, you're an army bobbie," she said, putting on her bogus English accent again.

"And you are a skanky scrubber?" he said with a sardonic smile.

She didn't understand his meaning. "What is that . . . domestic service . . . a maid or something?" she asked.

"Something like that," Jack said, his smile broadening.

"Manchester, indeed," he thought to himself. "She doesn't know Liverpool from liverwurst."

"No, I never done anything like that," she said reverting back to her Southern dialect. She studied her hands and then ran her fingers up and down her torso a couple of times. Jack couldn't tell if she was trying to be seductive or scratching an itch. She then touched her fingers to her cheeks as she spoke. "No, I go to school and work as a waitress part time," she said distantly.

"What school?" Jack prodded.

She regarded him for several moments. The rage he saw earlier was gone, replaced by bewilderment. She resembled a deer in headlights.

"The girls' school in Manchester," she said.

"Which one?"

"The main one," she said, the flame rekindling.

"Oh," Jack said, trying to hide his disbelief. He was not in the mood to argue or conduct an interrogation.

"Yes . . . that one," she said.

Jack was about to offer her the couch for the night, when Donna surprised him.

"Why do you think we can pass through the dark?" she said. Jack wasn't looking at her when she spoke. If he had, he might have noticed a knowing grin wash across her face.

"I don't know," Jack said. "Why do you think we can?"

"I think the things in the dark like us and give us a break," she said, nonchalant as if she were discussing the weather.

Jack raised an eyebrow. "Really . . . and why is that?" he asked.

"I don't know . . . a feeling," she smirked.

Jack had the same feeling. Although he did not trust the darkness enough to sleep with the lights off, he did find it calming. It was like wrapping himself up in a warm blanket, yet a blanket that he feared could smother him if he let his guard down. "Why do you think it likes us?" Jack asked.

"Because you know them and they know you. Y'all always have," she said with a tone of indifference.

"What the hell does that mean?" Jack demanded.

Donna shook her head and shrugged. "I think it means we have to keep a low profile. I don't think there are too many people who would understand our aptitude," she said.

Jack felt a knot in his stomach. He felt as if someone may be watching. This thought frightened him ever since he woke up with a bloody head. Someone would find out, someone would ask questions, and then someone would ask more questions. Then they would want to know all about him. He couldn't have it. Jack was careful, but he was not perfect. Someone would find out about his community service work and they would not understand. People were stupid. He avoided personal interaction as much as possible.

"Okay," Jack said, half serious and half playing along. "So, what do you think we should do?"

"Well, first of all, turn all these danged lights off," she said. "If this were summer, you would be attracting every bug within miles. As it is, you are just attracting questions you don't want to answer."

She gave him with a knowing grin. He was not sure why, but it sent chills up his spine.

Without another word, he got up and flicked off the outside light. He then turned off the kitchen light, plunging them into darkness.

"You want to sleep on the sofa?" Jack said.

"Well I'm sure as hell not going to sleep with you!" she said with a cold certainty. It was a stark contrast from her initial demeanor.

Jack felt a flush of embarrassment wash over his face. He was glad it was dark and she couldn't see him.

"Whatever," Jack said. "I'll get you a pillow."

"Thank you sugar, that's mighty sweet of you!" she said reverting back to her seductive, southern voice.

Jack didn't acknowledge her. He walked in his bedroom, retrieved a pillow off his bed, and then came back and tossed it to her.

"Here," he said before turning and walking back in the bedroom. He closed and locked the door behind him.

"Crazy urchin," he muttered as he reluctantly took her advice and shut off his bedroom lamp.

The room fell into complete darkness. Jack stood for several minutes listening to the hissing and clicking. Those ethereal noises sounded as if several people whispered in a strange language. Jack found it an intoxicating lullaby. He walked to his bed and stretched out. Sleep came, but not before he asked the same question a dozen times—*who or what is she?*

CHAPTER 17

THE UNLIKELY ALLY

"Some allies are more dangerous than enemies."
~George R.R. Martin

SALVATION. This single word had been in the back of everyone's mind since Musial announced his deepest desire hours earlier. Once the shock of President Garrison's broadcast wore off, the cryptic word was now first on everyone's mind. Only, Musial wasn't talking; in fact he had been in a deep sleep ever since the radio was switched off. Their best efforts to wake him were unsuccessful. When he did finally wake from his comatose slumber, who would they address . . . Andrews or Musial?

Everyone bedded down for the night, yet nobody slept. How could they when the only thing separating them from a horrific death was a few well-placed lights? Charlotte and Derek set up cots between the sofa and the kitchen. Cecil stretched out on the floor beside his traumatized wife on the couch. Burt and Sally settled a few feet away.

"Cecil . . . you asleep?" Burt whispered after thirty minutes of listening to the depraved chorus surrounding the cabin.

"What is sleep?" Cecil said, rolling on his side to face his friend.

"A sweet distant memory," Burt said, rubbing his bloodshot eyes.

He paused for a moment and asked, "Have you given any more thought as to what we are gonna do?"

Cecil shook his head. "I don't know, but we're going to have to do something in the next day or so. We've got maybe forty-eight hours of fuel left if we are lucky."

"I'll take a bunch of lanterns in the SUV and drive to get fuel . . . it's the only way," Burt said.

"The hell it is!" Cecil said. "If anyone is going, it's me!"

"No, you've got Barbara to take care of," Burt argued.

"You have Sally to take care of!" Cecil retorted.

"I don't have any kids . . . you have daughters to think about," Burt said, but the instant the words left his mouth he regretted them. "I . . . I'm sorry, Cecil . . . I didn't mean," he said shamefully.

The words cut Cecil, but not from insult. Instead, it was the sorrow of a painful memory.

"It's okay, Burt," he said. "I still have Abbs; she's just not here right now. So I do have more than one daughter."

Burt rubbed the back of his head and frowned. "Do you think . . . they will be back . . . the Impals?" he asked.

"Without a doubt," Cecil said as he rolled onto his back and put his hands behind his head. "Dr. Winder seemed to think that this was the 'eye' of the cosmic storm and, as with all eyes, it will pass and the storm will return. That's what I believe . . . it's what I have to believe."

"You forgot one important point," Burt said.

"What?"

"Your old man is full of shit," he said flippantly.

There were a few moments of uncertain silence before both men broke into a fit of laughter.

"That he is," Cecil chuckled, "as full as a septic tank."

"Yep, the White House needs an enema," Burt laughed

Cecil felt a sharp pang again deep inside. The pang was more numb and deeper than ever. This was good because he knew exactly what giving the White House an enema meant. His father would have to be removed and most likely it would take an assassination to accomplish it.

The most important thing right now was that it felt good to share a laugh with his friend; it was something they hadn't been able to do for a while.

"What joke did I miss?" Sally said, rolling over and peering through sleepy eyes over Burt's shoulder.

"Nothing . . . potty humor," Burt snorted.

The two men laughed until Sally finally turned in a huff with her back to them. Burt reached over and patted her on the rear, but she swatted his hand away.

"Not tonight," she hissed.

Burt glanced over his shoulder with a comical grin and then back at Cecil.

"You wouldn't mind if we did it tonight, would you?"

"Oh, by all means," Cecil said. "I'll close my eyes."

"Oh please don't," Charlotte called from the other side of the sofa.

They all began laughing again and were even joined by Sally and Charlotte, and then finally Derek.

"So anyone know any good dirty jokes?" Derek asked.

Burt was about to volunteer one when a foreign yet familiar voice broke the mood. It was Musial.

"You all seem rather chipper considering what horror you are facing," he said evenly.

They all turned their heads in unison toward the chair where Musial was bound. Terror seized them when they realized the chair was empty. A pile of rope and chain was coiled beside it. It didn't take them long to find him. He was standing in a dark corner of the room, an area dark enough to mean certain death to any of them.

"What the hell are you doing, Musial?" Cecil shouted as he leapt to his feet.

"The chair was uncomfortable," he said massaging his wrists. "I hope you don't mind me taking the liberty to stretch my legs."

Burt pulled his pistol and aimed it at Musial. "Get your ass back in the chair!" he barked.

Musial slowly stepped forward into the light with incredulity etched on his face. "Indeed, captain?" he said. "If I was a threat I can assure you one thing. You would all be dead right now."

"Really?" Cecil said, pulling his own pistol.

"Really, major . . . I have been free for at least an hour."

Sally retreated back to Charlotte and Derek. Derek stepped forward and stood behind Burt and Cecil.

"I could have flipped these at any moment. None of you would have known what hit you," he said, flexing his index finger up and down above one of the light switches.

"How did you get out?" Derek asked.

A warm smile washed over Musial's face. "I thought you would never ask!" he beamed. "You see, in life, my flesh and blood life, I was a magician and escape artist."

"Bull!" Burt retorted. "I bet you got one of your buddies outside to help you."

Musial shook his head in slow motion. "Major, I am disappointed in the intelligence of the officers serving under your command," he said. "Did we not already cover that the dark can't interact with the physical world, except through the mind. Once you step into the dark you are driven to death by the suggestion of those butchers," he said motioning toward the window. For one small instant the insidious chorus seemed to intensify. "They don't pick up a knife and cut your throat," he continued, "or hoist you up in a tree and drop you to your death like Dr. Winder. They don't do those things any more than they could come in here and untie me."

"So you were a magician?" Cecil asked.

"Yes."

"Where and when?"

"In Europe, about a hundred years ago," he said.

"Is Musial your last name?"

"Musial is my name."

"But what was your given name?" Burt asked, still holding the gun steady.

"Musial," he replied, annoyed.

"Huh, he thinks he's a rock star like Madonna or Sting," Derek muttered.

"Not a rock star, good sir," Musial said, making Derek jump with surprise. "But I was a star in my day!"

"So what did a star magician—escape artist do to wind up in the dark void for eternity?" Burt asked sarcastically.

"I loved my work so much that I wanted others to take part. I thought it would give me great pleasure, but I found it gave me more satisfaction when they didn't succeed."

"Succeed at pulling a rabbit out of a hat?" Burt sneered.

"No," Musial said casually. "They didn't succeed at escaping from chains underwater or from a wooden casket buried in three feet of earth."

"And you enjoyed it when they suffocated or drowned?" Charlotte asked.

"Yes, I did. It surprised me at first, but then I came to believe that it was serving a purpose. I began to choose my victims after a while, convincing them that it was completely safe and a most exhilarating experience. My selections were always racial in nature."

"What race?" Charlotte asked.

"It didn't matter . . . gypsy, African, Arabic . . . maybe an occasional China man. Anyone who wasn't, well, an equal."

Charlotte could feel rage building inside her, but she managed to keep it in check. Having grown up an African-American in the South she had experienced a small degree of racism. Although it was nothing compared to what her parents and grandparents endured.

"How sad for you," she said as she sat back down on her blanket.

Musial seemed hurt by her comment, yet he made no reply.

"So what the hell do you want, Musial?" Cecil asked. "What did you mean by salvation?"

"Exactly what it means, major. Salvation is liberation from ignorance or illusion. Most important, it is deliverance from the power and effects of sin."

"So . . . you want to repent?" Burt asked.

"In a manner of speaking, yes."

"How do you propose you do that?" Derek snapped. "Gather by the creek and have a good old fashioned revival and baptism?"

"No, that would only have worked when I was living and in the flesh. Now it is a little more complicated for me."

"Well why don't you un-complicate it for us?" Cecil said.

"I believe if I commit some good and selfless acts in my present state, then it just might be possible."

"That's it?" Burt asked.

"Not exactly, I can't just do a good deed or two and expect to be welcomed through the ethereal door. I have to be sorry for what I did."

"Are you?" Burt asked.

"I am working on it," Musial said flatly.

"How in the world can you know? Was it on a 'how to reach salvation' brochure handed out to you and your kind for eternal reading in your dark void?" Sally sneered.

Musial regarded her for several moments before answering. "I know my dear, that's all . . . I just know."

"So what good deed do you propose first?" Cecil asked.

Musial's face broke into an excited grin as he turned to face Cecil. "That's the beauty of it! I think we can establish a symbiotic relationship for the time being."

"How?" Burt asked.

"Well since I didn't have much else to do but listen to your yammering as I sat in the chair for the last several hours; I picked up on quite a lot."

"Such as?" Cecil asked.

"Well it would seem that I am the perfect candidate to solve your little problem."

"And what problem would that be?" Burt asked.

Musial turned his face up to the overhead light and closed his eyes as if he was basking in the glow of the sun. He then opened his eyes and pointed up.

"The most important thing to you right now, the thing that is keeping you alive," he said.

They all knew exactly what he was talking about. They needed to keep the lights on.

"You can pass through the dark?" Cecil more stated than asked.

"Yes," Musial said. "I can go and get the gas you need."

CHAPTER 18

SHOWERS AND BURGERS

"That which does not kill us makes us stronger."
~Friedrich Nietzsche

THE MAN KNOWN AS RUTH did not sleep; he did not need it. Although, the body he inhabited did. He watched all night through the pale and cataract-veiled eyes of the geriatric woman. Of course, he could see with perfect clarity. He stared at Rebekah and Malakhi, unable to look away from the only thing that both sides of his psyche desired most. The mother and child represented both satisfaction to his dark side and hope for his desire of salvation. He did not know which was strongest and which would win out in the end. Any time he felt himself giving in to his desire, he reminded himself of the dark void.

It was a never-ending void, sometimes crossing paths with the world he was now a part of again. Physical interaction was never possible. The dark souls' interaction was more similar to an interactive movie. It provided a small degree of satisfaction to those few fortunate enough to be a part of those intrusions. They took great pleasure in whispering their malevolent suggestions to their hapless victim. Of course, it was nothing compared to how it is now. It was analogous to the difference of looking at a picture of a steak and eating steak. Although they couldn't harm in the physical sense, the influence they now enjoyed was the next best thing. After centuries of dark and formless existence, this newfound freedom was intoxicating. Discrimination of victims was a distant afterthought in their new playground. Everyone must die.

Ruth resisted for several hours and for that he gave himself a metaphorical pat on the back. The prospect of salvation might be an assumption, a tall tale weaved in the minds of dark and desperate individuals; a false hope offered to an otherwise hopeless existence. There were many in the void who did not consider hope, nor did they want it. They were content in their anger and hatred, which had consumed them for so long. Yet, they did not realize the one thing that Ruth and Musial, and so many other dark souls, believed. The first step in a person's salvation is a knowledge and an acknowledgement of their evil. As much as Ruth wanted to return to his old ways, he came to understand over the centuries what he did was wrong. It did not serve humanity as his dark nature led him to believe. He believed if he helped someone in the world, salvation might be possible. How he knew, he did not know. Nor did he know exactly what salvation meant. Was it an escape from the dark void or was it something more? Perhaps the ability to join the souls known as Impals? But . . . move on to where? He was not sure, nor were any of the other salvation minded dark souls. One thing they believed was that it must be better than where they had been.

Ruth stood up at the first sign of light and listened as the sound of the darkness began to recede. He stumbled and caught himself on the flap of the tent. This old body was not only worn out by years of chemical abuse, it was exhausted and it had not slept. He would have to remedy that after breakfast, perhaps with a nap. The woman needed to eat and drink as much as she needed to sleep. She was also arthritic and he had no clue how to deal with it. He cursed himself for not finding a more fitting host, but this woman was in the right place, in the right condition, and at the right time. She was still present; he could feel her stirring in the back of her mind, a mind she was terrified out of at the moment. He harbored no desire to harm her, well . . . maybe a small one, but his intentions were to use her for his purposes, and then he would let her go. One thing he knew that the old woman didn't, was if she wanted to, now she was sober, she could force him out. He couldn't betray his secret, not if he had any hope of salvation.

"Ruth, are you okay?" Rebekah asked, sitting up and stroking Malakhi's back.

"Oh yes, yes . . . just stood up too fast," Ruth lied.

"Momma, I'm hungry," Malakhi said as he rubbed the sleep out of his eyes.

The two other women got up and folded their palettes. "Let's go find the chow line," one of them said as she scooted around Ruth and peered out the front flap of the tent.

"Where's the boy?" Rebekah asked, noting the empty palette on the far side of the tent.

"I don't know," the other woman shrugged. "I guess he is really hungry."

As they weaved through the forest of tents, they passed a field littered with a mix of body bags and white sheets in semi straight rows. The soldiers had gathered the dead from the perimeter of the base and were preparing a mass burial. A backhoe roared to life a few yards away making them all jump with surprise.

"My God," the heavy set woman said. "Why did they even bother with the bags and the sheets?"

"Because they still deserve their dignity!" Rebekah snapped.

The woman's mouth hung open, but she made no reply.

"Indeed they do," Ruth agreed. He surprised himself because he realized he wasn't just playing along, he really meant it. "Everyone deserves their dignity."

"Everyone other than harlots, single mothers, and their brats," Ruth thought to himself. He tamped this idea down deep. Old habits were going to be hard to change.

As they passed the field and headed through another row of tents, a sheet flapped in the breeze as if it were waving goodbye. This blood stained sheet covered the body of the teenage boy who slept in their tent last night, although, he hadn't slept. He got up in the middle of the night, grabbed one of the lanterns, and then lifted one of the women's flashlights. He had no nefarious plans in mind, other than to find his mother and sister whom he was separated from yesterday. The poor

126

boy made it to the perimeter of lights without the guards spotting him, but he only made it a few yards into the darkness beyond. The lantern and the flashlight were not enough protection from the moonless night. They found him sliced to bits on the razor wire coiled over the base fence. The lantern and flashlight lay a few feet from where the parade ground lights would have ended. The poor nameless boy, who only wanted to find his family, was scooped into a mass grave before their eyes.

Breakfast consisted of humus, bread, and chicken broth. Not exactly five star dining, but hunger has a tendency to enhance flavor and quell finicky eaters. After breakfast, Rebekah located the showers a short distance away. They were in a makeshift building with a canvas roof and plywood walls. The line was at least a hundred people deep. Even though the wait would be most of the morning, Rebekah, Malakhi, and Ruth staked their place in line.

"We can all use a good shower," Rebekah said.

Ruth didn't argue. He did not particularly care whether his host practiced good hygiene or not. Ruth would not let Rebekah and Malakhi out of his sight. They were his ticket to salvation, he was sure of it.

Jack awoke with a gasp as he heard a loud knocking. He squinted at the window, expecting the knocking to continue. All he saw was bright sunlight streaming in and an occasional bird flutter past. It was morning, but what time was it? He jumped when the knock came again, this time it was more of a pounding on his bedroom door.

"You up yet you stupid tosser?" Donna called in her fake British accent.

Jack jumped out of bed and stomped to the door. He considered throwing it open then decided to take a more cautious approach instead. He remembered he did not trust his tiny and unusual visitor. For all he knew, she could be standing there with a gun or a knife, ready to gut him the instant he opened the door. He stepped to the side, twisted the knob, and flung it open.

Donna made no move to attack. She just stood there with her hands on her hips, scowling at him. "You haven't got any damned food!" she barked in a half British, half southern accent.

"I don't eat here, I eat at the base," Jack said irritably as he opened the door all the way and stepped into the living room.

"How far is the base?" she huffed.

Before Jack could answer, the phone rang. It was his commanding officer.

Jack assured him he was fine and had managed to survive the night with a bunch of candles and flashlights. He declined the offer of transportation with a medic to check out his head. He finally convinced him he was fine and would be back within the hour. He hung up the phone and looked at Donna, who was sulking in a chair by the window. She seemed rough enough last night, but the sun revealed a deplorable appearance. The girl had been on drugs, there was no doubt. The evidence was on almost every square inch of her body. He pondered whether to take her back with him. Jack was somewhat confident she would not say anything about seeing him in the moors last night. She was like him in one way; they both could pass through the dark. This was a secret neither one of them wanted to let out.

"Get your crap and let's go!" Jack barked.

Her face lit up as she hopped from the chair. "Packed and ready," she said with a mock salute.

Jack winced when he saw her blackened teeth. She looked as if she rinsed with a bottle of ink, another terrible sign of drug abuse. He still distrusted her, junkies can never be trusted, but he did pity her.

They set out through the town with Jack in the lead and Donna following close behind. He didn't bother to avoid the whispering shadows as he did yesterday. What was the point? They passed through dark alleys and beneath the shade of buildings and trees. The dark whispers could be heard each time they walked through the dark, but it was nothing more than a friendly tickling in their ears.

Jack decided to leave town a different way than he came in yesterday. This alternate route was much more shaded. It was a narrow country road winding through dense forest and connected with the main road a short distance from the base. He wasn't sure why he wanted to go that way because it would take about thirty minutes longer. It was probably because they wouldn't meet up with too many people . . . not unless they were like them. This stretch was often referred to as the 'tunnel' road because the thick overhanging foliage.

As they approached the outskirts of town, Jack stopped and scratched his head. He hadn't been this way in several months and did not realize a new restaurant had been built. It was the first of its kind in England and Europe. The iconic flying saucer on the sign was enough to grab anyone's attention. Martian Burgers had come to town.

Jack paused and examined the gaudy sign. Peering inside, he could see the lighted menu sign, slightly obstructed by the painted green alien on the window. The plethora of space themed menu choices was endless. No one appeared to be inside. Of course, the whole town was either dead or evacuated.

"You hungry?" Jack said, glancing back at Donna.

"You better believe it!"

Jack was getting sick of her fake English accent, but he was in no mood to argue about it. He was hungry and he didn't want to wait until he got to base. First of all, the base food was tolerable at best, and second, he knew he was going to be questioned for hours. Technically speaking, he was AWOL last night. He also knew he would be getting a full examination from the base physician due to the blow to his head. It throbbed and stung each time a bead of sweat ran down the back of his head and into the shallow wound.

"Well, let's go in," Jack said, heading for the door.

"Is it open?" she asked.

"Probably not, but who cares? I used to flip burgers at a McDonald's in Manchester in my younger days. The concept is all the same."

At first, Jack thought the restaurant was locked as he pushed on the door and it didn't budge. Then he saw the body lying inside like a macabre door jam. The corpse was a young woman in her late teens or early twenties. She was overweight with a pear shaped middle, making it all the more difficult to work the door open. The poor woman wore the green uniform of a Martian Burgers employee, complete with flying saucer hat and hair net.

Once they scooted her out of the way, it was not immediately evident how she died. As they placed her in front of a trash receptacle, Donna noticed something. A thick liquid coated her swollen and blistered mouth.

The floor around her head was also thick with this viscous substance. She got down on her hands and knees and sniffed. A moment later, she sprung to her feet, gagging and covering her mouth.

"Oh, Jesus," she said. "It smells of burned pork, vomit, and cooking oil. I think she drank hot oil from the fryer."

"I would suggest skipping the Martian finger French fries then," Jack said casually as he made his way to the kitchen door. Death did not bother him; he was good friends with death. He just didn't care for the smell that sometimes accompanied it. He was determined to keep his distance from the pathetic woman on the floor. He couldn't help chuckling at the creative way the dark had chosen to claim this victim. What was whispered in her mind to get her to commit such a horrid act? He would never know, but it might be fun speculating.

Donna pulled some aprons out of a supply closet and covered the victim as best she could. Jack found the beef in the freezer and within a short time had grilled up a couple of custom flying saucer burgers. They each filled a 'Take me to your Liter' sized soft drink from the fountain and took a seat at a table on the far side of the restaurant. Jack was thankful that the building still had power. Although, he knew later today nowhere in a hundred mile radius would have power except for the base.

Jack devoured his burger, while Donna pensively nibbled at hers. She ate a few bites and then stared out the window. For someone who was complaining about a lack of food less than an hour ago, she didn't seem to have much appetite now. Jack watched her at first with curiosity, and then apprehension started to creep back in. Whatever trust he had gained for this small and mysterious woman was starting to erode. He believed she was like him, an analogous spirit in her own way. However, the longer he observed her, the more he could see that she was very, very different.

Jack did not know how she was different. The not knowing scared the living hell out of him.

CHAPTER 19

CARMELLA

*"Nothing in the world is more dangerous than sincere
ignorance and conscientious stupidity."*
~Martin Luther King, Jr.

PRESIDENT GARRISON MANAGED to get a few hours sleep, but not *where* he expected. He went to Steff's room to scold her for wandering about, but when he got there he found her sound asleep on the floor. She was curled up with a pillow and quilt from the bed.

He was angry. Angry at the Impals. Angry at what they had forced him to do. He was angry at his granddaughter for disobeying him. There was a part of him, now buried very deep, that felt ashamed of his actions. Perhaps more accurately, he was ashamed because Steff had witnessed them. Of course he still believed he was doing the right thing. Yet, as pure as he believed his motives to be, sometimes the work of the righteous is not glamorous. In fact, it can be quite unpleasant.

A dutiful soldier would not want his child witnessing his actions in battle. As well, the state executioner would not want them to see him insert the lethal needle into the arm of a condemned murderer. Garrison's family never witnessed his deeds. Now Steff had seen him gun down several people for seemingly no reason. There was a very good reason in his mind, but he knew that Steff was not privy to his divine insight. She was too young to understand and he couldn't afford to leave her unattended again.

She was so peaceful; he couldn't bear to wake her. He decided to take matters into his own hands for the time being. He locked the door, deposited the key in his pocket, and then stretched out on the blue comforter of the full size bed. He rolled on his side so he could see Steff. He thought about turning out the light, and then reconsidered. It occurred to him what would happen if the lights went out and she was not in his grasp. Steff was too old to snuggle with her grandfather, so he left the lights on. He wavered in and out of sleep for the remainder of the night because lights were not agreeable to his sleeping habits.

The one thing he did not know was that Steff did not sleep at all. The shock of seeing her grandfather act so violently weighed heavy on her. She found herself locked in a state of sickened insomnia, compounded by the terror of *him* sleeping a few feet away from her. The man she reached out to for help had proven he was not the man she believed him to be. She wanted her mother and father worse than anything. She would give anything, even if it meant living in the darkest and dirtiest hole, to be with them again. She fantasized about escaping and reuniting with them. How she would make it out of the most secure house in the world, and where she would find them, she did not know. Frustration overwhelmed her and by the time morning arrived, her eyes were swollen and her mouth dry as sandpaper. She had laid on a tear soaked pillow, listening to the incessant snoring of her grandfather all night.

He got up without disturbing her and left the room, locking the door behind him. Whatever hopes of her fantasy coming true evaporated with the click of the lock. There was no way to get out without the key. She studied the small windowless room and felt sick to her stomach. She got up and lay across the cool fabrics of the bedspread. A few moments later, she heard a knock at the door. Steff just stared. There was nothing she could do to unlock it and let this person in, so she chose to ignore it. A few moments later, there was another knock followed by the clicking of the key in the lock. She sat up as a tall, slender black woman carrying a silver tray came inside. She had short shoulder length hair and wore a beautiful blue dress and white blouse which was a compliment to her vivid white smile.

"Hello, dear . . . my name is Carmella. I figured you would be hungry this morning," she beamed.

Steff did not reply. She watched her suspiciously as she walked across the room and set the tray on the bed.

"I'm sorry I don't have a breakfast tray," she said. "Do you mind sitting on the side of the bed to eat?"

Steff shook her head. She was still in shock.

"No problem," Carmella said as she pulled back the lid, revealing a plate of scrambled eggs, sausages, and toast. There were also two large glasses of orange juice. Carmella picked up one and smiled. "I already ate," she said. "I hope you don't mind me joining you over a glass of Florida's finest."

Steff shrugged and mumbled. "No . . . I don't mind."

"Good . . . good," Carmella said as she took a seat in an armchair, and sipped her juice. "I'll just sit over here if it is okay with you darling."

Steff drank half the glass of juice before she touched her food. She was very thirsty. The breakfast was a little cold, but still quite good. She felt only a little better after eating. She was still dealing with a lot of issues that a good breakfast just can't fix.

"Do you work here?" Steff asked.

"Yes, for many years," Carmella said. "I am older than I look," she said brushing the side of her face with mock vanity.

This brought a smile to Steff's face. She couldn't help it. The woman exuded a relaxing and pleasing charisma, putting her immediately at ease.

"How are you, honey?" Carmella asked.

Steff shrugged. She was tired, she was frightened, she was disappointed, and she missed her family. However, she tried not to let on that anything was wrong.

"I am fine," she said through pursed lips.

Carmella was too perceptive and too empathetic to believe it for one second. Of course, anyone with eyes could have seen from the poor girl's gaunt face and haunted eyes that she was far from fine.

"It's okay, sweetheart . . . I know," Carmella said softly.

Those five simple words spread relief through Steff like sinking into a warm bath. She began to cry, this time not for fear and disappointment, but for hope. Maybe she would be okay after all.

Carmella placed her glass on the table and scooted the tray to the far side of the bed. She sat down and let Steff fall into her arms, stroking her hair as she wept.

"He's a monster!" Steff gasped between sobs.

Carmella patted her on the back and said, "Sweetheart, he is your grandfather. You must always remember that."

Steff pulled back a little. Was it possible her grandfather sent this kind woman to influence her? She was about to pull away when Carmella continued, "None of us is perfect and none of us is evil. Men do evil things because they are ignorant mostly. They believe they are doing the right thing, but their ignorance leads them down the wrong path. I doubt there are very many people in history who made the conscious decision to be evil, they didn't say, *I'm going to be evil today.*"

"How can anyone not believe that shooting down a bunch of people for no reason is evil?" Steff sniffled.

"To the un-ignorant, like you and I, it is most definitely evil. But for the ignorant it seems logical."

"How can he be ignorant?" Steff asked. "He has always been a very smart man."

"Honey, often times superior education breeds superior arrogance, which leads to superior ignorance. Some of the smartest people I have known have also been the most ignorant. You have to understand that ignorant is not the same thing as stupid. Ignorance just means they are lacking some key pieces of information to make an informed decision. Stupid means lacking intelligence. Your grandfather is not a stupid man . . . he just doesn't have all the information he needs to make the right decisions."

"But . . . he is a Christian," Steff argued. "He always goes to church and has me study Bible verses with him. I don't think there is a part of the Bible he doesn't know about."

"Do you know Ephesians 4:18?" Carmella asked.

Steff shook her head.

"Well, my memory is not perfect, but I believe it goes something like this— *They are darkened in their understanding, alienated from the life of God because of the ignorance that is in them, due to their hardness of heart.*"

"What does that have to do with my grandfather?"

Carmella pulled back and gazed into her eyes. She smiled and rubbed Steff's cheek. "Honey, your grandfather has lived a hard life. His heart has hardened over the years. To him, it seems as if God has toughened him up, made him ready to take on anything. But instead . . ." she continued with a sad tone. "It has hardened his head and muddled the true meaning of what he is trying to accomplish . . . what he is trying to accomplish in the name of God. There are few things more dangerous than an ignorant Christian with power."

Steff considered this for a while. "Why can he walk around in the dark now when most people can't?" she asked.

"I don't know baby, I don't know."

"Can he be saved?" Steff asked.

Tears brimmed up in Carmella's eyes and she clasped a trembling hand over her mouth. "Yes he can, honey . . . yes he can, but it won't be easy."

"How do you know?" Steff asked with hopeful skepticism.

Carmella brought her hand down and slowly unbuttoned the lower buttons of her blouse. She pulled it open and turned sideways for her to see. Steff gasped. There were very few areas of the kind woman's torso without the scars of long and terrible lacerations. Her body resembled a raised topography map of several mountain ranges.

"What happened?" Steff croaked.

"Ignorance," Carmella answered matter of factly. However, the tears streaming down her cheeks were a contradiction to her casual tone.

"Who?" Steff breathed.

"A man . . . a white man . . . many years ago."

Steff remembered studying about the Civil Rights movement in school. She was disgusted when she learned about the horrific treatment endured by blacks in the South. She swallowed hard before she asked her next question.

"Where did you live?"

Carmella pulled her blouse back down and began to work the buttons with her trembling fingers. She smiled ruefully. "A little town called Hackney in Alabama. I lived there until I was ten years old."

"How old were you?" Steff asked.

"When I got these scars I was only six years old."

"Why?" Steff asked.

"I was a black girl playing on the playground of a white church. The preacher came out and told me to leave. When I didn't, he went to work on me with a mimosa branch."

"Why did he tell you to leave?"

"Because I was a nigger at a white church and niggers were unclean animals according to the beliefs of that preacher."

Steff cringed at the use of the 'n' word. It was one of today's ultimate taboo words. Of course, when Carmella was six years old it was as common as saying 'hello'.

"He beat you for playing? But, but . . . you were only six!" Steff shrieked.

"It didn't matter," Carmella said, reaching out and stroking Steff's hand. "A nigger, was a nigger, was a nigger . . . it didn't matter how old or how young. He was doing God's work by punishing and removing the impurity from holy ground."

"I bet he is burning in Hell!" Steff snapped.

"I don't think so," Carmella said with a smile. This took Steff by surprise. How could he not be burning in Hell, and how could she seem happy if he was not?

"What?" Steff asked in disbelief.

"You see . . . this preacher, this man, was ignorant. It took many years, but he finally recognized his ignorance. He was so overcome with guilt of what he had done, he tracked me down to apologize and beg my forgiveness."

"Did you?" Steff asked.

"Of course I did, honey. If I couldn't forgive him for his transgressions against me, how could I ever expect God to do the same for me?"

Steff didn't answer, she had never considered this. She knew deep down that she would find it difficult to forgive someone for treating her so cruelly. Carmella must be a special woman.

"So you see, sweetheart . . . there is hope for everyone, even your grandfather."

Almost as if the very mention of his name summoned him, the door flew open. There stood Ott Garrison with a stern and unforgiving expression.

CHAPTER 20

THE ERRAND AND THE NEW ORDER

"Take no part in the unfruitful works of darkness, but instead expose them."
~Ephesians 5:11

BURT AND CECIL DIDN'T FORCE Musial back in the chair to be tied up again, but they did insist he remain on his side of the room. He complied with no argument and sat on the floor with his back against the wall, a pillow cradled in his lap. He continued to clutch it as he gazed back at his captors. His countenance did not seem vicious, it was more casual curiosity. Cecil and Burt got little sleep. What rest they did get was staggered as they took turns watching the allegedly penitent dark soul. It was funny how a much a different personality and demeanor can change a person's physical appearance. The longer they were around Musial, the easier it was to forget he inhabited the body of their alcoholic ally, Sam Andrews. But Cecil hadn't forgotten. Shortly after daybreak, he walked within a few feet of Musial. His hand grasped the butt of his weapon in case Musial wasn't as remorseful as he proclaimed.

"Is Sam still in there?" he asked.

Musial nodded. "Of course, and when I am done you can have your hot headed, chemically dependent friend back."

Cecil, or anyone else in the group, carried no real affection for Andrews. The man had been useful through the connection with his brother for the ships which evacuated the Impals. In all truthfulness, he was more of a hindrance and royal pain in the ass than anything. Still, he was one of their own.

"Is he still in there?" Cecil asked.

"Oh, yes," Musial said with an impatient shrug.

Cecil stared at him, finally driving the message home that his answer was unsatisfactory.

Musial sighed and stretched his legs. "His consciousness is asleep. It was easy enough to keep him this way . . . he had quite a lot to drink."

"But he should be sobered up by now . . ." Cecil began, but was cut short by a shameful clicking of the tongue from Musial.

"Major, major, major, I thought you understood. The body and the soul have little to do with each other. This body has been sober now for hours, but the soul, your dear Mr. Andrews's soul, is drunk with sadness, anger, and despair. To be blunt, he is an emotional abomination. It has been far too easy to keep him under, so to speak."

"Is he a dark soul, like you?" Cecil asked.

Musial seemed bemused. "I couldn't have taken him over, not if we were similar to me. No, Mr. Andrews is no dark soul. He is just . . . how do you say it nowadays . . . a hot mess."

Cecil didn't know whether to be pleased or upset. Pleased because Andrews was just a normal jerk, or upset that his father seemed to be one in the same with the darkness. Part of him didn't want to believe it. As hard as he tried for the last couple of months, he couldn't bring himself to completely hate his father. Sure he hated the things he had done, both now and when he was a child. He could hate him on the surface, yet deep down; there was a small ember of a son's love still burning for his father. It singed his heart. He wasn't sure he could ever extinguish the feeling and it made him feel guilty.

"Is there any hope for my father?" Cecil asked in a whisper; he didn't want the others to hear.

"Perhaps," Musial said stroking his chin. "If he overcomes his ignorance. However, with your alcoholic friend here," he said pointing to his own forehead. "The first step is admitting he has a problem. In his case, admitting he has been ignorant of the truth. The weakness of dark souls is pride. It comes before all else. If he can't overcome pride, admit he has been wrong and then seek honest redemption, well then . . . I am afraid he has no hope at all."

Cecil heard and understood what Musial said, yet he made no reply. Instead, he walked to the window and stared outside as the morning sun began to drive the darkness back into the woods.

"How did you overcome your pride?" Cecil asked.

Musial shrugged. "I don't know. Maybe I was tired of living in the void with all those other villains for years and years," he said then gave a soft chuckle. "Or maybe I had time to think . . ."

Cecil watched him expectantly, but Musial offered no more information. He leaned against the wall with his back turned to the room and began to breathe in and out as if he were sleeping. Cecil pulled up a chair and sat with his pistol across his lap, guarding Musial until Burt woke up.

President Garrison did not have the time or the inclination to chit chat with Carmella and Steff. He reminded Steff that he would expect her for lunch in the president's private office. He then ordered Carmella to make sure they were served chili. Not the weak stuff, as he put it, but the stuff that makes you sweat. He needed a 'pick me up'.

"Does that sound good to you, Steff?" he asked sounding more of a command than a question.

Steff didn't care much for chili, and hated spicy foods even more, but she was too scared to argue.

"Sure. Sounds good," she said, forcing a smile.

Satisfied, Garrison closed the door, leaving the two ladies alone and strode back to the Oval Office. The New Order was under way and he must get back to oversee the plans for the United States future. The new United States, with him at the helm enforcing his righteous agenda. When he thought about the accomplishments of his new allies within a few short hours of joining him, he smiled. Garrison failed to stifle a giddy laugh as he descended the stairs.

"God be praised!" he proclaimed to no one in particular, although anyone within fifty feet would have heard him. "They did it all in one night!"

A bystander in the bright halls may have thought he was quoting a line from Charles Dickens's, *A Christmas Carol*. He never read the holiday fable because ghosts were of the Devil. In his mind, he believed he was quoting an obscure verse from the Bible dealing with a timely miracle. He believed a miracle is what he received last night.

Robby Johns and Joan Titsworth had paid some strategic visits to various VIP's around the capital city last evening. In only a few hours, they eliminated most of the opposition to Garrison's coup d'état. They accomplished this with no violence, at least on their part. They just introduced their targets to the dark. The Speaker of the House, several members of Congress, and several military officers met their demise. The massacre was a bloody affair and a remarkable coincidence. It seemed all these high ranking dissenters forgot to stay out of the shadows at the same time. That's where Garrison's longtime friend, Avery, came in, along with geek extraordinaire, Sebastian Gardner. Avery created a speech worthy of a master spin doctor, while Gardner updated internet newsfeeds. This was done in anticipation of connectivity suddenly returning.

Internet and television had been useless since the storm arrived months ago. Nobody knew what the event was, no one knew when or if television and internet might come back. It was best to prepare for when it did. One errant news report could derail everything accomplished by Garrison's administration. They must be preemptive. Radio was much easier to control.

"So, what would you like us to do now, Mr. President?" Robby asked with thick sarcasm.

Garrison didn't notice, or refused to acknowledge, the mocking tone. He gave a quick and enthusiastic response. "Splendid work last night . . . splendid work!" he boasted, and then with excitement rising in his voice he asked, "Tell me . . . how did the Speaker meet his end last night?"

Robby and Joan exchanged glances, and then both of them shrugged at the same instant.

"It was the damndest thing I ever saw," Joan said with a tittering laugh. "We pulled him out of his lit up house into the dark yard. He then got the garden hose and tied a perfect hangman's knot. He tossed it over the limb of a big beech tree and started looking about for something. We didn't know what till he emerged from the corner of the house pulling a wooden bench. Then the idiot proceeds to climb up on it, sticks his head in the garden hose knot, and then jumps as if he was trying to take flight."

"It sounded like a pencil breaking in two!" Robby added with a laugh.

"How did he know how to tie that?" Garrison asked with amusement. "He did an actual hangman's knot?"

"Well, hanging is not my specialty," Robby said with a knowing grin. "But it seemed pretty damn accurate to me. It did the job."

"Yeah, it was definitely the most original of the night," Joan said. "Everyone else drank poison, shot or stabbed themselves, bashed their head into a wall, or jumped out a window."

"Oh, you remember the idiot Congressman who threw himself off the roof of his one story house?" Robby cackled. "It took the moron forever to die. He finally managed to crawl to a flower bed and impale himself on a landscaping light. I was about ready to take care of his sorry ass myself, but Avery said to let the dark do the work."

"I guess it was his final filibuster," Joan snorted, causing Robby to burst into laughter.

Garrison sat listening to their story and their laughter; he didn't join in though. Not because he found it offensive, no indeed, they were doing God's work to get rid of the dissenters. His attention switched to Avery and Sebastian as they entered the room.

"When is the radio address?" Garrison asked.

"Noon," Avery said with a wide smile. "Everything is set."

Garrison started to smile, but then it faded to a frown.

"I have a lunch date today, can it be later?"

Avery shook his head. "No, this is the best time . . . all the evac bases will be broadcasting on their public address speakers. The morons who were too stupid to evacuate, well, we figure noon would be the most obvious time they would be listening."

"Those morons will be dead tonight unless they have a generator, anyway," Sebastian said. "The power is going to be cut to most public areas at 3 PM Eastern Time today and diverted to the bases."

Garrison stood up and walked to the window, listening to the sound of distant heavy equipment. Beyond the iron fence of the White House grounds, a large front end loader deposited its cargo into the back of a dump truck. Bodies spilled into the bed like a bunch of discarded and bloody rag dolls. The Washington DC Department of Public Works and the National Guard were going to have their hands full today. The corpse clean up and removal across the entire world was overwhelming. Garrison said a silent prayer for those being collected outside and around the world. He pitied the poor people who had fallen victim to the dark, well . . . all those who didn't stand in the way of God's agenda. He knew it was not their faults; it was the fault of the Impals who were now in their true form. They were not blessed as he was. After all, didn't Psalm 82:3–4 say *Defend the cause of the weak and fatherless; maintain the rights of the poor and oppressed. Rescue the weak and needy; deliver them from the hand of the wicked?*

This clean up task would be far more daunting than the terrible blizzard that hit the East coast last winter. The bodies coated the streets and neighborhoods of the nation's capital like macabre snow drifts. But in contrast the storm of last winter, this one was worldwide. If the remains were not disposed of soon, they would have another problem on their hands almost as bad as the dark. Disease would run rampant.

"Contact the regular military and tell them to get their asses up here and assist the Guard. This mess has got to be cleaned up fast!" Garrison barked.

"Way ahead of you," Avery said, tapping his finger against his temple. "I ordered it an hour ago. We should have three hundred more dump trucks and loaders here by the time you go on the air."

"Thank God it is not summer," Sebastian remarked as he waved his hand in front of his nose and squinted. "If it were, the stench would already be unbearable."

"Good job, Avery," Garrison said. "I think before we begin the meeting we should open with a prayer, don't you?"

Avery nodded and reverently bowed his head, but the other three were incredulous. They rolled their eyes and sighed as Garrison rambled off a self-serving prayer lasting more than two minutes.

"Okay, let's begin," Garrison said as he raised his head and beamed at everyone.

"What a damn hypocrite," they all thought but did not say. However, for personal motivations, they would continue to wear the mask of sycophant. They all had their issues that made them dark souls, only none of them were hypocritical about it. They were what they were . . . take it, leave it, or shove it. Of course, they all knew why they held a special relationship with the dark. They felt the calm of their kinship each time the lights went out. Garrison saw things differently. What his companions saw as peace derived from a kindred existence, Garrison believed his calm came from God. His pride wouldn't let him consider anything else.

"How shall we carry out the Lord's will going forward?" he asked with a toothy grin.

CHAPTER 21

THE BASES

*"Suspicion is the companion of mean souls, and the bane of
all good society."*
~Thomas Paine

"Who in the hell is this skank?" Jack wondered as they trudged down
an old cow road on the way back to the base.

Their bellies were full with their custom made Martian Burgers,
but they didn't sit well. Jack's stomach burned as if a small fire kindled
in his gut. There was something very strange about this girl who called
herself Donna.

He thought about killing her when they got to the part of the road
known as the tunnel. Its lush canopy forming a cover high enough
for a tall truck to pass would be the ideal spot. It was secluded, it was
private, and nobody would be any the wiser. She knew about him
because she saw him at the moors. Even if she hadn't seen him dump
the body, she knew. A part of him believed she would turn him in first
chance she got when they reached the base. The MPs would arrest
him and throw him in a cage.

"How ironic," he thought to himself.

However, something stayed his hand. Something that tormented
him because he couldn't put his finger on it. She was a vexing enigma

and he couldn't harm her, not yet . . . not until he figured her out. He clinched his fists and bit the inside of his lip as he fought his homicidal impulses. She was no longer silent. This didn't help control his rage as she rambled on about nothing in particular.

"Would you shut up, would you please shut the hell up!" he bellowed as they passed into an especially dark area of the road. He wasn't sure if he yelled because he was trying to talk over the noisy hiss and click of the dark or because he was at his wit's end.

She glared at him. Eventually, Donna backed down and decided that 'shutting the hell up' was preferable to the rage she saw in Jack's eyes.

The rest of the journey was tense and silent. Jack found it the most enjoyable part of the day. He considered the relative silence and soothing whispers of the dark to be therapeutic. That's why it didn't anger him too much when he was seized and thrown to the ground at the gate of the base. He expected it; after all he was AWOL the last twenty-four hours. What angered him was when Donna pointed and laughed as he spit out a mouthful of grass and leaves.

Donna, of course, received better treatment. She allowed the guards to give her a perfunctory pat down before admitting her through the gate. They were both escorted on foot, Jack with his hands bound behind him and Donna with her hands in her pockets. They reached the base office where they were separated and each put in a different room with nothing more than a desk, chair, and lamp. A few minutes later, the door flew open on Jack's room and a large man in a military police uniform dragged in a heavy metal chair. He spun it to face the table across from Jack and then slid into the seat, keeping his eyes locked on Jack the whole time.

"Where did you pick up the girl, private?" he asked.

Jack swallowed hard. He couldn't believe he hadn't come up with some plausible story, one they could both stick to. He already told the commander and his friend over the phone that he suffered an accident and woke in a well-lit room. This was not entirely a lie; in fact the only false part was where he awakened. He knitted a plausible tapestry of deceit in his mind, and then delivered it as calmly as he could. "When I came too after my accident, she had broken into my house to get away from the dark," he said in a monotone.

The soldier's eyes narrowed with disbelief.

"What the hell was I supposed to do . . . kick her back out into the dark?" Jack asked, his face turning red with anger.

The interrogator did not reply, instead he glanced out the window. Jack followed his gaze and his heart sank when he saw another MP sitting across from Donna at a picnic table. They were in the bright sunlight, which any other day would have seemed unusual since there were so many other tables in the shade. The mood at their table was more laid back as they smiled and chatted.

"Did you have sex with her?" the soldier asked, turning his attention back to Jack.

The geyser of Jack's patience erupted and he shot out of his chair. "What kind of bloody question is that?" he screamed. "I'm no damned nonce!"

One might think he would have said something cheeky like "I may be a serial killer, but I'm no child rapist!" Of course, Jack did not believe his killings were wrong, he believed he was doing society a favor, yet he was no fool either. He knew people didn't understand because most were cowards. The one thing Jack did have in common with the normal world was that he believed child molestation was an abomination.

Before Jack could utter another word, he found himself sitting back in his chair. A throbbing pain burned his chest. The soldier pushed him back down.

"Don't get up again until I tell you to," the guard hissed as he leaned over the table, inches from Jack's face. "Do you understand, Private Abernathy?"

Jack stared at him in utter shock; he didn't know what to say so he just nodded his head. He threw his hands in the air and forced a calm tone of voice.

"Look, I have told you everything I can. Why don't you get the Doc in here to check out the back of my head!" he said, gently touching his wounded area.

The soldier glanced at Jack's head, and then frowned with indifference.

"I have just one more question, private," the soldier said, regarding him without emotion. "Were you walking about in the dark last night?"

Jack felt rage churning inside. Had they seen? Did the little rag-amuffin out there squeal? If she did, turnabout was fair play. He would fix her wagon by God, he would fix her good. No one could have seen him last night, not unless they were immune to the dark as well.

"If I did, I would be dead right now," he said.

The soldier examined him without blinking for a few moments. He then stood up and walked out the door. Jack couldn't tell if he believed him or not, the man was good at his job. Jack watched out the window as the soldier and Donna continued their conversation. His interrogator soon approached their table and summoned the other. He got up; leaving Donna with her elbows propped on the table, and joined him several feet away. The two men talked for several minutes. Their expressions and mannerisms didn't give any hint of the mood or subject of their discussion. Both men were stoic except for a couple of subtle hand gestures. Finally they parted ways and Jack's interrogator came back inside, this time with a friendlier attitude.

"Okay Private Abernathy, if you'll come with me I'll escort you to the base hospital so they can check your head out," he said.

Jack didn't know why he was being so formal. Everyone called the base hospital the dispensary because they got prescription drugs from there. Jack didn't argue, he followed the soldier across the parade ground and to the long, two story hospital. One of the base doctors immediately saw Jack. His name was Dr. Peter Kincaid, a man who Jack knew well. The doctor visited the Impal barracks most nights to hear stories from J.M. Barrie, the *Peter Pan* author.

"Jack, what did you bloody do to yourself?" he asked.

"Ah, it was pretty damned stupid," Jack said. He then proceeded to tell him the bogus tale of his clumsiness, omitting, of course, the part about the old woman in the cage.

"Well . . . you're going to need about three stitches," Dr. Kincaid said as he examined the wound. "You're damn lucky you don't have a concussion."

Dr. Kincaid administered a local anesthetic, and then proceeded to clean and suture the wound. As he worked, Jack took the opportunity to question him about the MP's strange behavior and equally strange questions.

"You know . . . he asked me if I was wandering about in the dark last night!" Jack laughed. "Isn't it hilarious?"

He expected Dr. Kincaid to laugh along with him, but the reflection of doctor's face in the glass cabinet in front of him was anything but amicable.

"What is it?" Jack asked.

Dr. Kincaid could not look him in the eye since he was stitching the back of Jack's head, but he wouldn't have done so anyway. He was too scared and confused.

"Last night . . . there were a few civilian deaths."

"What, they wandered into the dark?" Jack asked.

"Yes, but it was why they wound up in the dark in the first place. It was quite disconcerting."

There was a long pause as Dr. Kincaid retrieved a bandage to place over Jack's stitches. Finally, suspense goaded Jack into asking the obvious question.

"What?"

"There were three folks who lured them there."

In an instant, Jack knew where this conversation was headed. He knew he must play dumb for his own sake, so he asked a dumb question. "How did they get lured?"

"Well, there were three people who the dark didn't seem to have any effect on. They were wandering about in pitch blackness and taunting everyone. As in most large crowds, there are always one or two morons who can be convinced of anything, or have more balls than brains."

"What a bunch of idiots," Jack thought but did not say.

"They convinced about five people to come and join them. At least we think there were only five . . . we're still picking up body parts by the south tree line. One of them managed to get hold of a grenade and, well, there is enough mess out there to be two people." Dr. Kincaid grimaced and shook his head. "The others, . . . one of them managed to almost hack their own head off with a field utility shovel. Then there was a child . . ." he shook his head and trailed off. "Suffice it to say, last night was a bad night."

"Why were these people able to walk about in the dark without harm?" Jack asked with sincere curiosity. He didn't know for sure himself and wanted to know if the military developed some plausible theory. He also wanted to cover his own butt.

"I don't know," Dr. Kincaid said. "They're holding them in the stockade until they get some answers."

"Do they consider them threats?" Jack asked.

Dr. Kincaid revered at him as if he were mad. Jack realized he was overplaying his hand.

"Well . . . they did invite those poor people to come out there with them so . . . yeah, I guess you could say they are a bloody threat!" Dr. Kincaid snapped.

Jack stared at the floor. "Of course," he muttered.

Jack's mind raced as he thought of what they could be doing to those three special individuals similar to himself. They were locked up just because they were different? Well, okay, they shouldn't have tempted people to come out with them. That was pretty ignorant, but it wasn't as if they dragged the people outside and threw them into the dark. These people, these morons, had done so on their own free will. Isn't it what his grandfather used to call 'chlorinating the gene pool'? Of course, Jack saw himself as one of humanities' pool boys, a job in which he took pride. A job which he thought he might be getting fired from when two beefy military policemen entered the exam room.

"Is he done, Doc?" one of them asked harshly.

Dr. Kincaid nodded and stepped back from the table.

"Private Jack Abernathy, please come with us," the other MP demanded.

"Where?" Jack asked as he got to his feet. Fear and anger surged through him like two competing poisons. He already knew where and he knew who to blame. He should have killed her last night.

"We're taking you to the stockade for observation," the officer replied without emotion.

Rebekah, Malakhi, and the man in a woman's body waited three hours for a shower. Rebekah thought it was well worth the wait. She felt much better and Ruth was much more tolerable to be around . . . at least in the physical sense. Ruth was strange in the questions she asked, but not as much as the way she watched Rebekah and Malakhi. It was always subtle, when Ruth thought Rebekah was not paying attention. It was starting to give her the creeps.

Rebekah's comfort level was so diminished; she talked to one of the officers at the base, requesting a tent transfer for her and her son. They told her the obvious . . . space was at a premium and they couldn't move people around now.

"But what if she does something?" Rebekah pleaded.

"Report it and we will deal with it. Until then, there is nothing we can do," he stopped and grinned before walking away. What he said caused Rebekah to turn red faced with anger. "Besides . . . she's an old woman, what is she going to do to a strong and firm woman like yourself?"

Rebekah wasn't sure what bothered her the most, his condescending attitude or his lack of empathy. She turned with clinched fists and strode to the edge of a large field where Malakhi was playing soccer with several other boys. She plopped down on the grass and absently stared at the game. She wasn't watching; Malakhi could have scored ten goals and she wouldn't have noticed.

This was the first time she had any time to reflect on the last couple of days. Her mind locked into a repeating playback of events from the last two days and the last few months. She was so thrilled to have her father back. After the initial shock wore off, it was like old times again. When he disappeared and the darkness gained a malevolent life, it was an indescribable pain. A pain she supposed millions were now experiencing; the pain of losing someone for a second time.

The dark horror and her concern for her son did not allow for any time to grieve and reflect, so she now made up for lost time. Tears began to flow down her cheeks as she hugged her knees and buried her head on them.

No one sat near her and she was alone in her own private world of grief. Of course, she was not really alone. Someone watched her from behind, out of sight around the corner of a tent. The same hungry expression washed over Ruth's face as he . . . *it* watched Rebekah wallow in her personal anguish.

CHAPTER 22

LESSONS

"You may be deceived if you trust too much, but you will live in torment unless you trust."
~Frank Crane

IN HIS MIND, Cecil was with his daughters again. They lay snuggled in an enormous hammock with Abbs under one arm and Steff under the other. He was happy, he was content, and love covered them like a warm and tangible blanket. Barbara watched from a nearby lounge chair as they swung to and fro in a lazy summer breeze. There was no storm, there had never been a storm, the world was as it always was . . . perhaps better.

Cecil inhaled and closed his eyes, pulling his daughters tight. As he listened to the wind rustling the leaves and the faint babble of a nearby stream, it slowly started to change. The more he listened, the more the joyous paradise began to slip away. A dreadful sound began to morph out of the perfect ambiance of the woods. It was the dark. Cecil felt his girls slipping away. He saw Steff's pleading eyes, her face agape with horror. He tried to speak, but no words would come. He grabbed her as tight as he could and turned to Abbs. To his surprise, her face was calm and serene.

He tried to call out to her, yet his voice still wouldn't work. He tried to pull her tight and was shocked when he realized that his arm was slipping right through her. He felt the strange mixture of warmth and cold as the living get when they penetrate and Impal. He saw she now exhibited a luminescent glow. His arm had almost passed completely through her when she said, "I am okay, dad. Take care of mom and endure, it will be okay."

The next instant, she faded from sight. Yet, unlike when she disappeared before, she did not seem afraid. She was anything but afraid.

Cecil turned his full attention back to Steff, but it was no use. Regardless of how hard he tried to hold on to her, she still continued to slip until she fell over the edge. Cecil lunged for her, but she was gone too. He then turned to Barbara. She lay motionless in the lounge chair, her eyes closed and her chest rising and falling. He cried out and was startled when he felt a couple of gentle hands grasp his shoulders.

"Cecil . . . Cecil . . . it's Sally," he heard a soft voice say.

A second later, he breached the gap between waking and dreams. He found he was sitting in the floor of the cabin. Bright sunlight streamed in from every direction, but he could still hear the faint call of the dark in the woods, as in his dream. Most people awake from a nightmare and are relieved they have been dreaming, but Cecil was just the opposite. His daughters were gone, Barbara was still catatonic, and they were surrounded by deadly darkness. Recalling where he was, he jerked his head towards Musial. He was gone.

"Where . . . ?" he began, then Sally stopped him with a soft pat on the back.

"He's outside with Burt and Derrick. They are giving him lessons," she said.

Cecil stared at her, dumfounded. She shrugged and indicated he should join them. He eased to his feet and tried to shake the cobwebs from his head.

"You passed out right after Burt started watching that thing. You were exhausted and you needed your sleep, so we left you alone."

"How long?" he asked as he walked over and knelt by Barbara, stroking her hair.

"A couple of hours . . . long enough . . . we already ate breakfast."

"I saved you some!" Charlotte called from the kitchen doorway.

"Thanks," Cecil muttered, not taking his eyes off Barbara. He wasn't hungry, even though he probably should be. Stress and fear make a formidable appetite suppressant. When it came to food he didn't think of himself, he thought of Barbara.

"We've got to get some food in her," Cecil said, fighting back tears. She looked gaunt, even though it had only been a little over a day. The experience and the after effects were taking a toll on her.

"I already thought of it," Charlotte said. "I'm cooking up a special broth for her. If she can swallow water, she can swallow broth."

Cecil smiled. "Thank you, Charlotte."

She blushed, and went back to her cooking. Soon a hearty, rich aroma drifted from the kitchen.

Cecil tended to Barbara's private needs. Sally and Charlotte had fashioned a makeshift diaper for her yesterday. He changed her, cleaned her, and redressed her in a pair of sweat pants provided by Charlotte. He couldn't help crying as he worked. It wasn't supposed to be this way. She was supposed to tend to him in his geriatric frailty, but not for at least another forty years. He never considered Barbara would ever be in this position. She was too strong, too beautiful, and to him, she was an immortal goddess.

When he finished, he kissed her and then went outside to join Burt and Derrick in their training session with Musial. They were teaching him how to drive. Burt was sitting in the passenger seat, giving instruction, while Derrick sat in the back. His gun trained at the back of Musial's head. They had no idea if shooting Andrews's body would stop Musial or not. It seemed the prudent thing to do. There was a day and a half, maybe two days, of gas left. Musial was the only one who could make it through the woods unmolested. The only way he could do this and get back in time is if he drove.

A knot formed in Cecil's stomach as he stood and watched the herky-jerky maneuvering of the SUV in the large circular area of the drive. It reminded him of when he gave Abbs driving lessons only a few short years ago. He took a seat on the porch to watch.

The lesson continued for another ten minutes with abrupt stops and an occasional curse word from Burt. Cecil gazed up at the sky and took in the lazy motion of the clouds and silent rustling of the breeze. The sky's unusual reddish tint with orange clouds was a stark contrast to the lavender and yellow to which they were accustomed. He never thought about it before, but it struck him as a color contrast between Hell and Heaven. They were certainly in Hell now; in spite of the peaceful and serene setting. The macabre whispers from the woods left no doubt.

Charlotte brought Cecil a plate of scrambled eggs, toast, and fried Spam. He picked at it for a while; he was not hungry at all. He wished they had a dog, and then he could at least take care of the fried meat. He downed his coffee in a single gulp. He was thinking about how nice it would be to have a 'Take me to your liter' sized soft drink from Martian Burgers when Burt called out to him.

"Well, what do you think of Stan the Man's driving here?" he called out the open window of the SUV. Musial didn't understand the reference to the St. Louis Cardinal's great, Stan Musial.

Cecil held out his hand, palm facing down, and then twisted it back and forth to indicate Musial was a 'so-so' driver.

"He should be all right," Cecil said. "Considering there shouldn't be a whole lot of other people on the roads."

Most people were 'voluntarily' evacuated to military bases, but none of them were sure just how voluntary it was. Of course, if they didn't go they were dead without a generator and fuel.

"True," Burt said. "We shouldn't have to worry about him hitting anyone . . . unless they are an idiot."

"No, all we have to worry about is whether or not he'll come back," Cecil thought.

"I want to show him one more thing," Burt said and held up a finger to say give me a minute.

Cecil could hear Derrick and Burt having a heated argument. A few moments later, the back door swung open and Derrick rolled out, a deep scowl on his face. He walked around to the front of the vehicle. He didn't point his pistol at Musial, but kept it at a forty-five degree angle in front of him so he could bring it up and fire at a moment's notice. Burt leaned out the window.

"I haven't showed him about backing yet. Once he masters it, he should be good to go," he called.

Burt turned and gave instructions to Musial. He pointed at different areas on the dashboard and the rearview mirrors. He then acted as if he were adjusting an invisible gear shift. Derrick turned and shrugged at Cecil.

It was obvious he did not trust Musial and he trusted him even less now that he wasn't able to guard him up close. No one trusted Musial, but Burt needed Derrick out of the back seat. He couldn't teach Musial about the fine art of backing with Derrick's head in the way.

After he finished coaching, Musial shifted the SUV into reverse and it lurched backwards. What happened next was unclear. It brought Cecil out of his seat and Derrick's gun to bear on the vehicle as it sped away in reverse.

Burt screamed and tried to grab the wheel, but it was no use as they careened down the slope next to the driveway. They were heading toward the darkest spot in the woods.

"I told him this was a bad idea!" Derrick screamed as he ran after the vehicle. "I told him!"

Cecil was in pursuit on Derrick's heels, without a clue to what they intended to do. It wasn't as if they possessed super powers and could grab the bumper and stop the SUV's wild jaunt. Running after it was all they could do until it stopped.

"Burt . . . jump!" Cecil shouted as the vehicle approached the woods.

Derrick kept trying to aim a shot, but the way the vehicle jostled from side to side, he stood a good chance of hitting Burt. They heard the screams of Sally and Charlotte behind them. Their focus was on getting Burt out of there somehow, some way. When it became obvious there was no way the vehicle was going to stop before hitting the woods, Cecil did a dangerous and foolish thing. He tackled a man with a loaded gun and an itchy trigger finger.

"What in the crap are you doing?" Derrick spat as they tumbled and slid together on the wet grass.

"We can't do Burt any good if we go charging into the dark after him . . . that'll just leave the women with Musial! Do you want that?"

The logic had a hard time penetrating his adrenaline charged head. Before it began to sink in, Burt began to scream. Not a pain filled or terrified scream, it was an anguished scream, eerily similar to what they heard from Dr. Winder. They saw the SUV had come to rest against a large pine tree, in the center of the dark spot in the woods. The tires continued to spin in reverse as the tree refused to give an inch.

"Burt!" they called in unison, mixed with the mingled screams of the women who were approaching from behind.

Cecil had to jump to his feet and tackle Sally or else she would have traipsed right in after her husband.

"Let me go you, bastard," she screamed. "He is going to die!"

Cecil ignored her rages and glanced back over his shoulder at the vehicle. His heart lifted for a moment when he saw Burt's door open and him roll out onto the ground. Then his heart sank as Burt knelt and proceeded to slam his head in the heavy SUV door.

"Jesus," Cecil croaked and buried his head on Sally's heaving chest, covering her eyes with his arms.

Charlotte dropped to her knees beside them and began to sob with her hands covering her face.

"You bastard!" Derrick shouted and a single shot rang out. Cecil could tell by the sound that he didn't hit anything. The bullet whistled away through the underbrush.

A moment later, the sound of the slamming door ceased. They all knew that the eerie silence now engulfing them meant only one thing . . . the dark had done its job. Burt was dead.

CHAPTER 23

IN THE SHADOWS

"Am I not destroying my enemies when I make friends of them?"
~Abraham Lincoln

STEFF SAT ALONE in the president's private dining room. She nervously picked at a bowl of chili, refusing to take a bite. It was too damned hot, thanks to her grandfather. Much to her relief, she would not have to endure the discomfort of his company. Her grandfather would not be attending their lunch date because he had more important matters to attend. His noontime radio address would be in a few minutes. President Garrison took "waste not, want not" to the extreme. He had always insisted that Steff and her sister never take more food than they could eat, and always clean their plates. This might have been sound advice except he always dictated what they ate.

When Carmella heard Garrison would not be at lunch, she brought Steff a peanut butter and jelly sandwich with French fries. Carmella took the steaming bowl of chili and flushed it down the Executive toilet before returning the empty bowl to Steff. If he came in, it needed to appear as if she had indeed cleaned her plate.

Steff gobbled the sandwich and fries up before Carmella could leave the room. She had not eaten anything substantial in a couple of days. Her grandfather tried to force a meal of veal and garlic mashed potatoes on her yesterday. He said it was in 'celebration' of his victory over the resistance. Steff found veal revolting when she discovered what it was a year earlier in class. She did enjoy mashed potatoes, but garlic made her sick to her stomach. She didn't have much of an appetite even if she did care for what was on the menu. In spite of her youth and naivety, she understood that a victory over the resistance was a victory over her father.

"Besides, he hadn't really beaten the resistance," she thought, licking jelly from her finger. "Mom, Daddy, and Abbs are still out there, along with a bunch of others."

She did not know that her sister was killed in the raid, and had now disappeared with the legions of other Impals. If she did, she would have already tried to escape . . . darkness be damned. This was why Garrison concealed the truth from her. In his mind, he was protecting her. Carmella was right; Grandpa Garrison is an ignorant man.

Steff listened to the address on a small radio. There was nothing new. Government good—Impals bad, go to bases for your protection. He once again reminded the public that the power grids would go dark at nine o'clock tonight for an indefinite period of time. All energy would be conserved and diverted to military bases. He mentioned the tragic deaths of key government and military leaders, placing the blame on the Impals. There was one thing different, something Steff did not catch. Social studies and US Government were never her strongest subjects in school. Near the end of the speech, he introduced Avery Cooper as the new vice president. The ring of cronies lounging around the Oval office would be his new cabinet. He announced their immunity to the dark, proclaiming them as a deliverance from God to assist him in the country's most trying hour. This was his most blatant usurping of the Constitution yet. However, people were so frightened; there would be little more than a whimper of protest. It was the perfect storm for their agenda, both literally and figuratively.

"Carmella," Steff asked as her new friend cleared away the dishes. "Can you help me get out of here?"

Fear flooded Carmella, causing her hand to shake and clatter the dishes. She glanced around as if someone were listening. She sat down beside Steff and leaned in till her mouth was less than an inch from the girl's ear.

"Don't answer me out loud, honey. Do you understand?" she whispered.

Steff nodded.

"Where would you go sweetheart . . . do you know where your parents are?"

Steff frowned and shook her head.

"Well, if you left . . . the only safe place for you to be is at a military base. He would find you there."

Steff slumped in her chair; she knew Carmella's was right. Without knowing where her parents were, she couldn't go to a single safe place where her grandfather would not find her. A feeling of complete hopelessness and despair washed over her as she began to cry. Carmella pulled her close and kissed her on the forehead. To Carmella's credit she did not say anything for a long time, she held her tight and let the crying run its course.

"What am . . . I going to do?" Steff muttered between choked sobs.

"For right now, you'll stay right here and we'll both keep our ear to the ground for news of your parents. In the meantime, I am here for you."

Steff tried to smile, but just couldn't manage one. Carmella's eyes lit up as she leaned in and whispered, "Let me know what you like. I'll make sure you never have to eat off your grandfather's nasty menu again."

Steff grinned, she couldn't help it. Carmella had a knack of putting her at ease.

"Thank you," she said.

Carmella gave Steff a hug and then stood up to leave just as President Garrison entered the room. He rudely announced he was ready for lunch and sent Carmella scampering for a warm bowl of chili. He asked Steff to join him in a self-serving prayer, and then tried to engage his granddaughter in one sided conversation. Steff nodded, offering only a simple yes or no response. If Garrison noticed she was upset, he didn't show it. He rambled for a half hour about God's plan, the new administration, and his vision for the future of our country. By the time she went back to her room, Steff felt sick.

Before Cecil could push himself off the hysterical Sally, something startled him, causing him to flinch and roll to the side. Someone ran past him. He could tell by the quick glance of the lower legs and shoes it was not Derrick, it was Andrews's clothing.

Derrick screamed a litany of obscenities mixed with incoherent rambling. "Drop!— I'll—kill you!"

Cecil jumped to his feet and saw Musial making his way up the hill to the cabin with Burt draped over his shoulder. He sprinted after him as the women continued to scream.

As they reached the parking area in front of the cabin, Musial stopped and gently lowered Burt to the ground. He knelt down beside him and began to check vitals. Cecil arrived and gaped at his injured friend. Burt's head was covered in blood, making him unrecognizable.

Derrick did not stop. Instead, he sprung like a linebacker trying to stop a runner at the goal line. He flew through the air sending Musial tumbling across the gravel. A second later, he was sitting on Musial's chest, his gun pressing between his eyes.

"You tried to kill him you sorry psycho!" Derrick spat.

Cecil was torn between tending to his injured friend and stopping a potential homicide.

"Derrick, back off!" Cecil warned.

"How can you say that when you saw what he did to Burt?" Derrick hissed.

"Derrick, it was an accident. If he wanted Burt dead, do you think he would have pulled him out and carried him up here? Thank about it Derrick . . . just calm down and take a moment to think before you do something you'll regret. Don't forget this body belongs to Sam Andrews."

"The major has impeccable logic, sir," Musial said casually. "It was an accident and I am truly sorry."

Cecil wished that he would keep his mouth shut. Even when Musial was trying to be polite, he came off as arrogant and condescending.

"Burt needs our attention now, Derrick. He is still alive, but he might not be for long if we don't help him."

Cecil breathed a sigh of relief when he saw the tension relax in Derrick's muscles. He loosened his grip on Musial and started to get up, but not before bringing his fist down with a sickening crunch on Musial's nose.

As they tended to Burt's injuries, Derrick had no idea how close he was to death. If the men had looked, they would have seen hellish rage burning in Musial's eyes. It took every ounce of strength, every ounce of resolve, and the constant reminder of his motivations to keep Musial in place. He so wanted to pick up a rock and bash in Derrick's skull. He had not experienced such a strong desire to kill someone in a long time. The temptation to return to his nature was intoxicating. Somehow, someway, he resisted as he wiped blood from under his broken nose. He could feel the pain just as if this was his own body and Andrews felt it too. He could hear his agonized screams somewhere in the background of his mind.

This was new territory for Musial and he wasn't sure what to do. Killing had always been a natural, calming experience. While he hated his victims and believed they needed to die; he never killed out of anger. He found this impulse both exhilarating and disturbing at the same time. There was no justice in his desire, only revenge.

It did not take long for Sally and Charlotte to join them. Charlotte ran inside to get water and towels, while Cecil and Sally examined his injuries. He was unconscious, but still breathing and his heartbeat was strong. Most of the blood was from a large gash on the front of his head. They used the towels and water to wash away the blood and then compressed the wounds until the bleeding stopped. Derrick went inside and found a first aid kit. They were able to do a makeshift patch on Burt's injuries with butterfly bandages and gauze. Ten minutes later, he resembled a slumbering swami with a sloppy head turban.

Sally held him in her arms whispering in his ear while everyone milled about with uncertainty. Derrick kept a wary eye on Musial whose nose was now swollen to the size of a lemon. Derrick's heart skipped when he caught a brief glimpse of the fury struggling to come out of Musial. He gripped his weapon a little tighter as the repentant dark soul turned away from him. He became so intent with watching Musial, he did not even notice when Burt began to stir.

"Sally?" Burt muttered as his wife planted a kiss on his cheek.

"Burt!" Cecil said, "How are you feeling, buddy?"

Burt blinked at him with bleary eyes as if he were trying to focus on some distant object, and then shrugged. "Which one of you idiots ran over my head?" he asked with good-natured humor. However, the humor melted as the recollection of what happened sank over him like a slimy blanket.

"Oh Jesus . . ." Burt muttered as terror engulfed him. He remembered, he remembered every ghoulish detail. He and Cecil now shared a terrible kindred sympathy.

"I'm sorry, Cecil," Burt said in much the same way one would tell a friend they are sorry for the death of a loved one. He took Cecil's hand and squeezed as cold understanding passed between them.

"Well Mr. Golden, how was the Führer?" Musial asked as he walked over to them.

"Shut up you bastard!" Sally hissed. "He wound up in there because of you!"

"Don't pay attention to him," Cecil urged. "He's full of crap."

Cecil could tell by the haunted countenance on Burt's face, Musial was not full of crap, not in the slightest. Musial took a few steps further and Derrick raised his weapon. He pulled back the hammer with a menacing click.

"That's far enough!" Derrick barked.

Musial raised his hands as if to say I surrender and held open his palms in supplication.

"I apologize," Musial said. "I should have chosen my words better."

"You're damn right you should have!" Sally shrieked.

Musial knelt down in the grass with his head lowered, giving Derrick ample opportunity to take position behind him.

"I'm sorry, but he was there wasn't he? I thought I could feel his presence when I pulled you out," Musial said.

Burt glanced at Cecil and then took a deep breath, tracing the edge of his bandages with his fingertips.

"There were at least a hundred of the most vile and despicable things I have seen in my life. I can't imagine they were ever human, but . . ." he paused for a moment. "I guess they were in the flesh and blood sense."

Before anyone else could respond, Burt turned to Musial who was still staring at the ground. "Yes, you were right. Adolf Hitler was there, and yes he wanted me bad, but . . ." he paused until Musial turned his face up and looked at him. "He wants you more."

CHAPTER 24

ROAD TRIP

"If my ship sails from sight, it doesn't mean my journey ends, it simply means the river bends."
~Enoch Powell

MUSIAL STARED THROUGH BURT for several moments. He surprised them all by breaking into a broad and crafty grin.

"I don't swing that way," he said flippantly, and then shook his head and folded his arms over his chest. "Besides, he can't do anything to me . . . even if I decided to abandon this poor drunkard's body and rejoin the dark. But . . . he could make my eternal existence difficult," he said, exhaling a deep sigh of satisfaction. "Thank you, Burt!"

"For what?" Burt mumbled.

"Why . . . for reinforcing my motivation, of course. You see, you don't know how close I almost came to relapsing a few minutes ago. Mr. Vandeputte there," he said pointing at Derrick, "barely almost got his head bashed in for his troubles."

"And who in the hell was going to do it . . . you?" Derrick said through gritted teeth.

"Yes," Musial said, and then pointed at a smooth rock about the size of a bread loaf. "With that rock," he finished with such a cold and certain finality, Derrick felt frost condense on his spine.

The truth was, his former colleagues of the dark could harm him, perhaps not in the physical sense, but a wounding of the soul is much worse. Musial knew it too, yet it was not in his nature to show weakness. Besides, as long as he occupied Andrew's body, he was safe. He was not completely sure of it until he pulled Burt to safety. He had lurked in dark corners of the cabin, but he had not interfered with the desire of the dark souls to satisfy their nature, not until now. They were furious and they wanted to punish him, but they couldn't.

A grumbling followed by a loud pop drew everyone's attention. A sinking sensation ran through them all. It was a terrifying reminder of the predicament they now faced . . . the generator had run out of gas. There was enough in the tanks to last another day and a half or maybe two if they were careful with their energy consumption.

"How much is left?" Charlotte whispered.

"Enough. We will be okay for a while. We need to get Musial on the road as soon as possible," Cecil said. "Are you up to it?" he asked, turning to Musial.

Musial gave his customary sardonic grin. "Of course, major," he replied. "As long as I don't have to drive in reverse."

"Try to avoid that gear, huh?" Burt said, massaging his temples with his index fingers. Then to everyone's surprise, Burt and Musial began to chuckle as if they shared some unsavory inside joke.

"Indeed sir, indeed," Musial said as they continued to laugh.

Everyone else exchanged incredulous glances. They wanted to laugh along, yet none of them could quite bring themselves to do it. It was like laughing at a plane crash. People often use humor to diffuse tension, but this was different. They could only muster a polite smile.

"So where do I need to go, major?" Musial asked, turning to Cecil.

"I think that is a question best put to Charlotte," Cecil said. "This is her family's cabin. I'm not familiar with this area."

"So, where's I need ta' go, Miss Charlotte?" Musial said in a loud pickaninny voice.

They knew Musial was an admitted racist. Especially since race played into his selection of victims. Yet, they were all surprised by this sudden outburst. In the 1930s it wouldn't have received a second thought. Now, it was a verbal slap to the face. To Charlotte's credit, she handled it well, ignoring his tone and answering his question.

"Well, the Ever So Quick station is about ten miles from here. If they are cutting back power, they were probably shut off because it is in such a rural area."

Cecil felt his stomach twist in knots. This was something he had not considered. If the power is cut, how were they going to be able to pump gas?

"From there is Manassas about thirty miles away. There are a lot of gas stations there."

"Power is going to be cut tonight," Cecil said. "After tonight, you won't be able to get gas except on a military base and I doubt they would let you leave."

"Well then," Musial said rubbing his hands together, "I better get going then . . . daylight is wasting."

His final comment was as true as it was unnecessary. It served no purpose other than to raise everyone's blood pressure.

"Help me up," Burt said, holding his hands up to Cecil.

Cecil took his hands while Sally supported him from behind as they brought him to his feet. He clung to both of their shoulders while his legs wobbled like a new born calf. Burt glanced at Musial and, with his right hand draped over Cecil's shoulder; he motioned for him to come.

"You have the basics down. Just remember the red octagon sign means to stop. The yellow triangle means yield, a red light means stop and a green light means go. You shouldn't have much, if any, traffic to deal with. If you see a cop, tell him you are going to Quantico for evacuation. Remember, you are Sam Andrews so use his identification," Burt said, nodding at his shirt pocket.

Musial stuck his hand in the pocket and pulled out a thin brown leather wallet. He opened it up and thumbed through the plastic pages. Out of six potential pages, only two contained anything. One held Andrews's driver's license and the other his military ID. He squinted at the pictures and gave an exaggerated wince.

"I suppose it wasn't in my cards to find a more handsome host," he said.

"Do you have any questions?" Burt asked.

"Yes, where would I find a red light and a green light? In my day, a red light signified an area of ill repute. A green light, well, I think it meant the coast was clear . . . I never paid attention to such things."

"Let's stick to the basics," Burt said. "You can read, can't you?"

Musial folded his arms scornfully. "Of course I can!" he snapped. "Do you think just because I was a magician it means I am an uneducated, illiterate prat?"

"Good," Burt said, ignoring his wounded tone. He was certain that Musial was not upset at all, only toying with him. "As I said, keep it simple, keep it slow and remember the basics."

Charlotte drew a makeshift map on a piece of notebook paper. While the vehicle had GPS, they decided it would be too complicated to teach Musial to use it, not to mention it would waste valuable time. They were not sure if GPS would work in the storm either. Musial walked back down the hill and retrieved the SUV while Burt lay back down on the grass. The vehicle was undamaged except for a few scratches and a dent on the rear bumper.

Once he pulled in front of the cabin, they loaded all the empty gas canisters in the back. They also included an assortment of canning jars and containers from the kitchen. They packed anything capable of holding gasoline. Barring a miracle, this would be their one and only chance for procuring fuel. They just hoped they could collect enough to outlast the eye of the storm. How much they would need, God only knew.

Burt gave a few more last minute instructions, which went ignored, then Musial left with a wise remarks. "*See you in a few days.*" He then sped away clumsily. He still didn't seem to have the full grasp of acceleration. Even when he was gone from view, they could still hear the revving of the engine.

"Do you think he will come back?" Derrick asked.

Cecil shrugged. "I don't know, but we didn't have much choice."

"I think he will," Burt said as he squeezed Sally and Cecil's shoulders. "I think he was serious about wanting salvation. Not coming back would seriously jeopardize his goal."

"How in the hell can you be so sure?" Sally asked.

"I spent some time with him today in the vehicle, got to know him a little," Burt said.

"I didn't hear you discussing anything. You yelled at him about how he was screwing up," Derrick interjected. "And I was with you the whole time."

Burt acted as if he hadn't heard him. "Anyway, I feel like my head is going to explode. Can we go inside and sit down?" he asked.

They had refueled the generator before loading the canisters. With its current payload, it should last till mid-morning tomorrow. Then, they would have to use their last canister of gas, assuming Musial didn't return by then. If he didn't return, they would be powerless the following evening and the dark would have its way with them.

Cecil and Derrick helped Burt to his palette. They each donated one of their own pillows to help keep his head elevated as much as possible.

"How do you feel, now?" Cecil asked as he sat down in a nearby chair, his elbows on his knees.

Burt touched his hand to the bandages on his forehead, and then gave a half-grimace and half-smile.

"I feel like a tractor ran over my head. Otherwise, I'm in mint condition."

Cecil took out a flashlight and leaned closer.

"Look at me," he said. Burt obliged with a pained expression. His eyes squinted as if he was staring into the sun rather than a flashlight.

"You have a concussion," Cecil said. "I hope that's the least of your worries."

"Don't give me this doomsday vibe, jerk. Shoot me straight."

"I'm not a doctor and even if I were we couldn't tell anything without a cat scan or an x-ray. For right now, you should rest and keep your head elevated. I think Charlotte has more aspirin or acetaminophen," he paused and took a deep breath. "We should ice it too."

"I'll get some," Sally volunteered as she scampered into the kitchen.

A few moments later she returned with a handful of ice cubes sealed in a large sealable freezer bag.

"So that's it?" Burt asked. "Just rest and freeze my noggin?"

Cecil gave him a reassuring nod, but deep down he knew it was not the whole truth. He had given him the best-case scenario. Worst-case scenario is Burt might have brain swelling or hemorrhaging, which doesn't get better. If so, his headaches would grow to an agonizing level before he slipped into a coma, never to wake up again.

Cecil watched his friend as worry began to eat away at him. Burt was slowly fading.

"Do you know where you are?" Cecil asked as Sally changed positions with the freezer bag, moving it to his right temple.

Burt first regarded him with annoyance, as if it was the most stupid question he ever heard. His countenance soon faded to confusion, followed by panic. He looked around the room for some clue, some reminder. After several desperate moments, his gaze fell on Charlotte. His expression changed course as if he shifted into reverse.

"Her place," he said with a meek smile nodding at Charlotte.

Cecil glanced at Sally and saw her wearing a triumphant smile. He had gotten the question right, which must mean he would be okay. When she saw Cecil's worried eyes, her smile vanished.

"Try and keep him awake for as long as you can," Cecil said as he got up and walked out the front door.

He descended the stairs and stared up at the menacing red sky with its orange clouds.

"Where are you, Abbs?" he asked out loud.

Was she standing there beside him, just as the Impals had done for thousands of years before the storm arrived? He reached out his hand as if he were beckoning some unseen person to take it. He waited for well over a minute, but when the cold and warm sensation did not come, he began to cry. He had never felt more alone. For all intents and purposes, his whole family was gone. He squinted, trying to fight back the stinging burn of his tears, and saw the makeshift grave of Dr. Winder a few feet away.

Would he soon be burying another friend? Would they all be buried out here . . . save one last person. Or, would they die all together when the dark finally spilled in? Cecil walked as far away from the cabin as possible without going into the shadows. For a fleeting second, he considered running into the woods and ending it all, ending the misery. It would all be over and he would not have to worry about anything again. Maybe he would see Abbs. He could tell her he was sorry and beg her forgiveness. Then he thought of the rows and rows of sleeping Impals lined up at the base, ready to be dumped into the Tesla Gate. They were the suicides, the ones who gave up on life and took the easy way out. If he ran into the woods voluntarily, wouldn't it make him a suicide? He wouldn't do anyone any good.

"You damn coward," he muttered as he wiped a tear from his eye.

If he wasn't so distraught, so stressed, so disgusted . . . so terrified, he might have noticed a faint cold touch in the center of his back.

CHAPTER 25

THE WAIT

"Curiosity is lying in wait for every secret."
~Ralph Waldo Emerson

JACK SAT IN HIS CELL the rest of the day and all through the night with no contact from anyone. Of course, he had his companions in the dark to keep him company. They visited each time the guards flicked the lights off and on at five-minute intervals. When the experiments first started he tried to fake an insatiable desire to harm himself. This only lasted so long. After a minute or two, it was evident Jack was not affected by the dark. If he were, he would have been dead many times over.

Whoever administered this experimental light show seemed to take great joy in it. They sometimes blinked the lights in the rhythm of popular show tunes. By the time morning rolled around, Jack was exhausted. If he could, he would have murdered his mystery tormenter in front of the whole base.

"If I see the rhythm of *Copa Cabaña* tapped out again like some sort of hellish Morse code, I'm going to put a dull knife through the wankstain's throat," he thought to himself.

He was pretty sure the whole base knew his 'dark' little secret by now. The question was, did they know half of it or all of it? Did they send troops out to his house this morning to turn it inside out? He knew they would be desperate to find some important piece of information explaining his ability. He was sure a half dozen soldiers were going through his flat as he sat here. The more important question was, what *would* they find? Was he as careful and discreet as he believed? He thought so, but on TV didn't they always find some piece of evidence the killer overlooked? He still didn't believe he had done anything wrong. Perhaps his inner peace and his insatiable arrogance made him careless. This thought turned his emotionless guts upside down. He broke into a sweat, feeling as if he was going to be ill at any moment. He bent over and clutched his stomach as he rocked back and forth. He felt dizzy and knew he must channel his thoughts elsewhere, to focus on something else. Just as he thought it was going to be impossible, his thoughts came together. With laser focus, they coalesced into a single image in his head.

"Bitch," he said loud enough it echoed around his small steel cell.

He thought of Donna and her treachery. His twisted guts filled with a burning, homicidal rage. He was going to kill her the next time he saw her. Oh yes, he would put a dull knife through her throat, but only after he tortured her for a satisfactory amount of time. How long would that be? Well, the way he felt right now, it would be a pretty damned long time.

What Jack did not know was that the British Army was very much interested in him. Not because he was a murdering psychopath in their midst. They *had* sent a small platoon to his house and found nothing except for a few blood spots on the floor where he hit his head on the stool. They took blood samples and, when analyzed, they would confirm it was his blood. The cage, Jack's favorite killing stage, had been disassembled and put away after last night's bloody mess. He hid it well. He used plastic sheets under the cage which caught the excess blood. Jack had disposed of them when he disposed of the old lady's body. Forensically speaking, he was clean. However, their interest was in Jack's ability. Little did Jack know, he wasn't quite as unique as he thought.

The acting President of the United States shared this trait along with his current cabinet. There were also reports of similar people around the world. The base had two of them in confinement a few yards away from Jack's cell. These two were receiving the same rhythmic torment as Jack, but their tormenter was more partial to Slim Whitman tunes. The discovery of these individuals was via their own stupidity and arrogance. The scientists could not find a single factor that would make these two different from anyone else. Of course, if they dug deeper into their personal lives, they would find a common link as obvious as the nose on their faces.

Their dark behavior made them kindred spirits with the whispering lunatics in the shadows. They had committed their own terrible acts. The dark was now a litmus test of the arrogant psychopaths and sociopaths of the world, but the world had too many other things to worry now.

Yet, not all these people were the same either. Take the dark soul of a man who called himself Ruth; or Musial for examples. There were many others around the world committing corporeal hijacking. All done for the possibility of salvation from their eternal dark void. They did not have hope before the eye of the cosmic storm opened the door to their realm. These souls were desperate to escape their hopelessness. In the absence of hope their only purpose was to perpetrate their ignorance and arrogance.

Jack heard voices and shuffling of feet outside his door. Shadows passed by his tiny portal window and he stood up. The veins stuck out on his neck and he dug his fingers into the steel door, breaking a couple of nails. A trickle of blood flowed down his fingers, but he did not notice. He focused on what he saw in the hallway. Donna passed by with two armed guards.

"You!" Jack screamed. "I'll kill you!"

The door was thick, but it was not sound proof. The soldiers faced forward, unflinching. However, Donna glanced over her shoulder as they passed. Instead of regarding him with contempt or gloating; she regarded him with pity. Even in his conscious free heart, he felt a sudden glimmer of the sorrow in Donna's eyes. It was as if all the wind went out of him at one time.

"You bitch," he whispered. He jerked his hands back from the door as if it scorched him. He tucked his fingers under his armpits as he plopped down on his cot.

He was blank and numb not from a lack of emotion, but from an overwhelming wave of emotion. It washed through him like the intimate touch of an Impal . . . soothingly warm and frigidly cold. He felt sorrow, he felt regret, and he felt guilt. He was not sure why. Jack leaned back and closed his eyes, trying to process these feelings. They were as foreign to him as physics was to an amoeba.

He closed his eyes as the emotional cyclone continued to rage within.

Ruth slept. He knew if he did not allow the woman's fragile body to rest, it would not last much longer. The one good thing about occupying a body was that even as the body slept, the occupying soul could still keep one eye open, so to speak. He had managed to keep an eye on Rebekah and Malakhi. However, even though they slept closely, it was similar to trying to watch someone across a wide field with binoculars. This gave him the strange sensation of being close, yet feeling far away from somebody. He had not felt this since the day he died.

This caused him to do something out of the ordinary, he thought of his friend, Dismas. He had watched him die several yards away as they both hung outside Jerusalem. He never saw Dismas in the void. For centuries, he wondered why. Some people are just slow learners and it took the man calling himself Ruth almost two thousand years to figure it out. Dismas was penitent for his evil acts when he died; he was not. In fact, he was downright belligerent in his ignorance and arrogance. He murdered, raped, and stole his whole life and had not felt a shred of guilt or remorse. He believed he was doing what he must to survive. To him, in his ignorance and arrogance, all his actions were justified necessities.

Ruth did want salvation, but the temptation to revert to his old ways was overwhelming at times. He wanted to take Rebekah out in the woods, rape her, and then slit her throat. What good would it accomplish? It might make him feel good for a few minutes or even a few hours. But, then where would he be? He knew his desire to have sex with this woman and murder her for his own well-being did not fly. He almost laughed to himself when he considered he was not equipped to rape a woman right now.

He watched and waited as the old lady and her body slept under his control. He was convinced his salvation somehow rested with them. He didn't know why. Maybe it was somehow atoning for his deeds by watching out for them.

As he thought about these things, a name ran through his head, his real name. His mother was Ruth, this much was true. In the void, he was just a nameless occupant of a nameless nothingness. He had to stop and think for a moment. It was such a long time since he remembered. When he did recall, his face broke into a wide grin in spite of the sleeping body.

"That's my name and I will have salvation," he thought to himself. "As sure as my name is Gestas."

Musial did not return by nightfall, which worried everyone. However, when he didn't return by the next morning, panic began to set in. There was not enough fuel to last another night, especially if it was a cloudy day. They might not even make it to nightfall. This possibility was driven home by the distant rumble of thunder.

"You've got to be freaking kidding me," Derrick said as he stared out the window at the darkening sky. The perimeter of daylight was closing fast on their little cabin. "We are going to have to milk the generator for all it's got today. If this storm doesn't pass soon, we won't have enough gas to make it through the day, let alone tonight," he said, tapping his knuckles on the window with frustration.

"Shut up, Derrick!" Burt snapped. "He'll make it back."

Derrick folded his arms and turned to face him. "You sure got chummy with that murderer," he said. "What's the deal? Don't tell me you actually sympathize with him?"

Burt did not answer. He just stared at him with distant, glassy eyes as if he were trying to figure out who was speaking. Cecil watched pensively from the sofa as he sat next to Barbara. She had been exhibiting some encouraging signs this morning. Her mouth moved as if trying to form words. It wasn't much, but it raised his hopes a little. As he watched his two friends, his tiny amount of joy began to melt away. Burt was showing all the classic signs of someone who had suffered a severe concussion. The first occurrence of nausea and vomiting had begun at sunrise. Cecil hoped, they all hoped, Burt just got his bell rung a little. The longer they watched, the more they realized this was not the case. If he did suffer a severe head trauma, he needed medical attention, and he needed it now. Of course, it was not an option without taking him to a military base.

Cecil felt as if a stone was sitting in his gut as he watched his friend's eyes open and close as he tried to focus on Derrick. Did he have reservations about Musial's trustworthiness? Absolutely, but he knew Burt was right; they had no choice but to trust him. He also knew Burt was no fool.

"Well, if he doesn't come back it's all on you!" Derrick continued.

Cecil had heard enough. He saw the tears begin to roll down Sally's face as she rubbed her husband's arm. He stood up and stood between Derrick and Burt.

"Give it a rest Derrick," he muttered.

He looked in Derrick's eyes, expecting to see rage. Instead, he saw something he did not expect, he saw fear. His anger at Derrick started to fade into empathy. Cecil was terrified as well.

"Let's go outside," Cecil suggested.

Derrick blinked and then glanced around the room at all the eyes locked on him. He suddenly felt embarrassed. He turned and walked out onto the porch.

The wind began to blow harder; rustling the trees in the nearby woods. The sound was strange. The darkening sky had driven the shadows closer to the house. The dark whispers made the rustling leaves sound like background static. Cecil couldn't help thinking of the TV in the movie, *Poltergeist*. Judging by the approaching clouds, he guessed they had about ten minutes before the dark forced them into the house.

"I'm sorry, Cecil," Derrick said. "I don't think he is coming back. He's already been gone almost twenty hours. I could have driven to Denver by now."

Cecil didn't say anything at first, he just shook his head. Then he took a deep, shuttering breath. "I understand, Derrick but lay off of Burt, okay? He's in bad shape."

Derrick seemed shocked. Either he had not paid attention or he didn't understand the nature of head injuries. "Okay . . ." he stammered. "How bad?"

"I think he has a concussion and a pretty bad one. He needs a doctor."

Derrick rubbed the back of his hand across his upper lip. "Jesus . . . I had no idea," he whispered.

The wind picked up as lightning flashed, followed a few seconds later by an enormous clap of thunder. It rumbled through the woods, exciting the dark as their insidious hissing intensified.

"We better get inside," Cecil said, clasping Derrick's shoulder. "The shadows are going to be on us before we know it."

The two men turned and walked inside as the first fat raindrops began to splatter the driveway. The dark was coming and would soon be on the doorstep. It would be contained only by their interior lights. The lights which were now putting a tremendous and unplanned demand on the starving generator.

If they had stayed outside a few moments longer, they might have heard the distant approach of a vehicle deep in the woods.

CHAPTER 26

REGIME

*"There are three things in the world that deserve no mercy,
hypocrisy, fraud, and tyranny."*
~Frederick William Robertson

THE NEW CABINET ACCOMPANIED President Garrison to the large relocation base at Quantico. As far as they were concerned, DC was in hand. Last night, they introduced their final opposition to the whispering lunatics. It was now time to broaden the web, to shore up support, and to prune the tree of discontent beyond the capital. This time the military personnel who sympathized with the Myriad Resistance would meet the same fate.

The president brought his new cabinet because Avery was now the vice-president. He could deal with the unpleasant tasks since the president didn't need to get his hands dirty. Garrison believed himself superior to the individuals who had to leave the lights on after dark, yet he still knew the importance of plausible deniability.

"Looks like a hell of a storm heading this way," Robby said as he peered out the window. He had been biting the inside of his lip and clinching his fists for the last ten miles. He was seeking something to resist the temptation to rip Garrison's throat out with his bare hands. The president did not care for smoking and deplored the sinful act even more in closed quarters. When Robby tried to light up a cigar, Garrison slapped him.

"Who the hell does that idiot think he is?" he thought to himself. "If he wasn't the president he would be dead right now."

The presidential limo carried five people, not counting the Secret Service ride along. There still seemed to be enough room to play a pick-up game of basketball inside the spacious sedan. This car was identical to the presidential limo which vanished a couple of weeks earlier. The only difference was this car did not sit under a hundred feet of murky water.

Everyone stared out the window at the approaching storm. Actual weather related storms were a rarity since the cosmic storm arrived months ago. For some strange reason, it seemed to have a calming effect on meteorological conditions. Ironic, since it also had the effect of materializing souls and unleashing dark spirits on the Earth.

"What did you do . . . piss off God?" Joan asked, glaring at President Garrison.

Garrison glared back. It was clear to everyone that he didn't appreciate her disrespect or sacrilege. Avery moved in to diffuse the situation. "What exactly did you do for the government?" he asked her.

She kept her eyes locked on Garrison as she answered. "I screwed men to death," she said with no emotion.

"Damn," Sebastian chimed in.

"You come near me," Joan said with the guile of a poisonous snake about to strike, "and I'll cut off your root and feed it to you. Then I'll stab you in the throat, shish-k-bobbing the little worm while it is still in your gullet." She then muttered a host of curses while clinching her fists.

"Joan was one of our best operatives," Avery interrupted. "She did whatever she had to do for the mission."

"Sounds like she enjoyed it," Robby grinned as he chewed on an unlit cigar.

"What if I did?" Joan snapped. "What did you do," she asked, eyeing Robby's rather large mid-section, "sit on people?"

His face flushed red with anger and he turned toward the window as another brilliant streak of lightning spiked across the sky.

THE EYE OF MADNESS

Almost as if the ensuing thunder was his queue, Garrison said, "I think all of you need to shut the hell up! We are doing God's work. We are all chosen by God's will and all you can do is fight amongst yourselves and use language offensive to our Lord!"

"What does God have to do with anything?" Sebastian thought, but dared not say. He was an atheist and had spent his whole life despising the Christian faith. Sebastian was never sure why he hated Christianity. He was never molested by a priest, struck by a nun, nor was he ever berated by an overzealous evangelist for his sinful ways. He reviled the hypocrisy he saw in every Christian church he ever attended. He never believed the deeds he committed as evil or hypocritical. He was doing what he must in the grand scheme of the universe. He did things those hypocritical Christians would find offensive. He despised the hypocrisy breaming in the car around him, culminating with President Garrison. This zealot was the personification of every negative feeling he ever held about religion. For a moment, he wondered why he was here. He reminded himself that not everyone had the opportunity to be a presidential advisor. What else was he going to do?

Everyone took the president's advice and shut up, but no one was happy about it. The only thing that kept the rest of the ride from becoming a scowling contest was the sudden onset of rain. The rhythmic beating of large raindrops splattering against the roof and windows was soothing as the wind nudged the car from side to side.

The driver and Secret Service agents were saved at the behest of President Garrison's insistence. He demanded they bring plenty of extra lights. It wasn't because he cared for their well-being; he didn't want to have his driver engulfed by the dark while travelling at sixty miles an hour.

Even though it was a little after noon, it was as dark as dusk when they reached Quantico. A single guard remained at the post sitting in a tiny shack. What appeared to be a three hundred watt bulb burned inside. Of course, he did not come out; he couldn't. The guard waved them through when he recognized the car.

They arrived at the command center a few minutes later. It was lit up with brilliant white lights shining from every window and door. No one was outside. A dozen or so officers in full dress uniform stood inside the door ready to greet them. Garrison had been forward think-ing when it came to the lights for their support staff, yet he had not when it came to umbrellas. They got out of the car and sprinted the twenty yards to the building. The wind howled, the lightning arced, and the rain fell with enough force to sting.

Garrison glanced up moments before he made it under an aw-ning. A bolt of lightning arced like a spider web across the clouds. He couldn't help noticing how much it resembled the foreboding en-trance to the Tesla Gates. In an instant, an idea struck him. What if he could kill two birds with one stone?

In the course of eliminating dissenters, he could also see if the Tesla Gate would get rid of Impals in their current dark form. He could use the condemned dissenter as bait. It would have to be done quietly though. If it leaked, it would destroy any form of plausible de-niability. He was deep in thought as they entered the building. Gar-rison ignored greetings, respectful applause, and the offering of dry towels. He walked straight to the nearest conference room, entered by himself, and then locked the door behind him. He would have to think this over.

"Thank you God for giving me this insight," he muttered under his breath as lightning flashed outside. The thunder followed with an ominous "*You're welcome.*" At least, it's what President Garrison heard in his head.

Cecil's heart leapt into his throat as headlights flashed behind him, casting small shadows on the far wall. They gathered as close to the window as they dared. It was almost completely dark outside and the howling wind competed with the whispers of the dark. Burt was glassy eyed, but he smiled with triumphant vindication as the SUV driven by Musial bounced up the road. It came to an abrupt and jerky stop in front of the cabin.

"I tffld yof he wouff come bath," Burt muttered.

A chill ran down their collective spines. Not because of the dark souls, the presence of the ominous storm or even Musial's unexpected return. This sudden shared horror was due to Burt's slurred speech.

He sounded like Andrews after a six pack or two. He sounded much, much worse.

This new worry overshadowed any joy they may have felt by Musial's return. It may have taken him twenty-four hours, but he came through and came through in a big way. Every canister was filled to the brim.

"I say, what a welcome," Musial said stepping in the door as lightning and thunder simultaneously cracked.

"You better hurry," Derrick said. "We only have a few hours of gas left in the genny."

"Well, it's very nice to see you too," Musial said with a sarcastic sneer, and then he turned to Cecil.

"You have no idea what I had to go through to get this. It is as if every soul has disappeared from the planet. The damned pumps don't work if there is no electricity and I couldn't find a single gas station within fifty miles of here with power."

"Then how did you . . ." Cecil began but Musial cut him off.

"How did I get it? Well major, I may be a dark soul seeking redemption for my wicked ways. Nevertheless, I am not above borrowing, especially if lives are at stake."

"You stole it?" Sally asked.

Musial seemed hurt. "Why my dear, I merely accepted an involuntary charitable donation to save your lives, nothing more."

Cecil grinned and glanced at Derrick. He was surprised to find a smile creasing his face as well.

"Thanf yof Mufal," Burt stammered.

Cecil knew he needed help, but there was nothing any of them could do for him. Even if Musial could drive him to the base, there was no way Burt would make it through the woods alive. There were too many dark shadows.

Musial turned and jogged into the driving rain where he retrieved one of the gas cans from the back of the SUV. Lightning struck somewhere nearby, but he didn't seem to notice as he toted the can around the corner of the house. The sound following the lightning was quite unusual. It was like an ocean wave folding back in on itself at ten times speed. The dark souls hated the radiance from the lightning and they were temporarily driven back into the woods.

A few minutes later, Musial filled the tank. He walked back around front, setting the empty gas can under the covered front porch before coming back inside.

"Well even if this damned storm lasts all night, there is enough gas in the generator to last at least another day. There is plenty more where that came from," he said, pointing over his shoulder at the SUV.

"Thank you, Musial," Cecil said and extended his hand.

Musial regarded him for a few moments, then reached out and shook his hand. "You are welcome, major," he said.

This brought on an uncomfortable silence which Derrick soon broke. "I would suggest we gather up all flashlights, lanterns and such. We may be on a generator, but all it would take is one good strike to blow it out."

Cecil and Derrick gathered the lights and arranged them on the coffee table in the middle of the room. Musial sat back in the same chair where they had tied him up and propped his feet on a small end table and watched. After they counted six high beam flashlights, five camping lanterns, and three penlight flashlights, Musial gave a snort of laughter. "If the lights go out in here, do you think that is going to be enough to hold back the dark?" he chided.

Cecil ignored him as he walked back to the sofa and knelt beside Barbara. Musial shrugged and then stared out the window.

"How is she?" Charlotte asked as she bent over the back of the sofa and touched Barbara's forehead.

"No change," Cecil said. "I guess no news is good news."

"She'll be fine," Charlotte said. "I know she will."

They both had the uncomfortable feeling of someone watching them. They turned and saw Sally staring at them from the adjacent love seat. Burt's head was on her shoulder and she lovingly stroked his hair. His expression was vacant.

Cecil tried to give her a reassuring smile, yet he was not very convincing. She could see the fear and worry in his eyes. Sally ducked her head and kissed Burt on top of the head as tears rolled down her cheeks.

Nobody noticed the rain had stopped and there was an eerie quite outside. Even the whispers of the dark were absent. Musial noticed. He got up and walked out on the front porch. He stood still and silent for several long moments, before cocking his head to one side as if he were trying to hear a distant noise. He heard it seconds before everyone else did. A low dull roar in the distance, like the approach of a freight train. Cecil stood up and ran to the door. The roar slowly grew louder. Cecil almost fell down as Musial turned and ran back into the house. Everyone stared in disbelief as he began flipping furniture over and tossing a flashlight or a lantern under each one.

"Cecil, damn it, we have to move her!" Musial shouted as he grasped Barbara around the shoulders and motioned for Cecil to take her feet.

Under normal circumstances, Cecil would not have approved of Musial touching his wife. These weren't normal circumstances. There was no time to argue. He sprinted back and took her feet as they sat her on the floor and gently turned the sofa on top of her.

"What is it?" Charlotte shrieked as the roar grew louder.

"It's a damned tornado!" Musial shrieked. "One of those bastards killed me before and I have no intention of letting it happen again!"

CHAPTER 27

PROPER INTRODUCTIONS

"Mary, Mary quite contrary ..."
~English nursery rhyme

GESTAS AWAKENED IN RUTH'S BODY refreshed in the physical sense. The rightful owner of the geriatric physique still cowered in the background. The old woman was afraid to speak, afraid to act, and afraid to remind him she was still there. He knew she was there and, in spite of his nature, he left her alone. He still did not know the poor woman's name nor did he find it important. He did think it important to learn some etiquette tips from her. She did not come right out and tell him. He could sense her reaction, good or bad, to his actions. It had been a long time since he worried about such things as social etiquette. Of course, even when he was alive, it was not important to him.

The one thing he could sense from the old woman is, despite her flaws, she was an honest person. To continue a relationship with Rebekah and Malakhi would he need to be completely honest with them? Tell them he was not an old lady named Ruth, but rather a two thousand year old man searching for redemption? The only real question was how and where to deliver this shocking news.

Gestas thought of surprising them with breakfast in bed. He could talk to them in private after the others left for the chow line. Yet, when he sensed awkwardness from his host, he reconsidered his plan. For now, he would keep his distance and give them some breathing room.

Gestas got up and left the tent, making his way towards the growing crowd of hungry refugees. The chow line was not out in the open today. Instead, it was now inside a large tent the soldiers erected overnight. This seemed more practical, especially since there were darkening clouds in the distance. Could there be rain on the way? If so, it would be the first rain in weeks, maybe even a month. The distant rumble of thunder affirmed the probability.

When he reached the line it stretched about twenty yards outside of the tent. A couple of soldiers took pity and ushered him inside. He couldn't help grinning as a thought flashed through his mind.

"I could get used to being an old lady."

The grin evaporated when the bizarre nature of his notion sunk in. His masculine side couldn't get used to it, not one bit.

He filled his plate and took a seat at a bench table near the tent wall. He sat and ate, taking pleasure in act and taste. He had eaten in the old woman's body, but this was the first time he was able to just sit and savor the eating experience. For a moment, he had no worries about salvation or keeping his eye on a mother and son. He smiled and relished the pure physical enjoyment. He remembered how much he adored figs and pomegranates when he was alive. By his good fortune, figs were on the menu this morning.

He was thinking about his life when another rumble of thunder made chills run through him. His memory flashed to the day he died, the day he paid the ultimate price for his transgressions. There was thunder that day as well, but not like any thunder heard before or since. It was angry thunder. Each rumble seemed as if the sky wanted to shake the world apart. As he hung outside of Jerusalem and stared at his friend, Dismas, the rumbling shook them from side to side, adding to their agony. He remembered how he felt. Even though he was in extreme physical agony, he was also angry. Not at his accusers, his victims, or even his executioners. He was angry with Dismas.

Dismas had added insult to injury by betraying him, when he sided with the other criminal who hung with them. He berated Gestas for his insolence and told him he deserved to die and this other man didn't. Perhaps it was true, this other man had committed no murder or thievery. In fact, his one and only crime was so ludicrous it was almost laughable. But still . . . was it any reason to shun the one true friend who had watched out for you for years? All because of the absurd claim made by this man, the claim that he was the King of the Jews? A thought surfaced in his mind, one he never considered before. Perhaps the man was who he said he was. He was not in the dark void and neither was Dismas. Maybe, Dismas's last act of repentance saved him. Gestas felt a new hope rising within. Maybe he had done enough. Perhaps nothing else was required for redemption. Something told him this was not the case. He was not free yet, somehow he could sense that. He would spend the rest of the day thinking about it, and then he would tell Rebekah and Malakhi tonight. Deep down he was afraid of what the consequences would be if they were not supportive. Would he be able to contain his dark nature?

Jack opened his eyes and sat up. Why was someone knocking? He was in a prison for God's sake. As he opened his eyes he heard a muffled voice calling his name. An instant later, the latch in his door turned. With a deep grating of metal, the door swung open. His rage flared when he saw Donna entering the room. A beefy guard followed close behind. With a surge of energy, Jack flew from the bed. He hurled himself at Donna, wrapping his hands around her throat.

He felt her trachea collapsing beneath his thumbs when a brilliant flash of pain stabbed his ribs. The beefy guard booted him off of the tiny girl, sending him rolling. He slammed into the cell wall by his bed. Jack was stunned, but soon regained his focus. He was about to go after Donna again when he felt a sharp sting as if an unseen fist punched him. Every muscle in his body seized, causing Jack to collapse on the floor in the fetal position. He could not move. If he had been able to move, he would have seen the guard standing over him holding a Taser gun.

"Freeze you bloody bastard!" he said and then erupted into a high-pitched belly laugh.

While his body was paralyzed, his mind was not. He thought about all the ways he would kill both of them. Jack saw Donna kneel down in front of his face and place her hand on his cheek. If he could only move . . .

She spoke in a calm and sweet voice. "Jack, it's okay . . . I just need to talk to you for a minute," she cooed.

Donna glanced up at the guard and he shrugged. "Don't know why I'm doing this . . . both of you are eerie as hell," he muttered.

"You know exactly why you are doing this," she said, batting her eyes seductively.

The guard laughed and gave her a sly wink. "He should be out for about fifteen minutes," he said, tapping Jack's paralyzed leg with his boot. "When you get done, I expect at least fifteen minutes out of *you*."

"Is that all?" she said with a pouty frown.

He gave her a creepy grin and then stepped outside, closing the door with a loud clang. The instant the door shut, her countenance of a randy seductress faded to one of disgust. She would have to find some way to get out of her promise, but she would think about it later. Now, she needed to talk to Jack.

"Jack," she whispered, leaning close to his face, "I want you to know I did not tell on you . . . they just knew."

He rolled his eyes and tried to open his mouth to bite her face, but his body would not cooperate with his rage.

"Listen, I need to be upfront with you. I need you to know who I am. If I tell you and you believe I had no part in turning you over, maybe we can be friends again."

"We never were friends you stupid moron!" he thought to himself, yet her identity intrigued him. Donna wasn't who she said she was. His curiosity tempered his rage a little. He stopped moving his eyes and focused on her.

She took a deep breath while rubbing his head. Her eyes dropped to the floor as she spoke. "My name is not Donna. I don't even know what this poor girl's real name is," she said as she patted her face.

He kept his eyes trained on her as she continued to stare at the floor with her hand on his head. He felt an encouraging sign as he wiggled a couple of toes. It wouldn't be long before he could spring to life and strangle her.

Donna explained how she hoped to gain redemption by possessing the body of this wretched drug addict. The young teenage runaway was passed out in a dark alley when the eye of the storm arrived.

"If I hadn't been in the right place at the right moment, this young girl would be dead right now. I guess that is something positive I have done," she explained, and then paused as she rubbed a tear from her eye. "She is still here; I can feel her in the back of my mind. She is scared to death, but at least she is sober for the first time in a long while."

Jack moved his leg slightly.

"You better spit it out because I'm about to kill you!" Jack thought. He was almost able to move his lips with the words in his head.

He found her explanation pretty far-fetched . . . dark souls seeking redemption? True enough, there were dark souls. He had communed with them in dark places, gaining more of a comforting feeling than anything terrible or evil. He also saw their handiwork and admired their creativity, especially with what they did to the old lady in his cage. Yet . . . dark souls possessing someone? No one possessed him. He was who he had been for the last twenty-six years and nobody or no dark soul had changed him. Besides, for what did he need redemption or atonement? He had done nothing wrong. He performed a service to society and so what if he enjoyed it. Weren't you supposed to take pleasure in your work?

After Donna explained everything about dark souls and redemption, she forced herself to look into his eyes. She was noticeably shaken when she saw his maniacal rage still etched on his face. One of his legs moved a little. She turned her gaze back to the floor again. Still, she kept a wary peripheral eye on him.

"They know I can move about in the dark, Jack. That's why they are keeping me in a cell down the hall, but . . ." she paused and shifted her weight as she rose to her feet. "They don't know who I really am and I have no intention of telling them. I want you to be the only one to know, Jack."

One of his arms began to twitch and she took a couple of steps back.

"My name . . . when I was alive . . . was Mary," she said as his other arm began to move. She took a couple more steps toward the door.

"My full name was Mary Tudor and then I became Mary I, the Queen of England for a time after my father and half-brother died."

She watched Jack as he tried to struggle to his hands and knees. The clicking of the lock echoed through the cell as the guard entered. Before the door swung open, she said one final thing. Contempt and shame dripped from her voice.

"They called me Bloody Mary."

The world inside the cabin seemed to move in slow motion as the roar of the tornado reached a deafening pitch. Instinct took over as everyone scrambled for cover.

Cecil climbed under the flipped sofa with Barbara. He covered her with his body before pulling it on top of them. A moment later, he realized his mistake as the darkness engulfed them. He heard Barbara moan before his own nightmare returned. The snakes attacked with a vengeance. They bit and slithered, while they whispered their suggestions. He didn't care about anything other than getting away or dying, there were no other options. He was no longer aware of the terror now barreling down on them.

Cecil slammed his head as hard as he could against the sofa. In his mind, he was back in the canoe which had flipped over, trapping him in a nest of water moccasins. He had received about his thirtieth snakebite when there was a bright flash and he was back under the couch with Barbara. Her face now grimaced with terror. The thing was, he could see, really see everything. A couple of lanterns and a flashlight now flanked them, giving off their glowing shield of protection. He winced and grasped Barbara tighter as screams and yells of their companions erupted from outside. It was a hellish sound mixed with the maddening howl of the tornado. His friends were still out there and he was helpless to do anything to save them. All he could do was protect his wife and hang on.

The sofa rattled as if a giant hand was shaking it back and forth. Cecil hung on for dear life. Bits of debris and glass blew through the open areas between the sofa and the floor. They cut his arms and a large shard of glass embedded in his leg. He hung on, covering Barbara and uttering a silent prayer over and over. After an eternity, the noise dissipated leaving only eerie silence.

Cecil squinted as he was blinded by a warm trickle of blood into his eye. When his eyes adjusted, he could see light streaming in from outside. It was not artificial light, it was bright sunlight. He looked down at Barbara; the terrified expression was still there, but not quite as harsh. He kissed her on the forehead and then reached up with the shirtsleeve of his left arm. He wiped away his blood on her face. He then pressed his sleeve against his forehead to stop the bleeding from his head wound.

Once her face was clean, he rose up, pushing the sofa up with his back. A sharp pain in his leg caused his body to tense. He landed on Barbara with a huff. He reached down and found the glass shard sticking out of his leg and jerked it out. To his relief, it had only penetrated about an inch into his flesh, however the pain radiated all the way to the bone. He took deep breaths until the pain subsided. Gingerly, he began to push up again. The pain came back, but he gritted his teeth. The sofa rose in the air, spilling in an abundance of sunlight. With his uncut left arm, he pushed it over.

A sudden bizarre thought ran through his mind as shielded his eyes from the light. He thought of The Wizard of Oz when Dorothy disappeared in a dark tornado, only to find herself in the bright and colorful land of Oz. The tornado was gone, the storm was gone, and pure sunlight streamed in, yet something wasn't right. Even on the brightest sunny days, there was not this much light in the cabin. Some artificial light was still required to keep the shadows at bay. When Cecil finally looked up the reality hit him like a cold wave. The roof of the cabin was gone. The wall was gone as well, he might as well be sitting outside on a hardwood floor. Glass and debris were scattered all about him and stretched as far as he could see to the woods and beyond.

Cecil hoisted himself up and sat down on the couch. He wiped blood and sweat out of his eyes and looked about the room. Running on pure adrenaline, he bounced to his feet. Oblivious to the pain in his leg, Cecil bellowed a single horrified and sorrowful shriek.

CHAPTER 28

THE AFTERMATH

"To absent friends ..."
~Anonymous

STEFFANIE GARRISON SAT in an upstairs window of the White House watching the storm clouds in the distance. The welcoming sunshine beaming through a break in the clouds was akin to the way she felt at the moment. Her grandfather had left the premises and would be gone for a while. She relaxed for the first time since making the phone call to her grandfather a few days ago. A decision she now regretted more than anything.

She had made a new friend in Carmella. They were going to meet in the kitchen for dinner later. She still didn't understand why she wouldn't help her get away and search for her parents.

If her grandfather did anything right, it was shielding her from the atrocities surrounding them. He kept her confined as the corpses were being scooped up around the Executive residence. As she sat in the window, she could hear the sounds of heavy equipment in the distance. For all she knew in her twelve year old brain, they could be building a new theme park rather than scooping up decaying remains. She had no clue what reality existed a few blocks from her. She witnessed the chaos and the death from the window of her grandfather's house, yet she still had no concept of its scope.

Steff wanted to leave, she wanted to run away, and she wanted things to be the way they were before. She was scared. She also trusted Carmella. This trust was the one positive thing she had going for her.

She looked forward to their dinner tonight and decided she didn't want to wait another couple of hours; she would go and find her now. Steff slid down from her seat and slipped out the door. Carmella had told her to stay put until she came for her. She didn't consider it a real demand, as when her grandfather told her to stay put. The one time she disobeyed him, she regretted it. The massacre in Lafayette Square was like the remnant of an unforgettable nightmare.

She walked down the hall, passing several staffers and Secret Service agents. They either gave her a curt nod or ignored her altogether. Steff was glad they didn't try and corral her back into her room. She descended the stairs and was surprised to find the great entrance hall deserted. When she didn't hear any voices, she retreated up one floor and stepped into the center hall. To her left were the library and Vermeil room. She was about to go that way when she heard voices to her right. She turned and headed toward the far end of the hallway with her head cocked, listening for familiar voices. As Steff passed the China Room and the Diplomatic Reception Room, the voices got louder. She could tell it was several people, both men and women. By the time she passed the Map Room, she knew the voices were coming from a closed office door about twenty feet in front of her on the left. As she approached the door, she almost knocked. A single word stayed her hand:

"*Garrison.*"

It was a man's voice. As she pressed herself against the wall, she heard a woman respond, it was Carmella.

"For God's sake, would you keep your voice down! His granddaughter is here . . . do you want her to hear?" she said.

"What . . . are you afraid she's going to tell her grandpappy?" a deep male voice snapped.

"Of course not!" Carmella hissed. "But he is her grandfather and she is a little girl, show some consideration!"

"We don't have time for consideration!" another man interjected. "The old bastard is not here and he took his cronies with him. If we are going to act then we need to do it now!"

"He is at Quantico and we are here. Just what the hell do you intend to do?" a woman asked.

"I think a well-placed bomb would do nicely," the man responded.

"What . . . you intend to blow the Oval Office to hell and destroy hundreds of years of history?" the woman chirped.

"Better that then let him destroy this country and perhaps the rest of the world with it!" a man yelled. Steff didn't need to put her ear close to the door now.

"I told y'all to keep your damn voices down!" Carmella said in a hoarse whisper. "You dumb asses are going to cut your own throats and this will be over before it begins!"

A new voice entered the conversation, a deep male voice. It not only projected authority, but a soothing calmness as well. "We must be prudent above all else," the man said. "This house, and the presidency, mean a lot to the American people. This could end up being as detrimental as everything this accursed storm brought with it. Besides, it is foolish to burn down your house to kill a cockroach . . . and that is, after all, what we are talking about here."

There was a smattering of laughter from the others in the room.

"You are right, Mr. Midkiff," Carmella said. "We must be sensible with our actions."

There was a pause for several moments before the man with the golden voice continued. "Why don't we return to our normal duties for now and consider this carefully. Let's meet back here at 9 PM, shall we?"

There was a faint mumbling and the creaking of furniture on the old hardwood floors as everyone got up. Steff was in a trance when she heard the group's plans for her Grandfather. She was so lost in thought, she almost forgot where she was. They would be coming through the door any second. She came to her senses a few seconds before the door clicked open. Steff had barely enough time to scamper into the Map Room. She almost rolled underneath a large camel back sofa before she heard the excitement of the darkness beneath. Instead, she quickly scooted to a fully lit and obscured corner behind it.

Steff heard voices and footsteps pass, but never saw anyone because she curled up into a tight ball with her back to the door. She lay there trembling for several minutes. When she was sure everyone had moved on, she climbed out and took a seat in a large armchair by the fireplace.

Tears streamed down her cheeks as she tried to process all the feelings flowing through her. The thought of her Granddad blown to pieces horrified her. She also felt betrayed because the woman she trusted, the woman who was her friend, was plotting with the others to kill him. But the thing tearing at her heart more than anything was, deep down, she agreed with them. This made her feel ashamed. Yes, she believed her grandfather had done some terrible things, and yes, she believed he needed to be stopped. But, blowing him up? There must be another way.

Her tears flowed harder because she knew there was no reasoning with him. She had seen his stubbornness and arrogance first-hand. Anything short of God himself showing up in a flaming chariot telling him to stop would have no effect on the man. He was her grandfather and this single fact made it almost impossible to see the full reality of the situation. She just couldn't bring herself to condemn him.

Steff covered her eyes with the palms of her hands as she sobbed. "Stop being such a little girl!" she told herself. "You turned your family in because you didn't want to live in a stupid cabin, because you wanted a clean bed and better food. Well . . . you've got it now, how does it feel you stupid little girl?"

Whatever maturity she had in her, pinned her predicament squarely on her own shoulders. Her dilemma would have been difficult enough for the most mature adults. She didn't think it was possible to hold so much love and so much hate for one person at the same time. Her aching heart, churning stomach, and tortured soul were a testament.

She began to cry harder as images of her parents crossed her mind. They were hiding out like a bunch of rats in a hole. However, she knew the logical scenario suggested if they were hiding in dark places, they were dead now. She cried harder.

Steff was so lost in her own misery, she almost jumped out of her skin when she felt a hand on her shoulder. She looked up, blinking through a murky film of tears. Her heart sank to the floor when she saw Carmella standing over her.

Cecil shrieked again as he bolted from the couch. He tripped over a pile of debris causing him to sprawl headlong across the cluttered floor. He felt sharp stabbing pains on the palms of his hands. His hands slid out from under him as if he touched something slick. He brushed his hands on his shirt, leaving long streaks of blood flecked with shards of glass and wood. His palms continued to ooze blood.

Under normal circumstances, he would have stopped, cleaned, and dressed his wounds. Not today. He got back to his feet and then trudged to where outside the wall stood minutes earlier. He stepped forward, hopping two feet to the ground below. He knelt down and checked for a pulse on Derrick. Cecil already knew the answer his touch confirmed. It was grotesquely obvious. A jagged piece of wood protruded from his abdomen. Cecil couldn't tell if the blood soaked object was from a tree or a part of the house. It did not matter. Shards of glass, small branches, and even a picture frame protruded from his body. They penetrated deep into his flesh, demonstrating the sheer power of the twister.

Cecil stood up, wiping tears and blood from his eyes. "Burt! Sally! Charlotte!" he yelled.

He paused, listening with bated breath. His heart hammering in his ears made it difficult to hear. A moment later, he heard muffled shouts. They were coming from the kitchen. His initial adrenaline rush was starting to wear off and the pain of his injured leg was beginning to throb. He limped to the kitchen as fast as he could. Musial stood beside the kitchen table. A pile of rubble covered it. Musial had one arm stuck inside the pile and he beamed at Cecil with satisfaction.

"Glad to see you're no worse for wear, major," he said pleasantly.

"What the hell are you doing Musial? Where are the others?"

Musial smirked and shifted his wait as if he were trying to adjust for comfort. "Burt and Sally are under here," he huffed.

"Then what the hell are you doing?"

"I'm keeping my dark companions away from them until you can pull this debris off. Do you think you can move it, major?"

The realization of what Musial was doing sank in; he was holding a light for them.

Cecil didn't waste any time as he hobbled across the room and began to pitch debris out the open wall. After several minutes, Burt and Sally emerged with bleary eyes. Aside from a few superficial cuts and bruises, they seemed uninjured. Cecil's heart sank when Burt spoke.

"Whe ah we?" Burt asked.

Cecil patted Burt on the shoulder, hugged Sally, and then turned to Musial. "How did you make it through?"

Musial smiled and pointed at the pantry door which was standing ajar on twisted hinges. It was near the center of the house. Aside from the hinges, it seemed one of the few places free of damage.

"Where is Charlotte?" Musial asked.

Cecil's heart sank. His faced flushed as he limped back into the living room.

It took a half hour before they found her. Musial tackled Cecil to prevent him from rushing into the woods. She was lying motionless in a dark area of the forest, a short distance away.

Musial entered the woods and soon returned cradling Charlotte's lifeless body. He lay her down in the grass and Cecil knelt beside her. What he saw was shocking. Not from the grotesque nature of Charlotte's body, but from the absence of it. There was not a scratch, bruise, or mark anywhere on her. It was as if she were in a deep and breathless sleep.

"Was it the dark or the tornado?" Cecil asked as he touched her cheek.

"Well, I'm pretty sure the tornado put her out here, but beyond that I do not know." Musial said and then frowned before continuing. "It is not like them to be this gentle."

"What the hell did it matter anyway?" Cecil thought to himself. "The tornado, the dark . . . Charlotte is still dead and nothing will change that."

Cecil stood up, a sharp pain ran through his leg and it almost buckled. His stomach twisted when he turned back toward the house. This was the first time he had taken in the whole cabin at one time.

The upstairs was gone. The bottom of the staircase, two external walls, and three internal walls were all that remained of the downstairs. Horror suffocated him when he checked the side of the house where the generator rested. It was gone. They had lost two people, but the even colder reality was none of them would survive the night without the generator. He glanced at his watch and noted it was a little over three hours until sunset. Only three hours until they all joined their absent friends.

CHAPTER 29

THE TRAIL THROUGH HELL

"Curiosity is natural to the soul of man and interesting objects have a powerful influence on our affections."
~Daniel Boone

GESTAS WAITED IN THE TENT for Rebekah and Malakhi to return. He felt he must tell them the truth. He believed it was not only the right thing to do to help them; it was also the right thing to do to quell some of his old desires. He couldn't control it forever.

Mother and son arrived from the mess hall a little after dusk. Gestas had bathed and managed to procure a new dress along with a pair of sandals. In fact, he had stolen them from a woman on the far side of camp. He guessed if it was his worst sin thus far he was doing okay. He felt odd about putting on women's clothing, though it was not much different from the robes he wore in life.

Gestas also found a folding chair and set it against the far wall of the tent. The geriatric body he inhabited was no longer able to sit in and get up off the floor.

"Hello," he said pleasantly as they entered the tent. "Did you have a good dinner?"

They stopped in their tracks and stared. Rebekah thought the old woman was a bit off her rocker, but this sudden presentation was completely out of character.

"Yes," she said. "Why?"

"Just asking . . . did you have pomegranates? I adore them."

"No, Malakhi is allergic to them. We had some apples, bananas, and lintel beans."

"*Great, of all the food I could have brought up, the kid has to be allergic to it,*" Gestas thought to himself. However, he did not let it dissuade him. He was determined.

"I wanted to apologize for my behavior the past couple of days. It's been quite an ordeal. I think I have been in a little bit of shock," he said. "I'm starting to get over it now."

Rebekah smiled, putting Gestas a little more at ease. "Yes it has," she agreed. "I haven't been as friendly as I could have either."

"You have been great!" Gestas said. "I am glad I found the two of you."

They chatted for an hour while Malakhi rested on his mat and flipped through a picture book. Rebekah had indeed warmed up to the man masquerading as an old woman. She was starting to have second thoughts about her first impression. Gestas sensed this and decided now was the appropriate time.

"Do you know what the darkness is?" he asked.

Rebekah shrugged. She thought she did. Their brief encounter in the hallway when the menorah dropped exposed them. In her mind, they were devils and nothing more.

"Maybe," she said glancing around, wondering where the other women were. "I think they are tayvls or lapitut," she said using the Yiddish word for devils and demons.

As hard as he tried to suppress it, Gestas chuckled. "No . . . no my dear, nothing so extreme," he chortled. "Although I do see why you might think so."

She glared at him, her jaw starting to clench along with her fists. In spite of their recent rapport, she was starting to feel uncomfortable again. She didn't appreciate his patronizing laughter.

"Well then . . . why don't you explain it to me," she snapped.

He felt his face reddening. Was it embarrassment? It was an emotion he had not experienced in two thousand years, and only on rare occasions.

"I'm sorry . . . I didn't mean to offend," he said. It surprised him how easy the apology flowed. To the best of his recollection, he had never apologized for anything in his life.

Rebekah did not answer. She scooted closer to Malakhi and put his head in her lap, keeping her eyes fixed on Gestas.

"Your interpretation of the dark might not be far from the truth," Gestas said, staring at the floor with forced humility. "We are tayvls I suppose, in one form or another."

"What do you mean 'we'?" Rebekah asked, tightening her grip on her son. Malakhi grunted and went back to his book.

Gestas seemed startled, he did not intend to use that pronoun, at least not yet. He leaned forward and stared at the ground, clasping his hands together as if in prayer. In a calm, peaceful voice, he told her the true nature of the dark and his own history. When he finished, he looked up at her, expecting to see horrified incredulity on her face. Instead, he saw something else. She was upset, yet she seemed curious.

"So, you are saying you were one of the men crucified with the prophet who claimed to be the Messiah?" she asked skeptically.

"Yes," Gestas said.

"Well . . . was he the Messiah?" she asked, this time with a little more curiosity than skepticism.

Gestas shrugged. "I don't know. I have been part of the dark void since that day. All I can tell you is my friend, Dismas, and this Messiah were not in the void. I'm sure of it."

Rebekah paused and frowned. Several emotions danced across her face at once. "So you expect me to believe you are some kind of dark soul who possessed a poor old lady in an attempt at redemption?"

"That's the truth," Gestas said calmly.

Rebekah started to rise to her knees, pulling Malakhi along with her. It was as if Gestas was a venomous snake about to strike at any second. She wanted to get away before given a chance to bite.

"I don't believe you!" she shouted when she reached her feet. "You're just some crazy old lady who needs help!"

Rebekah turned to dart out the door with Malakhi, but a sudden jolt sent her sprawling backwards, landing on her butt. Malakhi cried out in pain as he hit the ground and his mother rolled on top of him. She sat up, dazed and blinking, expecting to see a brick wall. Instead, she saw the heavy set woman who had shared their tent the past few days. A wave of relief washed over Rebekah, now she had an ally, a quite solid ally, in the event Gestas tried to do something.

"Oh thank God!" Rebekah said. "Help us out of here!" she pleaded, holding her hand up to the woman.

The woman kept her eyes fixed on her for several moments before she spoke.

"He's telling the truth, honey," the woman said.

Rebekah's wave of relief turned to a wave of ice.

The woman glanced at Gestas and shook her head while clucking her tongue.

"Why the hell did you have to tell them, Gestas?" she hissed. "Now we're going to have to kill them."

Seconds after the cell door slammed with a deafening clang, Jack was able to get to his feet. He stumbled toward the door, slamming his shoulder into it as if he intended to knock it off its hinges.

"Bitch!" he screamed and peered out the small window.

He couldn't see anyone, but to his right he did see shadows moving as if people were walking down the hall. The hallway was darker than it was the last time he checked. There was a large window to his left, at the west end of the hall, facing a grove of elm trees. The shadows of dusk stretched down the hall like a taut rubber band, threatening to break and surrender to the dark as the sun went down. Jack was on the verge of breaking himself.

He shook the residual cobwebs from his head, and kicked the cot, causing it to lurch sideways with a metallic squeak.

"The stupid nutter is crazier than I thought," he muttered to the room. "I'm going to rip out her bloody throat!"

Jack burst into laughter over the irony of her statement. "Bloody Mary," he spat. "What kind of a fool does she think I am?"

Although he found her story humorous, he could not bring himself to relish in the humor. A part of him had its doubts. Could she be telling the truth? All the times in the darkness he felt at ease as if a warm blanket embraced him. However, that wasn't quite accurate; it was more like a web. Similar to a spider's edifice, individual threads made up the whole of the dark. They coalesced into a single minded purpose of malignancy. There were individuals there; he knew it because he sensed them. This sudden realization made him question his skepticism of Donna's story. It still didn't change the fact he wanted to kill her.

Jack lay down on his cot and tried to get some sleep because he expected another night of loud music and flickering lights. His anticipation proved correct as his lights switched off thirty minutes later. Michael Bolton would be the music of choice for the night.

As Cecil surveyed the damage, he turned in the direction of Derrick's body. His legs were just visible protruding from behind a pile of rubble. He looked back down at Charlotte. Her pale and peaceful expression made his heart ache.

"We've got to bury them. We at least owe them that much," Cecil said, glancing at Musial, but not making eye contact.

"Damn it man . . . are you giving up? We don't have time. It is going to be dark in about three hours," Musial shouted.

"That gives us plenty of time and then . . ." Cecil said.

"And then, what?" Musial interrupted. "Die yourself?"

Cecil's cheeks flushed as he rounded on Musial. "I don't know what the hell you want from me. The cabin and generator are gone. We have no way to produce any light at all except for some cheap ass lanterns and flashlights. Outside of a sudden air rescue or the eye of the storm passing, I don't see any hope, do you?"

Musial gave him a knowing smile. It made Cecil want to punch him in the nose, until he saw that Musial was not looking at him, but past him. Cecil glanced over his shoulder.

At first he didn't comprehend. There were the woods and a huge downed pine tree. He couldn't see anything else until he took two steps to the side and looked from Musial's angle. A feeling of hope washed over him.

The tornado was devastating. It destroyed their cabin and genera-tor, yet in the process it also cut a jagged path through the woods. It was not a short patch, it was a long swath stretching for miles. The path was not clear, the remains of various sized trees littered it, but it was a path and it led all the way down to the main road. Cecil could see the gray asphalt and yellow lines of the road.

"My God," Cecil rasped. "We can leave, we can get out of here today."

"I don't think so," Musial said studying the path and then glancing at the SUV. "There's no way you can drive this down there. Walk yes, drive no."

"By the time we could get everyone together and carry Burt and Barbara down there, it would be about dark," Cecil observed.

"Exactly," Musial said. "There is no choice other than to wait until morning and try then."

"Are you crazy?" Cecil asked. "With no generator and no house, there won't be anyone left in the morning except for you."

"Why, major," Musial grinned. "You have everything you need."

Musial picked up a piece of wood that used to be part of the front porch. He pointed it at Cecil. "You have wood," he said and then pointed at the nearest gas can scattered in the yard. They had been tossed, but they were sealed and still filled to capacity. "You have gas," he said and tossed the board toward the cabin. "And I am sure we can find a match or a lighter," he paused again and said, "I'm sure you must have been a Boy Scout at one time, major. I am confident you can rub two sticks together."

The horror and the genius of the plan hit Cecil. It scared the hell out of him and it also gave him new hope. It just might work.

"How many bonfires do you think we'll need?" Cecil asked.

"Several," Musial said. "Let's get to it."

CHAPTER 30

THE TIP

"I pledge allegiance to the flag ..."
~American Pledge of Allegiance

THE RAIN FINALLY STOPPED pelting the window of the empty conference room where President Garrison sat. The storm spawned several tornadoes and his staff urged him to seek shelter in the bunker. He refused. God had brought him this far, God had shielded him from the dark. Did they really think something as trivial as a tornado could harm him? He sat and watched as the clouds began to dissipate. A few rays of sun shone through, penetrating the semi-darkness of the room. The shadows hissed in protest.

He took a moment from his deep meditation to offer a single taunt. "Take that you bastards," he said.

Garrison had been thinking about the three reasons they came to the base. This was the biggest base, with the highest number of refugees, and he wasn't sure if he could trust all the officers. Once he whipped them in line, or out of the way, he was sure the enlisted men would follow. The question was, how could he do it without appearing to act without discrimination? More important, how could he do it without getting his hands dirty?

Garrison considered individual interviews. Of course, it might seem sinister if the officer never returned from the conference. Perhaps something benign . . . a social gathering? He could talk to them one on one in a less threatening environment. Yes, that might work. What would the occasion be? There didn't seem to be anything to celebrate at the moment. He glanced around the room and noticed a calendar hanging on the far wall. A wry smile creased his face as he compared his watch to the date on the calendar. Today was Halloween, the grinning jack-o-lantern by the date confirmed this.

He hated Halloween since he was a child. Halloween was Satan's holiday, or so his father said. It was a belief passed down for several generations, a belief fostered by their family church. Cecil had grown up deprived when it came to Halloween fun. There was no candy allowed at the Garrison household let alone, a jack-o-lantern.

Garrison shook his head in disgust. This was the opportunity presented to him and if it served God, he would do it. There would be an impromptu Halloween party tonight for the officers, but it would be strict dress formal . . . no masks. Garrison wanted to see their true countenance to determine who to invite to the *after* party. He walked to the window and peered out across the parade grounds at the large hanger in the distance housing the Tesla Gate. A vacant smile crossed his face when he heard a knock at the door.

He turned to see his staff enter, except for Sebastian. He had demanded to inspect the cyber security at the base. With a great deal of reluctance, they admitted him to the mainframe building. Of course, his true intentions were not for security, he could care less. His true intent was to search for any dissent on the base. He was good at what he did, and if there was anything there, he would find it.

"What's the plan, sir?" Avery asked as he took a seat near Garrison.

He turned and regarded the group now scattered around the conference table, with Robby at one end and Joan at the other. He stepped forward and sat in the middle so they were an equal distance from him. Avery pulled his chair up beside Garrison and took a seat.

"As much as it pains me to say it, we're going to have a Halloween party," Garrison said with a grimace.

Robby had run out of cigars and he was now chewing on the tip of an ink pen. He began to tap it on the tabletop.

"A Halloween party? A costume party?" he asked.

"Now that would kind of defeat the purpose, wouldn't it?" Garrison said.

"You want to have a social gathering so you can get a read on who is with you and who is not," Avery said.

Garrison nodded.

"How will you know?" Joan asked.

"Oh, I'll know," Garrison said. "The Lord will guide me."

"So what are you going to do with the dissenters?" she asked.

"That's where you come in," Garrison grinned.

Joan scowled as comprehension dawned on her. "If you think I'm going to have sex with half the base, you're damn crazy! I may be good at my job, but I have my standards!"

Garrison let out a mirthful belly laugh, causing Avery and Robby to join him. They were not sure what they were laughing at.

"I'm not asking you to screw them to death!" Garrison guffawed. "Just make them think you are."

"You want me to make all them think it at one time?" Joan asked, knitting her brow.

"You stupid bitch," Robby said. "The president will let you know and you take them off one at a time."

Joan's stare at Robby suggested she wanted to rip his head off and use his skull as a gravy boat.

"I told you . . . I'm not screwing everybody! You all can go to hell!" she hissed.

"You really are stupid!" Robby laughed. "You lure them away and then you kill them. Take them in a room and turn the lights off . . . the dark does the work for you, badda-bing, badda-bang!"

If Robby Johns had known they would be his last words, he might have thought of something more profound to say.

Before anyone could react, Joan was on her feet. In one fluid motion she grabbed a nearby flag stand with a brass flora lee on top. She hurled it like an enraged javelin thrower at Robby. The top twelve inches of the staff penetrated his throat with a sickening crunch. A second later, there was a whooshing noise like someone letting the air out of a water logged balloon. Gurgling persisted for a few moments as air wheezed in and out of the wound from Robby's dying lungs. His eyes stared at Joan before clouding over with the vacant stare of death. The American flag draped his chest and the table top in a gruesome patriotic bib.

"Damn . . ." Avery muttered.

Garrison stared for several moments with mixed surprise and satisfaction. He shook his head and addressed Joan. "Well, are you going to clean this mess up?" he said, half tongue in cheek and half serious.

"How the hell are you going to explain this?" Avery demanded. "This kind of takes our subtle approach and tosses it out the damned window!"

"He was worthless anyway," Garrison muttered and got to his feet. He felt vulnerable remaining in a seated position with this raging woman nearby. Avery joined him by the window.

Joan huffed with rage, taking deep and rapid breaths. Her face twisted into a malicious scowl. Perhaps she was showing her true face, the face of her dark soul.

"Ms. Titsworth, I am glad you are on our side," Garrison said, beaming.

She made a move in their direction causing Avery to jump, but Garrison remained cool. She brushed the hair out of her eyes with one swipe of her hand and exhaled. "That'll teach him to piss me off," she said, her contorted features morphing back into a beautiful woman.

Garrison walked over and inspected the body. "He was definitely dead weight, but Avery is right . . . how the hell are we gonna explain this?"

"What do you care?" Joan retorted. "You're the damn president aren't you?"

"It's not that simple!" Avery said, doing his best to suppress a shout. "If one of the president's advisors was killed in a staff meeting, well I think we could lose a lot of credibility."

"Why don't you just introduce the lot of them to the dark and be done with it?" Joan snapped.

"Because we can't kill everybody, we need some of them to run this base and this country!" Garrison said.

"Make the arrangements for the party," Garrison said to Avery and then turned back to Joan.

"And you . . . you go get cleaned up and make yourself presentable for tonight," he said waving his finger.

The rage had not left her, not by a long shot. She turned and stormed out the door, slamming it hard behind her.

"Is she going to be a problem?" Garrison asked.

Avery shook his head. "No, she's loyal but . . . damn," he said grimacing at the bloody mess, which was Robby Johns.

"Yeah . . . damn," Garrison agreed. He said a silent prayer seeking forgiveness for his profanity.

Garrison and Avery managed to drag Robby's body into a small storage closet. They had a difficult time getting the door closed with the flagstaff protruding from his throat. The flora lee was hooked too far into his spine to pull it out. Avery unhooked the flag from the pole and used it to mop up the blood now starting to dry on the table and the carpet. Fifteen minutes later the room seemed normal to the casual observer.

"Why didn't we just tell them he wandered into the dark and he did it to himself?" Avery asked.

"Because they know. They know we can pass through the dark. They saw us all come in together when it was pitch dark. Remember the damned storm?" Garrison said. He wanted to finish it with 'idiot' or 'dumb ass' but he refrained. He had to get control of his troops back and insulting his second in command wouldn't help.

Avery left to go about party arrangements while Garrison went back to the window. He smiled at the large hangar silhouetted in front of the woods. He intended to perform some experiments tonight.

Steff felt as if her heart would pound out of her chest. Carmella had changed. In her eyes, she was no longer the caring and loving soul she came to trust. She wasn't any better than her grandfather.

"Get away from me!" Steff howled as she darted across the room and took refuge behind a large plant.

Carmella followed and stopped a few feet away. She held out her hands, palms up, in supplication. "Sweetheart, will you please listen to me a moment," she pleaded.

Steff wouldn't look at her, She sat behind the pot with her knees pulled close to her chest, rocking back and forth as if she was going to be sick. Carmella knew she may not want to listen, but she could still hear her. She was going to say what she needed to.

"Honey, believe me when I say that hurting anybody is the last thing I want," she said. Carmella took special care not to mention anything about killing.

Steff continued to stare at the floor.

"I want to make sure nobody gets hurt, but sweetheart . . . I know you understand your grandfather has done some bad things. He has to be stopped."

Steff's first impulse was the childish reaction of *'don't you talk about my grandpa.'* Nevertheless, she didn't have enough faith in her grandfather's benevolence. Instead, she glanced at Carmella and then continued her brooding. She knew he did some terrible things, some horrific things. Perhaps she could dismiss it out of hand as vicious lies told by his enemies, but she couldn't. She had seen it first-hand.

He gunned down several people in cold blood outside the White House. She tried to forget it, tried to tell herself it was only a bad dream. Deep down, she knew it wasn't. But kill him . . . blow him up? She didn't think she could have any part of it no matter what he had done. Locking him away in prison didn't seem very appealing either, but she could live with it. At least he would be alive. Maybe he could be rehabilitated?

"You said you were going to blow him up," Steff sobbed.

"No baby, I didn't say that. A man with a very big mouth said it. I think we need to arrest him and have a peaceful transition of power, the way it should be."

"Who?" Steff asked.

"I don't know, we'll have to work it out. Most of the people in the legal line of succession are dead."

"Did my grandpa do it?" Steff asked, her body trembling.

Carmella felt sick. She knew the answer to the question, yet she remained tactful for Steff's sake. "I don't know honey, I just don't know."

Steff frowned and turned away, feeling ashamed. She could read the answer on Carmella's face.

They remained in silence for a couple of minutes until Steff jumped to her feet. Without a word to Carmella, she ran out of the room, down the hallway, and up the stairs.

CHAPTER 31

THE SWITCH

"O, what a tangled web we weave when first we practice to deceive!"
~*Walter Scott*

THE WOMAN WAS ON TOP of Rebekah before she could scream. Pudgy hands clutched her neck and the thumbs pushed against her windpipe like two large walnuts.

"Momma! No . . . don't hurt her!" Malakhi pleaded.

Her son's cries began fading as unconsciousness dawned. She was going to die. All of a sudden, Rebekah felt a violent shake as the weight of the woman's rotund body and the pressure of her thumbs lifted. Air flowed back into her lungs in a shrill whistle as her damaged windpipe struggled to expand. She rolled on her side in time to see Gestas deliver a crushing blow with a folding wooden chair to the head of the fat woman. Her limbs turned to Jell-O and she collapsed in a heap.

Gestas had just raised the chair again to deliver another violent strike when Rebekah let out a whistling, "Noooo." He turned and glared at her, causing the little breath she had to leave her lungs in a single gasp of terror. For the first time, she saw the true countenance of Gestas, full of hate and fury. He seemed to be taking great delight in this violent act. She rolled over, trying to catch her breath again. If she had continued to watch, she would have seen disgust wash away all the satisfaction on Gestas's face. He caught himself at the last minute. The woman was dead. He dropped the chair and crawled to Rebekah's side.

Rebekah tried to get away, but she didn't have the air or the energy to do much more than emit an airless whimper. Malakhi cowered in the corner, staring at Gestas as if he were a hungry bear about to devour his mother.

"It's okay, Malakhi . . . I'm here to help," Gestas said as he raised Rebekah's head and shoulders, placing them in his lap.

The boy did not seem convinced by the assurances of this old woman. He scooted around the perimeter of the tent until he found a loose section. With the speed and agility of a rabbit, Malakhi squirmed under the wall of the tent and was gone.

Gestas stroked Rebekah's hair and leaned close to her face.

"You're son is running to get the soldiers. They will be here soon," he whispered. "You must listen to me and you must trust me."

Rebekah regarded him as if he were crazy. Whether she believed him or not, it was foolish to trust him. Besides, she didn't believe him. Ruth was just a crazy old woman. Either way, unless he changed her mind before the soldiers arrived, his chance for redemption would be gone. He would spend the rest of the storm in a stockade.

Gestas continued, "You know I am telling the truth because the dark soul inhabiting the woman confirmed it. I saved your life, please remember."

Rebekah's breathing was labored, but her throat was starting to open. "Why?" she wheezed.

"Because I'm sorry for what I have done and realize that my ignorance nurtured arrogance in me. It drove me to a life of hate and misery. It took two thousand years of living in a dark void with other arrogant souls to realize this. I just want redemption, a chance for salvation."

Rebekah shook her head as she took a deep and shuddering breath. "No . . . why us?" she asked.

Gestas said, "I'm not sure, a feeling . . . I can't explain it. When I saw you and Malakhi alone on the street, something inside told me to watch over you. I'll admit, it was hard at first. My dark nature was still there in the background, tempting me to return to my ways. I was able to resist because I felt different. Knowing what I know now . . . it is amazing how the removal of ignorance takes arrogance right along with it. Two millennia was quite an educational experience."

Rebekah continued to consciously push air in and out of her lungs. Her face was no longer one of a drowning woman. She was an exhausted woman, who had a lot to think about.

"Please, when the soldiers arrive . . . tell them the truth. Tell them I saved your life. Please don't tell them anymore."

The woman twitched, causing Gestas to jump, but it was a single movement. He reached over and checked her pulse. She was dead . . . probably a post mortem nerve impulse, but he wasn't taking any chances. He lowered Rebekah's head on a pillow. Her eyes rolled and she appeared to lose consciousness, but her breathing was steady. He placed an ear on her chest. She had a strong and steady heartbeat. Satisfied she was fine, he leaned over and whispered in her ear.

"I'll be right back, I have to check on something," he said and then crawled over and put his ear between the woman's shoulder blades. Her torso was as silent as a bag of flour. She was dead, there was no doubt.

"What happened to the dark soul inhabiting her?" he wondered.

Even though he was a dark soul himself, he had no answer for this question. This was new territory. He guessed it left her body and retreated to the dark shadows of the nearby woods.

"What happened to the soul of the woman?" was the next question in his mind. Again, he had no answer. He would assume she went wherever the Impals are now. He wasn't sure if that was a good or bad prospect, but it seemed the most logical explanation.

He had just crawled back to Rebekah when two soldiers burst through the flap of the tent, their weapons drawn.

"What the hell happened?" one of them demanded as he kept his weapon trained on Gestas and Rebekah while the other soldier checked the deceased woman.

Gestas put on his best, terrified old lady act as he explained the horrific events.

"I don't know what came over me," Gestas swooned. "I just grabbed the chair and swung . . . I don't know where the strength came from."

After pronouncing their former tent mate dead, the soldier moved over and checked on Rebekah.

"I think she'll be fine," he said. "A little bruising around the neck."

Rebekah was beginning to come around and the sat up groggily.

"You need to come with us to see the base physician," the soldier said as he slung his weapon over his shoulder.

Rebekah shook her head. "No," she croaked.

"Where's Malakhi, her son?" Gestas asked.

"He's safe. We can bring him back once we have everything squared away here," the soldier with the weapon said as he glanced at the woman's body.

"Can you tell us what happened, ma'am?" the other soldier said, addressing Rebekah.

Rebekah shrugged. "She went crazy and Ruth saved me," she said, pointing at Gestas.

"Do you know why?" the soldier asked.

"No," Rebekah said and lay back on her pillow. "I'm very tired; I want to rest for a moment."

"Sure you won't come see the doctor?" the soldier asked again.

Rebekah shook her head and then closed her eyes.

The soldiers worked as quietly as they could, zipping the woman up in a body bag. They tried to be discreet as they carried her through the tents to a makeshift morgue on the other side of camp.

A peppering of gasps and screams filled the night air as the soldiers toted the body through the maze of tents. As it turned out, this was not the only death in the camp; there were three others, each with mysterious circumstances. They were killed by someone claiming self-defense. It could have been a coincidence. After all, this camp was sizeable with around ten thousand inhabitants. A good portion of these were Palestinians who were now relocated in the same camp with Israelis. In many cases, the same tent. The dark had enjoyed plenty of amusement with this old and tiresome conflict.

A soldier stuck his head in the door. "The other woman who was in here, when she found out what happened, she asked to move. So, we accommodated her," he said.

Gestas nodded and glanced at Rebekah. He was glad they were going to have some privacy after everything that happened tonight.

"We'll bring your son back in a few minutes," the soldier said and then ducked outside.

"Why don't you get some rest and talk to Malakhi for a while," Gestas said and pointed at the far wall of the tent where the other women had slept. "I'll rest over here and give you some privacy."

As Gestas was about to get up, Rebekah grasped his arm. At first, he thought she wanted him to stay close. When he turned and saw her face an inch from his. He felt terror for the first time since entering the dark void. It was Rebekah's features, but what was behind the eyes was not her. Fury and hatred burned through, leaving little doubt this was not her. Her mouth contorted into a hateful sneer as she pulled him even closer. He did not know the name, but somehow he recognized it as the same dark soul that had inhabited the body of the fat woman. She spoke in a raspy, hate-filled voice.

"If you kill me again . . . I'll kill you and make sure you are tormented for eternity in the void!"

When darkness fell over the Virginia mountains, there were enough bonfires blazing to signal the International Space Station. Sally, Musial, and Cecil had managed to accumulate enough debris to keep their fires going all night; at least they hoped so. Burt tried to help, but he stumbled and fell so many times Cecil convinced him he needed to guard Barbara while they worked. He took a seat beside her in the grass and kept a diligent, if groggy, eye trained on her.

Cecil was worried about his wife, but he was starting to become more worried about Burt. What they first thought was a mild concussion was something much more serious. Cecil knew if Burt didn't receive medical care soon, he wouldn't live much longer. His plan of escape had morphed into one much more dangerous, yet practical.

He knew the only possible way for him to get the medical care he needed was to take him to a military base. The nearest one was

Quantico, the place from which Burt helped him escape prison a month earlier. It sounded insane to return to the lion's den, but they were out of options. Cecil knew for his wife to recover and Burt to survive, they would all have to return to the base. That being said, he wasn't willing to let anyone take the rap for aiding in his escape and assisting the Impal refugees. He, and he alone, would accept all blame. Of course, there weren't many left to take the blame. The majority of the people who joined the resistance had already paid the ultimate price. This fact weighed heavily on him.

Once he made sure Barbara and Burt were secure, Cecil and Musial sat in the center of their bonfire circle. They talked for a while out of earshot. Cecil gazed across at the two fresh mounds of earth next to the semi-fresh grave of Dr. Winder. It seemed an eternity since they buried the former National Science Advisor. In reality, it was only a few days.

"I want to leave at first light," Cecil said.

Musial made no reply.

"How much do you know about Sam Andrews?" Cecil asked.

Musial shrugged. "Bits and pieces, I know he thinks he is going to explode if he doesn't get a beer soon," he said and then gave a humorless laugh. "His body wants one too . . . it's about to drive me crazy," he said rubbing at his arms as if bugs crawled on them.

"Well, when we get to the base tomorrow, I need you to be him. You think you can manage?"

Musial stared at him. "Why in the devil would you go there? Don't you know they will kill you?"

"Because I forced you to go with me on threat of death to you and your family. You finally saw your opportunity to escape and you took me prisoner," Cecil said. "But one thing you must remember, Burt was my prisoner too."

"Ha!" Musial said, "they will never believe that about either of us in a million years. Weren't Burt and Sam the ones who broke you out?"

Cecil frowned. He hoped their peers at the base wouldn't know, at least not right away. Not before Burt got the treatment he needed. All Cecil could do was hope because they had no other options, not if Burt were going to live.

"Cecil, do you believe things happen for a reason?" Musial asked, sounding more like a familiar old friend than a useful, albeit shady, dark soul.

"A lot of times, I guess . . . sure. Why?"

"This whole thing . . . the storm enabling me, and I'm sure others like me, a chance for salvation. Many people have died because of this storm, but it has given a second chance for many. And then, this storm," he said pointing at the tornado trail through the woods. "A couple of your friends died, yet it gave you an opportunity to get away. You have a chance to save your wife and Captain Golden."

Cecil couldn't wrap his head around a divine plan that could cause the death of millions to save a few dark souls. On a personal level, the thought angered him. The very idea they had been given a way out for the bargain price of Derrick and Charlotte's lives was an audacity he could not accept.

"I think it just happened and some bad things came out of it, that's all."

"Really?" Musial asked skeptically.

"No, I don't believe my friends lives were taken so we could get away. They were in the wrong place at the wrong time and it was just dumb luck the tornado cut a path."

"I thought you were a Christian, major? Aren't you supposed to believe in a divine plan?"

Cecil was starting to become agitated. "What are you getting at Musial?" he snapped.

"Nothing . . . nothing . . . it's just I never was religious. I always thought religion was something people clung to because they were scared of life. They were frightened and needed something to believe in." He paused a moment and stroked his chin. "Then there are those who think *everything* is a sign or a message from God. Everything from their brand of toothpaste to their worldview is shaped by this belief. I have seen it drive some people quite mad."

"My father," Cecil muttered.

"What's that, major?" Musial said, cupping his hand to his ear.

Cecil suspected Musial had heard him and was trying to rub a little salt in an old and deep wound. He wasn't going to let him, so he changed the subject.

"Here are my thoughts about tomorrow," Cecil said and flicked a twig into the blazing fire while wiping sweat from his brow.

They discussed their plans until the wee hours of the morning. Cecil couldn't sleep, he had to make sure none of the fires died. More so, he was worried about Barbara and Burt. He was worried about all of them.

Cecil sat in silence, poking a stick into one of the fires after Musial lay down and shut his eyes. He seethed and cursed his father for putting him in this situation. Thanks to him, his oldest daughter was dead, his youngest was a captive, and his wife was in a vegetative state. This was no divine plan, this was just an old man who was crazy. Ignorance and arrogance had consumed him long ago. He couldn't bring himself to call him father or even old man anymore. Those days were gone.

"Damn you, Ott Garrison. Damn you to hell!" he muttered.

CHAPTER 32

THE GIVER OF THE LAW

*"The foundation of morality should not be made dependent
on myth nor tied to any authority lest doubt about the myth
or about the legitimacy of the authority imperil the foundation
of sound judgment and action."*
~Albert Einstein

STEFF LOCKED HERSELF IN HER ROOM for the night. She refused to come
out no matter how much Carmella persisted. When Carmella left her
dinner at the door, she ignored her. She was angry, upset, afraid, and
hungry. She was also mad because, deep down; she suspected they
may be right. Maybe the only way to stop her grandpa was to kill him.

This comprehension brought on a crescendo of negative emotions,
most of which she was not mature enough to handle. The only way she
could deal with these feelings was to put them out of her head, but that
was proving more and more difficult. Her favorite memory was the
one when her dad took her to Marian Burgers a couple of weeks ago.
She felt safe and important in this memory.

She sat and watched from her bedroom window as Carmella escorted a group of three men and one woman to a limousine. They
loaded several large duffel bags in the trunk. As one of the men shoved
the trunk shut, Carmella waved at Steff's window. Like a child, Steff

jumped back behind the curtains. She knew Carmella had seen her, did she think hiding now would change it?

What was in those bags? Bombs, grenades, guns . . . thermo nuclear weapons? Maybe it was only gym clothes. Steff did not believe the latter as much as she wanted to.

A few minutes later, Steff heard a knock on the door followed by Carmella's calm and pleading voice. "Sweetheart, we need to talk," she called.

"About what?" Steff thought. "What kind of casket you are going to put the pieces of my grandpa in?"

Carmella soon gave up. As she walked away, a bizarre thought came into Steff's head.

"I wonder if my grandpa would be nicer as an Impal?"

If Steff only knew what happened the previous evening, she might have been on board with the 'bomb squad' staff at the White House. One hundred and ten officers attended the Halloween festivity in the grand ballroom. Only about sixty of them went home. The unfortunate fifty were not all dead, at least not yet. Garrison still had a use for them. Of course, the use would result in their deaths. He intended to run experiments with the Tesla Gate, using these condemned men as guinea pigs or, in this case, bait.

If the Tesla Gates could absorb and get rid of Impals in their deceitful form, why couldn't it do it now in their dark form? He envisioned gates similar to large bug collectors on the back of enormous trucks, boats, or airplanes. They would snatch up these abominations and send them back to where they belonged. Perhaps destroy them all together. Yes, total annihilation was Garrison's preferred result.

Aside from the one hundred-ten officers, Joan had taken care of several other men last night. She invited them one by one into a private conference room. There were several conference rooms because the dark was quite violent last night. When the lights came back on after each victim, it would have taken an industrial cleaning crew to get them presentable again. Joan got rid of about twenty minor officers. She didn't lift a finger against them, except to beckon them inside and then switch off the lights.

Sebastian identified these officers as he searched the base's data base and email records. There was a resistance forming and there would be some required visits to at least six other bases, but they would have to do it fast. He would try to control communication in and out of the base, yet he knew he could only control it for so long. Sooner or later, word would get out about the executions. When this happened, some resistance members might pull the trigger early. This might cause a chaotic mess for President Garrison and his administration. They needed to be swift, they needed to be thorough, and they needed to be efficient.

Sebastian and Joan would head out tomorrow to Fort Bragg in North Carolina. They would be a tag team tandem of the nosy geek and the slutty executioner. Sebastian wanted Avery to join them, if for nothing more than to give their visit more clout. His request was denied without reason.

President Garrison was in the hanger before first light. Thirty angry and confused officers huddled outside. Power had been redirected there from other noncritical areas at Quantico. The hanger hummed as power surged through the massive conduits to the Shredder. As the Tesla Gate fired to life again, a thrill ran through his body. Today was going to be a fun day.

Jack Abernathy slept most of the night and almost to noon the following day. He was exhausted and when his captors realized he would not succumb to the music and light show, they left him alone.

"They are banging the little slag, Donna," he thought to himself.

Was it a twinge of jealousy he felt? Perhaps, but the question is, was it jealousy of her carnal exploits or jealousy of her freedom while he sat in jail? He was pretty certain it was the latter.

He shuddered and laughed out loud at the thought. "Preposterous. I hate the treacherous slut," he said to the room.

Then he shuddered again. Something deep inside disagreed. It was a feeling alien to him and he didn't know how to process it. He didn't want to process it, but there it was, festering inside . . . a small spark of affection.

"Damn her!" he muttered then rolled over and tried to go back to sleep.

* * *

The vehicle couldn't make it down the swath cut by the tornado. There were too much debris and downed trees for it to navigate, even in four-wheel drive. The driveway, as far as they could tell, was still navigable, but there were too many dark patches to make it a safe option. They decided Musial would drive the vehicle to the road and Cecil would lead everybody down the tornado trail. They would meet Musial down at the main road.

"No, you can't do that!" Sally protested when she heard Cecil's plan to go back to the base. "They will kill you!"

Cecil led Sally away from Burt; he was lying on his back and staring at the sky, resembling a man with a terrible hangover.

"Sally . . . listen to me," Cecil whispered as he gently tugged on her arm. She was staring at her husband. Sally turned and looked into Cecil's eyes. "Burt needs medical attention and he needs it now," Cecil said. "We have to go for his sake!"

Sally began to shake her head, but she was so distressed she resembled a bobble head doll. "No . . . Burt would never allow it," she stammered. "He would never forgive himself if something happened to you . . . he would never forgive me if I let you do this."

"Sally," Cecil said firmly. "This has nothing to do with me and Burt's friendship. I am Burt's superior officer and this is an order. It's not open for negotiation."

"But you aren't in the military anymore . . . the two of you gave it up when you started helping Impals," she protested.

"Sally, I had a meeting with the president the night he was murdered. Do you know what he told me?"

She blinked with surprise and then glanced at Burt.

"He told me he thought Burt and I were heroes for what we were doing to help the Impals. As far as he was concerned, we still held the title of captain and major. Then someone shot him."

There was an uncomfortable silence between them for several moments before Cecil continued. "As far as I am concerned and the Constitution is concerned . . . he was our last legitimate leader. So yes, Burt and I are still in the military and I am ordering him back to base."

"But—," Sally began to protest before Cecil cut her short.

"Don't forget . . . Barbara needs help as well."

Cecil and Sally aided Burt down the path. They rigged up a rescue sled for Barbara made of two straight limbs and a few salvaged sofa cushions and pillows. They made frequent stops to rest. Burt could walk on his own, yet he still required a lot of support. There were also several areas where thick fallen trees blocked their path and Cecil had to pick up Barbara and carry her. Even though the path was wrought with obstacles, it was a short walk. Under normal circumstance, it would have taken maybe a half hour to traverse. It took Cecil and Sally over two hours to maneuver Burt and Barbara down to the main road.

"Are there any wooded areas or tunnels between here and the interstate?" Cecil asked Musial as they loaded Burt and Barbara into the cargo area on a soft palette of pillows and sofa cushions.

"Not that I recall, major," Musial said. "Of course I wasn't paying attention when I came this way before."

Cecil glared at him.

"Of course, you are driving, major," Musial said. "I wouldn't have it any other way."

It was Musial's way of saying he wasn't going to take the heat if he drove them through a tunnel or a shady forest. Cecil wouldn't have it any other way either. He took the keys and slid into the driver's seat.

"I'll drive until we are a few miles from the base," Cecil said as he turned the key and shifted into gear. "Then you are going to take over."

Cecil glanced in the rear view mirror and saw Sally on her hands and knees, leaning over the backseat. She kept her feet up as much as possible because the back floor board was full of dark patches, especially under the seats. They put one lantern in the back floor board, one on the floor between the driver and passenger, and the rest around the cargo area. The goal was to eliminate any random dark spot. The lights in the vehicle were probably unnecessary, considering it was a bright sunny day, but it was better to be safe than sorry.

There must be a certain degree of darkness to harbor the dark souls, but nobody knew just how shadowy it was. One thing was certain, the hellish hiss and click of the dark thrummed in the woods as they drove by. It was loud enough to be heard over the engine. Cecil was certain he also heard the same sound coming from somewhere in the vehicle. Maybe under the seats or in the glove box. The noise outside sounded angry. The noise inside was scarier . . . more plotting and patient, as if it was waiting for the right opportunity to pounce.

Cecil's first impulse was to ask Sally to buckle up, after all, it was the prudent and legal thing to do in the 'normal' world. Nothing was normal anymore.

About noon, they drove through a small town whose only claim to fame was a Post Office in a mobile home. As they turned right at the crossroads, they passed a Virginia State Trooper heading in the opposite direction. Cecil's heart leapt into his throat as he saw the blue lights flash to life and the car make a tire squalling U-turn.

He thought of trying to out run him, but he reconsidered when he thought of Burt and Barbara unsecured in the back. Besides, he was in unfamiliar countryside and he could easily find himself in a dark area. It was now early November and Cecil cursed the fact the trees had not yet dropped their leaves. Despite some chilly, fall days, everything was still as lush and green as early summer.

Cecil and Musial both shrugged. He pulled over on a sunny, graveled shoulder and put the vehicle in park. He left the engine running. The patrol car pulled up behind them and stopped. Its blue lights reflected off every glass surface in the vehicle. After several long moments, a single officer got out and began to stroll towards the SUV. As the officer approached the rear driver's side of the vehicle, Cecil glanced at Musial. He was gone.

"Cecil. Where's Musial?" Sally whispered from the back seat.

Before he could answer, his door flew open. As he spun to face the officer, he was grabbed by the arm and slung out onto the pavement with surprising force. He raised his head to find himself staring down the barrel of a .44 automatic.

"Don't move you low life piece of crap!" the officer barked. "Lie face down with your hands behind your back!"

Once Cecil complied, he slapped a pair of handcuffs on him. He then reached up and threw open the back door.

"Get your ass out here and kiss the pavement you fat hog!" he growled at Sally.

Cecil felt a sudden urge to rise up and put his fist down the officer's throat. "She didn't do anything, leave her alone!" he yelled.

As Sally clambered out, the officer shoved her to the ground and gave Cecil a kick to the ribs for his disrespect. He slapped another pair of cuffs on the bawling Sally and then flung open the hatch of the vehicle.

"Freeze you scumbags!" he shouted, pointing his gun at Burt and Barbara.

Cecil was furious. He pushed up with his shoulders, springing to his knees and then with one more thrust he sprung to his feet.

"They are injured, they can't freeze or get on the ground or anything . . . we're trying to take them to a hospital!" Cecil screamed.

The officer rounded on him and gave him a paralyzing blow to the gut, causing Cecil's body to stiffen and slump to the ground. He lay still, trying to catch his breath.

"So, they are injured, huh?" he said glancing in the back at Barbara. She was not moving and her eyes were shut. Burt's eyes still swam. "I'll tell you what I think happened," he said, keeping the gun pointed at them as he checked their pulse. He stepped back, apparently satisfied with the story. The officer walked over and stood about six inches from Cecil's face.

"Me and a few other officers have been patrolling the area every day to make sure there aren't any looters out," he said. "I think y'all are damn looters." He paused for a moment as he removed his sunglasses, polishing the lenses on his sleeve. He stuck his jack booted foot out and tapped Cecil on the nose. It was not hard enough to do any damage, but hard enough to remind Cecil that his nose was recently broken. "I think you and the fat sow here are looters. You took those two hostage back there after you robbed them. How am I doing so far?" he sneered, as he leaned over Cecil and spat in his ear.

Cecil did not answer. He knew it would not do any good. This officer was one of a minority of police officers around the world who harbor insecurities. They use their position of authority to compensate for those short comings. Cecil said nothing.

"I tell you what," he said, bending over and patting Sally's butt. "I wanted to do a little hogging before I carry out judgment, but you ain't my type. I prefer my hogs a little more lean . . . you've got too much cushion for the pushin'," he said and then let out a loud braying laugh.

"Get your ass up!" he screamed at Cecil.

Cecil slowly got to his feet.

"Come on!" he ordered, giving Cecil a kick in the butt.

Once Cecil was standing tall, the officer spun him around and drew himself close to his face. He was shorter than Cecil so his eyes were even with his chin.

"By the authority vested in me by the honorable President Ott Garrison and the Commonwealth of Virginia, I find you guilty of sedition and larceny. You are hereby sentenced to the shade!"

The meaning of the officer's words did not sink in at first. Then he spun around and pointed with his pistol at a very dark patch of woods across the highway.

"Get your ass in there . . . march!" he screamed as he gave Cecil a shove in the back.

CHAPTER 33

THE SWING

"A really great talent finds its happiness in execution."
~Johann Wolfgang von Goethe

"IF YOU KILL ME AGAIN . . . I'll kill you and make sure we torment you for eternity in the void!"

It was the last thing the dark soul now inhabiting Rebekah said to Gestas before cradling Malakhi in her arms. The spite radiating from her face would have frozen a blast furnace. She stroked Malakhi's hair while staring at Gestas.

The first question Gestas wanted to ask was how this dark soul was able to accomplish this. He believed he may know the answer. A dark soul can leave a body at any time they choose, but entering is a different matter. The person has to be in a weakened state when they come in contact with the dark. This typically pertains to a person who is drunk or under the influence of drugs. In Rebekah's case, her semi-conscious state brought on by the strangling was all this dark soul needed.

They played a grueling game of chicken for the better part of the night. Gestas was afraid to act at first, fearing this dark soul would do something to Malakhi. Still a few hours from sunrise, the old woman's body could not hold out much longer.

"What do you want?" Gestas asked.

"The same as you, my kindred . . . I want salvation, redemption, escape . . . I'm never going back to the wretched dark abyss again."

"You have a funny way of showing it," Gestas said. "You were going to kill the woman you now inhabit because you thought she was going to give away our dark secret."

"Well . . . yes," she said with raised eyebrows. "She would have revealed us. If that happened, I would have gone back to the void."

Gestas felt anger burning inside of him. "What is your idea of salvation?" he asked.

It replied in a matter of fact tone. "To inhabit this body so I will have something to cling to as a life preserver when this storm passes. You know it will in time. When it happens, the void will seal again and we will be back in miserable purgatory. I would expect forever this time."

"You ignorant fool!" Gestas hissed. "It's not salvation or redemption . . . that's theft. In truth, it is murder!

"How is it murder?" it frowned. "She is still here, somewhere. . . . Her body is still very much alive. Why, it's not murder at all."

"You intend to keep control of her body, even after this is over. You are destroying the person who was Rebekah and replacing her with yourself. Don't you see?"

It shrugged. "Well, this is best for both of us. I think her life will only be better with me and my many years of experience. We can do great things. Besides, you can't make an omelet without breaking a few eggs, or so the expression goes." It paused and grinned before glancing down at the sleeping Malakhi. "Speaking of omelets, I'm kind of hungry." She shook the sleeping boy a little harder than she should. He jumped up with a cry. "What say we go and get some breakfast, son?" it said with a sappy, forced smile.

Malakhi frowned at Gestas who agreed with a shaky nod. He didn't see much choice at the moment. They got up and left the tent, the dark soul in Rebekah flashing a devious smile before ducking under the flap. Before it closed the flap, it turned and whispered. "And I thought the Spanish Inquisition was fun. I never understood why I was in the void after all the good I did for the church."

Gestas sat up, the heart in his geriatric chest pounding as if he ran a marathon. He felt ignorance is something he had overcome in two millennia. He knew what he must do for redemption. In his case, he needed to help someone without regard for himself. He didn't know why he suddenly knew this. It wasn't as if some booming, omnipotent voice had spoken great words of wisdom to him or he learned some sacred wisdom in the void. There was only an eternity of darkness and hate-filled lamentations. The occasional small rabbit hole to the mind of a gullible individual in the outside world was the only break in monotony. Time passed differently in the void. Still, two thousand years was a long time to wait. It was also a long time to think, rethink, and observe some of these jaunts into the heads of the weak minded. A lot of ignorance can be overcome in twenty centuries if one is willing to put their arrogance aside.

Gestas knew for sure that stealing a person's identity was not the way to go about anything. He was borrowing the old woman's identity, but he intended to return her to her life once he reached his goal. He wanted to move on and be like the other people who had the choice to stay or move on after death. Where would he move on? Could it be the paradise that the man who called himself the King of the Jews spoke of to Dismas? He didn't know. He believed freedom from the dark void was as good as any paradise.

He believed his ticket to redemption lay in helping Rebekah and Malakhi, but he now felt his hope fading. Perhaps this was his opportunity. He had never figured out before how Rebekah and Malakhi needed his help. He felt compelled to stay near, just in case. This was the quintessential definition of needing help.

The problem was, he didn't know how to help. Whoever this dark soul may be, they now enjoyed full control over Rebekah. To make matters worse, they had participated in the Spanish Inquisition. From his experience with the dark souls, they were some of the most arrogant and ruthless beings in existence. Their self-important pride in their belief made them almost impossible to reach. This was Gestas's opportunity, but he did not know how to act. He couldn't leave the body of the old woman without returning to the darkness. Even if he could, he didn't know if he could get inside Rebekah's head and drive this arrogant wretch out. The one thing he could do right now is continue to watch and stay close. Gestas got up and headed towards the mess hall, watching for Rebekah and Malakhi.

President Garrison had to shoot the first officer to make his point. Participation in this experiment was mandatory.

"You are all guilty of treason!" he proclaimed, holding up printouts of emails given to him by his tech guru, Sebastian Gardner. "You may well survive the experiment," he lied. "If you refuse to participate, you most definitely will not survive!"

The remaining officers bravely lined up in the bright sun outside the hangar and awaited their turn. Joan and Sebastian stood guard with the MPs. They pointed their weapons with enthusiasm at the condemned men. The MPs did not seem so enthusiastic, yet they were obedient.

The hangar was a large building with acoustics ideal for an outdoor concert. Even through the massive closed doors, the electric hum of the Tesla Gate vibrated the metallic walls. The terror filled screams of the men added to the horror.

Garrison was not sure if the experiments were having any effect. He was glad he selected twenty men as test subjects because less than ten would not have been enough. He had rigged up a platform in front of the Tesla Gate, with a long rope hanging from a rafter high above. On first glance, it would have appeared as a gallows. However, instead of a rope tied around the man's neck, it wrapped under his shoulders. Avery stood behind the condemned until the lights in the hangar turned off. As the man screamed when the darkness closed in, Avery shoved him off the platform. The unfortunate officer made a perfect swing into the glowing blue arcs of electricity in the center of the Gate. None of them survived. The darkness followed the men in their flight as the tormented screams never ceased. It was unclear after three such drops if the electrical field at the heart of the Tesla Gate had any effect on the dark souls. It certainly had an effect on the poor men; their bodies were fried to a crisp.

The sick sweet, acrid smell of burned flesh lingered in their nose and mouth more akin to a taste than an odor. The remaining doomed men began to wretch at the pungent odor as they were brought in one at a time. Garrison was undeterred. He ordered each man forward while preparing to extinguish the lights. It was if he were wearing an invisible gas mask. Garrison would proclaim he was shielded by the hand of the Lord.

The dark souls couldn't be seen, except as a shadow by the naked eye. Once the switch flipped, the only light left in the hangar was the bluish luminescent glow of the Tesla Gate. Avery thought it resembled a giant TV set tuned in to the Twilight Zone. With each new victim, the dark souls swarmed like bats seeking prey. Their wild fluttering in front of the pulsing Gate enhanced its already horrific appearance. It was too difficult to see if the experiment was actually working. There was no way to perform a census before and after each experiment to see if the dark souls were consumed by the Tesla Gate. Garrison decided he needed a closer look. He climbed down from his podium to the right of the Gate and stood a dozen feet in front of the opening. It once bore the nickname the Shredder when it consumed a steady diet of Impals. Now it seemed prudent to change the nickname to the Fryer. The hangar reeked with burned flesh, yet it didn't bother Garrison.

Garrison took the remote switch and pointed it at the ceiling as Avery readied the next man to swing. Once the man was bound under the arms, Garrison hit the switch and waited till he heard the blood curdling screams.

""Now!" he shouted, as he had done a half dozen times before.

He could see the man jerking and kicking as he swung toward the Gate. It was almost like watching a strobe light performance. The ebb and flow of the electrical pulse blinked the condemned man in and out of relief. He could see the dark souls encircling and swarming the man as he got closer. Garrison watched, leaning back towards the Gate as he watched for some sign the dark souls had been shredded.

When the man hit the Gate, there was a tremendous crackle and buzz as his body cooked with voltage. Pieces of burning flesh and clothing flew from the corpse like a ghastly Roman candle. Garrison didn't see any dark souls disappear into the Gate. He did see a large fireball of burned flesh and material flying directly at him. There was

JOHN D. MIMMS

no time to react and Garrison was pelted in the right eye with a sear-
ing pain. He howled in anguish, shouting several phrases the Lord
would not approve of, before falling to his knees. He passed out from
the agony.

Cecil didn't see any alternative other than move forward. This cop was
either unstable or ignorant. He believed he was doing the right thing
by acting as judge, jury, and executioner. He also seemed to take sadistic pleasure from inflicting misery on his prisoners. Cecil's mind
worked feverishly for a way out, yet he knew if he resisted, the cop
would take it out on Sally after he was dead. Then what would happen
to Barbara and Burt? A moment later, he heard a sickening crunch
and a moan behind him. Cecil turned to see the sadistic State Trooper
collapse to his knees. He then toppled forward and slammed face first
into the pavement.

As he hit the ground, the gun went off sending a bullet careening inches from Cecil's chin. As he checked to insure his face was
still intact, he saw Musial standing over the trooper brandishing a
tire iron. Rage and satisfaction swam behind his glaring eyes. Before Cecil could say anything, Musial sprang forward. He delivered
another crushing blow to the back of the troopers head. If he wasn't
already dead he was now. Bits of brain and bone oozed in a bloody
puddle on the pavement. Musial moved to strike again, but Cecil
grabbed his arm.

"It's done," Cecil said. Musial struggled in his grasp so he gripped
him harder and pushed him back against the SUV. The rage in Musial's
eyes was murderous. There was also elation, similar to a junkie who
finally got a hit of their addictive poison after a long hiatus.

"Thank you, Musial," Cecil said. "You saved us all . . . thank you."

The mention of saving seemed to break Musial's crazed trance. He
blinked and then looked from the body to Cecil.

"Sorry major, I hope I didn't get any on you," he said as he casually
wiped blood splatters off of his face with his sleeve.

Cecil helped Sally to her feet. She wrapped her arms around his
neck. He was not unsympathetic. He knew she was worried about Burt
and she feared she was about to get raped and murdered by the vile

234

police officer. On the other hand, he was tired of her excessive wailing every time something bad happened.

"Suck it up, be a man!" his father used to say to him.

This recollection washed over him in a sickening wave. He wasn't sure what made him feel worse, that he was projecting the attitude on Sally, or because his father said it. He bit his lip and pressed his mouth into a thin line.

"Get back there and check on Burt and Barbara," he muttered, urging her towards the back seat.

Sally blinked as if she had been splashed with cold water. Cecil knew he had scared her, but if that was what it took to get Burt and Barbara the help they needed, then so be it. He was tired, he was worried about his wife and friend. He was also worried about what his father would do to them when they arrived at the base. Cecil was also in anguish about his two daughters, one alive and one not; yet both were in pain. Manners and politeness were not the slightest of his concerns.

"She's a bawler, isn't she?" Musial said as he gazed in the driver's side mirror to get the rest of the blood spots off with an old towel he found under the seat.

"Shut up," Cecil muttered as he began to walk back towards the police car.

Musial let out a little hoot of a laugh, not taking his eyes off the mirror.

Cecil checked the interior of the police car and then wondered what to do. They couldn't just leave it here on the road. Whoever he was reporting to knew his exact location. He considered taking it with them, he could drive the SUV while Musial drove the police car. He gave it up when the stupidity of this occurred to him. If they could track the car then they could track them. They could have a dozen cops converge on them with an appetite for heavy women and a strong desire to feed the dark's hunger. No, they would have to ditch the car and the cop someplace dark and not accessible.

Cecil and Musial loaded the officer's body in the trunk of the police car. Musial drove the car down a narrow path between the trees, running over brambles and downed limbs as he drove. When he came to the area where the whispers of his brethren were the loudest, he parked it and hiked back.

Sally had calmed down and was leaning over the backseat talking to Burt. He seemed on the verge of losing consciousness at any second, so she did her best to keep him awake by engaging in conversation.

"Keep talking to him, Sally," Cecil said as he shifted the SUV into gear and pulled back on the road. "We will be there soon, keep him talking."

To call the noises coming out of his friend's mouth talking may have been a stretch. You could catch a word here and there, but most of it was a garbled mess. At least he was conscious. Cecil knew with a head injury of this magnitude, he could go under at any second and never regain consciousness.

A little over an hour later, they passed the sign announcing Quantico as the next exit. Cecil pulled over in the parking lot of a deserted Safeway to exchange positions with Musial. The plan was that Musial was Sam Andrews who was taken against his will. He managed to escape and rescue Burt and Sally who were also hostages. Barbara was forced into rebellion by her husband. The blame would fall on Cecil's shoulders . . . he hoped. There were still a lot of variables, a lot of things that could go wrong.

A few minutes later they rounded a corner and came upon a security checkpoint. It was the same one where Andrews and Burt helped him escape a little over a month ago. A block of ice slid into Cecil's stomach. What if the same guards were there from the night of his escape?

CHAPTER 34

THE PRODIGAL SON

*"The pattern of the prodigal is: rebellion, ruin, repentance,
reconciliation, restoration."*
~Edwin Louis Cole

GESTAS FOLLOWED REBEKAH AND MALAKHI for the better part of the day.
To the casual observer, there did not seem to be anything wrong. She
behaved as a loving and doting mother. This dark soul was either very
good at deception or really did relish the role of loving mother. Gestas
didn't believe it was the latter. He saw the fury burning behind Rebekah's pretty green eyes. He knew this soul entertained no desire for
redemption. It only sought escape from the darkness at any cost.

Gestas was in uncharted territory. He did not know if it was possible to get a dark soul out of someone without killing the body. If
salvation was possible, he was pretty sure that cold-blooded murder
was a deal breaker. The only thing he could do was watch and make
sure no harm came to Malakhi.

The increased physical demands on the old woman's body were
starting to take its toll. He believed he either strained or broke a rib
when he saved Rebekah from their possessed tent mate. The legs of the
old woman throbbed with protest. He found he must rest frequently.
As a result, he lost them a couple of times. He managed to stay a safe

distance behind until nightfall. Tonight, he was not sure the physical limitations of his elderly host would be enough.

Jack was awakened around mid-afternoon by the click and squeak of his cell door. A fat, older gentleman, wearing a brown smock, waddled into the room. Behind his multiple chins, bushy eyebrows and shocks of white hair above his ears, there was a kind and gentle countenance. He was a stark contrast with the two armed guards accompanying him. The man reminded Jack of Alfred Hitchcock or perhaps Winston Churchill.

Jack sat up on his bed and rubbed his eyes. He watched the man as he took a seat in a small metal chair a few feet away. Jack glanced from the man to the soldiers. The man adjusted his long smock and tried to balance his rather ample fanny on the narrow chair seat.

"Good afternoon, Jack. I am Dr. Turnberry," he introduced himself with a polite nod. He didn't offer his hand.

Jack didn't say anything; he just glared at Turnberry. After several long moments of tense silence, Jack said. "Why are you holding me here?"

Dr. Turnberry straightened the wire-rimmed glasses on his button nose and then cleared his throat. "I thought it was obvious, Jack. You have an ability few people seem to possess," he said, then narrowed his eyes and lowered his voice. "You also seem to have a propensity for violence which we were not aware of."

Jack's heart rate accelerated. Had they discovered his secret? He knew what the reaction would be if he was found out. There would be no medals, no glorious media interviews, no parades, or parties. The only pedestal he would be on is a gallows. These imbeciles were too ignorant to understand the good he served.

Jack's pulse subsided as Dr. Turnberry said, "You were ready to kill that young woman. It wasn't just a momentary burst of anger, it was visceral rage I saw in you."

Jack glanced around the room, wondering how this obese clown had watched him. He soon spotted a tiny camera mounted in a dark corner.

"Does it have sound?" Jack asked, pointing.

Turnberry shifted his weight nervously and said, "No, I'm afraid not. That's why we were wondering what the girl, Donna, said to you."

Jack breathed a sigh of relief and experienced a flash of inspiration. They hadn't heard. There was no telling what she told them, but now this was Jack's opportunity to discredit *her*.

"You know who the crazy brat said she was? Queen Mary."

Dr. Turnberry jumped with surprise. "Mary, Queen of Scots?" he asked.

"No, no . . . the other one . . . Bloody Mary."

Turnberry raised an eyebrow and then folded his arms. "Why would she make such a claim?" he asked.

"How the hell should I know?" Jack said. "She's a nutter."

Dr. Turnberry smiled a little.

"You know she can move about in the dark too, don't you?" Jack said.

Turnberry regarded him for several long moments before responding. "Yes, she was open about it. You weren't quite as forthcoming so we tested you."

"You were in charge of that rubbish?" Jack said, remembering the relentless light blinking and music from his first night in the cell.

"Well, not hands on," Turnberry said. "But I did authorize it."

"Wanker," Jack muttered.

Turnberry's mouth creased into a thin line. It seemed his sense of humor only stretched so far. "So what is your connection with Bloody Mary? Are you Henry VIII?"

Jack wanted to explode. He wanted to bash this arrogant jerk's skull in and then go do the same to Queen Mary. Nevertheless, he restrained himself.

"No, I'm just Private Jack Abernathy. What you see is what you get," he said mustering as much humility as he could.

"You haven't seen my cage, have you?" he thought, but did not say.

"You never knew this Donna before?" Turnberry asked.

"No, as I have said before, she showed up at my door the night I was stuck at my house. That's the first time I saw her in my life."

"But you weren't really stuck . . . were you Jack?" he asked with a straight face, yet accusation shone in his eyes.

"I didn't know it at the time," Jack said.

"When did you know it?"

Jack studied him and then the guards as the stitches on the back of his head began to tingle. He reached his hand back and touched the bandage.

"Right after I woke up from this," he said.

"Yes . . . yes, your injury," Turnberry said like a professor contemplating a difficult concept. "Exactly how did it happen again?"

Before Jack could answer Turnberry scooted his chair closer and then pointed at Jack's head. "May I?" he said.

Jack turned his head and let Dr. Turnberry exam it. He did not remove the bandage or even touch it. Instead, he seemed more interested in the area of Jack's head where the injury occurred.

"Mmm . . . occipital lobe . . . vision . . . perhaps . . . yes," Turnberry muttered. Jack was no doctor, but he understood him well enough to know the doctor thought he might have gotten some brain damage from the fall.

Maybe it affected his immunity from the dark. He avoided the dark until he was kicked by the old lady in the cage. He woke up in the dark, yet he never considered it unusual. He felt at home, at peace among the dark whispers. Perhaps he did suffer some brain damage since the most obvious solution eluded him. He and the dark are the same.

"So you think my injury caused this?" Jack asked as Dr. Turnberry scooted back and began to stroke his pudgy chin.

"At least a possibility," he murmured, and then blinked. "Makes me wonder if your friend Donna suffered a similar blow to the head, making her immune."

"And knocking the sense out of her to where she thinks she is Bloody Mary?" Jack asked.

"A possibility," Turnberry agreed. "I will need to examine her further to make a determination."

Jack laughed inside while suppressing a grin. This guy didn't know a bloody thing. He was interested in the medical aspect of Jack's 'condition', nothing more.

"I knew I was careful," he thought. "Even if they check the moors near my house, they can't prove I had a damn thing to do with any of them."

Dr. Turnberry got up to leave after offering Jack dinner. He had not enjoyed a decent meal since they stopped at Martian Burgers a couple of days ago. Jack accepted and the doctor promised him a steak, baked potato, and a Coca Cola.

"I'll have someone bring it to you within the hour," he said, motioning the guards to meet him at the door.

As Jack's stomach grumbled, he smiled and got up to shake Turnberry's hand. The doctor stepped behind one of the guards who delivered a forearm causing Jack to stumble backwards. He quickly recovered, ready to respond to another blow, yet none came. Dr. Turnberry peered at him from behind the two soldiers.

"I'll be back shortly with your meal, Jack. In the meantime, I would like an answer to a question when I return. I don't want an answer now because I want to give you time to think about it," he said and then paused. "Always remember, honesty is the best policy."

Jack felt a sinking feeling in the pit of his stomach; he didn't care for Turnberry's tone. "What question?" he asked.

Dr. Turnberry nervously removed his glasses. With growing angst, he slowly told Jack the question. "I would like to know what the cage was for."

The same guards from the night of Cecil's escape were not at the checkpoint, but it didn't matter. They knew his name all too well. Major Cecil Garrison was public enemy number one. The soldiers responded with the same zeal as if Bonnie and Clyde had just waltzed into FBI headquarters. They dragged him from the SUV and threw him to the ground. This time, he managed to avoid another broken nose. However, he did have the wind knocked out of him.

Even though Musial tried to explain that he was Sam Andrews, the guards did not buy it. They hauled Cecil and Musial to the same jail where Cecil resided before. It could have been coincidence, fate, or just cruel irony; but they were thrown into his previous cell.

When he was here before, the Impals were still about, being fed into the Tesla Gate a short distance away. Now that the eye had arrived and the dark souls ruled the shadows, Cecil took note of how dim the jail was. There seemed to be a threshold of light the dark souls occupied. Fortunately, the shadows in the jail were not dark enough, but they were close. The whispers of the dark echoed all around them like a thousand mice scratching inside the walls.

Cecil sat down in the most well lit side of the cell while Musial sat on the bed, which was under a dark shadow. That seat would have been fatal to Cecil. Sally, Burt, and Barbara were taken elsewhere. Cecil was grateful that at least they were not here in this hellhole with him. He hoped Burt and Barbara received the help they needed.

"So what do we do now, major?" Musial asked.

"Wait," Cecil said. "I'm sure they have gotten word to my father in Washington by now. He'll do one of three things. He'll have us executed, he'll have us rot in this cell, or he will come to see me so he can gloat before having us executed."

Cecil had no idea his father was currently being treated in the same base infirmary with Burt and Barbara. When he learned of the presence of the traitors, not even God knew what the lunatic would do. President Garrison worked outside the prevue of God in his own private religious fairyland.

"Well I must say you are a lovely cell mate, major."

Cecil shrugged and didn't say anything. His mind was elsewhere. It was with Steff, it was with Burt, Barbara and Sally. It was also with Abbs, wherever she may be. He possessed a natural fear of death, though it did not terrify him. He didn't care what his father did to him. Not as long as everyone else was okay. His biggest regret was that he would not be there for his family, although . . . maybe he could. The Impals who stayed did so by choice. He could see himself making the same choice if he died today. Of course, the world had changed since the Impals were here. Where would his soul go now and, wherever it was, would he have a choice? The more he thought about it, the more it scared him. What had happened to the Impals?

"Oh, Abbs," he said as he pinched the bridge of his nose to quell tears. If alone, he would not have cared, but he didn't want to give Musial the enjoyment of seeing him cry. He decided to change the subject.

"What did you mean right before the tornado hit when you said one of them killed you before?" Cecil asked, jumping as the dark responded with increased agitation. Musial's head flew up and his eyes narrowed on Cecil.

"I had rather not talk about it, major," he said. "I may have been a bad boy in life which earned me a plunge into the dark void. Yet . . . there are some things I would rather not discuss."

"It bothers you more to talk about that then all the people you killed?" Cecil asked.

Musial didn't reply. Although Cecil couldn't see his face in the shadows, his heavy breathing echoed through the jail. Finally he took a deep breath and said, "I was on my way back from getting rid of some nigger's body. I don't even remember his name and I didn't care what it was. This storm blew up out of nowhere and I tried to hide under a big oak tree outside the town where I had been performing. I heard the roar of the damned thing approaching. I thought it was a steam train, but I remembered the steam train didn't run through the little piss ant village. By the time I figured out it wasn't a train, it was too late. The damned twister snatched the tree up as easily as someone weeding a garden . . . with me clinging to it."

He took a deep breath and shuddered before continuing. "The last thing I remember seeing before I found myself in the void was the god-awful nigger staring down at me from one of the branches. He was smiling and swinging his feet as if it was a sunny day. I don't know if he was enjoying the weather or enjoying watching me die."

"Was it his Impal?" Cecil asked.

Musial shook his head. "Hell, I don't know. I have never seen an Impal. I've only heard you living folks talk about them."

"You couldn't see them before the storm?"

Musial huffed, "I thought I told you we couldn't see anything before then."

"You said you broke through sometimes to influence the weak minded."

"It was rare and it was more like trying to talk to someone through a knothole in a fence. You couldn't see much and you were lucky if they heard you," Musial said and then stretched out on the cot. "I told you I didn't want to talk about this, major," he said.

Cecil's started to suggest that referring to black people with a racial pejorative was not a good start on the road to salvation. He held his tongue. The story fascinated him and he could see Musial was shaken by its retelling. Besides, being a racist paled in comparison to Musial's other deeds.

Suddenly, a booming voice echoed through the jail, filling Cecil with dread. Aside from his wife and daughters, there was none as familiar.

Cecil saw a dark form walking down the hall. A moment later, his father glared through the bars at him, smiling triumphantly. His left eye bore a hole through Cecil, while the right eye was concealed behind a wad of surgical tape and gauze. Two people stood behind him in the shadows, but Cecil could not see their faces.

"So . . . the prodigal son has returned, God be praised!" he shouted.

CHAPTER 35

THE PERIMETER RUN

"Indeed, without emotion it seems unlikely we can even have morality."
~Julian Baggini

STEFF WAS GETTING HUNGRY. She sat in her room for the better part of the day avoiding Carmella, which also meant avoiding meals. She didn't feel like eating. She didn't think she would ever eat again. Her stomach twisted in knots so tight, she felt there was no room for food. Her grandfather was an evil man, yet he was her grandfather. She still loved him. Those were two concepts she couldn't reconcile in her young mind.

The longer the day progressed the more she felt as if the walls were closing in on her. As the afternoon wore on and the hunger pangs intensified, she found it harder to breathe. Steff began to pace the room like a caged animal. She wanted nothing more than to leave, to be back with her family. She wanted to go someplace a long, long way from her grandfather. She thought Carmella was a friend and perhaps she was. After all, she was the one who opened her eyes to her grandfather's shortcomings. Even after the shooting of the people in Lafayette Square, it still didn't sink in. What had she said . . . he is an ignorant man? Yes, that was exactly what she said, and Steff almost laughed at the time.

When she thought of an ignorant person, she thought of someone stupid like Forrest Gump, not her grandfather. She decided to Google the word and then remembered the Internet was still down. Steff took the old fashioned way and found a dictionary on one of the White House's many bookshelves. She thumbed through the pages until she came to the I's, and then scanned a couple of pages until she found the word.

Ignorant
1. Lacking education of knowledge.
2. Showing or arising from a lack of education
An ignorant mistake
1. Unaware or uniformed

"Well that didn't sound so bad," she thought to herself. "It means there are some things he doesn't know about."

Steff knew what he did to the Impals. She also knew what he did to ascend to the presidency. Those, along with what he did to those defenseless people with a rifle was much worse than a mere ignorant mistake. It was horrible. Could her grandfather really do all those things just because he was ignorant? Did he not know it was a sin to kill people and steal something that doesn't belong to you, in this care the presidency?

But Carmella also said the ignorance breeds arrogance. Steff considered this and flipped to the front of the dictionary until she came upon the word.

Arrogant
1. Having or displaying a sense of overbearing self-worth or self-importance.
2. Marked by or arising from a feeling or assumption of one's superiority toward others.
An arrogant contempt for the weak.

Steff gasped after reading this part. Her grandfather definitely felt superior to everyone. He was God's chosen leader. She stared at the page and read the definition over and over. It was not too difficult to see how ignorance could lead one to a state of self-importance. After several long minutes, she put the book back on the shelf, but not before soaking several pages with her tears.

The more she paced the room, the more she felt she must get away, yet sanity held her back. However, sanity took an unscheduled break, somewhere between her 150-160th lap around the room. When it departed, there was only panic left to fill the void.

There was no other option left in Steff's troubled mind than to get away from this place and get back to her family. Her mental image included all them, even Abbs. Perhaps the only decent thing her grandfather did was not tell her of Abbs death. It didn't matter now though because she was hell bent on getting away.

The simple, salient thoughts did not occur to her such as it would be dark in two hours. She also did not know how she would get to them, and no idea where they were. No, the first and only order of business was to get out of her prison. To Steff, the White House was nothing more than Alcatraz Island, surrounded by a menacing sea of dark souls.

She knew she did not want to go back into the hallway because Carmella or the Secret Service would stop her before she could make it to the door. She decided her only option was to try and make it out a window. She was on the side of the White House facing Lafayette Square. As she studied her possible escape routes, she noticed something gruesome. The bloodstains from her grandfather's spree gleamed on the brick and concrete street like a demonic sign, reinforcing her grandfather's guilt. Her resolve tightened and she began to try the locks on the window.

Steff pushed until her thumbs were sore, but the window lock would not budge. She considered breaking the window with a wooden chair, but changed her mind. She remembered hearing her grandfather say one time that all the White House windows contained bulletproof glass. If they could repel the bullet from a high-powered sniper rifle, it would certainly deflect the weak attempts of a little girl swinging a chair.

She searched the room and found a shiny brass letter opener. With heaving, panicked breaths she carried it back across the room and began to dig at the lock; it still would not budge. Her breathing became more labored as anxiety started to course through her. It was as if the very air was turning to water and she was drowning, fighting to get to the surface. The surface was on the other side of the window. Finally, after several strong jabs from the letter opener, the lock moved about a half-inch. She hit it several more times, causing her knuckles to bleed as they smashed against the sash. Finally, it swung clear. She did the same thing with the other side, attacking it with much more fervor. Sweat began to pour down her face and her trachea constricted to the size of a straw. Each breath was a high-pitched whistle. Just as she felt as if consciousness were about to leave her, the lock popped free with a loud crack. She grabbed the sash and jerked the window upwards with a couple of hard tugs. The semi-cool evening air wafted into her face filling her with promise. Her relief was short lived as something else hit her in a cruel wave. She had been sealed inside the White House since arriving with her grandfather. She was not prepared.

While the city and military performed an admirable job of cleaning the corpses out of the nation's capital, it was not perfect. The stench of death was still heavy in the air. As it wafted into Steff's nose and mouth; the odor seemed to have a putrid taste. She felt as if she was going to vomit. This, coupled with her starved lungs, was more than her poor brain could stand. As consciousness left her body, she thought of her family. A brief and pleasant image bloomed in her head of her birthday party a year ago where everyone was together. Everyone was happy and all was right with the world. She never loved them as much as she did at that moment.

Steff was unconscious for what happened next. She tottered forward and fell headlong out of the window, plummeting almost thirty feet before landing on her head. Her short life ended with a terrible snap.

Gestas followed Rebekah and Malakhi all day as they wandered about the camp. They didn't seem to be doing anything out of the ordinary, but that is what scared him. He knew this dark soul was self-serving and held no regard for Malakhi. His only concern was to escape the dark void by any means necessary. Even if it meant clinging to Rebekah for decades like a corporeal life raft. Of course, Gestas knew how the dark souls thought. He knew sooner or later Malakhi would become a useless burden. It would cut him loose by the most efficient means available . . . death.

Shortly after dusk, the dark soul and Malakhi left a play area. They began to walk in the general direction of their tent. Gestas followed a good distance behind, but it was too far. Perhaps in the young male body of his former life it would have been close enough. In the broken down, geriatric body he now inhabited, it was impossible. The old heart in his chest almost seized when the dark entity turned and headed toward the darkness beyond the perimeter. Gestas pushed the old woman's legs as hard as he could, but only managed a fast totter as he tried to weave through the tents to catch up.

The harder he pushed, it seemed the further they drifted away from him. The dark soul pranced along pulling Malakhi by the hand like a mother lion bringing dinner to her cubs. The old woman's body resisted his efforts. Still, he pushed forward.

They were less than twenty yards from the darkness when something unexpected happened. Malakhi pulled loose from the dark soul's grasp and began running towards the camp, towards Gestas.

Gestas held out his arms in a beckoning gesture, but Malakhi did not trust the crazy old lady either. She had murdered someone in the tent right in front of him. He turned without thinking and bolted the other way. When he saw what he already suspected was not his mother, he stopped abruptly and lost his footing, landing on his back. It was on him in an instant. Grabbing him by the hair, it started to drag him toward the perimeter. It shouted curse words loud enough to be heard across the camp. It was hell bent on throwing the boy into the hissing gloom.

This short delay gave Gestas the time he needed to catch up. He wrapped a bony arm around Rebekah's neck and pulled her to the ground. Malakhi fell forward with them as it tightened its grip on his hair. He let out a scream of pain. The cries got the attention of the guards a short distance away and they came running with their weapons drawn.

Gestas saw the guards out of the corner of the woman's cataract eyes. He had no intention of being arrested and thrown in jail. The thing inside Rebekah could then feed Malakhi to the darkness at its leisure. He tried something desperate. He grabbed Rebekah's head between his hands and held on for dear life as the dark soul raged, cursed, and spat at him. The countenance on Rebekah's face was inhuman. Gestas was bringing the dark soul to the surface to reveal its true identity. Keeping a single minded focus, he moved his face closer until their foreheads touched. With all his spiritual might, he leapt forward. For a few moments, he was in a disorienting darkness, and then he began to adjust to his surroundings. The dark faded and he realized he had somehow accomplished his goal. He was inside of Rebekah. He could see her cowering in the background, just as the old woman did when he inhabited her body. There was something different. Something he should have expected. Somebody else was there.

Gestas hoped when he entered the body of Rebekah it would force the dark soul out. He wasn't completely sure how he had been able to enter her body since she was not incapacitated. Yet, in a way she was. The rightful owner of the body remained in the background. This dark soul now stood in front of him. Gestas didn't recognize the man. The void was a large, dark, and formless place.

The dark soul's eyes bulged from underneath a mop of black stringy hair. His lips peeled back to his gums, exposing a line of teeth so misshapen, they seemed pointed. He wore a generic tan tunic with long leather boots disappearing underneath. His fists clinched at his sides. Gestas knew this soul couldn't harm him, not physically. However, it was still in Rebekah and he could do considerable damage to her if he chose. Gestas knew he must tread carefully.

"So, what were you in for?" Gestas asked.

"For skulling do gooders like you," he growled.

This brief introduction yielded no name. It left no doubt in Gestas's mind that this was going to be a difficult task. He didn't think he possessed the strength to force him out, not by sheer will. Maybe there was somebody who did. The only way a dark soul could inhabit a body is if the owner agreed to it or were incapacitated.

The rightful owner was always so incapacitated with fear afterward, they were incapable of fighting back. This was the state where Rebekah now found herself. If Gestas could get to her, he hoped he could shake her from her fear; perhaps he could help her force it out.

It was as if the dark soul read Gestas's mind. It began running towards Rebekah who cowered in the corner of what appeared to be a large room with a hazy white floor, walls, and ceiling. Gestas, now unencumbered by frailties, took off at great speed. Even though the setting was all inside of Rebekah's mind, the stakes were every bit as high as if they were in the physical world.

The dark soul got there first, pulling at Rebekah with violent fervor. She screamed and covered her face. Gestas was there an instant later, flying headlong into the sadistic hijacker. It was not a collision of two bodies hitting each other. The impact was more like two waves colliding. Their spirit mass rippled across the room of Rebekah's mind in strobe lit shadows. After a few moments, they each recomposed themselves and dashed back towards Rebekah. She shrieked and buried her head under her arm when she saw them coming.

This time Gestas arrived first and embraced her, shielding her from the dark soul with his body.

"Rebekah, everything will be okay, trust me. You have to tell him to leave, you have to make him leave . . . you have to resist."

"Gestas?" Rebekah asked.

She did not recognize him since he was now outside the old woman's body. His long hair and stern features, not to mention his knee length brown tunic and sandals were unfamiliar to her.

"Yes," he said and winced as the dark soul struck him from behind. This time he did not go careening across the room, he grabbed Rebekah tighter and hung on.

As he pulled her closer, incredible horror and disgust distorted her features. This close vicinity to Gestas caused all his memories and thoughts to pour into her at once. She saw, knew, and felt every bad deed he ever committed. A sickness washed over her. She thought she would rather die than live with the memories of Gestas's sins. She tried to get away, but Gestas pulled her closer.

"No . . . I saw the things you did . . . you monster!" Rebekah wailed.

"I'm sorry!" Gestas pleaded. "That's why I have been helping you and Malakhi. I was wrong and I want to atone for it."

Rebekah thought Gestas had lot more to atone for than helping a woman and her son would cover. Nevertheless, something made her pause. Maybe it was the mention of her son's name. It was only part of the reason. She felt something else coming from Gestas. Despite all his horrible crimes, it made her feel pity for him. She felt sincerity. Rebekah began to empathize with him.

"Please help me," Gestas pleaded. "I can't get rid of him myself. This is your body, it's time you took it back."

Rebekah stared blankly for a moment. Soon, comprehension dawned on her delicate features and she rose to her feet.

"I'm going to kill your little bastard," the dark soul taunted from across the room. "While you two have been cuddling in the corner, I already started taking him back toward the woods. We're almost there!"

CHAPTER 36

A FATHER'S CHOICE

"He who spares the rod hates his son, but he who loves him is careful to discipline him."
~Proverbs 13:24

CECIL THOUGHT HIS FIRST MEETING with his father would be one of snide indignation. He would tell the old man what he thought about him. Then he would make some heroic proclamation such as 'do with me what you will' before throwing himself on his father's mercy. Of course, this would be under the sole condition he not mistreat Steff or Barbara. It did not work out quite the way he planned. Much to Cecil's shock, his first emotion was pity for his father. He gaped at the bandage covering the old man's eye. Tiny spots of blood blossomed on the sterile white surface making a macabre polka dotted monocle. The face staring through the bars was ashen and sallow, not to mention livid from pain. When he saw the rage burning in his father's good eye, his pity melted into fear. It was like seeing the gaping jaws of a stealthy shark emerging from the deep.

"Where are Barbara and Steff?" Cecil asked.

President Garrison did not respond. He continued to glower at his son.

"Where are they?" Cecil demanded after almost a minute of silence.

"Do you know how you made me look?" President Garrison sneered. "My own damned son acting against me!"

Cecil stared at him, incredulous. This is what it boiled down to? He was more concerned with the embarrassment he felt than the health and well being of his two granddaughters. He knew the old man didn't see it that way. Everything that had happened since the night at the camp was due to the actions of his ungrateful, disloyal son. The prodigal son . . . the one who his father believed would burn in Hell for his betrayal of him and God.

The long shadow of President Garrison's silhouette extended into the cell as he leaned further in. As the whispering of the dark souls dwelling in the silhouette of the ignorant man got nearer, anger exploded in Cecil. He leapt to his feet. His first instinct was to spring forward and seize his father by the throat, but the shadow prevented it. Instead, he hurled the only weapon available. Cecil spat in his father's face. It was a miraculous shot from almost six feet away, striking President Garrison in his good eye.

Garrison cursed as one of the veiled figures behind him stepped forward and offered a handkerchief. Cecil recognized the individual as Avery Cooper. He never met the man, but he knew the alleged nefarious relationship with his father. President Garrison snatched the handkerchief out of Avery's hand and wiped the saliva from his eye. He then wadded it up and chunked it back at Cecil, hitting him in the chest.

"I don't have a lot to say to you . . . *son*," he said with sarcastic emphasis. "I'll make this quick and to the point."

He cleared his throat and asked his two companions to leave. They did so, but under protest. The other person was Joan, who offered to gouge Cecil and Musial's eyes out before cutting out their hearts with a screwdriver. When they left the building, President Garrison turned and addressed Musial.

"What is your name?" he asked.

Musial remembered his instructions from Cecil before they arrived. "Lieutenant Sam Andrews," he said, shooting to his feet and standing at attention.

"So, am I to understand my son here forced you into being a traitor?"

Musial glanced at Cecil. It was a split second, but the short delay spoke volumes.

"Correct, sir," Musial said.

"Son, do you know who I am?" President Garrison asked.

"Yes sir. You are the President of the United States."

A satisfied grin washed across Garrison's face. This caused the bandage to bunch together, crinkling some of the blood spots into a single crimson blemish. He seemed pleased with Musial's response, yet there was something underneath the twinkle in his good eye. Something that threatened to explode at any second.

"Indeed I am soldier, indeed I am. Chosen and ordained by divine providence. You do believe in God, don't you soldier?"

"Of course, sir." Musial replied.

The truth was, neither Musial nor Sam Andrews were religious men. In fact, Andrews was closer to being an agnostic than affiliating with any religion. Musial had never considered the possibilities one way or the other, not until the dark void gave him plenty of time to reconsider. Garrison squinted his eye skeptically.

"I have a strong personal relationship with God, lieutenant. Did you know that?"

Musial was not sure how to reply, so he gave a single nod.

"I stepped out of line when I got too close to my work. God punished me for it," he said, pointing to his eye bandage, which was now much more red than white. "But he has blessed me far more than I could ever hope."

Musial watched him stone faced, waiting for him to continue.

President Garrison glanced at Cecil and then said, "In spite of the curse of a blasphemous child, the Lord chose me for great things. I am now the most powerful man in the world. I am charged with the task of defeating Satan's armies which hide like cowards in the darkness."

Musial was finding it difficult to keep from laughing. A flat thin smile creased his face as he suppressed a chuckle. Garrison must have taken it as a smile of agreement because he continued. "These Impals are now showing themselves for what they really are. Nevertheless, I, and a handful for other good servants, are immune to their influence," he said. He stepped back into the darkness of the hall to prove his point. The whispering and clicking grew louder as he penetrated the dark, and then fell silent.

"You see, they can't hurt me. God protects me from these foul beings so I can protect the world," said President Garrison from the shadows.

Musial was good at concealing his secret life when he was living, but he was never any good at holding his tongue. Especially when someone made claims that were downright false. He began to laugh; he couldn't help it. This brought President Garrison back from the gloom and he grasped the bars.

"What the hell is so damned funny?" he demanded.

"You," Musial snorted. "First of all, those aren't Impals in their true forms. They are dark souls who didn't work and play well with others while they were living. I'm guessing they probably pissed *your* God off."

"Shut up, Musial!" Cecil shouted, forgetting the identity ruse they were supposed to uphold. It didn't matter. Musial was about to blow it to smithereens. Musial ignored him and continued his tirade. "And you aren't immune to them, you ridiculous one-eyed jack! You are one of them! You know . . . birds of a feather and all that crap!"

President Garrison didn't seem to comprehend the meaning of Musial's words. He did comprehend the tone. "You watch your tone you little prick and remember who you are addressing!" he hissed.

"Musial, shut the hell up!" Cecil yelled again. It was no use. The argument was on.

"Who? A delusional old fool who thinks God is on his side? You aren't immune to the dark souls you pompous imbecile. They don't hurt you because you are one of them! You are a dark soul, *Mr. President*," Musial finished with heavy sarcasm.

In Garrison's book, it was the worst insult he could have endured, without outright calling him a child of Satan.

Cecil shook his head. All hope of them making it through this alive disappeared on Musial's words. He knew his father and he knew vengeance wasn't in his father's vocabulary because vengeance is not providential. However, he did practice it, but under another name . . . penitence. Each person must pay for their sins as prescribed by God. A knot formed in Cecil's stomach when he thought of Barbara and Steff. He remembered a sermon his father delivered one time about how the sins of the father are redirected on the children. Yes, there was little doubt that Barbara and Steff would be paying for his so called sins.

Before President Garrison could respond to Musial, Cecil interjected with a plea. "Punish me, I'll take anything you want to do with me. I will ask for repentance if it will satisfy you. Please let Barbara and Steff go. They had nothing to do with anything. For God's sake, let them go!"

His father's stare was icy.

"I think it would be scriptural to give Steff a pass since she repented and turned in all you evil doers. As for your wife, I am sure she was right there with you. Don't try and tell me she wasn't!"

"She wasn't," Cecil half-pleaded and half-screamed.

Garrison closed his good eye and tilted his head as if he were listening for a distant sound. "God has spoken to me about your guilt and he has entrusted me to carry out what must be done. I'm sorry son, but you know God comes before all else."

He actually sounded empathetic. Perhaps even a vestige of affection left for his prodigal son. If it were true, it was all lost in what he said next. "I think it is only fitting that you die the way deceitful Impals do. The Tesla Gate is running and I will be back for both of you soon. May God have mercy on you, but I wouldn't count on it!"

He turned and walked down the hallway, slamming the door shut behind him.

The military police found the cage in Private Jack Abernathy's home. As careful as Jack thought he was, there was still blood residue. The local police department long suspected a serial killer was operating in the area. Now, over 80% of the local police was dead. Manpower aside, it was impossible to mount a proper investigation under the current conditions. They would wait, and so would Jack, alone in his cell with only his hatred of Donna to sustain him.

Donna became the unwitting host of Mary during a heroine-induced stupor. She was many things, a drug addict, a prostitute . . . an enigma. More than anything else, she was terrified. Her body had suffered from the withdrawals of the last several days, but Mary handled it. The dark souls shared little connections to their inhabited body, outside of normal body functions. This was a good thing for Mary and Donna. The very fact of her presence was a saving grace for the young girl who would have died in a short time from an overdose. She smiled as she considered the young girl who might be scared straight from this ordeal. Her smile faded when her thoughts turned to her former life.

Mary was many things, but one thing she was not was a liar. She told Jack the truth of her identity. Whether he chose to believe her or not was up to him. She did her best to help him. Maybe her best was just getting him off the streets so he wouldn't harm anyone again.

As Jack wasted away in his cell, she sat in her private room a couple of buildings away, reflecting on her past. She shuddered when she remembered the ignorance of her former life. Her arrogance sent two hundred eighty-three souls to their deaths during her short five-year reign as Mary I, Queen of England. These poor souls died for the crime of being protestant. They refused to recognize the Catholic Church as the supreme religious authority of England. She had hated her father, King Henry VIII, for taking England out of the good graces of what she believed to be the one true church. She was determined to rectify his error once she assumed the throne. Her hatred consumed her. It led to the genesis of her ignorance which soon birthed the most arrogant queen Britain had ever known . . . and the bloodiest.

This was not the worst of it. She enjoyed the executions, most of which were burnings at the stake. She could imagine the soul receiving purification from the flames as the condemned screamed. The smell of burning flesh was a scent she soon began to associate with redemption and purification. It was an aroma that began to give her pleasure, not only spiritually, but corporally. Her notorious nickname, which was well earned, was the only thing that bothered her about the whole affair. How could anyone say such vile things about someone who carried out the will of the church?

There was not much physical connection between the dark souls and their body, but this time was an exception. Mary started to feel nauseous as she thought back to the horrific scenes which had earned her nickname. She dwelled on these images many times in the dark void. Yet without the aid of the olfactory senses, she had almost forgotten the smell of cremation. The more she thought, the more the memory of the smell came forward. The unmistakable aroma of burning pork and almonds filled her head and nostrils like a smell from a nightmare. It no longer brought her pleasure. If not for a convenient trashcan in the corner, she would have vomited all over the sterile white tile of her room.

When she finished, she walked over to a small sofa on the far wall and stretched out. Mary lay on her side, clutched a pillow to her churning stomach, and then she began to cry. She had not cried in over four hundred years. It felt good to cry. It was liberating and relaxing. Donna's body needed sleep and Mary needed rest. After several minutes of steady weeping, she fell asleep. It would not be a restful sleep; her slumber would be filled with the horrific screams and the tormented faces of her victims.

"How could I have been so wrong?" she asked herself.

She had asked herself the question many times in the void. Now, wrapped in the flesh of her host, it resonated through every pore with agony. She knew she was being watched, more from perversion than security. She was not going to give them the satisfaction of seeing her lose control.

The visual images were bad enough in her dreaming mind, but the smell also followed her into sleep. She didn't think she would ever forget the smell.

CHAPTER 37

LOST AND SAVED

"Blessed are the hearts that can bend; they shall never be broken."
~Albert Camus

THERE COMES A MOMENT in everyone's life when inspiration takes over. It is a momentary flash, an instant of an instant, but in that small moment a life can change forever. Rebekah had been cowering in her own mind the last several hours, too afraid to act or move. She feared any action on her part would cause herself harm, or even worse, harm to Malakhi.

This dark entity made one fatal mistake. It left her with no option but to fight. If soul and consciousness possessed such a thing as adrenaline, it coursed through her now. She flew across the space within her mind and hit the dark soul in the back. She then jumped on top of him. He buckled and fell forward, spinning to meet the challenge. She attacked faster than he could have imagined. Rebekah attacked with the fires of fury burning in her eyes; the raw instinct of a protective mother fueled her rage.

"Get out of my body and leave my son alone you damned dark bastard!" she roared.

Gestas watched with utter incredulity. He wasn't sure if he was more shocked by Rebekah's aggression or the language coming from her mouth. Either way, he found himself enjoying it very much.

Rebekah raised her octave to an ear splitting pitch. "Get the hell out of me and go back to your dark friends you piece of shit!"

The dark souls gaped at her in terror. Before he could retaliate, Rebekah wrapped her hands around his throat and squeezed.

"Get out of me now!" she growled, squeezing as hard as she could.

Choking or suffocation was not a fate that any non-corporeal entity could suffer. However, the point of the action was every bit as potent. The dark soul's face shifted in a kaleidoscope of terror, rage, surprise, and hatred. Over and over again it changed as Rebekah increased pressure. Rebekah fell forward and landed on her hands and knees as the dark soul vanished in a wisp of black smoke. Similar to waking from a deep anesthesia, Rebekah began to feel herself regaining control of her body. She was utterly exhausted. Gestas rushed forward and pushed her out of the way.

"Let me handle this, before it is too late!" he said.

Rebekah was too weak to do anything other than step aside. She knew she was in no condition to be of any good at the moment.

Gestas came forward and peered through Rebekah's eyes. He took control of her arms and legs, however he hadn't meshed with the rest of her body yet. The right hand grasped Malakhi. To his horror, the whole right side of Rebekah's body lay beyond the lighted perimeter of the base. Malakhi was shrieking in the dark. It was all Gestas could do to hold on as the child thrashed about and slammed his head into the ground. As Gestas fought to pull the flailing boy towards him, he saw lights and movement to his left. He turned towards them, hurling Malakhi before him. An instant later, they were lying face down on the grass, heaving and panting. Gestas barely registered the sound of soldier's boots surrounding them. He was more concerned with the artificial light now bathing them from head to toe. It was like escaping a raging inferno into an ice-cold pool.

"Don't move!" one of the soldiers shouted.

Gestas was staring at the ground and could not see. He heard the click of an assault rifle and knew it was aimed at him. When satisfied Malakhi was safe, he retreated into Rebekah's mind.

"Malakhi is a little shaken up but he is okay. It's time for you to come forward now," Gestas said, taking Rebekah by the hand and pulling her forward.

She seemed reluctant. "What are you going to do now?" she asked.

Ruth was being carried away by two soldiers to the medical tent. They would have taken her to the psychiatric tent if one existed. She kept babbling about the ghost in a tunic and sandals. When examined, they would find traces of drugs and alcohol in her system. Her incredible stories would be chalked up to one big delusional dream of an addict in withdrawal. The one good thing was, whether it was scared straight or a major epiphany, she remained sober for the rest of her life. Regardless of the old woman's condition, Rebekah knew Gestas could not return to her.

Gestas looked at her sheepishly as he asked. "Would it be okay if I remain? You know, just until the eye of the storm has passed."

Rebekah gave him a wary frown.

"I promise I will stay out of the way. If I don't, you know how to get rid of me," he said and then pretended to choke an invisible neck.

Rebekah smiled. "Okay, but please give me my privacy."

Gestas nodded. "Of course," he said.

Rebekah came forward and took control in time to feel herself seized by strong hands and jerked to her feet.

Carmella had not wept as hard in her life as when she went outside to see Steff's body lying amongst the azalea bushes on the north lawn. Even her own mother's passing did not invoke such an emotional response. Perhaps it was because her mother's death was expected. She was ninety years old and in declining health for years. This was part of it, but not all. She felt a tremendous guilt because she was supposed to be watching over the poor girl. She failed. In the short time she spent with Steff, she developed a real affection for her. They formed a kinship of two tormented souls who had both faced hardship in their lives under the banner of ignorance.

"Oh you poor dear child," she wailed, dropping to her knees beside Steff's body and stroking her long, blood soaked hair.

A few guards and Secret Service milled around nearby. They seemed more interested in the pedestrians who stopped to gawp at the scene.

There was nothing more Carmella could do or say so she just cried until another White House aide came out and ushered her back inside. The Secret Service transported the body to nearby Bethesda Hospital. It was one of the few buildings in the city left with power after the mandatory black outs. Those who weren't dead were now in one of a dozen bases surrounding the nation's capital.

Carmella spent the next hour composing herself. She gave strict instructions that the president was not to be disturbed in any way. "He is on important business," she told them. She did know it was important to the president's attempt to squash dissent.

Even though Carmella was around the mid-range level in authority at the White House, no one questioned her. Everyone who would have been above her were now dead or in the company of President Garrison. Those with him at the moment would have killed her if they were there.

As Carmella sat alone in her office, a strange emotion started to take hold. Not that the emotion itself was strange, but rather it was strange to feel it in her current state. She started to feel hope and a little bit of relief. Carmella felt guilty about these new emotions. Yet the more she considered them she began to realize it made complete sense.

Carmella knew, and so did Steff, that President Ott Garrison must die. It was the right thing for the country and it was the right thing for the world. Death was the only thing that could break his ignorance and humble his arrogance. The car Steff saw Carmella loading was not loaded with traditional duffle bags. These bags contained high powered explosives. Two of her conspirators were Secret Service Agents and they would insure the car got to Quantico and picked up the president. The next leg of his journey would be to another base. There, he would weed out more rebels. The agents' plan was to weed out Garrison himself and as many cronies as they could take with him. The car was scheduled to leave Washington that evening to pick him up for the trip to Camp Lejeune in North Carolina.

As Carmella wiped her tears, a memo caught her attention. It had been placed on top of her work stack on her desk. She reached over and picked it up, squinting through swollen tear filled eyes to read.

> To: White House Sr. Staff
> From: Vice President Avery Cooper
> Please be advised, the president has scored another great victory today in the fight to keep America free. He will not stop until every evil spirit is put down along with every traitor who supports them. Today, at approximately 1430 hours EST, public enemy number one was captured. Major Cecil Garrison, the president's dishonorable son, along with four other conspirators were captured. They are now held in maximum security at Quantico where they await judgment for their crimes. More information will be forthcoming as these traitors face justice.
> Long live President Ott Garrison and long live the United States of America!
> Signed,
> The honorable Avery Cooper

Carmella felt a sudden sting of anger. The memo dripped with hypocrisy and downright ignorance. Not to mention, it disregarded one of the primary tenants of the Constitution. Weren't they innocent until proven guilty? This memo not only angered and sickened her, it added more fuel to the hope she felt. As much as it disturbed her, she felt relieved that Steff was gone. This freed her up to do what must be done in regards to Garrison. An emotional cyclone raged within her as she shifted from hope to disgust to relief to self-loathing. Finally, she summoned enough strength to pick up the phone and make a call.

Carmella was determined to be in the car when it left tonight, not for a suicide mission but rather a rescue mission. She saw an opportunity to do right by Steff. She could at least save her parents. If nothing else, she also owed it to them to deliver the news of their daughter's passing in person. This was not a task she relished, yet it needed to be done.

They would be there to pick her up within the hour. They must move fast because it would be dark in three hours. Carmella pulled a small hand mirror out of her desk and began to compose herself. She found it quite difficult as her hands trembled, so she set it face up on her desk to complete the task. She knew the chances were good she would not succeed in even getting close to Steff's parents. She would probably die in the process. She took a deep breath and fought through the fear. She had not been afraid of death before, especially after the Impals appeared. Their presence gave a hope and certainty of something beyond our existence. But now the eye of storm dictated a new reality; a reality where darkness and death ruled. How did it affect beliefs? What did it mean to the soul? If she died now, in the eye of the storm, would she be condemned to join the darkness? Was it Steff's fate? Tears streamed down her cheeks as she tried to convince herself it wasn't true, it was only pure imaginative fiction. However, fact and fiction had become interchangeable since the storm arrived. Four months ago, she would have thought ghosts were fiction. What if all the tens of thousands, if not millions, of people who were killed by the darkness not been victims, but recruits? Perhaps the dark demanded their suicide while pulling the soul into the shadows. She didn't think this was the case and did not want to believe it, but the mere thread of a possibility scared the hell out of her.

She finally grabbed the mirror and flung it across the room. Hundreds of glass shards rained onto the carpet when the mirror made contact with the far wall.

"Screw it!" she muttered.

She gave up on making herself presentable. Who was she trying to impress? Presenting a professional appearance was the last thing on her mind at the moment. In fact, there were not many in the White House now who didn't look as if they hadn't slept or bathed in days. Staying in the light and staying alive was everybody's priority. The vulnerability of a private bath and sleep was too much to risk.

Carmella grabbed her Bible from a nearby shelf and ran her fingers over the smooth leather surface. She took a couple of deep breaths and then walked downstairs to meet her fellow conspirators. They would take the short trip in the same limousine she hoped would give Ott Garrison his last ride.

CHAPTER 38

AT THE GATE

"And capital punishment, however ineffective it may be and through whatever ignorance it may be resorted to, is a strictly defensive act,—at least in theory."
~Benjamin Tucker

CECIL AND MUSIAL SAT IN SILENCE as the afternoon sun began to cast long shadows from the single window at the end of the hallway. The hiss and clicks of the dark drew ever nearer. Cecil felt as if he would explode if he could not break free from his cell and rescue Barbara and Steff. Standing and facing the wall, he made tight fists and pressed them hard against the cinder block surface. He channeled his frustration into the immovable wall. A foolish part of him hoped a sudden burst of adrenaline would give him the strength needed to push through to the outside. He began to tremble. He wasn't scared, not for himself. The thought of Barbara and Steff in the clutches of the man he considered a psychopath enraged him.

"Your dad is a real prick, isn't he?" Musial said.

Cecil did not acknowledge him, instead he continued to stare straight ahead.

"With all due respect to your mother, I think the man needs to get laid," Musial continued.

266

Musial didn't intend any disrespect towards Cecil; he was just trying to lighten the mood in his own crass way. Cecil did not find it humorous. He pushed off the wall and rounded on Musial who was sitting on the bunk.

"My mother is dead!" Cecil hissed as he leaned down inches from Musial's face. "And my father doesn't give a damn. I'm sure he thinks she deserved to die because of some sin she committed . . . that's why he believes I deserve to die."

Musial's mouth opened and closed as if he were trying to form words, but none came.

Cecil's eyes narrowed and his teeth clinched as he said, "You said you used to be a magician?"

Musial nodded.

"You also said you were seeking forgiveness . . . for salvation?"

Musial nodded again.

"Well, Mr. Magician, what kind of tricks do you have up your sleeve now to get us out of this and redeem yourself?"

Musial's face was etched with defeat. Yes, he was a magician. He was a small time magician over a hundred years ago when crowds were much less sophisticated than they are today. He might be able to do a card trick, if they had some cards, or pull a rabbit out of a hat, if they had a rabbit and a hat. Otherwise, he was at a loss. He did perform escapes, but not from a modern jail with modern locks. Musial did the only thing he could do; he stared at the floor and shook his head. For the first time since inhabiting the drunken Sam Andrews, he felt lost and unsure. Had he done enough to get out of the dark void? There was no way to say for sure. There was hope, but fear was always a more powerful motivator in Musial's life. The enigma of the storm was as much an unknown to him as it was to the rest of the world.

Cecil turned when he got no answer from Musial and returned to his wall, resuming the pressure with his fists. He leaned in and pressed his ear against the cool surface. Even though he knew better, he imagined Barbara on the other side of the wall, waking up from her traumatic slumber. She would be calling out for him. Maybe Steff was in there with her and they were both calling for him.

Cecil pressed against the wall until the whole side of his face was numb. He didn't hear anything other than his own breathing and the darkness in the corridor. As he was about to switch to his other ear, Musial spoke. It was quiet, but clear and calm.

"You will see your mother and daughter again, I have no doubt."

"What did you say?" Cecil asked.

"There is an upside of death . . . for you anyway," Musial said. "You're a good man, major, and I have no doubt your death will bring the liberty that mine did not. You can stay here or you can move on. In any case, you can be with you mother and daughter."

"What about my wife and my other daughter?" Cecil snapped.

Musial shrugged. "If you all die, then you will all be together. I have no doubt your wife and daughter are good people. If your wife wasn't, she wouldn't be in the state she is in now. The dark would not have harmed her."

"It seems kind of twisted doesn't it?" Cecil said.

"The dark souls are not here to judge and condemn, they are going about their nature. What seems like judgment is simply, let's say . . . professional courtesy to their kin."

"So my wife is lying somewhere in a catatonic state, Burt has a terminal injury, and Dr. Winder is dead because they are good people?" Cecil laughed without humor.

"Yes, they are," he sighed.

Cecil grimaced. He pressed his other ear to the wall and listened in vain. He heard everything Musial said, but hearing and accepting are two different things. His worry for his family gave little room for acceptance. He did not have long because a few minutes later they heard the metallic clank and squeak of the outside door. The door remained open as a long ray of afternoon sunlight flooded the hallway, driving the darkness away. The sunlight settled like a spotlight on the half solid, half opaque, infinity symbol across the hall. Cecil had seen this painted Myriad symbol weeks earlier when he occupied this cell. It was a sign, a harbinger of something, but of what he did not know. He didn't have long to ponder. A second later, three people stood outside the bars, obstructing his view of the Myriad symbol.

"Major Garrison, Lieutenant Andrews," a vaguely familiar male voice said. The speaker stepped forward out of the glare and Cecil recognized Avery Cooper.

Cecil and Musial said nothing.

"Under Article 106a of the Uniform Code of Military Justice, you have both been tried and convicted in a court martial hearing. The charge was treason against the United States of America. Your sentence will now commence in accordance," Avery said pompously.

"I don't recall any court martial hearing," Cecil snapped.

"You weren't invited, son," President Garrison said as he stepped forward. He stood shoulder to shoulder with Avery. He made 'son' sound more like an expletive than a term of endearment. He wore a fresh bandage over his eye, but it still had some blood spots. President Garrison needed more medical attention than a gauze pad taped over his eye. Nevertheless, he wasn't going to worry about it until he carried out justice.

"Isn't it my right?" Cecil snapped.

"Not when you are a danger to yourself or to the court, which you are," Avery interjected. "We reviewed the evidence and voted on it by a jury of your peers."

Cecil was angry and desperate, but he knew that arguing with the man was pointless. He doubted if there was a hearing, at least one in the traditional sense. He knew the sentence, it was a foregone conclusion. His father decided it long before he arrived at the base. What Cecil said next gave Avery a moment of shocked surprise.

"So, how am I to be executed . . . hanging, firing squad, lethal injection?"

"Since you tried to save Impals from the Tesla Gate, I think it is a fitting punishment," President Garrison said.

Cecil had not expected this. He knew what the Tesla Gate would do to a living person per his conversation with Dr. Winder. The world was full of irony and Cecil seemed cursed with it.

Musial said, "Would it make any difference if I told you I am not Sam Andrews?"

Avery laughed. "Who are you then?"

Cecil wished Musial would shut up. He knew no matter what Musial said, they were both going to face execution. He didn't want his father and Avery to be entertained in the process.

"My name is Musial. I was a magician in Europe in the late 1800s. I inhabited Mr. Andrews's body in an attempt to redeem myself from the darkness."

There it was, the truth was out. The truth in this case amounted to little more than comedic fodder for their captors.

"Damn you, Musial," Cecil thought

"Musial, huh?" President Garrison said with a wry grin. "Well tell me, Stan the man," he said. "If you're a magician, why don't you make yourself disappear? Can't you get out of something as simple as a prison cell?"

Musial did not answer. There was no way out of this. His father and Avery stood just outside their cell, armed with pistols. A soldier behind them waited with his assault rifle ready. At first, Cecil thought the sunlit hallway was for their benefit, so they could walk unmolested to the Tesla Gate. Then he saw the soldier. The distant expression and sallow face left little doubt this man could not enter the dark.

Cecil considered his own moral dilemma as well. If they tried to resist, they would be gunned down. At least it would not give President Garrison the pleasure of placing them in the Tesla Gate. Cecil considered the option for a few brief moments, until Barbara and Steff came to mind. The longer he was alive, the better chance he would have of getting to them.

"I want you to show me your backs now!" President Garrison demanded. "We are then going to enter the cell and bind your hands. Any issues and Sergeant Newland here will blow your head off . . . understood?" He said, gesturing over his shoulder at the poor recruit drafted into this despicable duty. Cecil thought he saw the barrel of the rifle begin to tremble in the man's hands. They might get shot anyway from nervousness.

"It's okay," Cecil said in a calm voice, speaking more to the sergeant than anyone else. "There will be no problem, right?" he said, cutting his eyes at Musial.

Musial shrugged. "Not if you don't think Lieutenant Andrews will mind if I get him executed."

There was laughter from behind them as they turned and faced the wall. A moment later, they heard the click of the cell door and the sudden screech of metal as it opened. Then they heard the unmistakable click of an assault rifle. Their wrists were bound with zip ties which cut into their flesh. Cecil bit his lip to avoid crying out.

"Can't use metal cuffs," Avery said as if discussing the weather. "The iron cuffs on the Impals caused a few problems Metal doesn't mix too good with the Shredder."

"But we do?" Cecil thought but did not say.

"Why don't you get them a little tighter," Musial said, sticking his bound hands back toward their captors. "I'm a magician. You don't want me to escape, do you?"

Musial screeched with pain as Avery grasped the end of the twist tie and jerked it tighter.

"Thank you," Musial said. "That should add to my difficulty level."

"Shut up you ass," Avery growled and then grabbed Musial's arms. With a hard yank, he steered him into the hallway.

"Let's go, son," President Garrison said as he grabbed Cecil by the arms and followed behind Avery. There was no gentle or sympathetic prodding as they walked. Cecil may as well have been a mean and vicious animal the way his father jerked and pushed him.

A few moments later, they emerged in the bright sunshine. They stepped over a smattering of small limbs and leaves cluttered on the grounds. They were no doubt from the storm that brought the tornado down on their cabin. As Cecil screwed up his eyes, he saw the menacing form of the hangar housing the Tesla Gate. He tried to inhale as much fresh air as he could and soak in as much sun as possible during their short walk to the hangar. This would be his last chance to enjoy those simple pleasures of life because he knew he wasn't coming out of the hangar alive.

CHAPTER 39

DISTANT THUNDER

"Disappointments are to the soul what a thunderstorm is to the air."
~*Friedrich Schiller*

REBEKAH WOKE UP TO FIND HERSELF LYING on a cot in a crude medical tent. Patients occupied rows of cots lining the walls. The smell of alcohol, sweat, and excrement filled the air in a pungent fog. It was a warm early morning and the only relief was from a few large box fans. Rebekah tried to get up when she remembered what happened, but she could barely move.

"Malakhi!" she called out with a dry and parched throat.

She heard a voice and jumped. Her heart hammered until she remembered her guest. It was Gestas speaking to her in her mind.

"Malakhi is okay," he said. "But . . . they think you tried to throw him into the dark. It's going to take some convincing to get you out of this."

"How do you know?" Rebekah asked.

"While you were sleeping I couldn't see anything, but I listened. There is a guard posted outside the door over there."

"Where is Malakhi?" Rebekah demanded.

"I don't know," Gestas admitted. "I just know they took him somewhere safe."

272

Rebekah tried to sit up again and discovered the reason for her inability to move. She was hand cuffed to the cot, both hands and both feet. Anxiety began to drive the air from her lungs. She felt as if she were going to drown in the hot and arid air.

"Calm down," she heard Gestas say. "Everything will be okay, you must stay calm."

Gestas reflected for a few hours while Rebekah was unconscious. In that time, he had a startling revelation. When he first took control of the old woman, his mindset was quite different. While he craved release from the void, he still harbored a strong desire to return to his nature. If he were honest with himself, his initial motivations were selfish. He wanted to get out of the void and move on, no matter what the cost. He also wanted to rape, murder, and steal. The drive remained with him because he struggled with it daily. He was not sure when the change started or when it took hold. The selfish desires were now almost gone. It was similar to the sudden and miraculous recovery from an illness. He didn't know when it started, he just knew that the desires were now buried deep in the back of his consciousness. They were still there, yet they no longer owned him. The most incredible thing was he realized his concern for Rebekah and Malakhi was no longer directed at what they could help him do. He cared for their well being.

"I can't be calm, Gestas," Rebekah said. "Not now, not when my son is away from me."

Before Gestas could reply, a noise like violent thunder rattled the tent making it sway as if in a high wind.

"What was that?" Rebekah cried, raising her head up as far as she could.

Gestas did not answer immediately, but when he did, chills ran through her body.

"Oh my God," he said, and then she could feel him drifting away from her until she could no longer sense him.

Jack awoke from a dream. In the dream, he threw Donna in his cage then pummeled, prodded, and bashed her to death. He felt good until consciousness coalesced. By the time he was wide awake he was no longer excited or satisfied; Jack was pissed. He got up and paced around his cell.

He was starting to feel caged and trapped. He knew he would never be free again. They found the cage. As soon as it was possible, they would check the marsh near his house and uncover his great service to humanity. It *was* a great service after all, but he didn't expect them to understand. Mankind was flawed and imperfect, not to mention ignorant. Man's arrogance would not allow them to understand the great works he accomplished. He was sure he would die an unappreciated man, yet he could make peace with it. The dark appreciated him; he felt it. Jack started to get a small fuzzy feeling in the pit of his stomach, but it was short lived.

He was jolted out of his brooding trance by a rumbling noise. It shook the building and vibrated his furniture across the room. It was as if a bolt of lightning ripped the sky in half and struck outside the wall. There was no bright flash nor a burning smell of ozone, yet the thunder persisted for several long and deafening moments. He heard agitated whispers and frantic clicks coming from the dark hallway. Jack's warm fuzzy feeling went out as fast as dropping a match into a bucket of water. It was soon replaced by terrible fear and dread.

Two Secret Service agents rode up front. David Fields, a White House junior secretary, rode with Carmella in the backseat of the limousine. Carmella was fidgety. Perhaps it was because David Fields was the most notorious sexist and narcissist she knew. Under normal circumstances, she would rather have a root canal with no Novocain. Today was not normal. David sat uncharacteristically stoic, saying nothing as he gazed out the window at the monuments. Carmella was sure he was thinking the same thing as she was— "*Is this the last time I am ever going to see this town?*"

She gazed out the window too and said a silent prayer. Her stomach churned, but it was not just because they were on their way to kill Garrison. It was also because a few feet behind her back, sat about eighty pounds of explosives in the trunk. The road was pocked with more pot holes than she ever noticed before. They soon passed the

Lincoln Memorial and headed out of town towards their date with destiny.

Carmella studied the massive building and thought of the kind man who lived in the White House for a short time during the storm. He soon left, forced out by his own sense of morality and decency. Where was he now? She did not know the answer. She hoped and prayed all the Impals had moved on.

A half hour later, they arrived at Quantico where they were quickly flagged through the gate. As they made their way to the administration building, no one noticed the people in the distance trudging across a field toward a large hangar. There were five of them in all. If Carmella had seen them, she might recognize one of them as President Garrison.

They pulled up at the administration office where Joan and Sebastian met them.

"You stay and drive!" Joan shouted, pointing at the Secret Service agent behind the wheel. The agent glanced with horror at his companion. What could he say? Any argument would raise suspicion and this would be their one chance to get to Garrison. The other agent was about to open the passenger door when Sebastian slammed it shut.

"What the hell are you doing?" he snapped. "We are going to need a security detail . . . keep your ass in your seat!"

Joan flung open the backdoor and ducked her head inside, glaring at David and Carmella.

"Who in the hell are you?" she growled.

"I'm Carmella Danson. I'm the president's executive assistant and this is David Fields. He is a junior secretary in the Executive Office."

"Nobody asked for you to come!" Joan shouted. She reached in and grabbed Carmella by the hair and jerked her outside. She rolled across the sidewalk before slamming her back into a concrete planter. Carmella let out a moan and lay motionless.

"Get your ass out!" she yelled, lunging at David.

David was no idiot. He jettisoned himself out the far door, landing on his hands and knees before crawling away.

Sebastian Gardner leaned in the front driver's window and relayed instructions to the driver. He then climbed in the back and sat beside Joan.

"What did President Garrison tell you?" he asked, leaning towards Joan.

She took his posture as a little aggressive and glared at him. "First, you stay on your side of the car, understand?" she said then hit the window power button and stuck out her head. She yelled at Carmella who was starting to get up. "You better get your ass inside, it's going to be dark soon!"

Carmella had the wind knocked out of her. Her aged joints and muscles ached. She cursed Joan in her head and wisely nodded. Carmella did not know Joan at all aside from a brief introduction at the White House.

This was not going according to plan at all. Tip Saunders, the Secret Service agent driving the limo, was to be the president's chauffer. He would also be a probable suicide bomber. His first priority would be to make sure that Garrison died, even if it meant he went out with the president. A remote switch would activate the bomb. Not a sensitive automatic detonation switch, rather one that would arm a one-hour countdown. This might give the agent the opportunity to distance himself from certain death if given time and opportunity. Agent Saunders would not have the opportunity. Everything happened so fast, the activation remote was not handed off to Agent Saunders. It was still in someone else's possession. The uncomfortable bulge in Carmella's slacks pocket confirmed this.

As the limousine turned the corner and disappeared from sight, she reached down and pulled it out of her pocket. She drew it close to her face, squinting in the bright rays of the descending sun. It was not yet activated.

"Do it!" David said, scrambling to her side. A handful of soldiers came out of the administration building to investigate the commotion.

"But he's not in there," Carmella protested.

"He will be in a minute," David said. "They are scheduled to arrive at Camp Lejeune about midnight."

David cut his eyes at the approaching soldiers then turned back to Carmella.

"Do it now, you won't have another chance!"

Carmella believed Garrison needed to die. However, believing it and serving as the instrument of someone's death are two different things. Several thoughts flashed through her head at one time, most of them were of Steff. This was her grandfather. She knew Steff loved him in spite of the things he had done. Carmella loved Steff. Of course, Steff was gone now. Was her Impal standing nearby and watching to see what she would do? She knew she couldn't let conjecture influence her. As the soldiers approached, she held the remote against her chest and took a deep breath. Carmella closed her eyes and said a quick prayer. She then opened them and stared straight ahead. "I'm sorry, sweetheart," she whispered.

Carmella closed her eyes again and pushed the button. In one hour the car would explode killing whoever was in it.

CHAPTER 40

TRICKS

"Tricks and treachery are the practice of fools, that don't have brains enough to be honest."
~Benjamin Franklin

CECIL GARRISON HAD VISITED the enormous hangar housing the Tesla Gate once before. He was familiar with the infamous Shredder. This time, it was like entering an unfamiliar location in a convoluted nightmare. Today, the Gate crackled with hungry intensity. The archway no longer resembled a benign construct; it was the gaping maw of a leviathan, ready to devour whatever came close. The blue light dancing around the hangar made Cecil think of a violent lightning storm. Perhaps it is why he or Musial didn't notice the sudden thunderous rumble coming from outside. President Garrison and Avery noticed. They glanced at each other as they marched their prisoners up the wooden platform in front of the Shredder. The platform swayed as the dark corners of the hangar hissed with venomous anger.

"We are not going to waste a lot of time with you traitors," President Garrison proclaimed. "At least your deaths will serve a purpose."

"What purpose?" Cecil spat.

"Perhaps you will take a few of these demons with you," President Garrison said.

278

It dawned on Cecil what his father had in mind. "You're going to turn the lights out and then swing us into the Tesla Gate?" he asked, noticing the two ropes dangling from a beam high overhead.

"You may have been a disappointment, but you were always intelligent," President Garrison said.

"Don't we get last words?" Musial asked with a wide, snarky smile.

"You can save those for God, son. I'm really not interested." President Garrison said.

"I'm sure God doesn't care what either one of us have to say," Musial said, regarding President Garrison with disdain. "He has someplace dark in mind for you," he said with a twinkle in his eye. President Garrison backhanded him. Musial stumbled backwards. "Fascist," he muttered under his breath.

"I guess you get the honor of going first," President Garrison said. He motioned for Avery to bind the rope under his arms.

Musial shrugged and stared at Garrison with cool defiance. He offered no resistance as Avery slid the rope under his bound arms. He then pulled it tight, squeezing Musial's lungs in the process. Musial did his best to avoid gasping as air puffed from his pursed lips. President Garrison did the same with Cecil. He postured himself more akin to a military official presenting a medal than an executioner presenting a rope.

A few moments later, the clanging of a metal door shutting echoed through the massive structure. A solitary soldier marched across the floor; stopping to salute President Garrison. He then walked over and took a seat at a long console of buttons and monitors. After several minutes of inspecting the controls, he gave Garrison the thumbs up.

"Is he the man you interviewed last night?" Avery asked.

Garrison nodded. It seemed they had found another kindred soul in the military population of the base.

"Yes, another Godsend," President Garrison said. "God be praised."

Of course, Garrison did not care about his peers who shared the trait of immunity to the dark. In his mind, God had put them there in order for him to pick and choose. The ones who did not serve his purpose were discarded like diseased cattle. If allowed to live, they might damage his unique stature in the world. He could not allow it.

President Garrison pulled Cecil back and lashed the slack in his rope around a post protruding from the back of the platform.

"Can't have the darkness make you do anything premature after we turn the lights out," President Garrison said. "You wait your turn," he said, wagging his finger under Cecil's nose.

The only way for Cecil to get comfortable, was to slump to the ground. He slid down, planting his haunches on the deck and his back pressed against the pole.

President Garrison and Avery conversed quietly in the middle of the platform. Cecil's mind raced with thoughts of his family. He would go quietly into the Tesla Gate if only he knew his family would be okay. A moment later, his worst nightmare was visited upon him. Another metallic clang echoed through the hangar as another door opened and closed. This time the echo was underscored by a strange squeaking noise. Cecil strained hard to see, but could only catch a glimpse of the silhouette of a hospital gurney pushed by a person in military fatigues. The curvature of the shadow on top of the gurney suggested someone lay upon it.

President Garrison noticed Cecil straining for a peek. He turned to face him with his hands open in supplication. "I'm sorry, I should not have tied you down so soon," he said. "Not until you had a chance to see your coconspirator."

Cecil's heart palpitated so hard he felt as if his head were throbbing. Who had he brought on the gurney? The most logical choices were Burt or Barbara. He hoped his father wouldn't be *that* cruel.

"Who is it?" Cecil croaked.

His father's face beamed with satisfaction.

"You have been a poor example to my granddaughters," President Garrison scolded. "But it's not all you. Your harlot wife had a hand in their upbringing too."

"Please," Cecil begged. "Please spare her. I'll do whatever you want. I'll sign a confession. I'll even go on the radio and proclaim I was wrong. Just please let her live."

President Garrison shook his head and spoke completely devoid of affection.

"Son, the only thing that is going to make this world better is the elimination of the evil in it. This includes anyone who harbors and supports it."

The sound of thunder rumbled again, this time it was much closer. The ropes which the two men were now attached quivered as the support beam above vibrated.

"What the hell is that?" Garrison snapped at Avery.

Avery shrugged. "I don't know . . . another thunderstorm maybe?"

Garrison watched until the vibration ceased. When convinced it had stopped, he turned back to Cecil. "Sorry, son. I'm sure in her catatonic state she won't suffer much," he said.

Cecil raged against his binding and uttered a string of expletives at his father. President Garrison didn't mind killing or torture when it suited the situation. However, profanity was something he just couldn't abide.

"Shut your disrespectful mouth!" Garrison growled and delivered Cecil a good swift kick to his abdomen. This accomplished the desired effect of shutting him up as he gasped for air.

"Another word out of you and I'll make that Jezebel wife of yours go first! I'll make you watch!"

Avery's phone rang. He reached in his pocket and answered it. After several short answers, he hung up and put it back in his pocket.

"It was Sebastian and Joan," he said. "They were confirming you wanted them to go on without us."

"What did you tell them?" Garrison asked.

"I said, yes and we would catch a military flight in the morning."

Garrison nodded and gazed back and forth to Musial and Cecil. "Good, we have a lot we need to do tonight."

"Well, shall we get on with it?" Garrison asked, clapping his hands together. "Colonel Kimbrow is expecting us for dinner and I am starving."

"Of course," Avery said, giving Musial's rope a quick jerk.

"When you turn . . . the lights off, . . . the dark is going . . . to go after Barbara. . . . How are you going to . . . protect her if you . . . want to kill her last?" Cecil managed to rasp out between labored breaths.

"She's strapped down," Avery said with a dismissive wave. "The dark can't do anything to her that she can't do to herself."

"Oh, by the way, son," Garrison said in a distant voice as he seemed to stare beyond the maniacal gate. "You can lie to me all you want about your companions. You and I both know the truth."

"What—do you mean?" Cecil gasped.

"Captain Golden, the one who tried to beat his own brains out. Well, I have it on pretty good authority, he was the one who broke you out of your cell. That in itself is a traitorous act; never mind what he has done since then."

Cecil's stomach churned like a stormy sea as his heart began to sink into its turbulent depths. He didn't say anymore because what good would it do? He knew his father was going to finish his story; it was too rich for him not to.

"I ordered the base surgeon not to treat him. I saw no point in wasting precious resources on a traitor." He laughed without humor. "God told me that resources were too valuable to waste on the unfaithful."

He glanced at Cecil for a response. When none came, he checked his wristwatch.

"He's dead you know. Got what he deserved about an hour ago."

Cecil's outrage seethed inside, yet he held his tongue and composure. He wasn't going to give his father the satisfaction. Susan crossed his mind. What had they done to her? He decided he didn't want to know. What good would it do him now?

Another blast of thunder rolled through the hangar. This one was much closer than the previous two. For whatever reason, it seemed to instill Garrison with a heightened sense of urgency.

"Let's get to it Avery," he said as he motioned at Musial, then stepped beside his condemned son.

Avery pulled Musial forward and stood him inches from the edge of the platform. The plan was to shut off the light and when the dark souls tormented Musial a while, he would shove him into the Gate. They hoped to take a number of them with him.

"I hope you've gotten right with the Lord," Avery hissed in his air. "Because you aren't welcome here anymore."

"I hope *you* have," Musial muttered, but Avery didn't hear him over the crackle and hum of the Tesla Gate.

Avery held up a hand and pointed at the soldier sitting behind the control panel. He nodded to indicate everything was ready. A moment later, Avery dropped his arm and the hangar plunged into complete darkness. Only the ethereal blue and gray light from the Tesla Gate remained. Musial jerked and cried out in agony. Cecil jerked backwards as the dark enveloped him. He was in the canoe again, the nest of water moccasins engulfing him like a cold and slimy hand.

His body radiated with pain from head to toe with every venomous bite. He wanted to escape the anguish. If death were the best option then so be it. This time was every bit as potent as the last two times he found himself in the dark, yet it was different. He was seeing a whole new horde of dark souls, along with each and every one of their sins. Each a disturbing example of the evil man is capable of. If this kept up much longer, madness would set in before he could partake of the sweet release of death. He wanted death and nothing else, not even Barbara, his girls, or his friends occupied his thoughts.

Cecil, in his own nightmare, hadn't heard Musial's screams, Musial's fake screams. They were cries that Avery enjoyed at first, until they became his own screams. When Avery began to scream, Garrison shouted for the lights. It did not happen right away. Between the screams echoing through the hangar and the strum of the Gate, the hapless soldier did not hear him at first. The soldier who wheeled in Barbara on the gurney sprinted to the station and relayed the command.

By the time the lights came on, Garrison stood on the platform a few feet from Musial and Avery. His mouth hung open with incredulous disbelief. Avery was now bound with the rope under his arms. Musial grasped him by the back of the shirt, ready to give him a shove off the platform and into the Shredder.

"How? What?" Garrison stammered.

"I told you I was a magician in my former life you arrogant prick," Musial said.

Without another word and without waiting for a response, Musial shoved Avery with both hands. He screamed, but for only as long as it took him to reach the Tesla Gate. A moment later, the Shredder hummed and buzzed like a bug zapper frying a large insect. Avery died on impact and his body continued to swing back and forth. He bounced against the electrical field, his flesh burning with every jostle. The rope soon burned away and the charred mess dropped to the floor with a wet plop.

"You!" Garrison screamed.

Musial moved toward him, but it was no use. He had no weapon and Garrison did. A single shot struck him in the abdomen. Musial slumped to his knees. He heard Sam Andrews screaming in the back of his mind. This was it. He tried to get up, but another shot echoed through the hangar, this one catching him in the chest. Musial/Andrews toppled off the podium and struck the concrete floor at an awkward angle. The fall may have killed them if the gunshots did not. President Garrison's rage made the other two soldiers almost take flight. He screamed with anger, putting a few more slugs into the body of Sam Andrews for good measure. Then, with wild-eyed intensity, he turned his rage back towards his son.

Cecil was coming around from his encounter with the dark and he staggered as President Garrison pulled him to his feet. The fuming president uncoiled the slack from around the pole and yanked his son inches from the edge of the platform.

"Now!" he shouted, waving his arm at the soldier.

The lights went out and darkness fell yet again.

CHAPTER 41

ILLUMINATION

*"There are dark shadows on the earth, but its lights are
stronger in the contrast."*
~Charles Dickens

PANIC SET IN ON REBEKAH as the thunderous rumble grew louder.
It shook her cot as if it were a vibrating bed. Gestas was gone, she
couldn't sense him anymore. She called out in her head and shouted
at the top of her lungs. There was no answer. Despite the thirty-plus
occupants of the tent, she felt alone. The noise outside was terrifying.

Rebekah called out for Malakhi. There was no response. In fact, no
one paid her any attention. They were too focused on what was going
on outside. A glowing white light permeated the thin cloth of the tent
making it seem as if a brilliant sunrise were happening outside. It was
still at least an hour until dawn and this light came from everywhere,
not just the east.

The blinding radiance made Rebekah squint her eyes, but it also
made her feel warm from head to toe. Her heart fluttered when she
heard what could only be called a unified scream erupted outside. It
didn't vibrate the air, it vibrated her soul like icy fingers plucking a
harp. She recognized the voice of the scream, if you could even call it
a voice. It was the terrified shriek of the darkness.

* * *

Jack looked about his cell in terror as another rumble vibrated the building. Were they under attack and, if so, from whom? He dismissed this thought because as another peal of thunder rang through the building, he knew it was no explosion. It was not thunder either. This sound was different and more frightening.

His heart rate quickened and sweat dripped from his brow as the dark night outside his window filled with a blinding white light. This brightness did not give him any comfort. He found it disturbing. Jack crouched in the corner of his cell, out of view from the doorway, as the blazing light began to fill the hallway outside. He covered his head as the lurid screams of the dark erupted all around him, his dark allies were not angry, they were scared. Jack shivered as the curdling scream mixed with the other worldly rumble. His bladder let go as the light flooded into his cell.

Carmella rested in a conference room of the administration building. An ace bandage covered her forehead where she made contact with the sidewalk. A heating pad warmed her lower back where she made contact with the concrete planter. Tears streamed down her cheeks. Not only because of Steff, but also because of the information just passed on to her by a member of the clerical staff.

President Garrison and Avery were not going to North Carolina tonight in the limo. They would go in the morning. He sent Sebastian and Joan ahead of them. The only good news Carmella could determine from the situation was that the two Secret Service agents had been put out at the gate. What good would they have been to the travelling ambassadors after dark anyway? One of them was in the infirmary nursing a bullet wound to the shoulder. Joan decided to take pot shots at them as they drove away.

Everybody was sympathetic to her treatment at the hands of the president's lone female henchman. None of them liked Garrison's cronies. Even fewer liked the president himself. Carmella could sense it, but she also knew they were guarding their feelings. She was one of the White House secretaries. No one knew how warm or cold her relationship was with the president and his administration.

For the time being, all she could do is wait. She knew there would be repercussions when the bomb went off and it wouldn't take Garrison long to determine who brought the car. When that happened, she would be joining Steff. She wasn't afraid of death. Her faith refused her the notion of fearing death. Almost as important as her faith, she had taken a peek behind the curtain, so to speak, and knew the promise of eternity was real. The Impals proved it. The one thing keeping her from squashing her fears was the wildcard of the eye of the storm. Did it change the nature and disposition of the soul? This uncertainty vexed her. Even as David brought her a cup of coffee and took a seat across the room, she could not manage a smile.

While she appreciated David's efforts, she wasn't in the mood for company. All Carmella wanted was to be alone and to contemplate her life in the short time she knew she had left. She was about to get up and seek solitude when something made her freeze in her tracks. Her tears shut off as if someone turned a faucet. She propped herself against the arm of the sofa as the room began to vibrate. A glowing white light began to drive away the approaching dusk outside. It was like the most brilliant sunrise ever, projecting radiant daylight in a surreal dream. She gasped in amazement, then fell back on the sofa, shielding her eyes from the brilliance.

Cecil's eyes had just become accustomed to the light when they were plunged back into darkness. He was no longer aware of his father, the platform or the Tesla Gate. He was ten years old again, in a canoe filled with vile snakes doing their best to torment him into taking his own life.

Cecil was aware of the sensation of falling, yet in his tortured mind, it was only the canoe sinking deeper in the water. As he cried out and tried to claw his way out of the canoe, he heard a wild shriek. It was around him and inside of him at the same time. The malignant sound chilled him as much as the snakes. However, now the snakes were gone, replaced by a warm and bright light covering him as a warm blanket, driving away the chill. He felt safe and secure. As the screaming faded, Cecil opened his eyes. What he saw convinced him the dark souls did their job. There was no other explanation.

He was still hanging from the rope by his arms and twisting with his feet a yard or so off the ground. The fact he was still hanging from a rope was what confused him. He felt a cold touch on his arms, but it was not disquieting like the serpents. It was pleasing, especially after he started to feel the unusual sensation of hot and cold. Standing beside him with bright smiles were Abbs and Steff. Cecil was overcome by joy, but he was also tempered with confusion. He expected to see Abbs again when he died or if the storm happened to bring the Impals back. Why was Steff glowing with silvery luminescence?

"Steff . . . what, what . . . happened?" he stammered.

Before she could answer, his reunion was interrupted by the booming voice of a man insane with rage.

"Demonic filth!" President Garrison screamed. "How dare you impersonate my granddaughters!!"

In a flash, Garrison jumped off of the platform and grabbed a nearby iron chain which had been used to herd Impals. In one quick motion, he swung the chain and struck Steff in the head. She went sprawling across the floor and came to rest less than a foot from the Tesla Gate. The backlash knocked Abbs into the platform and struck Cecil across the arm. Garrison jerked the chain back and took aim at Steff. This time determined to finish the job and knock her into the Gate. Then he would turn his attention back to the demon posing as Abbs and give it the same treatment.

Garrison was so focused on the abominations, he didn't notice the light flooding the hangar. It was due to much more than two rogue Impals. As he reared back to swing again, he cried out with surprise. The chain dropped to the floor with a clatter, echoing through the hangar. Cecil twisted so he could swing sideways and see in President Garrison's direction. He was both relieved and horrified.

Garrison resembled an enraged angel as he hung above the ground. He was bathed in the shimmering light of the half dozen Impals who seized him and lifted him in the air.

"Get thee behind me, Satan!" he screamed as he kicked and writhed. His efforts were futile. They carried him forward and held him a few feet from Cecil and his daughters.

Another Impal walked up behind Cecil. He turned and stood between him and his father. Cecil blinked in surprise because he recognized this Impal and knew him well.

"How are you?" Cecil croaked, his mouth agape. Part of him felt as if he was in a dream. This was too real to be a dream and the rope too painful for him to be dead.

The man stepped forward and smiled as he placed his hand on Cecil's lower arm.

"I'm fine, major," Thomas Pendleton said softly. He then turned and beckoned to a group of Impals out of Cecil's line of sight. "Please, let's get this man down," he said.

Cecil felt the warm-cold touches of Impals as he was lifted in the air and the rope pulled loose from his torso. A moment later, he was set back on the ground. Cecil massaged his sore ribs for a few moments before his father began to shout again.

"You are all under arrest . . . you are all traitors . . . how dare you defy my authority and the will of the Lord!"

Cecil stepped forward and gazed up into the face of the raving lunatic he once called father. Garrison spat in his son's eyes before muttering, "You disgrace, you should have been aborted. The world would have been a better place."

The words hurt, yet Cecil ignored him. He stepped back and put his arms around his daughters. He tried to address his father with some affection, but it took every ounce of resolve to utter the first word.

"Dad . . . these are my daughters, your granddaughters. They are not demons."

"I know for a fact Steff is alive and well at the White House, the most secure location in the world. This can't be her! The deceivers will go to any means to test our faith!"

Cecil felt the odd warm and cold sensation like tiny shooting stars moving through his shoulder. Steff's tears rolled off her cheeks in shiny drops as she placed her forehead on her father's shoulder.

"It is me, grandpa," she said. "I tried to climb out a window and fell. I followed Carmella out here when they brought your car."

"Lies," he hissed. "Go back to Hell, demon!"

The full meaning of Steff's presence sunk in with Cecil and he began to cry.

"My poor girl," he said stroking her cold head. "I'm so sorry I wasn't there for you . . . for both of you," he said, pulling Abbs into their embrace.

"I'm sorry I let you down, Dad. It's all my fault," Steff said as silvery tears continued to sheet down her cheeks.

"No sweetheart, it's mine," he whispered.

Cecil wanted the moment with his daughters to last forever, but his father had other plans.

"Please let me down," President Garrison asked. He sounded quite lucid and calm. A far contrast from the hate filled zealot from moments earlier.

Cecil paused. He never heard this voice from his father, not even when he was younger.

"I don't think so," said one of the Impal men holding him up.

"Please," said President Garrison, pleaded. "I only want a moment with my granddaughters, God bless them."

"You just thumped them with an iron chain," the large Impal of an 18th century black man growled. He then helped hoist Garrison even higher as if making a demonstration of their resolve.

Cecil was so dumbstruck with the Impals return, coherent thought was an impossible notion for him at the moment. He was intoxicated with joy to see his daughters again. As a result of all these competing feelings, his inner sense of goodwill took over his common sense. His affection and trust for his father had disappeared a long time ago. Yet, a small flame still burned inside him like a dying match. The unconditional love of a child for their parent is a flame that's difficult to completely extinguish. Cecil's tiny flame still kindled a small hope for reconciliation. He hoped this more for his daughters than himself.

"Let him down," Cecil said.

The Impals detaining his father, a group of a half dozen men or so, all turned to him. Their clothing was a stark contrast. Each man was from a different period in history ranging from colonial to the 1940s.

"I don't think it's a good idea," Thomas said, stepping closer to Cecil. "You remember what he did to me and Seth?"

Cecil did remember. It had haunted him every day since his failed attempt to rescue the father and son. Thomas earned his respect and admiration for the sacrifice he made for his son.

"Where is Seth?" Cecil asked, becoming aware that there were more Impals in the hangar. There were hundreds of them. The lights were still off and their bright luminescent glow lit up the whole of the structure. The soldier who manned the controls and the one who wheeled Barbara in fled. Barbara still rested on a gurney a few yards from the Tesla Gate.

"Seth is back there," Thomas said, pointing towards the far wall of the hangar. Dozens of Impals covered the distance. "He is with a friend. I didn't want him to see up here."

"Please let me down," Garrison pleaded again, this time he sounded as if he were on the verge of tears. "Please, I just want to see my grand-daughters . . . to tell them I am sorry."

Thomas shook his head at Cecil, but his common sense still had not returned. The small flame was still bright enough to blind him for an instant.

"Let him down," Cecil requested again. "But make sure he doesn't have any weapons or iron on him."

Perhaps it was Cecil's prudent suggestion that led the Impals to relent and lower Garrison to the ground. After several long moments of debate, they dumped him on the hard concrete floor.

Garrison got up and regarded Cecil and the girls with a wide sheepish smile. He began to walk towards them, his arms opened with his palms turned up in supplication.

"I'm sorry girls, please forgive me," he said and opened his arms wider.

Thomas moved to intervene, but Cecil urged him to step aside. Garrison moved closer and when he was a few feet from the fright-ened girls, his smile faded into a scowl of hatred. He charged them.

"I'm sorry I didn't do this earlier!" he screamed.

Impals are capable of passing through most solid objects except for iron, but they have to concentrate. It takes focus and determination.

Abbs and Steff had no time to prepare. He caught each of them under their arms and began to drive then towards the crackling mouth of the Tesla Gate.

Cecil and Thomas tried to grab Garrison, but he was too quick. Two flashes shot from the far corner of the platform and raced towards Garrison. He was less than ten feet away from the Gate when the flashes intercepted him. He was jerked backwards and the girls dropped to the ground. They began to crawl towards Cecil as he and Thomas ran towards them. Each reached a girl and pulled her to safety. A moment later, President Garrison was hurtling towards the Tesla Gate. Cecil turned his head as the disgusting crackle of a body hitting the current resonated through the building. The stench of burning flesh flooded Cecil's nose, making him want to wretch.

His father had become the latest victim of the Shredder. Even though this would have been celebration for most, he could not bring himself to celebrate. The small, weak flame burning inside managed to produce a few tears which rolled down his cheeks. He wiped them away as he covered his nose to suppress the smell.

He turned to look, it was unavoidable. His father's body lay smoldering on the floor. Standing on either side of him were two Impal men, one of which he recognized immediately, the other not until he spoke.

CHAPTER 42

THE STORM ROLLS ON

"Darkness cannot drive out darkness; only light can do that.
Hate cannot drive out hate; only love can do that."
~Martin Luther King, Jr.

"I'M SORRY, CECIL," Sam Andrews said.

"I am too, major. Quite regrettable," the other Impal said. He wore a nineteenth century, three-piece suit. It consisted of a sack coat with matching vest and trousers. He didn't resemble the stereotypical magician with top hat and cape. Even so, he definitely fit the appearance of a showman.

"Musial?" Cecil asked. "You're an Impal now?"

"Yes," said Musial trying to keep up his cool and sarcastic persona. He was so elated, he could not conceal it. Tears of joy rolled down his cheeks like silvery shooting stars, disappearing into the gray concrete floor.

"I'm sorry, major," Musial said, then turned away. He walked behind the platform for privacy.

Musial was right. It was possible to redeem yourself, no matter how dark one's transgressions may have been. Did he make himself right with God? Cecil could not say, although he did have his own beliefs on the matter. The only thing he knew for certain was that overcoming ignorance and arrogance seemed to free the soul in more ways than one.

"Sam, are you okay?" Cecil asked.

Sam grinned and put his hands on his hips. Cecil noticed he was wearing the same clothing his body was clothed in. It was curious to see the vast garment variations among the Impals. There didn't seem to be any rhyme or reason to their attire. Perhaps it was a favorite garment in life and they incorporated it into their eternal wardrobe.

"I've never been better, Cecil. I haven't felt this good in years." He paused for a moment and stroked his chin, smirking with satisfaction. "You know, I don't have any desire for a drink, not one little bit."

Something changed about the Impals since they walked the planet before. Cecil couldn't quite put his finger on it. They still had the same tinny sounding voice and a glowing silvery ethereal quality, but there was more. They seemed much brighter than before. Perhaps it was the close proximity of so many of them together that gave this illusion.

When Cecil noticed the girls standing beside their mother's gurney, his heart sank. He knew they walked close to their grandfather to get there. Their attention was too focused on their mother to notice his macabre presence. A large American flag hung from a nearby pole so Cecil walked over and took it down. He carried it to his father and covered the corpse. It seemed both reverent and disrespectful at the same time. He covered his father with a flag, but Cecil didn't believe his father deserved that privilege. A part of him, a rather large part of him, thought it disrespected the flag more than anything. The important thing was, his body was now covered from view of his daughters. As Cecil was about to turn away and join his girls, something dawned on him. His father's Impal was not here.

Cecil whirled about as if a wild animal might be stalking him when he heard a voice a few feet away. Musial said, "I told you major . . . he is not here. He is with the dark"

"Where?" Cecil asked.

Musial gazed up at the ceiling distantly, as if he were pondering the size of a planet in the night sky. He then frowned and glanced about the hangar.

"The dark souls are gone," Musial said. "The eye has passed."

Musial didn't have to say any more. The former general, former president, and former father, had joined his kindred spirits. Cecil couldn't help feeling a little sick thinking of his father confined to the dark void. He also felt safe. He pushed the thought aside, took a deep breath, and joined Steff and Abbs with their mother.

Barbara's condition broke his heart ever since the day she was ravaged by the dark. Now to see his daughters, his two deceased daughters, regard her with forlorn sadness. It shattered his heart into a million pieces.

"Mom," Abbs said, reaching out and taking Barbara's hand.

Steff didn't say anything as she took her other hand. Both girls wept.

Cecil stood there for many moments watching his daughters. Salty, mortal, tears dripped from his face and formed a wet spot at the foot of the gurney. He was vaguely aware of the crowd of hundreds watching them. Right now, he did not care. His life would soon be an empty and lonely one. He had not thought of Barbara's condition as serious until now. With every passing day, and every passing moment, his hope of getting his wife back grew weaker.

Cecil was startled when there was a loud crackle and pop as the hangar grew darker. One of the Impals figured out the controls and managed to shut down the infernal Gate. He turned and looked at the empty archway, still emitting a low hum as it powered down. He jumped again when he felt cold hands on each shoulder. He turned to see Thomas and Sam standing there.

He suddenly remembered hearing the disturbing tale one night from an inebriated Sam Andrews's. The story of how his parents were murdered in a home invasion when he was only eight years old. He had witnessed it all.

"Being drunk is the only way I can talk about it," Andrews had told him with slurred speech.

Cecil resented Andrews drinking problem because of the safety concerns it presented for others. Yet, he tolerated it. He thought alcohol might be a necessary evil if it helped him cope with the tragedy. Andrews's tragedy was aggravated like an old wound when the storm arrived. He realized his parents did not stayed behind to watch over him, they had moved on. Cecil knew both Sam and Thomas had dealt with tragedy. Their sympathy was genuine and heartfelt. As Cecil turned back to his girls, something incredible began to happen.

It was Barbara. She was still lying with her eyes closed. The same steady and rhythmic breathing continued, yet her whole appearance seemed improved. He could not explain it, yet he knew it was happening all the same.

"Momma?" Steff said, bending closer. Her luminescent tears fell straight through her mother's chest.

As both girls leaned closer, Barbara's breathing started to accelerate. Hope started to build. Barbara's mouth began to twitch and her eyelids rolled back and forth as her eyes began to move rapidly underneath. A few moments later, her hands began to move. Both girls hung on to their mother as their dejected faces bloomed into a countenance of hope. Barbara's eyelids fluttered opened as if waking from a bad dream.

Barbara squinted into the glowing faces of her girls with a blank expression. Her vacant stare soon morphed into a loving smile of recognition.

"My girls," she croaked. As much as they had tried to get fluids in her, she was on the verge of dehydration.

He tried to be patient as the girls doted over their mother, but he couldn't stand it any longer. Cecil stepped forward. "Sweetheart, how do you feel?" he asked.

Barbara smiled at him. "Better now," she squeaked, then held up her arms for him to come and join in the reunion.

Cecil wasn't sure how long they embraced, but it wasn't long enough. He was overjoyed to have his wife back. He wondered if Barbara remembered what happened to her in the darkness. He knew better than to dwell on it. She was back. She was the same old Barbara in most respects, but in one way she was different. The haunted emptiness behind her eyes was all the proof one needed. She did remember and would never forget.

Sometime in the middle of their emotional reunion, an explosion tore through the night air. It occurred about sixty miles south on Interstate 95.

A large limousine burned and smoldered for hours since everyone who wasn't dead was now relocated. There was no one available to respond. The charred bodies inside would remain there for a few days until discovered. There were no Impals at the scene, only fire, smoke, and darkness.

Rebekah sat up as people began to stumble past her. Everyone who was able got up and rushed to the door of the tent. She felt a strong need to find out what was happening. Before she could beg someone to unfasten her restraints, three individuals entered the tent. Her heart leapt with delight when she saw the smiling face of Malakhi. He walked toward her followed by the other two persons. Her son's return so absorbed her, she didn't notice the others at first. When she tried to focus, she found it difficult at first. The individuals emitted a very bright light. As the last horrific screams of the darkness faded, one of them spoke. Tears of joy sheeted down her face when she recognized the voice. "Hello my dear, I'm so pleased to see you," her father, Nehemya, said.

"Dad!" She shrieked and tried to embrace him, yet she could not move.

Nehemya touched her arms and feet, releasing her bonds. She sprang up and hugged him. There was the same sensation of warmth and cold as before, only there seemed to be a lot more warmth. As she hugged her father and sank into his form, she felt more happy and secure than she had in a long time. She felt Malakhi grasp her leg so she bent down and picked him up so he could join in the embrace with his grandfather.

"Dad, I am so glad to see you. Where have you been? Are you okay?"

"I have been close," Nehemya whispered in her ear. "I have been so close, yet so far away."

"I missed you, Saba," Malakhi said.

"I missed you too, my little man," he said. "I could see you, you just couldn't see me. You have been brave and strong protecting your mother."

Malakhi and Rebekah both pulled back and frowned at Nehemya.

"How did you see us? We saw you vanish," Rebekah asked.

"It felt strange at first when I disappeared. It really wasn't much different than the way it was before the storm arrived," he said, then disgust washed across his face. "I could see them," he said and glanced sideways at the third person.

Rebekah turned and gasped in surprise. The last time she saw Gestas was in her head. Now he stood in front of her. The only difference now was he boasted the same luminescent glow as Nehemya. Gestas was now an Impal.

"I guess redemption is possible," she said with a sheepish smile.

Gestas did not speak, he nodded and stared at his feet. After a time, he said, "Yes it is. Thank you for your help . . . both of you," he said, patting Malakhi's head.

Rebekah nodded. She wanted to thank him for helping them, but here was something else she wanted to ask. "So, the darkness is gone?"

Gestas nodded.

"Back to where they came from?"

He nodded again. "Yes, they are all gone."

"It was terrible to see the true face of those souls dwelling in the shadows," Nehemya said. "I am glad you made it out, sir. Thank you for taking care of my family."

Gestas felt guilty for accepting thanks. There were a few times where he almost snapped and reverted to his former nature. The fact he even considered those temptations left a bad taste with him. He didn't feel worthy and perhaps he wasn't; yet he had managed to gain his freedom from the void. He did something right. Gestas smiled and then walked across the tent to give the family some private time together.

The small family pulled apart and walked to the door. They stepped out into the bright pre-dawn air. Rebekah was overwhelmed by what she saw outside.

CHAPTER 43

THE IMPALS

"O, come, be buried
A second time within these arms (They embrace)"
~William Shakespeare, Pericles

CARMELLA SAT UP AND SHIELDED HER EYES from the blinding light coming in through the windows. David got up and sprinted out the door. The rumbling sounded like an enormous stone rolling away from a tomb, a stone large enough to cover the entire planet. The odd thing is, Carmella found it comforting. She sprang to her feet and trudged toward the door with her hand cupped over her eyes. She could see several people in front of her, all crowding around the front door of the building.

Many people gathered around the door. They all talked with excitement and pointed outside. Carmella stepped forward and peered over the shoulder of a short, balding man. She cried out and clasped her hand over her mouth. Her whole body trembled. A countless multitude of Impals milled about outside. They surrounded the building, stretching all the way to the forest. They seemed lost and confused. Carmella elbowed her way past the others and exited into the middle of the ghostly throng.

"Steff!" she called. "Steff, honey; are you here?"

The Impals surrounding her said nothing, they all kept moving. It was as if all of them were trying to get somewhere, yet none of them knew where they were going. Carmella continued to call for Steff until she was hoarse. As she was about to give up, she felt a cold hand grasp her elbow. She turned around, expecting to see Steff's smiling face. Instead, she received the shock of her life.

"Mom?"

She had not seen her mother for almost twenty years, when she passed away with Alzheimer's disease. After the storm arrived, Carmella assumed her mother had moved on.

"Yes baby, it's me," she said as silvery tears dripped from her round cheeks. "I have so wanted to see you for such a long time."

Carmella threw her arms around her mother and squeezed hard. She ignored the warm cold sensation as she relished having her mother back.

"Where were you? I never heard from you after the storm arrived," Carmella said.

"I was at our home, honey. I never left it."

"But . . . why didn't you contact me?" Carmella asked. She knew the question was a stupid one as soon as the words left her mouth.

"I didn't think your boss would like it too much," her mother said.

"Oh my God!" Carmella exclaimed. She forgot where she was for a moment. "Where is he?"

Carmella's mother responded through gritted teeth. Her luminescent glow seemed to shine red for a moment. "I hope he is burnin' in Hell," she muttered. She then turned and pointed at the hangar. "He is out there, deader than a doornail."

Carmella was dumbstruck.

"Dead?" Carmella repeated, a little surprised at how pleased she sounded.

"Yes," her mother said. "I guess this last part of the storm moved on just in time, takin' those foul excuses for souls with it, includin' your boss."

A hundred questions spun in Carmella's mind, but one came to the forefront. "The dark is gone?" she asked. She suddenly realized that where she was standing would be pitch dark now if not for the light of the Impals.

"A few minutes ago. It was like a mess of frightened snakes slitherin' into a hole. I guess the hole is the doorway between here and where they come from. The opening closed up tighter than a frog's butt once they were all in."

"You could see them?" Carmella asked.

Her mother nodded. "Every God forsaken second they were here. I hope to never see nothin' like it again."

"You said Garrison is dead?" Carmella asked again.

Her mother nodded.

"How?"

"Not really sure," her mother said. "Heard he got a taste of his own medicine."

Carmella was about to ask another question when her mother interrupted.

"I think the little girl you were callin' for is out there. I saw her ride in with you in that big ol' car a couple of hours ago. She made a beeline out there."

"Steff!" Carmella shouted, then took her mother by the hand to lead her to the hangar.

Her mother pulled her hand through Carmella's, almost making her stumble forward.

"No baby, you go on ahead. I'll be right here waiting when you get back," she said.

Carmella gave her mother a hug. "I'll be back, Mom. Please don't leave," she said before turning and trudging through the multitude of Impals. Light penetrated the crack between the hangar doors. Carmella focused on it and pushed through without courtesy as she passed through a number of Impals.

Mary stood on the dark perimeter of Jack's base. Her former host, Donna, lay a few feet away under a tree. She stirred as she tried to sit up. Mary knelt and spoke softly.

"I'm sorry I had to do that," she said. "I want to thank you from the bottom of my heart. You will never know how much you helped me."

Donna's eyes widened at the sight of a glowing Impal woman dressed in the clothing of sixteenth century British royalty.

"Where are my parents?" Donna whispered.

"I don't know dear. When I found you, you were not in a very pleasant place."

She sighed and then placed her hand on top of Donna's head. The girl flinched at the cold touch.

"You had so many chemicals in your body when I found you, I'm surprised you are still alive."

Donna frowned. She remembered some things, but not all. The drugs had robbed her of a great deal of her memories since leaving her parent's house a few months earlier. She could almost remember her home. Her head had not been this clear in a long time. Her craving for the poison was no longer present. She found she didn't want another hit, another blow, or another drink. Donna wanted something to eat, and she wanted to go home.

Mary stopped stroking the girl's head and turned to the prison a short distance away. Screams erupted through the thick walls again. Jack sounded as if he was frightened out of his mind. Where Mary and Donna watched was still dark. The area around the prison and many other buildings on the base glowed with the light of several hundred Impals. They were back, but wandering.

"Poor Jack," Mary said with sincere empathy. "I really hoped he would see his errors and atone." She paused and then rubbed her chin. "I don't see why he is so distraught. The dark is gone and surely a man like him is not afraid of Impals."

Mary was right. Jack was not afraid of Impals, at least not every day, run of the mill Impals. What she did not know was that Jack always kept a small tether to the dark void, as most dark souls. In fact, everyone has the tether. The ignorant and arrogant were just more responsive to it than others. It was not a permanent pipeline, but rather like a party line for the darkness to speak if the conditions were right. The line was cut for Jack and he felt alone and terrified. This was enough to make him uncomfortable, but not enough to send him into a frenzy. What horrified Jack was that his sins were revisiting him, in the most literal sense of the word.

The Impals of seven elderly women stood inside Jack's jail cell. They did not regard him with anger or hatred, they moved past these

THE EYE OF MADNESS

emotions. The women, who now appeared a little younger than they had in the last days of their lives, spoke to him in one unifying voice.

"*Why* Jack?"

He did not answer. The only thing he knew was he would kill them again if he could. Screw them all. The damn wretches got what they deserved and the world was better for it. He did not intend to give them an answer or an apology. Jack cowered under his bed with a pillow clasped tight over his eyes and ears. He wanted them to go away, he wanted those stupid old diseased skanks to leave him alone.

"Oh, what I wouldn't give for a good iron bar right about now," Jack thought. "I would teach them a lesson."

The women did not stay long. Seeing Jack in this state was enough for them. They knew he would never repent or confess his evil acts. He was too arrogant. They would have to do it for him. None of them moved on because they thought it necessary to stay behind to stop Jack. They were unable to act before because they were rounded up shortly after the storm arrived and shipped to an island in the Channel. During the dark period, they were able to make their way back to the base where they waited and watched Jack. There were six in all, now seven after joining with Matilda, the poor lady who Jack put in his cage the day the darkness arrived.

The women passed through the jail wall as Jack continued his infantile screaming. As Mary and Donna watched from afar, the women walked up the narrow path to the base commander's office. Justice would be done, they would see to it.

Seth Pendleton had been playing with some new friends. He was in the back of the hangar and away from the terrible and triumphant events at the Tesla Gate. He did not see the gruesome deaths of Avery Cooper, Sam Andrews, and Ott Garrison. Nor did he see the miraculous recovery made by Barbara Garrison. Seth had matured since his exodus with his father through the Tesla Gate. Thomas wasn't sure if it was a good or bad thing. Maybe it was a result of living on the next level of existence for a while.

"Can we go out and play now, Daddy?" Seth asked, referring to a group of Impal children nearby.

One little boy smiled hopefully at Thomas. He was a child who would have been condemned by most a short time ago. Like Thomas and Seth, the young boy wearing the green Lego Star Wars t-shirt had changed. Not by appearance or personality, but by an attitude adjustment. The next level of existence brought on a change in all those who entered. Patrick may have turned them in to the authorities at the Air and Space Museum due to sheer jealousy, but now envy was an expired emotion. It disappeared after he entered the Tesla Gate shortly after Thomas and Seth.

"Sure you can," Thomas said. "But first, I have some people I want you to meet . . . both of you," he said, giving Patrick a wink.

Patrick smiled as he and Seth wrapped their arms around each other's shoulder like they were buddies for life. They marched along shoulder to shoulder behind Thomas as the sea of Impals parted for them.

The bodies were hidden behind the wooden platform in front of the Tesla Gate. A group of Impals carried out the task while Cecil and his girls talked to Barbara. It wasn't done to hide them from Seth and other child Impals, but to hide them from Sam Andrews. He couldn't take his eyes off his own corpse.

Thomas arrived beside the gurney just as Barbara tried to get up. She plopped back down with an exasperated "*humph.*" It would be a while before she would be able to get up and move around. In spite of Cecil moving her arms and legs on a daily basis, her muscles needed a little time to wake up again.

"Major Garrison, I want to give you a proper introduction to my son, Seth. Also to his friend, Patrick."

"Hello, Patrick," Cecil said with a warm smile as Patrick stepped forward to shake his hand. After he accepted Patrick's frigid handshake, he turned his attention to Seth. He met Seth under less than ideal circumstances when he tried and failed to rescue him from the Tesla Gate.

"Hello Seth," Cecil said as he accepted another cold greeting from the boy. "It is so good to see you again!"

Seth gave him a puzzled frown before recognition dawned over his glowing features. "You're the Army man who tried to get me back to my daddy," he beamed.

"I tried," Cecil said with a sad smile. "I'm sorry."

"Why?" Seth asked with a goofy grin. "Mission accomplished!" He said, reaching out and grasping his father's hand.

All hints of a speech impediment were gone now.

Cecil took the opportunity to introduce Seth and Patrick to his daughters, who agreed to go and play with the boys. As they talked, Thomas walked to the side of the Tesla Gate. He stared in horror at what lay behind the monstrous structure. No one knew what the future held and how long this storm would last, but the situation behind the Shredder must be addressed soon. Cecil soon joined him.

"Oh, Jesus," Cecil gasped.

A large and glowing mound started a few feet behind the Tesla Gate. It was as high as a man and stretched through the back wall of the hangar. The logistics of the mound were not important, its composition was. Cecil estimated there to be almost a thousand sleeping Impals piled on top of one another. They were the suicides tossed through the Gate, lying unseen until the eye passed a short time ago.

CHAPTER 44

JUSTICE

"The dead cannot cry out for justice. It is a duty of the living to do so for them."
~Lois McMaster Bujold

ABRAHAM LINCOLN ONCE SAID, "I have always found that mercy bears richer fruits than strict justice."

In the last century and a half, President Lincoln had seen much in his invisible presence at the White House. The lessons he learned since the storm arrived were far more valuable than an extra two hundred years of unseen study. Lincoln would say the two piles of burned flesh behind the wooden platform were some of the richest fruit he had ever seen. He came to realize that sometimes mercy is not deserved, nor is it beneficial to society. Like rotten flesh from a body, some people must be removed from humanity.

Lincoln was still around, yet he was a long distance away. There was no judgment on the island he had come to call home. There were only Impals, all relocated by the brother of Sam Andrews. They barely left American waters when the eye of the storm passed over the Earth. As the Impals disappeared, the crews of the two boats succumbed to the darkness. It was terrifying for the Impals to stand around, unseen and powerless. They watched, helpless, as their liberators were forced

into more and more heinous forms of suicide by the dark. The evil
countenance of the dark souls was burned into the heart of each Impal
like a branding iron heated in the depths of Hell. The Impals could
see them. So could the unfortunate fleshers who found themselves
trapped in the darkness.

The Impals of the slaughtered sailors and the payload of Impals
washed ashore a day later. The two boats crashed on the rocks of an
uninhabited island somewhere in the Atlantic. There they stayed,
unseen and alone, until the eye passed. Some considered duplicat-
ing the method they used to traverse underneath the Chesapeake
Bay. Of course, they had no idea how far from land they were. The
middle of the Atlantic is much deeper and darker than the Chesapeake Bay.

Cecil went about the task of removing the bodies and placing them on
the tarmac outside. He didn't move his father's body. He tried to distract himself from the unpleasantness by thinking of Lincoln and the
other Impals. He remembered faces, but a few names stuck with him.
Of course, there was Lincoln and the recently assassinated President
of the United States. His friend, Colonel Danny Bradley, who died
in the evacuation. Cecil's childhood science idol, Nikola Tesla, was
also part of the group, as well as the famous Chief Powhatten. Cecil
thought of these people, as well as a few who were not so famous. Mrs.
Fiddler and her daughter, along with little Chester Henry stood out in
Cecil's mind. He especially remembered Chester, the poor child who
was buried alive in an iron casket for a century. He wanted to see all
these people again, and began to make plans in his mind to find them.
He jumped when someone behind him spoke.

"Have you seen Steffanie Garrison?" Carmella asked.

Cecil frowned and asked, "What do you want with my daughter?"

Carmella's eyes widened. "Are you Major Cecil Garrison?"

"Do I know you?" he asked.

"I worked for you father in the White House," she said, staring at
the ground.

Cecil took a couple of steps backward as if Carmella's very presence was poisonous.

"My father?" Cecil said with disgust. "What the hell do you want with my daughter?"

"Please, I . . . I was trying to watch over her. I never meant for anything to happen to her. I'm so, so sorry," Carmella said. Tears began to pour down her face, but she composed herself and wiped them away. She took a deep shuddering breath and gazed up at Cecil. "I love your daughter, Major Garrison. Just ask her."

Cecil studied her face in the glow of the luminescent night sky. He then glanced at the bodies, all lined up and covered. He turned back to Carmella and gave her a slight nod. "Okay," he said. "Wait here, I'll be right back." He turned to go, then turned back to her. "What did you say your name was again?"

"Carmella," she said.

Carmella and Steff had their reunion a few minutes later. After watching their interaction, Cecil was satisfied that Carmella was a friend. He left them to their conversation and went back into the hangar. There was much to do, but he did not know where to start.

The next day, based on the testimony of six Impal women, Private Jack Abernathy was arrested for multiple murders. He laughed and scoffed at the judge for his idiotic proclamations of Jack's evil deeds.

"Yes, this man is just another fool," Jack said pointing to the judge. He turned to everyone in the small conference room, as if he was seeking their approval. There was none, only disdain and disgust. The most sickened face of all was from his former friend, Private Sean Poindexter. Jack made eye contact with him, expecting support from his old friend. Sean was determined not to break eye contact, to show resolve in his displeasure for Jack's actions, but he couldn't do it. The darkness hidden behind Jack's blue eyes for so long had now come to the surface like a dreadful oil spill. He couldn't look at the real face of his friend, it was too disturbing. He felt as if he was going to be sick, so he turned and left the room.

"Bloody coward!" Jack screamed as the door slammed shut.

The judge ordered he be returned to his cell to await trial in in three weeks. In the meantime, the bodies of the women would be excavated. Three weeks was a conservative estimate since the world was now in a new state of chaos and flux. The damage the darkness brought was incalculable. The uncertainty of the future was almost as terrifying as the darkness itself. A murder trial now seemed such a trivial thing. Yet, in his wisdom, the judge recognized the importance of quickly returning to a state of law and civility.

Jack was led from the room as he continued to scream his vile protests at anyone who was within earshot. Several bystanders, both flesher and Impal, lined the path to the prison. They watched in silence as the private, turned serial killer, marched past. The whole base seemed to have fallen into an eerie silence, making Jack's ramblings sound as if they were shouted in the mouth of a cave.

Jack had not been back in his cell more than an hour when one of the guards discovered him hanging beside his bed. He fashioned a makeshift noose from the bed sheets and tied them around a water pipe on the ceiling. His method of hanging was not as elaborate as Lieutenant William Langford's, but the result was the same. He was dead.

There was no Impal, sleeping or otherwise. His body dangled from the ceiling, a defiant sneer frozen on his face. The guard who found him swears that just moments before his gruesome discovery, the shadows in the prison seemed to move.

When Rebekah emerged from the medical tent, she found the entire camp engulfed with a mix of fleshers and Impals. The Impals seemed to outnumber everyone else at least two to one. They cast a brilliant bluish light that mixed with the orange rays of the rising sun. It gave the sky a temporary appearance of glowing blueberry and orange syrup. The morning sky was almost as mesmerizing as the luminescent ocean of Impals beneath.

They soon made their way through the throng, heading back to their tent. What would have been a five-minute walk took almost a half hour. Rebekah and Malakhi felt a chill at each frequent contact with an Impal, but they did not consider it disturbing. They felt it comforting.

Many of the Impals exchanged pleasantries with them, while others walked by in a confused trance. There were also a few who stopped to ask Rebekah questions, which she did not know the answer.

"Where is my husband?" an ancient Israeli woman asked.

"Where should we go?" a modern Palestinian family asked.

The oddest question she got was from a short man wearing the attire of a medieval knight. "What time is it?" he asked.

All Rebekah could do was give a polite smile and shrug. Even though she could tell they all spoke different languages, she understood them, yet she felt as lost as they did. Her head was so inundated with happiness and confusion, she did not notice something when they first entered the tent. When the unexpected presence sunk in, her jaw almost hit the floor. Sitting on a small stool in the far corner was the old woman she knew as Ruth.

Ruth and Gestas stared at each other for several moments. She did not regard him with hatred or fear, but Ruth seemed to study him as if viewing a piece of unusual art. Gestas met her gaze with a smile of gratitude. He walked over and knelt down in front of her. He reached out and grasped her right hand, and then kissed it.

"Thank you," Gestas whispered.

She began to cry. Gestas was confused. This was not the reaction he expected or imagined. If anything, he expected her to be angry with him.

Gestas glanced back at Rebekah for help then he felt Ruth squeeze his hand. He turned back to see her smiling at him, in spite of her tears.

"Thank you for saving me, Gestas," she said.

"I . . . I . . ." he stammered. He didn't know what to say so he said the first thing that came into his mind. "I don't even know your name."

She wiped her tears with the palms of her hands and said, "My name is Eliezra."

A couple of glowing tears dropped from Gestas's cheeks.

"Salvation," he said. "Eliezra means salvation."

Gestas ducked his head and began to sob with happiness.

"I don't understand," Rebekah said. "How did he help you?"

Eliezra released her grip and placed her hand on top of Gestas's head.

"My husband died almost a year ago. I had my daughter and her husband to take care of me, but they couldn't be there all the time. Even though I love her very much, she just wasn't a replacement for

Jacob," she blinked and rubbed her eyes as she sat up straight. "Jacob was my husband," she said as if Rebekah did not understand.

"I'm sorry," Rebekah said. She considered asking the obvious question, but before she could, Eliezra answered for her.

"I was moving on, but was still lost when the storm arrived," she said, then her face hardened and her mouth creased into a thin line. "The damn storm," she muttered. "I got my hopes up that maybe Jacob had stayed. I hoped I would get to see him again." She stopped and sighed as tears began to pour from her eyes again. "He wasn't here . . . I guess he was too smart to stay."

Rebekah took Eliezra's other hand. The poor old woman squeezed so hard, Rebekah winced.

Eliezra took a shuddering breath and said, "I saw others around me reunited with their loved ones and felt like I had lost him a second time. I just couldn't take the pain."

"So you began drinking?" Rebekah asked softly.

"Yes, but it was more than that. I was willing to try anything to get rid of the pain. I hadn't seen my daughter for weeks. I was passed out in an alley when Gestas found me." She glanced at Gestas who was listening to her with a sad smile. "He scared the hell out of me at first," she said as she patted his head. "I could see . . . I knew all the horrible things he had done."

She took her hand away and placed it in her lap.

"I could also see the goodness fighting to get out . . . his struggle for redemption."

Nobody said anything for a long time. Not even Nehemya understood the significance of their struggle. Only Eliezra and Gestas could appreciate it. They saved each other.

"I need to find my daughter now," she said with resolve. She knew there was a good chance her daughter had not survived the darkness, but she allowed herself to hope. She refused to consider the possibility that her daughter might be dead. Gestas may have saved her from her own hopelessness, but if her daughter was gone, she wasn't sure she could endure it.

"We will help you," Rebekah offered. She turned to her father and son. "We all will."

The world would be a delicate place in the coming days. Several people would search for lost loved ones, both Impal and flesher. Some would find happiness, but many would find themselves in a nightmare from which there was no waking.

CHAPTER 45

A NEW BEGINNING

"Much as we may wish to make a new beginning, some part of us resists doing so as though we were making the first step toward disaster."
~William Throsby Bridges

MARY TUDOR, FORMERLY BLOODY MARY, walked through the streets of a small hamlet about ten miles from the base. She led a nervous young woman by the hand. Donna had not been home for almost a year and didn't believe her parents would take her back. The drugs, the booze, and the promiscuity had driven her away. She thought it drove her parents away, but she didn't know the truth. Donna's parents spent months searching for her, never giving up hope that their daughter would come home again. Her mother refused to accept the possibility she might be dead. She very well may have died if Mary hadn't found her when she did. Her heart was beginning to fail from a massive over-dose when Mary came forward and took control. She was able to give Donna's body enough strength to live and become sober. Mary managed to give both of them redemption.

As they travelled the short path leading to Donna's cottage home, it reminded Mary of a house she used to visit as a child. It was a happy memory. One of the few pleasant memories before becoming entrenched in the arrogance of her self-righteousness royal duties. Mary tried to focus on the positive as they walked. She had witnessed too much blood and violence in her existence. She was responsible for it all. Even though she gained redemption for herself, she still couldn't slip the memory of her past. It was too painful. The innocuous nature of their serene setting drove the point home. Weren't her own deeds immortalized in the words of an innocent nursery rhyme?

Mary, Mary, quite contrary, How does your garden grow? With silver bells, and cockle shells, And pretty maids all in a row . . .

"Contrary" is one way to describe a murderous psychopath. This popular English nursery rhyme reads like gardening advice. In truth, it is a recounting of the homicidal nature attributed to Mary. A fierce believer in Catholicism, her reign saw the execution of hundreds of Protestants. Silver bells and cockleshells are torture devices, not garden accouterments. Maids, or maidens, was another name for the crude guillotine used in England at the time. Even as an Impal, she now found it difficult to escape the horrors of her past. She shivered and wiped a tear from her eye. Mary felt unworthy of this grace. She channeled her thoughts back to helping Donna find her parents.

She had a bad feeling about this trip from the beginning. Once they confirmed Donna's parents were not at the base, she knew the chances that they were still alive were slim. There was another base about thirty miles away, but reaching it alive would have been problematic at best. She walked a few steps in front of the expectant girl, hoping to shield her against what she feared they would find. She asked Donna to wait on the top step as she passed through the front door to make a perfunctory search of the home. At first, Mary found nothing, but then she looked out a back window and gasped.

Donna's parents were in the back yard. They were dead. Mary felt sick and hollow; it was almost as if the dark souls knew she would be the one to find the bodies. Besides torture and beheadings, Mary was well known for another atrocity; burning people at the stake.

A clothesline, bookended by metal poles a short distance apart, stood several yards from the house. Lashed to each pole were the charred remains of two people. Their blackened heads lolled forward over the binding as if they were paying their respects to the queen.

She knew they were Donna's parents. A gasoline can rested on its side halfway between the poles. The surrounding yard and shrubs were scorched. If it hadn't been for an excess of rain the past month, the house and woods may have burned down. She peered closer and saw several pieces of charred wood lying on the ground beneath them. They had gathered the kindling and placed it on the ground around the pole before tying themselves to it. A burnt line between the two poles suggested one of them lit the fire after they doused themselves in gasoline. She wondered how she ever allowed something so horrific and barbaric in her name, not to mention, God's. Silver tears began to stream down her cheeks. Mary lost herself in regret for a few moments, which is why she did not realize Donna had walked in behind her. She heard a gasp and then turned to see the horrified girl standing there.

"My parents?" she whispered.

Mary moved to block her view, and then tried to usher her out of the room. Donna resisted. She pushed right through Mary, taking no notice of the bizarre sensation. Donna stood at the large picture window with her palms pressed against the glass. If not for the occasional rise and fall of her chest, a casual observer might have thought her to be a mannequin. She didn't move, didn't blink, and didn't feel. This was the way she appeared on the outside. Inside, there raged a tempest of emotions, each fighting to come forward and seize the moment. Donna did not let them. At first, she felt guilty that her parents were dead and she was not. If she only hadn't left, if she hadn't been stupid then she would have been here with them. If she had, all three of them would be dead. In the end, the only real emotion surfaced. Donna burst into mournful tears.

"Why?" she sobbed. "Why . . . ?"

She was startled for a moment when she felt Mary's cold hand on her shoulder.

"My dear, I am sorry that you saw this," Mary said. "You do know your parents are still here, don't you?"

Mary's words did not register at first. Donna was too lost in her own grief. As the truth of what she said began to sink in, she wiped her eyes and took a deep, raspy breath.

"Do you think?" she asked.

"I know," Mary said.

Donna turned to face Mary and was surprised to see a radiant smile on the former queen's face. There was something else unusual, something she couldn't put her finger on at first. Then it occurred to her. The room was brighter than it was a few moments ago. It was a cloudy, overcast day and the power was out. Yet, it was as if someone turned on a bright lamp behind Mary, or . . . perhaps it was two lamps.

As Mary stepped to the side, Donna rubbed her eyes with the palms of her hands. She blinked and screwed up her eyes. As the world came into focus, her heart leapt. Standing a few feet away, glowing with silvery luminescence, were her parents. They smiled lovingly at her. Before anyone could speak, Donna rushed to them and embraced them both. She didn't notice the cold and warmth of their intimate touch. Nor did she notice the warm shooting stars streaking through her body that were her parent's tears. All she knew was unconditional and unbounded love. Mary had saved her from her own arrogant stupidity and brought her home. Perhaps not quite as expected, but she was home.

Many of the Impal men spent several hours placing the sleeping Impals in straight lines at the back of the hanger. They carried out the task with a great deal of respect and dignity. After all, they were still people regardless of how they died.

Cecil spent time with his wife and daughters, but not as much as he wanted. Even though the darkness seemed to have passed, the world was still dangerous. It would take strong leadership from a benevolent military to restore order. He considered it his solemn duty to begin the healing right away. Cecil left the girls in the trusted hands of Thomas Pendleton as he and a few other officers made their way to the base headquarters. He did not consider it his own personal mission, he realized he would be one part in a large and moving machine of reformation. He still felt somewhat responsible for his father's actions.

However misplaced his feelings may be, Cecil was ashamed to carry the surname of Garrison.

As he and a few other soldiers walked the dark trail between the hangar and headquarters, Cecil noticed something. A person watching from a well-lit window on the second floor of the infirmary, which stood next door to base headquarters. His heart sank into the pit of his stomach when he remembered what his father told him about Burt. The person watching in the window was Sally.

"Jesus," he thought to himself. "I need to get in there and talk to her."

Cecil broke off from the group with the promise he would meet them in the conference room in twenty minutes. Little did he know, it was the same conference room with a closet containing the corpse of a man impaled by a flagpole.

Sally met him at the door with a big hug.

"I've been so worried about you and your girls . . . what happened?"

"We're fine," Cecil said and then shook off the question. "I'm so sorry about Burt," Cecil said as he gave Sally another hug.

He felt as if he needed a hug himself. Cecil felt numb and empty on the inside because he had lost his daughters and now his best friend.

"Would you like to see him?" a woman in a doctor's lab coat asked from behind Sally.

Cecil looked to Sally for consent and she nodded her approval. He patted her on the back one last time before stepping past her, and then followed the nurse down the long, sterile hallway to the stairs at the far end. They went up one flight and then turned right, walking a short distance before pausing in front of a partially shut door.

"He's in here," the nurse said. "I'll come back for you in a few minutes."

They were in an area with several patients rooms. Cecil thought it a bit strange that his friend was not taken to the morgue or at least a private and secluded area of the building. He stood outside the door, feeling empty and alone. A tear rolled down Cecil's face, but he wiped it away when another thought occurred to him. Shouldn't Burt's Impal still be here? After all, he had seen Sam Andrews die and his Impal was still here.

Cecil stepped forward and eased open the door. What he found in the room, he did not expect. He presumed to see Burt lying in a state of eternal repose with his Impal standing beside the body. His expectations did not even approach the truth.

There was no bright light from an Impal, in fact there was no Impal at all. A standard hospital bed rested in the shadows a few feet away from a high, narrow window. There were several pieces of medical equipment humming beside the bed. Someone lay in the bed, but the darkness were too thick to make out any features. Cecil took a couple of steps forward before he stopped in his tracks. The person spoke.

"It's about time."

It was weak and labored, yet he recognized it all the same. His hair stood on end and his stomach felt as if it was on a runaway elevator. The notion of ghosts or Impals fled his mind as his thoughts turned to something more sinister, something 'undead'. The voice was Burt's, but yet, it couldn't be him. He was dead and there was not an Impal anywhere in sight. Cecil took a step backward and rasped, "Burt?"

There was several moments of silence as the machines beside the bed whirred and beeped. Cecil heard a long and labored inhale followed by an exhale.

"Yep."

Cecil walked to the side of the bed. The covers were pulled up to just below his neck and a large bandage encircled his head. In the faint glow from the heart monitor, he could barely make out his features. His eyelids resembled a turbulent ocean, bobbing and rolling up and down over his eyes. It was hard for him to focus. Cecil reached out and took Burt's hand. He felt a faint squeeze, not much, but enough to know that Burt acknowledged his presence.

"I'm here, buddy," Cecil said, trying to restrain the tears of joy. "I'm here and we won."

Cecil knew this was not exactly the truth. There was still a lot to be done before any victory could be claimed. Of course, he wasn't going to tell Burt. He felt another faint squeeze letting him know he had been heard. Cecil was trying to think of something else to say when someone spoke behind him. He almost jumped out of his skin.

"The doctor said, screw your old man," Sally said. "He wasn't going to let Burt die."

Cecil turned, his mouth agape. Sally mistook his shock at her uncharacteristic use of profanity as offense for mentioning his father.

"I'm sorry, Cecil," she said. "I know this has been hard for you . . . please forgive me."

He shook his head as if fending off a pesky fly.

"I'm glad he told him to 'piss' off," Cecil said. "I hope he didn't face any repercussions because of it."

Sally ducked her head and stared at the floor.

"The doctor's Impal is downstairs. He is still caring for Burt in spite of his execution."

The Impals stranded on the island in the Atlantic Ocean were fortunate to have such good leaders, not to mention the brilliant mind of Nikola Tesla. These men would help lead them back to civilization, but their good fortune did not end there. Since the eye passed, they had come to realize they were not the same as before the storm. They still looked the same, but they were not as dense as before. The Impals were able to pass through things with little or no concentration. They also seemed to have lost their desire for food. In fact, they suffered no more ties to physical existence, including the need to sleep. While this was curious and interesting, it was not the most incredible thing.

When discussion started about how to return home, of course the method they used to cross the Chesapeake Bay came up first, but was not popular with any of them. The argument continued until something happened by chance. Young Chester Henry was playing with a couple of other children when he jumped over a log. He kept going after he jumped, floating along like a soap bubble in the wind. Impals couldn't fly, but their mass had changed. They could pass over any surface without sinking, including water. The Atlantic Ocean was nothing more than an enormous puddle of water to them.

They huddled together on the beach with Lincoln, Danny, Tesla, and the president in the lead. One by one, they pushed off and began to glide over the churning surf. They resembled a large glowing fog bank heading west.

CHAPTER 46

CIVILIZATION

"We will never have true civilization until we have learned to recognize the rights of others."
~Will Rogers

THE WORLD MOVED SLOW and deliberate over the next few weeks. In almost every country, the respective militaries maintained order. It was difficult to bring the Earth to at least some small measure of what it had been before the storm. The task seemed overwhelming, but turned out not to be the case. The population of the world was cut by a third during the eye's presence. The optimist tried to frame it as two thirds of the population had survived. Yet, when one considered that one third of the population is about 2.4 billion people, it was hard to embrace optimism. Besides restoring order, the most important task was disposing of the bodies. Disease was now running rampant in several countries. Sickness added more corpses and more Impals every day.

The most sanitary and efficient means of disposal was fire. For weeks, the constant cremation pyres burned. Most of the atmosphere filled with dingy smoke. The lavender sky a deep purple bruise from the haze and the yellow clouds appeared greenish-gray. The Impals were the perfect candidates to help carry out this task. They were immune to disease and to the adverse effect of smoke, yet this idea was not as simple as first believed. The Impals were temporarily relocated to different clean up zones away from their homes. This was done so they should not have to dispose of their own body or the bodies of friends and family. However, this logistical issue was not the main problem; the Impals were different since the eye passed. Physically they were the same, but it was as if their light had dimmed a little. It was hard to see since there were so many new ones now than before. The Impals also now possessed the ability to fly, or perhaps more accurately 'glide'. They were no longer encumbered by gravity. Their fainter luminescence seemed to coincide with a fainter density.

Some might believe these to be desirable traits for the Impals, however it presented one major problem. They were unable to interact and influence their physical environment as easily. It took far more concentration to accomplish a physical task, and in some cases, it was not enough. Moving bodies was not easy for most of them and impossible for others. Only the sheer volume of the additional 2.4 billion Impals made the task possible.

The Impals were still wary of fleshers, but it soon changed after the world summit meeting in Little Rock, Arkansas. The United Nations building in New York had been destroyed during the eye of the storm. Most of its members died in an enormous explosion and fire which razed the building. It was still unclear what happened, but there was little doubt it was a result of the darkness. A few world leaders were exposed as a dark soul and jailed as their backgrounds were investigated. Surviving and recently appointed world leaders attended the conference. There were three of these leaders in the United States, not counting Cecil.

Many suggested that Impal leaders should attend. However, the idea was shot down. It was decided for the 'integrity' of the process, the fleshers be the only ones making decisions. Cecil considered this an outrageous prejudice. He considered boycotting the talks, yet he knew it would not do the United States, the world, or the Impals any good. He was selected by his military peers to lead the US delegation and he considered this his solemn duty. Thanks to the former General Garrison, the United States had few politicians left. The Constitution would require some improvising for a while and Cecil was a good choice. Despite his nefarious heritage, Cecil had demonstrated incredible character by standing up to his father. He sacrificed so much for the good of his country. The world needed men with integrity now.

Cecil settled his family back into their suburban Virginia home before he left. Both of his daughters were now Impals, but it didn't seem to make things any more difficult, at least for them. Barbara found it very lonely since now she would dine by herself.

Lincoln returned, along with the others on the island. He was given special consideration to live in the White House, as well as the most recent president, and Nikola Tesla. Albert Einstein showed up a few days later and he also received a special invite. Three of the most intelligent and influential men in history now resided in the most famous house in the world. It would prove to be a blessing to have these men together.

Carmella moved back to her small Georgetown apartment. Her mother moved in with her. They had years of catching up to do and Cecil saw to it that she was given as much time off her job as she needed. Of course, she and Steff also stayed in touch.

Thomas and Seth Pendleton accompanied Cecil to the summit in Little Rock. Arkansas's capital city was only about twenty-five miles from Conway. Both of them felt a strong desire to return to their home.

"Of all the places in the world, why did they choose Little Rock?" Thomas asked after they crossed the state line separating Virginia and Tennessee.

They travelled in a twenty vehicle military convoy with Cecil in the center car. It was suggested he fly for security reasons, but most air traffic had been grounded since the eye arrived. It would be another disaster if the darkness returned with planes in the air. Thousands of the dead were on planes when the eye arrived. In any case, Cecil insisted they drive. He wanted to see the devastation first hand.

"Because its central location and it doesn't have a lot of history on the world stage, good or bad," Burt said. "Most major cities around the world are all but destroyed. Little Rock suffered the least damage." He scratched the bandage on his head and frowned. His wounds were healing well, but they itched. The doctor, now Impal doctor, who saved Burt's life, recommended he take at least another week to rest. There was no way he was not going to be by Cecil's side in this important and historic moment. "Besides, there are two military bases nearby, the Little Rock Air Force Base and Camp Robinson."

Thomas nodded and wrapped his arm around Seth. Cecil glanced at Thomas, and then smiled at Seth. "Are my girls all right?" he asked.

Thomas rubbed Seth's head and said, "I know it is hard to understand unless you have experienced it," he said, then shook his head. "Don't take this the wrong way, Major Garrison, but they have never been better in their lives."

Cecil did have a small understanding of what Thomas was telling him. He wondered on more than one occasion what it would be like to be an Impal. He still felt a prejudice about death, based on his own mortal existence. It was still a horror in his mind, a definitive ending to the only existence he had ever known. Despite the truth surrounding him for so long now, he still found it difficult to cope. The Impals were not enough to quell his natural instinct to fear the death of his body. A part of him considered his daughters gone. This ate at him every day as he mourned their physical absence. He felt selfish because he always believed that mourning the dead is a selfish act. They are in a better place. What we truly mourn is their tangible absence from our life. This was how he dealt with death ever since his mother died.

Cecil smiled. It was the only response he could muster at the moment. He decided to change the subject and asked another question. "Are you a religious man, Thomas?"

Thomas regarded him for a moment and said, "Not as much as I should have been, but yes I am."

"Why do you think this storm happened?" Cecil asked.

He hoped to gain some special insight about what God's plan was in all this, but to his disappointment, Thomas shrugged.

"I don't know. I never saw anything outside of the dark souls that would give me a clue one way or the other. We were invisible to the world, watching a horror show unfold around us. It was a helpless feeling."

"I'll tell you what I think," Burt chimed in. "I am a religious man, a Christian, but I never have been as good as I should be."

"Didn't Hitler think you were Jewish?" Cecil said with a wry smile. Burt did not find it amusing.

"I would rather not talk about it," Burt said. "I believe what I have to say is important."

Cecil felt about three inches tall for his insensitive remark. He was open about his experience in the darkness, but Burt was not so willing to discuss it. He couldn't imagine it to be worse, but perhaps it was. "Please continue," he said.

"I've been thinking about this a lot and I think it is a reminder," Burt said.

"A reminder?" Thomas asked.

"Yes," Burt said. "A reminder from God that death is not the end, and we are eternal."

"You think God sent the storm?" Thomas asked.

"What do you think?" Burt asked, "you've seen more than any of the rest of us."

Thomas shook his head. "All I have seen is a world in which I was invisible. I have seen the horrors mankind is capable of. I saw no evidence of God."

"What about the doors Seth said he saw?" Cecil asked. "What is beyond those doors?"

Seth glanced up at the mention of his name. He gave his dad a sad smile, then ducked his head.

"His mother went through one," Thomas said. "He didn't follow so he doesn't know. The doors, if they are doors, are gone now."

There were several moments of uncomfortable silence as they sped down the interstate. Cecil gazed out the window, searching for something, anything, to change the subject.

"Has anyone noticed it is almost Thanksgiving and the trees have not changed?" he asked as they passed through a forested area. He first noticed this when trapped at the cabin in the woods.

"You know . . . that's true," Burt said, pointing out the window. "All these trees should be bare this time of year. They still look like we are in May or June. The grass is still green too."

"We've had some pretty chilly nights," Cecil added. "The weather is normal, in a meteorological sense."

"I don't know," Thomas said. "The weather doesn't seem as noticeable to me as it used to."

"I wish Dr. Winder had come with us," Burt said. "I kinda liked the little nerd. He was a plethora of knowledge."

Dr. Winder's Impal, along with Charlotte and Derek's, showed up about a week after the eye passed. Cecil gave them all a warm welcome and a prestigious residence in Washington, but only Dr. Winder agreed to stay at the White House. For him, it wasn't so much the prestige of the house. It was the access to Einstein and Tesla, not to mention his old friend, the most recent president.

Cecil did something unprecedented and controversial before leaving Washington. He insisted that the latest president, who was now an Impal, resume control of the Executive Branch.

"What if the Impals disappear again?" a general asked him.

It was a difficult question for Cecil. Especially since there were so many higher ranking officers looking to him. He realized this was a subject way beyond a simple meeting and agreement. It would take a change in attitude and perhaps beliefs by many world leaders. Of course, the unpredictable nature of the storm might make any political inclusion impossible. Cecil thought it would be appropriate for the United States to get its house in order first. However, there was too much pressure from the rest of the world to put a global policy in place as soon as possible.

They watched out the windows as crowds of Impals and fleshers lined the sides of the road to show their support as they passed. They all seemed supportive, although Cecil could have sworn he saw one sign reading, "Death to the Pythonians!"

Cecil shut his eyes and leaned back on the seat with his head cocked to one side. He closed his eyes as dozens of images flooded his mind. His thoughts began to mesh into one distorted image as he saw a serpent with many heads slithering about in his mind's eye. The heads of the snake consisted of his father's accomplices on each side of the slimy body. His father's head protruded in the dead center. He leered with a condescending smirk. As the abomination lunged, he shook himself awake and sat up. Was it a dream, or did the eye return?

He blinked into the bright sunlight.

Burt face was a mixture of sympathy and disgust. Before Cecil could say anything, Burt said, "I know . . . I know."

CHAPTER 47

THE PASSING

"Death is no more than passing from one room into another.
But there's a difference for me, you know. Because in that
other room I shall be able to see."
~Helen Keller

REBEKAH AND MALAKHI'S HOME was gone now, burned to the ground the day the eye arrived. Of course, the fire had been their salvation, enabling them to escape the darkness. For the past several weeks, they shared a small tent on the base with Nehemya and Gestas. Eliezra located her daughter a few days after the eye passed and went to live with her. Nehemya and Gestas did not need sleep anymore. They spent most of their nights walking the camp, visiting the guards, and playing an occasional game of Yaniv at the mess hall. It took several nights to teach Gestas the basics since cards were not around in his time. They even included Malakhi in some of their games when Rebekah was not around.

Gestas still felt the old urge deep inside to return to his wickedness. It was similar to the desire of a reformed smoker who still feels a twinge for a cigarette on occasion. However, the urge was weak and it grew weaker with each passing day.

The same day of the world summit in Little Rock, Rebekah received news that a small apartment was available. It was only a mile from their old one. They packed what little things they owned and moved in the same night. The apartment was indeed small and bare. If not for the loan of a couple of cots from a friendly army lieutenant, they would have slept on the floor. In comparison to their recent lodging, it was luxury. They enjoyed four solid walls and a roof over their heads, not to mention privacy. They invited Gestas to move in too.

Mary soon left Donna and her parents and began to wander the countryside. She had nowhere in particular to go so she visited many of the places she knew in life. St. James's Palace, the Palace of Whitehall and a country estate outside of London were her favorite places in life. She thought she may be able to capture some of the simple joys of her older life, but she found it impossible.

Whitehall had burned a little over a hundred years after her death. Only a few small parts remained. St. James's Palace was still a royal residence and security was too tight for her to get inside, even as an Impal. She thought about telling them who she was, but she didn't think it would go over very well with the current royals. The general public wouldn't be receptive either. She envisioned crowds of Brits pursuing her with lead pipes and chains, dealing some of the same justice Mary once used against her non-Catholic subjects.

The centuries had eroded her villainous stature. In truth, she was little more than a curiosity to her countrymen and the world, yet she was afraid to chance it. She thought it better to remain anonymous. Most people who encountered her smiled and nodded. To them, she was just another Impal from England's storied past. God knows there were enough of them wandering around already. There was no photography in her time and unless one possessed a keen eye, Mary didn't much resemble any of her portraits.

Her last hope of connection with her life was the country cottage. At first, she thought she was in the wrong place until she explored the nearby hills and valley centered with a lake. This is where the house once stood. The moss-covered rocks, which were the ancient remains of a foundation, confirmed it. She sat on the stones and stared at the distant lake where she once swam as a child. Sadness stung her when she remembered her friends. She recalled the wonderful, care free times she enjoyed here before the throne was thrust upon her. She didn't want to do what she did, not at first. Once it started, her arrogance convinced her it was justified. Every single day she spent as the sovereign ruler of England, she longed to be back here in this special place. Here, the cares of the world seemed hundreds of miles away.

Mary's eyes welled up and she began to cry. Large, silvery tears rained into the grass beneath her feet. She was thankful to be out of the dark void, yet she had never felt more alone.

The Headquarters of the 1st Signal Brigade in Gloucester was once again a busy place. Impals with nowhere to go made their homes there as the citizens of the nearby town began to move back and rebuild. Private Sean Poindexter helped facilitate the organized entrance of Impals. This time was different. This time, settlement on the base was voluntary. Poindexter was excited to see many of the Impals again, especially the great storyteller, J.M. Barrie. He was happy the darkness was gone. Although, every night since the eye passed, he had been apprehensive about turning off his lights before going to bed.

England declared Impals have the rights and privileges of any other citizen. Their temporary return to military bases was to expedite their reintegration into society. In fact, most of the first world countries had made similar decrees in the weeks since the eye passed, the United States included.

The summit in Little Rock was more or less to set international law and precedent for the Impals. It was also to help some of the third world countries come around in their thinking. There were still a few who considered them abominations to their religion. However, the recent encounter with the eye of the storm softened their stance quite a bit. Fortunately, none of these countries possessed Tesla Gates.

The news of the Gates had made it to Europe. Their nefarious legend spread quickly. J.M. Barrie even created a story around them which he told to both Impals and fleshers. In his story, the Tesla Gates were doorways to the Underworld. It was a horrible place that required a great deal of finesse and intelligence to escape. The Impals encountered many different adversaries such as evil fairies and ghost pirates. These stories projected a believable quality to the European

Impals. The ones who had fallen victim to the Shredder in America knew better.

Overall, Poindexter felt better, except for one thing. The situation with his friend of five years ate at him with guilt on a daily basis. Not because Jack was gone, Poindexter believed he got what he deserved. He felt guilty because he was friends with him, visiting his house on several occasions. He did not have a clue what Jack was really like, what he did in his home when nobody was around. No telling how many times he visited Jack's flat with the gruesome cage a feet away from him. He felt stupid because he could have prevented it, could have stopped it several victims ago. There should have been signs and Poindexter missed them.

Poindexter felt a chill every time he travelled to the quarter master barracks on the north side of the base to get supplies. Jack was buried in an unmarked grave a short distance behind the building. A small stick had been shoved into the soft earth, not as a memorial, but as a notice to avoid the area.

He tried to feel sorry for Jack, but he could not bring himself to do it. He felt far sorrier for all the poor women. Jack would be forgotten before long. He should be. The place where he now resided was far darker than the hole where his remains lay.

Poindexter picked up several crates of food and took them back to the barracks. It was a blessing that eating was no longer a function the Impals needed or desired. The base wouldn't have enough rations to last a week if they had to provide for the influx of Impals. He grabbed a ration pack and joined some of his fellow soldiers at an outside table. They listened to radio reports of the summit in Little Rock.

Poindexter had the good fortune of night duty assignment in the barracks. He barely listened to the radio as he thought about story time with J.M. Barrie. He felt a little childish, but he didn't care. Any positive diversion was welcome. Besides, he loved the stories.

After three days of deliberation, Cecil was exhausted. As he expected, minimal progress had been made. The whole thing was little more than a political show of who was the most compassionate and caring about the plight of the Impals. Of course, the United States was last in this category and deservedly so. Cecil hoped to change this perception, but it was going to take a lot of time to convince the world otherwise. There was too much baggage and too many open gates . . . literally.

The one unanimous agreement was that the Tesla Gates would be destroyed. This wasn't done only because of the Impals. The Gates could also become a formidable weapon if developed further. These devices were a political football, threatening to hinder any further progress. They agreed to destroy them and any blue prints in existence. Cecil called the president and let him know of this decision.

"It's for the best," the president agreed. "Those things are an abomination."

"How are you holding up?" Cecil asked.

"Great, never been better!" the president replied, a little too enthusiastically.

Cecil knew better. He knew the president was not receiving the same respect as he would have as a flesh and blood president. It was a sad reality and it was the main reason why Cecil asked him to step back into his post. If the United States could show the world that placing an Impal back in charge was the right thing, then it might send a strong message. Cecil asked Carmella to step in and check on him. She didn't want to leave her mother, not even for an instant, but she agreed to return to the White House during the summit.

The summit ended after a week. Besides the destruction of the Gates, the only item agreed upon is that Impals deserved the same due process as fleshers. What this meant varied a great deal from the developed countries to the third world countries. In the United States and its allies, it meant amnesty. Nobody was willing to go as far as granting citizenship, at least, not yet. This decision remained with individual nations.

Cecil was anxious to get back to Washington. The Constitutional government needed to be replaced. He knew it was not going to be easy, there would be several vying for power in the new government. In spite of all that had happened, man's desire for power and control was still strong.

The last day of the summit, Cecil walked outside the Arkansas State Capitol building to get some fresh air and to call Barbara. He intended to return home the next morning, but his last evening in Arkansas would be a short trip up the road with Thomas and Seth. He walked outside and breathed in the cool fall air. It was time for this kind of weather. After all, they were just a few weeks away from Christmas. The green grass and green trees made it a hard reality to accept.

The Arkansas State Capitol building was designed to resemble the US Capitol building, but only two-thirds the size. The large rotunda dome cast a shadow across the front of the building as the late afternoon sun sank low in the western sky. Cecil sat down on the shaded limestone steps and took out his cell phone to call Barbara. He was about to hit call when something caught his attention. Even in the shadow of the building, he could tell something was different above him. He squinted up into the sky and blinked several times. He slowly stood up as the phone slipped out of his hand and bounced down the steps.

The sky above had lost its lavender hue and was now a light blue. The once yellow clouds were now white. He started to walk down the steps, stumbling as his eyes remained focused on the heavens. Soon, something else grabbed his attention. Two large oak trees a few yards away dropped their leaves in a brown and thunderous crash. In fact, all the trees he could see, both close and on the distant hills surrounding the capital city, were bare in a few minutes. The millions of leaves dropping in short order from near and far emitted numerous muffled explosions. Cecil clasped his hands over his ears to shield them from the deafening roar.

Cecil jumped back towards the middle of the walkway as if he were trying to avoid stepping in something dangerous. The grass, which was a lush green moments ago, was turning brown as if painted by an invisible brush. The noise attracted people inside as delegates, security, and state police streamed outside.

Cecil stood in dumbstruck shock as security and Burt approached asking him if he was okay. He shook his head. "The—the storm . . . has p-passed," he stammered.

His heart throbbed as he scrambled for his phone. Abbs and Steff were foremost on his mind.

CHAPTER 48

THE ETHEREAL INSTINCT

"Trust your instinct to the end, though you can render no reason."
~Ralph Waldo Emerson

CECIL COULD NOT BREATHE as the phone began to ring. An eternity passed between every maddening pulse. A few moments later there was a click followed by a female voice. "Hello."

He sucked in a huge lungful of air when he recognized the sweet, tinny voice of Steff.

"Hello, Daddy," Steff said, "Are you coming home soon?"

"Are you and your sister okay?" Cecil gasped.

"Yes, we are fine . . . what's wrong, Daddy? You are scaring me."

"Scaring you?" Cecil thought. He then began to laugh.

"What's so funny, Daddy?" Steff asked, her voice rising with frustration.

"Nothing . . . nothing at all, sweetheart," he said between chuckles. "I am just so glad to hear your beautiful voice."

"Mom . . . Dad is acting weird," Steff called out. He heard shuffling footsteps and then Barbara took the phone.

"Cecil, is everything alright?" Barbara asked.

He confirmed again that both of the girls were fine before telling her what had happened in the past few minutes.

Barbara walked to the window and gasped.

"My God, it is true," she breathed. "Girls come here!"

Abbs came from upstairs and joined them at the window. They all stared with disbelief at a sight which would have been ordinary a few months before. The world was normal again.

Barbara walked to the TV and clicked it on. The first couple of stations she tried broadcast a test pattern indicating they were off the air. She soon came across a local Virginia station with a message scrolling across the screen.

"*It appears the cosmic storm has passed over the Earth. The Impals are still here. We will follow with a live broadcast as soon as the staff is assembled . . .*"

Barbara plopped down in a chair in front of the TV. The message offended her, saying everything was normal other than the Impals were still here. To her, it now seemed completely normal and she couldn't imagine a world without the Impals. Especially not a world without her daughters. She was relieved the girls were still here, but terrified when she considered that they could be gone at any minute.

"Mom, are you alright?" Abbs asked.

She and her sister knelt down beside their mother and placed a hand on her arm. Their cold was as comforting as a warm embrace. She almost forgot about Cecil on the other end of the phone.

"Cecil, are you still there?" she asked after several long moments.

"Yes, is everything okay?" he asked.

She smiled at both of her daughters and touched their ethereal faces with her free hand. "Yes, everything is fine. When are you coming home?"

"I was going to see Thomas and Seth Pendleton before I started back in the morning, but I'll come back tonight."

"No," Barbara said. She had grown fond of Thomas and Seth the past few weeks. She was quite attached to Seth. She thought he was the cutest and sweetest little boy.

"No, go check on them. I want to be sure Seth is okay," she said.

"I can call," Cecil suggested, but Barbara was insistent.

"We are fine here," she said. "Go check on them."

Cecil sighed, but he did not argue. Barbara felt a small pang of guilt because she knew he wanted to get home as soon as possible to see the girls. This storm was anything but predictable. The Impals could be here forever or they could be gone in a few seconds. There was no way to know. As hard as it was for Cecil to wait, they both knew that checking on Thomas and Seth was the right thing to do.

"I'll catch a flight first thing in the morning," he told Burt.

Air traffic was starting to return to normal since the "eye of madness", as it was now called, passed. He would catch a military transport from the nearby Little Rock Air Force Base. Cecil soon departed Little Rock with a military escort for the thirty-minute drive north to Conway. He found Thomas and Seth well and in good spirits.

Indeed the storm had passed over the planet. Fear and panic gripped people around the world, but this time it seemed unwarranted. The sky had changed, the seasons changed as they should have almost two months ago. Much to the delight of most people on the planet, television and internet signals returned. The one thing that did not change were the Impals. They were still here, as before, only . . . the people who died after the storm passed were gone. There was no Impal, no nothing. Death seemed to have returned to its ways before the storm. It was not clear where these recently deceased were. Perhaps they were able to move on.

Life went on as normal for several weeks. Rebekah, Malakhi, and Nehemya celebrated Hanukah with Gestas. Thomas and Seth celebrated Christmas in Conway with his boss, Don Lewis, and his family. Lincoln, Einstein, Tesla, the president, and a host of others celebrated Christmas in the White House.

The president still served in his executive capacity along with the vice president who died during the eye. The remaining members of the government agreed on a special election to occur the third Tuesday in January. This would fill over half of the vacated seats in Congress and several state government positions. It would also elect a new president and vice president. The government officials who perished during the eye were still here. Most wanted to return to their position, but they were denied. Even though the Impals now enjoyed some rights, their nature was too unpredictable. They could be gone in an instant, leaving the government vulnerable.

Most elected governments around the world were doing the same thing in January. The United Kingdom had to replace their Prime Minister and over half the members of Parliament. The royals were miraculously spared except for one obscure Duke who was on a hunting trip near Kent. He took his own life with a shotgun at the behest of the darkness.

One sad royal, who died a long time ago, did not have such a great Christmas. Mary spent Christmas Eve and most of Christmas Day with a group of homeless Impals. At least she had company, but each of them were miserable. They had no connection with their former lives. They sat in a small abandoned country church singing Christmas carols. They pretended to toast a Merry Christmas to one another. This only made their mood all the more depressing considering the Impals no longer had a need or desire to eat.

Mary wondered what Donna was doing. She imagined her sitting around a large table garnished with all sorts of food. The house and living room festooned with all sorts of Christmas decorations. It made her happy to think of Donna that way, but it also made her sad with envy. Donna was still a flesher and could enjoy everything about Christmas. Mary's mental picture of Donna was not too far off. She did have a nice Christmas with her parents, even though they did not eat with her. It was the best and most peaceful Christmas they had enjoyed in years. It was the same for Private Poindexter. He enjoyed the celebration with his fellow soldiers and his favorite storyteller.

Cecil woke up on New Year's Day to a dusting of snow. The trees and the grass outside his bedroom window twinkled in the morning sun. As he admired the view, the disturbing feeling that something had changed washed over him. Everything looked the same though. The sky was still blue with white clouds. He flicked the TV on and saw it was working. The Today Show was running a story on the coming special elections. The year had changed overnight, but it was something more. A thought sprang forth in his sleepy brain and he bolted from the room.

When Cecil reached the stairs, he stopped in his tracks and breathed a sigh of relief. Abbs and Steff were on the top landing looking down at him. His spirits lifted at first until he saw their faces. They seemed haggard, as if they needed sleep. Their sad eyes stung his heart.

"Girls . . . are you okay?" he asked.

The sisters exchanged glances and shook their heads in unison.

"We don't feel right," Steff said.

Abbs nodded in agreement.

"W-what's wrong?" Cecil asked, his heart sinking through the floor. He expected them to disappear at any moment as Abbs did when the eye arrived. Moments before she vanished, Abbs knew something was not right.

They both stared at him, but did not move until he held his arms apart, inviting them into his embrace. They descended the stairs and sank into their father's arms.

Barbara came out of the bedroom and stopped when she saw them.

"What's wrong?" she asked.

Cecil tried to give a reassuring smile, but it was impossible. He shook his head and mouthed, "*I don't know.*"

Barbara walked over and kissed both girls on the top of the head.

"What's wrong, sweethearts?" she whispered.

"I don't know, Mom," Abbs said. "Something doesn't feel right . . . something . . . we don't belong here."

Thomas and Seth had been playing a board game all night as part of their New Year's festivities. Father Wilson came by early in the evening and visited with Thomas before playing a few hands of Rook with Seth.

"I'm sorry about my insensitivity before," he told Thomas. "I know my mouth often gets ahead of my brain. It's not a good trait for a priest to have."

"It's fine," Thomas said. "It was a stressful time for us all. I appreciate you checking on Seth and me."

Father Wilson smiled. He then glanced at Seth and rubbed his chin as if he were trying to think of what to say.

"Thomas, do you mind if I ask you something?"

"Not at all," Thomas said.

"Please feel free not to answer if it makes you uncomfortable."

Thomas nodded and waited for his question.

"Well, the darkness was here for a while . . . do you think they were demons?"

Thomas grimaced and shook his head.

"No, they were the darkest evil that mankind ever produced. I saw their countenance as they lurked in the shadows. They were human, but humans who were rotten and arrogant to the core."

"Do you think they were what the Bible proclaims to be demons?"

"Well, you are the priest, you should know," Thomas said with a half-smile.

"I don't," Father Wilson admitted. "We have seen such miraculous things the past several months. We have seen definitive proof of the soul's existence. Even so, I feel as if I have more questions now than before."

"I guess the next thing you want to ask is if Seth and I have seen God?" Thomas said. He said it jokingly because he knew where Father Wilson's questions were headed.

Father Wilson raised his eyebrows with hopeful expectancy.

"No, we haven't, but I am certain he exists," Thomas said.

"How?" Father Wilson asked.

"Look at me, look at Seth . . . look at the other Impals, can you explain this any other way?"

Father Wilson shook his head and sighed.

"I just wish I knew what God's plan was in all this," he said.

"I do too," Thomas said. "I do too."

Thomas did not bring it up with Father Wilson, but he had a singular thought since he discovered Seth after the storm arrived. He wondered what was beyond the doors. What secrets did they hold? Were his parents waiting there to embrace him with open arms and welcome him into paradise? Was Barbara there? Was God? Thomas only knew one thing for certain. Barbara was beyond those doors. He would volunteer for a beating with an iron pipe if he could just see her again, if only for a moment.

Thomas had been thinking of Barbara all night and as dawn broke, a strange feeling came over him. He got up and walked to the window, uncertain of what he expected to see. Something hidden in the recesses of his psyche, pulled at him with a subtle, yet urgent tug.

His son stared up at him with a frown.

"Daddy . . . I . . . I . . . we . . . don't," he said trailing off, unable to form the words.

"I know, son," Thomas said, pulling Seth close. "We don't belong here."

CHAPTER 49

A SELFISH PRAYER

"Selfishness is the greatest curse of the human race."
~William E. Gladstone

THE FEELING TO EVERY IMPAL was subtle as the onset of a cold. It sank into their being, giving them all definitive revelation. None of them knew exactly when this feeling started. Perhaps it was when the eye passed or maybe it was yesterday. All Impals were now consumed with the strong feeling that they didn't belong. They needed to be somewhere else. The problem was, none of them knew where.

"What do you mean you don't belong here?" Rebekah asked Nehemya and Gestas. "This is your home, Dad. Of course you belong here!"

Nehemya shook his head and glanced at Gestas. They both felt the same way, but Gestas was not going to get involved with the conversation. This was between father and daughter. He walked across the room and sat down by Malakhi.

"I know it is, my dear," Nehemya said. "But I cannot explain this feeling to you. It is the most certain I have ever been about anything in my life."

Rebekah began to weep. "Where will you go?" she sobbed.

"I don't know my sweet daughter. I just don't know."

* * *

Mary felt it at the same time, but it did not have the same effect as it did with most Impals. She already felt alone and out of place since the eye passed. This new feeling deepened the despair she already suffered. Mary was by herself in a small park a few short miles from Buckingham Palace when she began to cry.

The Impal community now existed in a heightened state of agitation. Not agitation that would lead to violence, but more like a caged animal desperate to escape. It has been said the heart just knows when it comes to love. Perhaps the soul just knows when it comes to belonging.

The famous resident Impals of the White House were no exception. They all knew they no longer belonged. They didn't know why they felt this way, but at least a couple of them had an idea of where they might belong. Einstein and Tesla had discussed theories for weeks now, long before this feeling took hold.

"What is your opinion, Albert?" Tesla asked.

Einstein crinkled his bushy mustache and ran a hand through his unkempt hair. "I think the energy from the storm made all us visible. It then closed the portal, so to speak, for anyone else to move on after death. I think it is why everyone remained here after the storm arrived." Einstein paused and nodded at Tesla. "Do you think the Gates worked?" he asked.

Tesla said, "I think so, but there is no way to be sure. There were no doorways when the Impals went through the Gates. When we faded back onto that plane of existence during the eye, we saw no Gates then either."

"None of us know anything for sure, my friend," Einstein said with a grin. "That is what makes science so interesting."

"Where do you think the people are now who have died since the storm left?" Tesla asked.

Einstein took a long pause and closed his eyes. He seemed to be in a state of meditation. "I think . . ." he began. "I think it is not unreasonable to assume things have returned to normal."

"Then why are we still here?" Tesla asked.

"I have always believed if you cannot explain something simply, then you do not understand it well enough. I could say our energy was affected, or something is blocking us from passing over. Perhaps it is even some higher plan of the universe. In short, I don't know why we are still here."

This conversation continued after, what many called, "the Impal flu" arrived. The Tesla Gates had worked, in a sense. Perhaps not in the way General Garrison hoped, yet they worked all the same. The Impals returned to another level of existence.

Einstein and Tesla engaged in a heated discussion with Lincoln and the president. It was scientists against politicians. A battle of wills heightened by their agitated sense of feeling lost. Lincoln and the president did not like what their scientific counterparts suggested. However, something deep down in their ethereal existence knew they were right. After a couple hours of debate, Einstein addressed the group. When he finished, it was as if a light clicked on. They knew where they belonged. The question was, could they get there?

"My friends, you know me not to be an irrational man. Everything I have ever done has been with a great deal of thought and deliberation. Believe me when I tell you that Nikola and I have put a great deal of thought and discussion into this. We believe it is the only way to get where we want to go. I am tired, you are tired . . . we are all tired," he said making a circle with his arms to represent the whole world. "If we don't try, I feel we will never know peace."

"How do you know the doors will be there?" the president asked. "This is taking one hell of a risk."

"Life, or in our case, existence is all about risk. I believe the worst case scenario is that we would be as we were during the eye of the storm."

"A pretty grim scenario," Lincoln said. "I existed that way for over one hundred and fifty years and I would not recommend it."

"I will go first," Tesla said.

"Great," the president said. "But how the hell are we going to know whether it worked or not if we can't see you anymore?"

"Electromagnetic fields," Tesla said casually. "I worked with them all my life and the one thing that does seem to traverse from one realm to another is electrical energy."

"You guys are the scientists so I wouldn't presume to debate you," the president said. "I just don't feel comfortable with this."

"It is my risk to take," Tesla said. "These infernal contraptions have made my name synonymous with the evil they have perpetrated. Perhaps they can now be used for something good."

"Is that vanity speaking?" Lincoln asked.

In his life as a politician, he had uttered many things he wished he could take back. This was one of those times. He understood Tesla's reasoning. He wouldn't want his name associated with something so nefarious either. Tesla glared at him and Lincoln quickly apologized. "I'm sorry . . . I'm a little on edge," he said.

"We all are," Einstein agreed. "But, I think Mr. Tesla's plan is our most viable option."

Tesla smirked. "Trust me, I do not relish the thought of this not working. If the doors are not there, I could wind up in eternal solitary confinement or worse."

The first call from the White House went to Cecil Garrison. He was having a rough day trying to comfort his daughters. There was absolutely nothing he could do for them.

"Cecil, please tell me that all the Gates have not been disassembled yet," the president said.

There was a long pause on the other end of the phone, and then Cecil cleared his throat and said, "Not all, not fast enough. Why?"

The president relayed their discussion and explained they needed to test their theory. Not all the Impals of the world knew why they felt out of place yet. They soon would and then it would be overwhelming. Cecil felt as if his own soul left his body as he sat listening to the president. He felt empty, he felt hollow and, worst of all, he felt hopeless. He knew what this meant. His blank eyes drifted to his daughters who were sitting on the sofa next to their mother. He wanted to scream. Finally, after several inquiries if he were still there, Cecil uttered a few words just above a whisper.

"I will meet you at Quantico tonight," he said and then half hung up and half dropped the phone.

Barbara watched him with a worried frown, but he ignored her. Cecil hurried up the stairs and into the bedroom. He closed and then locked the door behind him. He fell to his knees beside the bed, leaned over it, and began to pray. Tears blotted the dark bedspread as he uttered the same prayer over and over. A prayer which he feared would go unanswered.

When Cecil arrived at Quantico that evening, he met Burt outside the hanger.

"My God, Cecil. You look like Hell! What's wrong?" Burt said.

Cecil felt lightheaded. His legs felt as if they were filled with sand. When he spoke it was as if he were hearing himself speak from a distance.

"We've got to turn on the Shredder," he murmured.

"What the hell for? I thought those damned things were destroyed!"

A large SUV pulled up. The back doors opened and Lincoln, Tesla, Einstein, Dr. Winder and the president got out. A few Secret Service agents accompanied them.

"Tell him," Cecil said, jerking his head in Burt's direction. Then he turned and went through the dark opening of the hangar.

Dr. Winder stayed and explained to Burt while everyone else went inside.

A few minutes later, all the lights were on and the dull hum of the Shredder powering up reverberated around the hangar. Einstein and Tesla walked behind the Gate as it fired to life, casting blue, flickering light. Einstein placed a small black box on a table about thirty yards behind the Tesla Gate.

"What is that?" Lincoln asked.

"An EMF meter," Tesla replied.

"A what?" Lincoln asked.

"It's a device for measuring electromagnetic fields in units called milligause," Tesla explained.

"I see," Lincoln said, "I'll take your word for it."

"Is this how you are going to communicate with Nikola once he goes through?" the president asked.

"Yes . . ." Einstein said. "If all goes as planned."

"So how will you know if the doors are back?" the president asked.

"A simple pattern," Tesla said. "If they are back, I will try to manipulate the electromagnetic field between realms. I will attempt to produce milligause readings in a sequence of 30-40-72-60-100. If they are not back, I will do the pattern in reverse starting with 100."

"Are you certain you will be able to do it?" the president asked.

"Yes, we are certain," he said with confidence, yet he gave Einstein a furtive glance.

The Gate soon ramped up to full power. Nobody in the crowd had seen one before, except one. Cecil saw it kill his father and devour Impals. He knew that if this worked, it would soon be taking his girls away from him. He hated the damned thing and, for an instant, he thought about taking out his pistol and shooting the control panel to Hell.

With no fanfare, and only a brief adieu, Tesla ascended the platform with his head held high. He stepped forward and dissolved into the cracking arcs of electricity. An instant later, he was gone without a trace.

A minute passed, then two minutes . . . there was no activity on the EMF meter. Everyone, including Cecil, walked behind the Gate to check. Einstein stood there, staring intensely as if he were trying to will the meter to move. When they were about to give up, they heard a beep.

"Thirty!" Einstein proclaimed.

There was another louder beep.

"Forty!" Einstein shouted.

Cecil's heart began to sink with each progressive beep. He knew the number thirty started the sequence confirming the doors were back.

The loudest beep of them all finally sounded, echoing around the hangar. To the Impals it was a joyous sound. To Cecil, it was the sound of the last nail hammered into his daughter's coffins.

"One hundred!" Einstein cried. "The doors are back!" he bowed his head and clasped his hands together. "Thank you my friend," he said to the unseen Tesla. "Thank you my brave friend. Now go . . . be at peace."

The meter beeped one last time in acknowledgement to Einstein, and then it fell silent.

"We should go through now!" Dr. Winder said, anxious to put an end to his longing desire to move on. He walked toward the platform.

"No, we should be the last ones to go through," Einstein said.

"That's right," Lincoln said. "Einstein is the only one of us who understands this, plus he is a familiar face. We are familiar faces," he said pointing to himself and the president. "As much as Impals might want to move on, there will be many who are distrustful and frightened. Not too long ago, this contraption was viewed as an execution chamber. Now it may very well be the instrument that brings them peace. They will need familiar faces telling them all is well."

"Agreed," the president said. "I have talked to some other world leaders today, and this is a global issue. All the Impals are restless. I have a feeling this country is about to be inundated with Impals since we have the only two Tesla Gates left."

"Where is the other one?" Burt asked.

Cecil knew the answer. His grandfather was interned there as an Impal.

"Arizona," the president said.

Cecil felt as if salt and alcohol filled his already festering wound. He turned and walked outside then toward the forest. When he reached the tree line, he bent over and grabbed his knees, trying to catch his breath.

CHAPTER 50

HOPE

"In this sad world of ours sorrow comes to all and it often comes with bitter agony. Perfect relief is not possible except with time. You cannot now believe that you will ever feel better. But this is not true. You are sure to be happy again. Knowing this, truly believing it will make you less miserable now. I have had enough experience to make this statement."
~Abraham Lincoln

THE MAJOR NEWS CHANNELS broadcast the announcement in the morning. All the Impals who did not know where they needed to be soon did. Cecil had stayed out late and was just coming in the door when the news broke. Abbs and Steff met him with hugs.

"Daddy, we know where we need to be. Do you think it is safe?"

Cecil wanted to tell them more than anything it was not safe. They should stay here with him and Barbara forever. He didn't tell them though. He thought about it a lot last night. As much as he wanted his daughters to stay, he held a stronger desire to see them happy. He nodded and said, "Einstein and Tesla think so."

Cecil wondered where his grandfather was now. He entered the Tesla Gate in Arizona months ago. He had not heard anything since the eye passed.

"Look for you great-grandfather when you go through the door. I hope he is there with you."

Cecil excused himself and went upstairs to check on Barbara. He found her lying in bed and crying into her pillow. The news recapped the president's speech on the small TV by the dresser.

Rebekah and Malakhi had the same reaction to Nehemya's desire to go.

"I love both of you," Nehemya told them as he embraced each with a luminescent arm. "But I just don't belong here."

Gestas stayed out of the discussion. He was the only one who understood. Rebekah and Malakhi were heart broken and devastated. Yet, in the end, they agreed to go with Nehemya and Gestas to America.

Mary was happier than most when she heard the news. She had never felt she belonged and now the feeling was ten times worse. She travelled back to Donna's house. There, she met them leaving for the base in Gloucester. Donna was as frail and fragile as she did when Mary found her during the eye. Only this time, it was not due to any foreign substance. It was from the grief of losing her parents again. Their reunion was brief and this time Donna knew she would lose them for good.

Donna was happy to have Mary accompany them to the base. From there, they would soon go to America. They understood each other better than anyone can understand another person. Mary was a godsend for the distraught girl.

They arrived at the base after waiting in traffic for hours. The line stretched almost three miles at one point. Millions of Impals would assemble through the base in the coming weeks before shipping off to their destiny.

Over the next week, the Impals already in the United States flooded into Quantico. They entered the Gate with some hesitation, but with determination. They needed to move on. Friends and family stayed with their loved one to the end before they stepped through. This slowed the process down quite a bit. Cecil knew of the issue, but he dismissed it.

"I don't care if it takes ten years. They can have their family with them," he told them.

Cecil didn't want all this authority thrust upon him. Representing the United States at the summit was one thing. Now he seemed to be the supreme authority and guardian of the Tesla Gates. He loathed this responsibility. Besides, there were many higher-ranking officers at the base, so why was it put on his shoulders? He knew the answer to the question although he did not want to admit it . . . his old man. Was this a legitimate confidence in his abilities? Or, was this a punishment for what his father had done? The answer to the question was not an objective one. He carried out his responsibilities, but from afar. He refused to enter the hangar unless necessary. The girls stayed home with Barbara and he came home early every night to be with them.

Cecil asked the girls to stay with them as long as possible. He used the excuse that he did not want to give the appearance of nepotism by letting his family go first. He knew it was selfish, but he could not help it. He loved his daughters too much. The thought of letting them go ate at him every second of every day. He found himself wishing for death so he could join them, but he was healthy and, barring an accident; he knew it would be fruitless. He would be just another eternal sleeper. No different from the ones who were now gone from the hangar, carried by other Impals as they passed through the Gate. At least he might be free of the pain from losing them, but what good would it be if he couldn't ever be with them. For all anyone knew, the sleepers were living in their own personal Hell as they slumbered. For two weeks this debate raged in his head until he got a knock at his door one evening. When he opened it he was not surprised to see his friend, Burt, standing there. Abraham Lincoln with Thomas and Seth Pendleton stood behind him.

"Hey buddy, sorry to drop in on you like this. Mind if we come in?" Burt asked.

Cecil absently shook his head and shuffled to the side. He was too numb and too shocked to do anything else.

"Thank you major for welcoming us into your beautiful home," Lincoln said and extended his hand.

Cecil stared at it for a few moments as if he were examining an alien object. He reached out and shook the former president's hand. Thomas stepped forward next.

"Thank you for seeing us, Major Garrison," he said as they exchanged handshakes.

Cecil nodded and then looked down to see Seth beaming up at him. The boy raised his left hand and shook Cecil's left hand. Seth wasn't versed in handshake etiquette. Cecil had grown very fond of the boy on their trip back to Arkansas. The mere presence of the child brought a smile to his face. Cecil said, "Hi, Seth. How are you?"

"I'm fine. Can I play with Abbs and Steboni?" he asked. It seemed his childish pronunciations had returned.

"Sure, they are upstairs. I'll call them."

Before he could call out, Abbs and Steff appeared at the top landing.

"Hi, Seth!" Abbs called. "Come on up."

In spite of their outward projection of good cheer, he could hear the pain in their voice. His heart ripped a little more every time he was with them. They were not happy and he knew why. He was the only one who could give them happiness, but he couldn't bring himself to it. He and Barbara desperately tried to think of some other way, but there wasn't any.

Seth raced up the stairs, or more accurate, he floated up. He leapt from the bottom step and resembling a small, luminescent astronaut as he glided up and landed at the top. The girls embraced him and then ushered him into a bedroom and closed the door.

Cecil's smile faded when the children disappeared. "So, what brings you here?" he asked.

"Do you mind if we have a seat?" Burt asked.

"Okay," Cecil said and gestured toward the sofa and recliner in the middle of the living room. Burt, Thomas and Lincoln sat on the sofa and Cecil took the chair.

"You know how we were discussing the storm and its meaning on our way to the Summit?" Burt asked.

Cecil nodded.

"Well, President Lincoln has some insight that we thought you should hear."

Cecil glanced at each of them in turn.

"What is this about?" he asked.

Lincoln leaned forward and gave a gentle smile. "I can only speak for my own personal beliefs, which I believe I share with most people in this room. I do think God allowed this storm to come. It served as reinforcement to our faith that man has a soul." He paused and then said, "perhaps a reinforcing truth to some and others, a chance of redemption," he said, nodding to Thomas.

Thomas smiled and said, "I agree."

He did not elaborate; he did not have to because everyone could hear the sincere emotion in his voice.

"What about the darkness, the eye . . . how do you explain it?" Cecil snapped. His mind flashed back to the horrific scene of Barbara's assault by the darkness the day the eye arrived.

"Well," Lincoln began cautiously. "I have to agree that God's intent is not immediately clear, but it did show us two things."

"What?" Cecil asked.

Burt jumped in and answered the question. "It showed there are consequences for evil."

Burt stopped and took a deep breath before continuing. "It also shows that God is always open to those who want to turn from their wicked ways. I think our friend, Musial, was proof."

"How do you explain the millions killed by these dark souls? What purpose did it serve?"

Thomas shook his head as he answered, "We don't know. We may be Impals, but we don't have any more answers than you. I don't understand everything that happens in this world, but I am certain it is for a greater reason."

Cecil rubbed his weary eyes and leaned back in his chair. He was a man of faith, but his faith had been stretched to the limits. He feared the day his girls left would be the day it snapped beyond repair.

"What about angels, what about demons . . . what about God? Have you seen any evidence of them?" Cecil asked.

"No," Lincoln admitted. "I have a feeling the dark souls may in some way associate with demons, but I am not certain. And God? Well no, not a personification, but I think the very presence of Impals proves his existence. I believe we will find the answers we are looking for when we reach the doors on the other side."

"You have to let Abbs and Steff go, Cecil," Burt said. "It is the only way for any of you to get peace."

Cecil flashed an angry eye at Burt. The very suggestion that he should let his daughters go . . . what nerve. Burt didn't have any children, so how could he understand? Before he could respond, Lincoln interrupted in a soothing voice. "I know how you feel, major," Lincoln said.

Cecil turned his heated gaze to the former president. How the Hell could anyone know how he feels?

"I lost two of my sons," Lincoln continued. "When I lived in Springfield, Illinois, my son Edward died of an illness. About twelve years later, my son Willie died after we moved into the White House. The death of my boys almost destroyed Mary and me. I know the pain you are feeling, major and I know the pain you are anticipating. It is hard, but I promise you will make it through. Even though I briefly had the pleasure of speaking with your wife, I can tell she is a strong woman. You will make it through."

Cecil's anger dwindled to shame. He sank back in his chair and pinched the bridge of his nose to stop the tears. He put his chin on his chest and muttered, "I love them so much."

"Of course you do," Lincoln said. "But be thankful, major."

"For what?"

"That you have gotten to spend extra time with them. Because you know for a fact they have gone on after death. They will be in a happy place where they will wait for you to arrive one day, and . . ." Lincoln paused and nodded to Thomas. "And we give you our word that we will take them through and make sure they get to where they need to go. I promise, major."

Cecil sat in his chair and wept with the palms of his hands pressed over his eyes. His friends sat patiently and waited. Finally, he looked up with red and swollen eyes.

"When?" Cecil asked.

"Soon, major. We will go with them soon," Lincoln said.

CHAPTER 51

THE OTHER SIDE

"I hope the end is joyful, and I hope never to return."
~Frida Kahlo

THE NEXT DAY, the boats from Europe began to dock at Newport News, Virginia. The ships from Asia, Australia and the Middle East began to dock in Los Angeles and San Diego. Regular air travel was still limited, so it wasn't feasible to transport the Impals by air. Besides, the large cargo ships could carry thousands of them. Phoenix, Arizona and Quantico, Virginia were the destinations of choice in the world at the moment. The government moved thousands of mobile homes to these bases to accommodate family members. Every single hotel and motel in these areas was booked solid for at least a month.

Mary arrived with Donna and her family on the first boat from Europe. They took a bus up to Quantico and spent the night in a used, but clean mobile home a couple of hundred yards from the Tesla Gate hangar. Donna's parents would be going through the next day.

Donna stayed up the whole night with her parents talking and reminiscing. There was a lot of laughter shared between them, but there were also a lot of tears. Mary found herself feeling out of place again, so she went outside and walked. She stared at the hangar, and then at the moon and the stars. She wondered which one she might wind up on when she went through the Gate in the morning. A light snowfall started and she began to walk with her arms spread wide, absorbing as much of the experience as she could. She giggled as the snowflakes passed through her. She began to feel better and her sadness seemed to drift away with the blowing snow. Mary felt more at peace with herself than she had when she was a little girl. She began to glide and spin across the snow as if on invisible ice skates. She leapt over a bush and came down in a graceful spin. Mary stopped when she heard applause behind her. She turned to see Donna standing a few feet away, smiling and clapping. Her parents stood behind her doing the same, and then they joined in with Mary. Three Impals glided and pirouetted across the snow like seasoned Olympians.

Donna laughed and clapped, then began to throw snowballs. Each time one passed through their body, they let out a tinny laugh. They spent the next hour building a snowman.

Donna went back to the mobile home to warm up and her mother made her a steaming mug of hot chocolate. She drank it down and sat on the sofa. A few minutes later, she was sound asleep.

"Shall we go?" Donna's father asked, looking out the window at the orange glow of the approaching sunrise.

"Yes," her mother said sadly. "Are you sure we did the right thing?"

Her father nodded.

"What did you do?" Mary said, stroking Donna's cheek. "Did you poison her?"

Her father didn't know whether to laugh or take offense.

"Of course not," he said. "It's only sleeping pills. She should be up in a few hours."

"But . . . why?" Mary asked, incredulous.

"Because we didn't want her to see us step through the Gate. We didn't want her to experience that finality. We want her to always remember tonight."

Mary understood their reasoning even though she didn't agree with it. There was no point in arguing now. "She wanted to say goodbye," Mary said quietly.

"She did," her mother said. "Tonight is the best goodbye anyone could ask for."

She bent down and placed a note in Donna's jacket pocket and then kissed her on the cheek. "Good bye, baby. We love you and will be waiting for you one day."

Her father bent down and kissed her cheek as well. "Goodbye, sugar bear. I love you."

Mary felt compelled to leave her a message of some sort. She asked for pen and paper which Donna's mom produced. She sat down at the table and scrolled out a quick note. She had to concentrate to keep the pen from passing through her hand. When she finished, she held it up and read to herself.

> *Thank you for saving me, Donna. You are a bright and noble young lady. I was glad to be able to know you and to save you. Your gift to me will not be in vain, as I move on to what awaits; please don't let my gift to you be in vain. Stay strong.*
>
> *~Mary Tudor*

Mary placed the note in her pocket. She bent and kissed her on the cheek.

"Keep strong, love," Mary said.

All three of them could not help shedding a few shimmering tears before they left. As the first rays of the sunshine broke through the window, they turned and walked out the door. The line was starting to form for morning departures. Less than fifteen minutes after they left the sleeping Donna, they passed through the Tesla Gate.

Rebekah, Malakhi, Nehemya and Gestas arrived a few days later. They lodged in a mobile home not too far from the hangar. Rebekah agreed she would not let Malakhi accompany them to the hangar. She didn't want him to see his grandpa go through a device once hated and feared as an instrument of genocide.

"He will try to follow," Nehemya said. "He is a strong willed little boy."

"I will stay with him," Rebekah said. "I don't want to see you leave."

Nehemya spent the morning with his grandson. He told him how much he loved him more times in a couple of hours than he had in Malakhi's whole life.

Rebekah took Malakhi to Washington, D.C. on a tour bus the afternoon that Nehemya and Gestas would move on.

"I'll see you tonight, Grandpa!" Malakhi called after he hugged his grandfather and stepped up on the bus.

Nehemya fought back a strong twinge of guilt as he waved goodbye. He knew they would not see each other again for a long time.

They had told Malakhi it would be the following morning when his grandfather and Gestas would leave. Rebekah found it hard to smile as they toured the capital city. Malakhi was a very perceptive kid and he knew something was wrong, but he thought it was the obvious. His grandfather would be leaving tomorrow.

When they returned that evening, Rebekah had already begun to cry before they were halfway back to the base. Her emotional outburst alarmed Malakhi. When they got back, he sprinted off the bus and into the mobile home. His panicked screams for his grandfather escalated as his calls went unanswered. Rebekah met him at the door as he tried to resume his search outside.

"Where is he?" Malakhi cried. He could tell the answer by his mother's tear streaked face.

He tried to break past her and make a desperate sprint for the hangar in the distance, but she held him tight.

"Your grandfather is fine," she told him. "He is happy and you will see him again," she told him over and over, but Malakhi continued to wail and struggle.

They cried together until they had no more tears to offer.

Cecil had seen this same scene on many occasions over the past few weeks. It was as heartbreaking now as it was when the Impals were forced to enter the Gates. Since he did not go in the hangar, he witnessed most of these anguished farewells outside. He heard even worse reports from inside the hangar. They were forced to increase security. There were several incidents where the flesh and blood family members tried to go through with their loved one. Two of them reached the Gate and burned in the arcing voltage. Their Impals were gone. Nobody knew whether they were gone because the storm had passed or because their momentum hurled their soul through the Gate.

Cecil could imagine the horror this caused their Impal family member when they found them sleeping on the other side. It was suicide. The fleshers were warned to stay clear.

The world was now in a mess, one he would be in the middle of for several years to come. There would be a major rebuilding, not only infrastructure, but the world economies as well. He was already slated to attend another summit next month in London. This one would deal with the world aftermath of the passing of the storm and . . . the Impals. He had not thought much about it yet, he was too worried about other things.

He thought of the summit the morning he went into his local polling place to cast his ballot for the new United States government. He thought about the irony. Today the United States would begin its rebuilding process with a special election. It was also the day he would have to say goodbye to his daughters. He left the polling place and drove home to spend his last few hours with them before he drove them to the base.

Thomas and Seth spent the morning in excited anticipation. The previous day, they visited the Air and Space Museum in Washington, DC. This time their tour was not interrupted as before. They even took Patrick with them, but he went back to the base with Lincoln. As much as he craved a father figure, he now craved finding his place of belonging even more. He knew Thomas and Seth needed their alone time . . . their father and son time. He was also nervous about going through the Gate. For whatever reason, Lincoln seemed to give him the most comfort.

There was a little fear because nobody knew for sure what waited on the other side. Sure, the correct sequence manifested on the EMF meter, but was it really Tesla? What if it were a mere coincidence . . . an anomaly?

"Do you think Mommy will be there?" Seth asked.

"I don't know son, I sure hope so," Thomas answered.

The one thing Thomas dreamed about ever since Seth returned was to see his beloved Annabelle again. He received another chance with his son and for that, he was forever grateful. However, he never felt complete, never felt whole. He thought about her every day since her death, both before and after he became an Impal. The one thing he learned from his experience is that love does not die with the physical body; it only grows stronger.

They watched Seth's favorite movie, Star Wars: The Phantom Menace, one last time that morning. Seth played with some of his action figures he brought with him, acting out scenes from the movie as they transpired on the screen. Thomas hoped Jar Jar Binks would not be anywhere in eternity. He didn't think he could handle it. Seth's crude, but accurate impersonation was bad enough.

When the movie finished, Seth asked a direct and blunt question. "Is God going to be in the door?"

"Maybe," Thomas said. "He is in there somewhere."

"Will he have any Star Wars stuff?"

"I think he will have even better stuff," Thomas said with a wink. "There will be all kinds of good stuff."

Seth half smiled and half frowned as he ducked his head.

"I'm kinda scared, Daddy," he said.

"I am too, buddy . . . but just a little. Remember we did it before and it didn't hurt."

"It didn't feel good, either," Seth said.

What they were most afraid of was *not* going through the Tesla Gate. They knew it wasn't painful and they knew it didn't shred them. What scared them the most was that they would not be able to find Annabelle.

A little after noon, Burt came by to pick them up. They were to meet Cecil and his family at the base around one o'clock.

Cecil arrived a few minutes late with Barbara, Abbs, and Steff. He resembled a man attending the funeral of his child. In one way, in his limited perception of things, he was. He would say good bye to his daughters, probably for a long time. When he got out of the vehicle and walked towards them; Cecil resembled a man walking through quicksand. Barbara looked the same as she approached with a hand on each girl's back. Burt knew this needed to happen as fast as possible, drawing it out would only make things worse.

"Everyone is inside," Burt said. "Follow me."

The world still faced weeks if not months left to send the Impals on their way. Ships arrived daily on the east and west coasts with thousands of troubled souls waiting to move on. The Gates ran almost constantly each day, shutting down only a couple of hours for maintenance and safety checks. Today Burt arranged for an hour of private time. The only people in the hangar were an operator and security officer, who retreated to the rear of the hangar when the party arrived. Today there would be a special exodus with some well-known Impals and several well loved ones.

The group consisted of Lincoln, Einstein, the president, the vice president, Dr. Winder, Thomas, Seth, Abbs, and Steff. The only fleshers present besides the operator and the guard were Cecil and Barbara, along with Burt and Sally. The Tesla Gate shut down ten minutes earlier while the circuits were checked. It now stood silent, a large benign metallic arbor. Cecil saw it as a silent serpent ready to strike. Burt motioned to the operator and he walked back to his station and flicked a few buttons. The Gate began to hum back to life.

The president, vice-president, Dr. Winder, and Einstein ascended the platform.

"We will go first," the president proclaimed as they turned to face everyone.

The vice-president gave a sheepish smile and nodded. He was a good man, but it was hard to believe that someone with such an introverted personality could have ascended so high in politics.

"Thank you, Cecil and Burt for all you have done," Dr. Winder said. He then turned and jumped through the blue arcs.

Everyone gasped at this unexpected move.

"Show off," the president quipped. He and the vice-president both waved and stepped backwards though the blue current. It was as if they were stepping behind a curtain after a campaign speech.

Einstein gave a short statement claiming how right they were to use the Tesla Gates to get to where they belonged. Then he turned and walked through sideways. He giggled as if the electrical currents tickled his translucent body. He was trying to be humorous to ease the tension of the fleshers present, but Einstein was not a comedian. It came across as awkward nervousness. Abbs and Steff gave an uneasy laugh before turning to their parents.

"I love you, Dad, love you Mom," Abbs said as she stepped forward and hugged them.

Steff was short on words. Her face spoke volumes as she ran to embrace her parents.

The little family did not move for the longest time as Thomas, Seth and Lincoln stood waiting. Barbara wept, but Cecil kept his composure. It was not an easy task holding back his emotions. It took every ounce of resolve to avoid an emotional meltdown. Even his die hard resolve was not enough to prevent a few tears from sliding down his face. Soon, the emotional trance was broken by a small voice.

"It's okay Mr. and Mrs. Garrison, I'll watch out for them," Seth said.

Cecil wiped a few tears away and motioned for Seth to come over. Seth looked up at his father. Thomas smiled and nodded. Seth half ran and half skipped to them, receiving a loving hug from each.

"It's time," Lincoln said. He gave Barbara and Cecil a pleasant smile, but neither of them got much pleasure from it.

Abbs and Steff pulled from their parent's embrace and walked toward the Gate. Cecil and Barbara embraced each other as they watched their girls leave. Burt and Sally walked over and placed a supportive hand on their shoulders.

Lincoln, Abbs, Steff, Thomas and Seth all assembled in a straight line in front of the Gate. They turned one last time and gave a final farewell, then they all stepped through together. They held a shared belief that they belonged in what lay on the other side. Their loved ones, their happiness, and their eternal reward waited. They could not have imagined what they found, nor could any of the Impals who went before them. They wished they could turn and go back through, fleeing back to the solid world in terror.

CHAPTER 52

THE DARK DOORS

*"Words have no power to impress the mind without the
exquisite horror of their reality."*
~Edgar Allan Poe

WHEN CECIL AND BARBARA WATCHED their girls disappear, they felt as if a part of them had gone with them. Burt and Sally were there to give comfort and support, but it was not enough to fill the vast hole in their hearts.

"Cecil, would you and Barbara join us for dinner tonight?" Burt asked.

Perhaps it was a little early, but Burt wanted to distract them from their pain. The question at first made Cecil angry. Did his friend really think a nice meal would fill his emptiness? Instead of getting mad, he turned and gave Burt a polite smile.

"No," he said, wiping tears from his eyes. "I think Barbara and I need to be alone tonight."

"Okay," Burt said, reaching out and touching Cecil's upper arm. "If you change your mind, let me know. Sally and I are here for you."

Sally wrapped her arms around Barbara's shoulders and whispered in her ear. "I love you sweetheart. I am here if you need me."

Barbara couldn't stop sobbing, but she nodded her head against Sally's shoulder.

Burt and Sally turned to leave so their friends could have some privacy. Soon after Burt and Sally disappeared through the hangar door, Cecil gave one last loathsome glance at the machine that had caused so much pain and misery. He then wrapped a shaky arm around Barbara's shoulders and walked to the door.

His expression may not have been so abhorrent if he had any idea that his daughters were right beside him, trying to get his attention. They were just feet away, but they may as well have been a million miles. He could not hear their cries, or the pleas from millions of other Impals. There was no way for them to come back and there was no way to warn the Impals who would begin going through again in the next hour. There was no way to warn them of the horror waiting on the other side.

Abbs and Steff started to go after their parents, but Lincoln restrained them. "It would be fruitless, ladies," he told them gently. "I can't let you get far, you might not be able to make it back."

From the Impals perspective. The doorways seemed to begin beyond and to the left of the Gate. The doors stretched to infinity through the back wall and far beyond. The Impals could see each and every one of the infinite doors. The Impals themselves stretched to infinity in the distance. The realm of the doors appeared as another world superimposed over the physical world. They occupied the same space, but were completely separate. The Impals could not only see the infinite doors stretching into the distance, but they could also see the world beyond the back wall of the hangar.

This seemed to be the common arrival place of the next existence because Impals passing through the Arizona Gate kept arriving at regular intervals. The recently deceased arrived in much shorter intervals as they experienced the death of their physical body and moved on. Could the Arizona Impals see the hangar and beyond in Arizona or the one in Virginia? Could the recently deceased see the room, hospital, or accident scene from which they just departed? These questions were never asked because the Impals were faced with a much bigger problem.

They all wanted to go through their door, but they could not. These infinite doors were not open as the Impals had hoped, but were closed tight. Evidence of a bright light on the other side could be seen permeating the thin line around the arched top and sides of the doors, making them resemble a sea of crescent moons. The doors were not only shut, they were blocked as well.

They were blocked by an enormous line of dark souls stretching as far as the infinite doors. They kept the Impals at bay, daring them to try and cross to the doors. The insidious hissing and clicking in this vast expanse of the ethereal plane was maddening.

"How the hell did they get here?" Lincoln asked as one dark soul hissed and flashed his red eyes at him. He could have sworn it was the actor John Wilkes Booth.

"I'm afraid it was because of me," a familiar voice said.

He turned to see Tesla approaching with a glum expression.

"What do you mean because of you?" Lincoln asked. "How?"

Tesla explained his theory to the best of his understanding, which, in this case, was not vast.

"When I got here, I saw the doors," Tesla explained. "They were all open and they were the most beautiful sight I have ever seen." He paused and shook his head," It was all I could do to keep from going through my door right then and there. Of course, I had to let you know it was okay."

"Why are they closed now?" Thomas asked.

"Because of the dark souls," Tesla said. "They slammed shut as soon as they began to arrive. It was a terrible and deafening noise," he said with a shudder.

Before anyone else could say anything, Tesla continued. He had to raise his voice to be heard over the ever increasing hissing and clicking. "When I was manipulating the energy membrane between realms to signal the EMF meter, something must have happened. Either my actions opened a portal into the dark realm, or . . ." he said pointing into the vast darkness opposite the doors. It was like looking into outer space with no stars, no moons and no planets. They were in a vast, eternal emptiness. "Or, they were already here in some dark and distant corner and my actions somehow summoned them."

"What can we do?" Einstein asked.

"I don't know," Tesla admitted. "Every time I approach, the dark souls mass in front of me to block my path. The threats uttered at me are most disconcerting and I would care not to repeat them in present company," he said, glancing at Seth and the Garrison girls.

They all stood in dumbstruck terror, staring at the line of evil keeping them from moving on. The maddening sound of the darkness mixed with the shrieks and gasps of the arriving Impals was disturbing beyond words.

Cecil and Barbara arrived home a short time later. In spite of the cold January day, Cecil sat in a lawn chair on the back patio. He was so numb, he did not notice the temperature at all. Barbara went upstairs and lay on the bed with the door closed, lights out, and the curtains drawn. She hoped the eye would return and put her out of her misery.

Both Cecil and Barbara had lost loved ones over the years, but never did either one of them felt such a deep seeded sorrow and despair. Millions around the world now found themselves in the grip of a similar unreasonable and unbearable sorrow. The grief seemed to grow stronger with each passing minute.

Two weeks later, when the last remaining Impal went through, this sorrow around the world had grown to a level of crisis. Many people would not leave their home or even get out of their beds. Society ground to a near standstill. If something did not change soon, the world would be in worse shape than it was when the eye of the storm wreaked havoc.

The Impals sense of time was different in their plane of existence. Typically, time went by much slower there than it did in the physical world. The two weeks since Lincoln, Einstein, Thomas and Seth, and the Garrison girls passed through the Gate would have only seemed like a couple of hours in the physical world. The growing sense of despair rising in each Impal, accompanied by the insidious noise and threats hurled from the dark souls made it seem an eternity. The real fear was that they would indeed be there for eternity, separated from their door forever.

The Impals, even though they numbered in the millions, were alone now. They could not go back and the physical world could not help them. The only thing they had left was prayer and they offered it up continuously onto what seemed deaf ears. The dark souls began to grow more bold, charging at groups of Impals with a hideous shriek. These Impals were either knocked backwards or retreated deeper into the dark space opposite the doors. It seemed they were trying to drive the Impals somewhere. Possibly into their dark void where the Impals would be imprisoned for eternity. However, they never fully committed to this task. They seemed more focused on blocking the way to the doors.

Abbs and Steff had seen their grandfather on more than one occasion. He was not taunting, but instead reprimanded them for being the demons impersonating his granddaughters. He seemed to be under the impression he was guarding the doors to Hell, preventing the demons return. Even after everything, his arrogance would not let him see the truth. If he held a mirror, he could see much more. He now more resembled a devil than any Impal ever did. It was terrifying for Abbs and Steff to see their grandfather. Even so, they still pitied him.

There was one Impal who did not show much fear. Perhaps it was the naivety of the young. Maybe it was a strong love for his Mom and Dad. He hated seeing his father frightened. It bothered him worse than anything. His dad was supposed to be strong and invincible . . . *rough and tough and not afraid of nothin'*, as his dad used to say about him when they would wrestle on the floor. He loved his dad and wanted to do anything he could to protect him, to keep him strong, and to make him happy.

His love for his father was compelling beyond words, but it was not the final catalyst of his actions. He loved his Mom every bit as much and he knew she waited behind the door across from them. He knew because he believed he could hear her calling to him. All the Impals knew which door belonged to them. Nothing would make him happier than opening the door and seeing his mother again. He also knew it would make his father happy as well.

Seth waited until his father was distracted in a conversation with another Impal. He paused and listened to the hiss and clicks of the dark. It echoed about the vast ethereal plane like a thousand rattle-snakes trapped inside a well. Underneath the clicking he could hear voices, hateful voices full of malice and rage. A few were directed at him, threatening things he could not even fathom in his brief existence. Seth did not consider the dark threats frightening, he found them disgusting. Over the malicious taunts, he began to hear something else . . . another voice. He listened for a moment then elation spread across him in a warm wave. It was his mother's voice. Seth glanced up at his father to see if he heard it too. Thomas continued his conversation with the tall Impal man, completely oblivious.

Seth turned back toward the doors, ignoring the thrumming mob holding them back. He cocked his head to the side and listened. Soon the voice came again, this time it was unmistakable in both sound and meaning. It was Seth's mother, Thomas's beloved Annabelle, and she was calling out in a strong and unafraid voice.

"Seth, come to me baby. You know the door." She said like the distant call of an angel.

Seth looked up at his father one last time, held out his chest, and then began making his way toward the doors.

CHAPTER 53

SUFFER THE LITTLE CHILDREN

"Courage is found in unlikely places."
~J. R. R. Tolkien

THOMAS DID NOT SEE SETH until it was too late. The boy was a few yards away from the dark wall when the man talking to Thomas cried out. "That's your boy!"

All the Impals in the immediate area turned and gasped in unison. A few men, who were much closer to Seth than Thomas, bolted after him. Before they could get close enough, they shrank back in fear. Seth did not. He continued to trudge forward with his chest puffed out. He intended to get to his door somehow even if he must go through all the dark souls to do it.

When Seth approached the line, he cried out in pain as a few of the dark souls lashed out at him. He was not hurt, at least his ethereal body wasn't, but the impact caused him a great deal of pain. He wanted to cry, wanted to drop to his knees and beg for his mother, but he knew it would do no good. He also knew the dark abominations would feed off of any fear or weakness he showed. He must be strong; he must be strong for his Mom and Dad. He forced his pain and fear down deep and turned to face the darkness again. Seth was determined to put an end to his misery, not just for him but for his parents. He could still hear her calling to him from somewhere behind the door. It did not occur to the boy that he might not be hearing the voice of his mother. Nor did he consider he might not be able to reach the door. He was heaved in the air by several dark souls and spun about. Every touch of their foul hands was like flames lapping at his body. He howled in pain, but he twisted and jerked, determined to somehow break free and make a run for the door.

Thomas charged, but before he could reach his shrieking son, he was engulfed by a wave of dark souls. He tried to contain the screams, but the pain was too great. He felt as if he were being impaled over and over by several daggers. He shrieked, but he forced each cry into a singular word. "Seth—Run—Away!" This he repeated over and over with each wave of pain. But Seth could not run, he could not escape the grip of his tormentors. He continued to spin in agony as the dark souls delighted in their sport.

Seth could no longer hear his mother above the hissing, clicking and ear splitting howls of delight from the dark souls. He was alone in his torment and, as much as he continued to fight, he was beginning to lose hope. Neither he nor Thomas was harmed, but their anguish was as real as if they still occupied a flesh and blood body. Was it possible for a soul to go insane?

Seth felt a strong lurch and then tumbled through the air. He landed on the 'ground' of the ethereal plane without a sound. It was soft and as warm as he remembered his bed at home . . . back in Conway . . . when his mother was still there. He heard his mother's voice again. He stared at his door and thought he could see movement in the thin line of light permeating the edges. He turned to find his father and saw his rescuer instead.

Musial and a man he did not know were fighting with the dark souls. The other man reminded him of several he had seen in pictures at Sunday school. He did not know Gestas. He recognized Musial from the day at the hangar when the Impals returned. These men seemed to have a special fight in them, one beyond the ability of most Impals when it came to dealing with dark souls. The crowd of Impals behind them seemed encouraged by Seth's bravery and the courage shown by these two Impals. They raced to Thomas's aid and knocked him loose, but it was all they could do as the darkness overwhelmed them.

"Go, boy!" Musial shouted as he tussled with a nasty dark soul. "Go to your door!"

Seth glanced at his father who nodded with encouragement as he crawled towards him. Seth smiled, but only for a moment.

"Daddy!" he shrieked as a dark soul grabbed his father by the ankle and pulled him back.

Seth was about to turn back to help his father when he heard his mother's voice calling once again. This time it was much louder. "Seth, baby . . . come to me!" she called.

He considered returning to his father for a moment. Thomas was screaming in agony as a wall of dark souls closed on him. Seth then got to his feet and ran for the door. A couple of dark souls spotted his bold act and made a dash for him, but they were too late.

A minute later, he touched the surface of the door and pushed it inward. Seth's door swung open and a brilliant light flooded out, as dazzling as a thousand suns. Before he could peer inside, something incredible happened. All the doors flew open at once. The full eternity of doors radiated blinding light. A great bang issued through the ethereal plane as it filled with light beyond light. Not an inch of shadow or darkness remained anywhere, except for the dark souls. They did not remain for long. With angry hisses and shrieks they were all driven away, fleeing like a massive thunderhead. A few moments later, they were gone, followed by an enormous distant explosion. No one knew what the noise was and nobody cared. They turned their attention back to their open doors.

The Impals approached with caution at first, but the closer they got to their door the stronger they were drawn to it. Seth waited for his father to get up and come to him. They smiled at each other with loving gratitude, happy they were both okay. Seth reached up and took his father's hand and they both turned to face their door. The light would have been blinding to the flesh and blood eye. To them, they found it warm and inviting.

They began to walk forward, giddy with anticipation, but still lethargic after the shock of their torment. The closer they got to the door, the more the lethargy disappeared. They soon stood in the doorway hand in hand. Thomas and Seth exchanged smiles, and then they stepped inside.

The light inside the door was akin to wrapping oneself in a tangible blanket of pure joy. They never felt so relaxed, happy, or at peace in their lives. The feeling only lasted a moment at the top of their list. As they took a few steps further in, both cried out with joy to see Annabelle standing before them, smiling her radiant smile. Seth ran to her and wrapped his arms around her waist.

"Mommy!" he cried. "I missed you!"

"I missed you too, baby," she said, leaning down and kissing him on the forehead.

Thomas stepped forward and wrapped his arms around her shoulders. He felt like crying for joy, but no tears came. This was not a place for tears. Instead, his joy seemed to flow through Annabelle and Seth, then back to him in an infinite current.

"I love you, sweetheart," Thomas said

"I love you too, honey," she said and kissed him. There was the electrical charge again. It was pure flowing happiness.

Indeed, he would have it forever. Annabelle led them further in, putting all worries of the world behind them. They entered the joy all souls crave.

All the Impals entered their door in a short time, each finding their fondest hope. Abbs and Steff were greeted by their grandmothers. The girls adored both of them in life and now the joy of being with them again was indescribable. They indeed found happiness

Cecil and Barbara did not instantly heal from the loss of their daughters nor were they suddenly joyous. Their transition was much more subtle. The feeling of desperation passed and they were finally able to reminisce about their daughters. They still shed tears for their loss, but they knew they would see them again. They knew it without a doubt.

So it was with the rest of the world. After the last stranded Impal entered their door and it closed behind them, the world finally began to heal.

www.ingramcontent.com/pod-product-compliance
Lightning Source LLC
Chambersburg PA
CBHW051525250626
47156CB00001B/234